CW00821777

THE GHOST DANCE

incorporating

The Ghost Dance
The Shrine

THE NIGHTHUNTER SERIES

Collection I: The Stalking

The Stalking
The Talisman

Collection II: The Ghost Dance

The Ghost Dance
The Shrine

THE
GHOST DANCE

ROBERT HOLDSTOCK

writing as

ROBERT FAULCON

C

CENTURY

LONDON MELBOURNE AUCKLAND JOHANNESBURG

© Robert Faulcon 1987
incorporating
The Ghost Dance
First published 1983
© Robert Faulcon 1983
The Shrine
First published 1984
© Robert Faulcon 1984

All rights reserved

This double volume first published in 1987 by
Century Hutchinson Ltd,
Brookmount House, 62–65 Chandos Place,
Covent Garden, London WC2N 4NW

Century Hutchinson Australia Pty Ltd
PO Box 496, 16–22 Church Street, Hawthorn,
Victoria 3122, Australia

Century Hutchinson New Zealand Limited
PO Box 40–086 Glenfield, Auckland 10, New Zealand

Century Hutchinson South Africa (Pty) Limited
PO Box 337, Bergvlei 2012, South Africa

ISBN 0 7126 1747 7

Printed and bound in Great Britain by
Anchor Brendon Limited, Tiptree, Essex

THE GHOST DANCE

For Wabi who does not approve

1

The car was a battered grey Cadillac, twenty years old, souped-up and noisy. It crawled through the wide, empty streets of Ridgeville making a sound like a jet engine. A plume of black smoke belched from its decayed exhaust, the acrid fumes blending with the foetid smell of refuse.

Even on a good day, Ridgeville, Montana, was a depressing, soulless place. It sat on the edge of twenty square miles of designated Indian reservation, just off the main highway between Westrock and Collinstown. From the shacks that bordered that highway, traffic was a silver blur, never stopping, passing by the Sioux town as if it were just a ghost town.

More shacks than pre-fabs, Ridgeville supported a population of over seven hundred men, women and children. Most of them worked in Westrock. A few didn't work, but stayed behind closed doors and drank iced Schlitz and watched the TV – morning, noon, evening and well into the night.

Like the Cadillac, Ridgeville bristled with aerials. They formed a silver fence against the sky, and through them, distantly, the hills known as Blue Snake Summit were uninviting, yellow swellings on the savage, hostile landscape.

The Cadillac turned left, into the main street. A few people walked here; a few more sat on the steps of their houses, knees drawn up, heads covered with ragged stetsons as they squinted at the noisy new arrival. A few acknowledged the driver. A few more didn't, just chewed on tobacco and spat dark saliva onto the cracked concrete pavement. Dogs roamed, active, angry, their barking a desolate sound on the hot day.

In the centre of town was the square, and in the centre of

the square was a water fountain and a single tree. The houses here were white-fronted, well built. Some of them had corrugated iron roofs, some had boarded-up windows. The sound of a radio playing country and western drifted from the open glass door of the bar, which was run by an Indian so miserable he was known simply as Old Sourface. The bar was a long, low shack, with outbuildings built around it, and connected. It made a warren of rooms: pool rooms, card rooms and talk rooms. They were all dark, smoky places, and the heavy, silent men who sat in them seemed never to come out into the daylight.

The car stopped by the tree. The young man who stepped out of the driver's side was tall, broad-shouldered and paunch-gutted. His hair was long and luxuriously black. His face was broad, his eyes narrowed, his mouth hard. There was something handsome about him, something wasted. His clothes were smart: pressed jeans, a sleeveless white T-shirt. He was an Indian who knew how Indians should look if they were to look cool. His Cadillac was his prized possession. He ran his broad hand over the hot roof of the car, as if stroking a woman's body. A gold chain glinted round his neck.

Frankie Laine Silverlock had work, and work that paid. And he wanted people to know it.

He leaned down and peered irritably into the car. 'Hey, move it! I gotta be back in Westrock by two.'

The girl climbed out of the car, looking miserable and frightened. She was shorter than her brother, but looked strong and swift. She was very beautiful, without the broad features of the rest of her family; rather, her nose was aquiline, her face narrow and quite sharp. Her eyes were wide and slanted. She looked a little like the country singer Cher, and that made her popular with the local menfolk. She was slim, and wore jeans and a T-shirt like her brother. Mary Jane Silverlock also had the natural feature that had given their family its name, three generations before: a lock of silver hair, running down the left side, from the crown. It shone brightly, contrasting elegantly with the ebony sheen of the rest of her hair.

10

'Why are you letting them do this to me,' she said quietly, and her brother turned on her sharply.

'You been picked, Mary. It's an honour. I don't like it in one way, but it's an honour. We Indians gotta respect honour.'

We Indians! Mary Jane thought bitterly, and looked at the sagging features of her brother. He drank, he smoked, he worked in the big town as a running boy to a white corporation. And all he ever talked about was white girls. Blondes. Sometimes the Scandinavian settlers mixed with the Indians, and some of the children were blonde, but with Indian blood. It was all he talked about, finding a girl like that: part Indian, but blonde, like Candice Bergen. His room was covered with pictures of Candice Bergen. He drank beer with the city boys, in their city suits, and laughed when they told jokes about blacks, and spics, and Indians. He told jokes about Indians himself. He got drunk and said 'The only good Indian is a drunk Indian who buys the next round'. Everybody laughed. They despised him, but they laughed. He was Frankie Laine Running Boy, and he had money, and he was big in Ridgeville. He screwed the girls, and told the boys how to handle the white man's world. The evidence of his success was the fistful of dollar notes that he could slip from his jeans pocket.

He was twenty-one years old. He was dead.

'I'm frightened, Frankie.' It was true. He put his big arm around her as he walked her towards the bar. She felt helpless, she felt like crying. She wished she had someone to turn to, someone strong, someone wise. She thought of Snake Man but he was up in the hills. It was too late to think about him now. All she had was her brother.

'It's gonna be okay,' he said, leaning down to give her an affectionate kiss. His breath smelled of beer. 'I'll be with you all the time. They just want to see you. They're gonna talk to you. I been here before, Mary Jane, there's nothing frightening. You been picked, right? And that's an honour. There's nothing to be afraid of.'

She let her body rest in the lee of his. She felt his muscles move powerfully, his brawny arms squeeze her reassuringly. She felt small and frail beside him. He took after their late father. Protective but stupid. When the elders said 'jump', he jumped. It was an honour. He didn't question. He would hurt inside, he would cry inside, but he never questioned. He knew that he was losing his sister. He *had* to know that. She was going to be Mary Jane Walk On the Sky. She was going to Walk On Water. She'd been told this, and that meant she was going a long way away. He knew he was losing her, and the small shack on 4th street would be an empty, silent place. It would fill with discarded cans of beer, empty wrappers. It would start to smell. There would be no Mary Jane to tidy up after him. She would be Walking On Water, and he would weep for her, but it was an honour.

There were five men in the bar, all sitting on high stools, leaning against the bar top. They looked round as Frankie Laine Silverlock led the way inside. Old Sourface turned away. His hair was tied back in a pigtail. It was very grey. He fussed with a new bottle of bourbon. He didn't want to acknowledge the newcomers.

'Hi Frankie,' said one of the men at the bar, and raised his can of beer. He was young, maybe twenty years old. His hair was cut like Donny Osmond's. Meticulous hair, no style. He'd worked as a cab driver for a while, but he couldn't bear to miss a baseball game on the TV, and he was never available. Now he hugged the Ridgeville bar, and waited for girls. His eyes narrowed, his lips twitched into a half smile as he stared at Mary Jane. 'Hi, Mary Jane.'

She ignored him. Frankie led her past the bar, and the five men turned to watch, their eyes lowering as their gazes, to a man, fixed on the girl's backside. One of them whistled. The young man at the edge of the bar said, 'How's work, Frankie?'

'Work's good,' he said. 'I gotta get back for two. Work's good. Pay's good.' All this without looking round. Girls and work, two things he was always prepared to talk about.

'They're through in the card room,' said Sourface. 'Been waiting an hour.'

Frankie glanced at him. He hoped he didn't look too worried. 'Had to get back from Westrock. Can't rush these things.'

Mary Jane felt the change in her brother. He had been strong, confident: now he was nervous. It made her nervous too, and her knees started to shake. She licked her lips. Her skin goosed up, and she crossed her arms across her body as Frankie gently propelled her through the corridor to the room at the end.

'I don't want to Walk On Water,' she said softly, and felt tears sting her eyes. *She wanted Snake Man. Snake Man would know what to do.* 'Get me out of this, Frankie. Please!'

His face set grim. He took her arm and squeezed and the grip was painful, almost angry. 'I can't, Mary Jane. You been chosen. I can't change that.'

He opened the door to the card room and they stepped inside. There was a murmur of conversation which died away as they crossed the threshold. The room was yellow, dimly lit from a piece of corrugated plastic slung across a hole in the roof. Smoke coiled and floated in the air; heavy, acrid fumes from the cigarettes and pipes that the men here smoked.

There were four of them, and they were very old. They sat around the card table, and moved very slowly, dealing out the cards for a hand of poker, then turning to look at the youngsters. Frankie knew three of them. Mary Jane recognized two. The oldest of them all, who was also the thinnest and the hardest looking, was a stranger. He wore a small hat, with a narrow brim. His shirt was black, and his fingers were covered with tattoos. He faced the door and his gaze lingered on Mary Jane. A small cigar was stuck in the corner of his mouth, and every few seconds smoke coiled from his nostrils.

'This is Coyote,' said one of the old men from Ridgeville, and the stranger raised a hand.

'Frankie Laine Silverlock,' said Frankie, and pushed his sister forward. 'This is Mary Jane.'

Coyote's eyes never left the girl. His fingers flexed and

13

the tattoos changed their shape. Mary Jane watched the symbols and they seemed to dance, to writhe, as if the pattern on his skin was a living thing.

'My real name is Jimmy Springwater,' said Coyote. 'Coyote is my magic name. You look frightened. Coyote is frightening, but it's just my magic name. You can't be frightened of an old man called Springwater. I'm just the magic man. Coyote is my guardian spirit. He's wily, is Coyote. A real trickster. But I got him tamed. No need to be frightened of old Jimmy Springwater.'

'I'm not frightened,' lied Mary Jane.

The old men watched her. Simon Grey Bear was the town's Chief. He had been a good friend of her father's. He said very little. He had a warm face, much wrinkled. His white hair hung down to his shoulders, very ragged. There was a patch missing above his right temple where he'd been hit by a car, years before. The other man she knew was Old Billy Once-Rode-Horse. His original name was long forgotten. He had owned a horse for years. Mary Jane could just remember watching him ride through Ridgeville, so proud on horseback, even though the steed was old and decrepit. He had taken the name Once-Rode-Horse because he wanted the young folk to remember how glorious it had been to ride the wind on horseback, rather than puffing out black smoke from a Cadillac. Frankie Once-Owned-Cadillac. The thought made Mary Jane smile.

'This Coyote,' said Once-Rode-Horse slowly, emphasizing each syllable and prodding his small, briar pipe at the visitor, 'He's come from the west. He's the magic man. We're very honoured to have Coyote with us. You've been chosen to carry the thread over the water. We're very honoured by that too. We're very proud of you, Mary Jane. I'm sure Coyote thinks you are right for what he needs.' He turned to the visitor and raised a questioning eyebrow. Coyote nodded, smiled thinly. Once-Rode-Horse said, 'There is a great force at work. Too big for Once-Rode-Horse to know, too big for Grey Bear, too big for Ridgeville. A great force. It's called The Great Spider. A great spider weaves a great web. All the Long Forgotten

14

are attracted to that web, like flies to a web. The Long Dead. The Great Forgotten. They come up through the earth, up through the mountains, up through the deep rivers, through the cracks in the ground, down from the moon, down from the stars, all to the web. All to the Great Spider.

This Coyote,' again he hesitated as he stabbed his pipe at the visitor, 'he's a magic man. He's a part of the Great Spider. But you. You're the little spider. You're Mary Jane Walks On Water, Walks On Sky. You carry the thread of that web, and you carry the voice of our dead. It's a great honour. It will be a long journey.'

Frankie nudged her gently and whispered, 'Say something.'

Mary Jane watched the old men, stared at Coyote, whose gaze held her like a fish speared on the end of a stick. His eyes went through her. He was searching her mind, poking around in the grey stuff, looking for feelings, for doubts. He would see everything. He would know that she didn't want to go.

She said to him, '*Why* was I chosen?'

Coyote said, 'You are strong. You are young. You are innocent of the ways of time . . .'

'I'm not innocent,' she said truthfully. 'I've had two lovers.'

Coyote smiled thinly. The old men laughed silently. 'There will be many more. You will be Mary Jane Walks On Water, and when you return there will be many lovers, a long life of love and success. You are the little spider. The Great Spider will look after her own.'

'I'm frightened,' she said. She didn't believe Coyote. She knew about Coyote, the old trickster god. He was wily. He had a dog called Rattlesnake. He let his friends die because it added chaos and confusion to the order of things. He was not a god of the Sioux, but she knew about him, how he made life hard for the ordinary folk. He was malicious, mischievous, a trouble-maker and a liar. How could a magic man adopt the name of the trouble-maker God, and pretend that he was innocent? She was quite sure

15

that the journey would be one way. Quite sure. She was to be sacrificed, but that would bring honour to her family, to her tribe.

'There is nothing to be frightened of,' said Coyote, and his wrinkled face grew soft and charming as he smiled. The other old men puffed on their pipes and cigarettes and smiled too. Grey Bear said, 'Tonight, in the Lodge. Go home, now, and tidy up your things. But don't eat. You will eat later. Go for a walk. Be happy. And come to the Lodge tonight at nine o'clock.' He looked at Frankie Laine Silverlock. 'Stay with her until then.'

Frankie looked uncomfortable. 'I have to go back to work. I have to be at Westrock at two.'

Once-Rode-Horse shook his head. 'This is more important. Stay with your sister until tonight. Make her happy. Help her.'

Desperately uncomfortable, Frankie nodded a quick acknowledgement then backed out of the door, reaching to tug Mary Jane after him.

'I'll lose my job,' he whined as they walked from the bar. 'I'm supposed to be at Westrock at two. They'll fire me.' He pounded his hand angrily against the top of his car, stared into the distance. Mary Jane watched him.

'Go to work then. I'll be all right.'

'I can't. They said to stay with you. I gotta do that. *Shit*! I should be back at work at two!' He looked at her, a sudden thought occurring to him. 'Yeah. You come with me. That's an idea.'

'I'm not going with you,' she said defiantly. 'They said make me happy, right? Well, I want to go up to Blue Snake Summit.'

'Why, for God's sake?'

'I just do. And I want to go alone. You go to work. I shan't run away.'

But he shook his head; he was uncertain, and worried. He glanced back at the bar. 'I gotta stay with you. *Shit*! It took me two years to get that job. I got the morning off, but not the afternoon. Damn!' She stood, waiting for him to calm down.

16

'I want to be on my own, Frankie.'

'You heard what they said . . .'

'I'm not going to make trouble for you. I just want to go and see someone. The old man, up on the summit.'

Frankie didn't understand. His face was kindly, puzzled. He watched his sister carefully. He knew about the Snake Man who haunted the rocks of Blue Snake Summit, but what the hell would his sister want with him?

'It's too dangerous,' he said. 'That Snake Man's mad.'

'I've been there before,' she said defiantly. 'Lend me the Cadillac, and borrow a car to go to Westrock. I'll see you later this evening.'

'I don't think I'd better,' he said.

Damn you! she thought. *I don't want you around!* It was years since she'd seen Snake Man. She'd been a tiny girl, maybe six or seven, and she'd gone up to the hills with her parents, she didn't know why. Wandering off, she'd found the shack, and its withered occupant. He'd been kind to her, talked to her, even given her a tiny wooden doll. Later she'd heard the stories about him, how he was an Indian chief from before the time of the European colonization of America, an undying relic of the old race, kept alive by magic and a diet of snake and sandstone. Nobody took much notice of Snake Man, but occasionally people would go to him for spells, or cures. The elders frowned upon the activity, but as long as he stayed on Blue Snake Summit, twenty miles away from Ridgeville, then there could be no harm to him.

I need him, Mary Jane Silverlock thought. *I need his help. He'll know what to do to make this thing easier. But I don't want Frankie around. He'll tell. He'll spoil it all.*

'Follow me, then,' she said angrily. 'But borrow another car. I want to be alone for a while. I don't want to have to speak to you, or to anyone. Is that clear? Lend me the Cadillac, and follow me if you must. But don't come near me! Not until after I've seen him!'

2

The house whispered to him.

The voice of the house was like a gentle breeze. It rustled papers, ruffled curtains, made doors swing to and fro. The voice passed through the house from top to bottom, pausing in corridors, hesitating in the deserted rooms upstairs, hovering about the supine form of the man who lay sleeping on the floor of the lounge.

Try harder. Try harder.

The man was in his thirties, dark, gaunt, unshaven. He looked strong, but there was sadness in the lines around his eyes. His chest rose and fell with a slow, steady rhythm, thirty seconds between each breath. Behind his closed lids his eyes moved rapidly. Dream sleep . . . or something else.

Nearly there. Nearly there, urged the strange voice.

The house shifted. Its beams creaked and groaned as night passed away. Grey dawn broke. Light crept into the room through gaps in the curtaining. It formed streaks of brightness across the man's dark face and motionless body. The house murmured. The voice of the house was like that of a bird, then of a breeze, then of a woman. It came from the chimney and the open fire grate; it came from the hall; it came from the corners of the brightening lounge. Always that voice was directed at the man who lay on his back on the floor, his hands so calmly placed by his sides.

Can you hear me? Can you hear me? called the house.

The man murmured. It was an incoherent, throaty sound, the word 'yes' spoken without his lips opening. His head turned.

Harder, urged the house. *Closer.*

'I'm trying,' Daniel Brady said, soundlessly, wordlessly.

The room closed in upon him. The whole house seemed to shake with triumph. *You heard. You heard.*

Brady's head turned from side to side. His fingers clenched, clutching the carpet as if in pain. His unshaven features, which a moment before had been so tranquil, almost peaceful, now creased and darkened. He began to look more like the haunted, tired man he was. He cared nothing for the way he looked, however. His mind twisted and shifted within its fleshy frame, loosening its hold, rising above the ground. Rising . . . rising . . .

It happened abruptly, and lasted only seconds!

One moment he was in the darkened room, awake behind his closed eyelids, concentrating hard. He was aware of the physical presence of the floor below him, and of the metaphysical whispering which grew loud, then waned, like a tide.

The next moment, all physical pressure went away. He felt as if he was floating. His eyes remained closed, but he achieved vision. He saw the room in shades of colour, and patches of light and dark, that did not actually exist.

'My God,' he said as he floated above his body. Around him there was noise. It was laughter, delighted laughter. It came from the colours, from the shades. A woman's laughter. He hovered about the room, blown on a breeze that he could not feel, turning slowly, glimpsing movement in the patches of light.

He was out of his body!

'Where are you?'

I'm here. I'm here.

He saw her, then. She was standing in a patch of light, in one of the corners of the room. He glimpsed her only briefly. She was naked, slender. Her arms hung limply by her sides. She gleamed in the spectral light, and smiled.

'Alison . . . I can see you . . . Alison!'

She became diffuse, reaching towards him, but fading from his vision.

'Alison . . .' he said again, and even as his spirit spoke he knew that it was *not* his wife . . .

19

He was aware of something moving around the room, and tried to follow it with his gaze, but he had no real control over his spectral form and obtained only sensations: the sensation of a female shape, trying to get close to him; the sensation of sound, her voice, whispering his name, expressing joy, triumph . . .

The sensation of warning. She was trying to warn him. *Danger. Threat. Approach.*

It was all too confusing. It was all too fast. Her words didn't lodge with him. There were too many sensations . . .

Seconds only had passed in this, his first controlled mind movement out of his own living body. He felt himself tugged back towards the earth, saw the room become dark, felt the warmth and security of his flesh enclose the momentarily liberated spirit.

And abruptly, horrifyingly, the images came!

They came out of the haunted part of his mind, the dark recesses where he had pushed the terrors of a Christmas Eve, just scant months before. The joy at this successful liberation of mind from body was pushed aside as the screams of his family echoed and shrilled in his memory, reminding him that his was not a life that could *ever* luxuriate in comfort. Not until they were safely back . . .

He cried out loudly, vocalizing his terror. His body thrashed where it lay on the floor, the eyes squeezing tightly shut. He wanted desperately to wake up, to sit up, to get up and run from the room, denying those awful memories a place in his conscious mind. But how could he? The memories were too strong, too sad, too important for him to deny them.

The ghost of the woman who haunted the walls of his house drifted away, frightened by the horrors that flooded Daniel Brady's waking mind. She watched from the shadows as Brady's body became as rigid as steel. She listened as his voice became a keening, desperate cry . . .

She watched, helpless, as Daniel Brady remembered . . .

★

'Where's Marianna?' Brady was perched on the stepladder, decorating the Christmas tree. He turned as he spoke to his son Dominick, and saw the boy crouching by the fire. It had snowed earlier and the children had been playing outside. Now it was after dusk and time for them both to be in.

'Dom? Where's Marianna?'

The boy shrugged. 'There was a man outside . . . she was talking to him.'

His wife, Alison, glanced up, stared at her son, then at her husband. In her dark eyes there was an agonized look of alarm and she slowly rose from her seat, repeating the words, 'A man?'

Brady felt cold. He came down the ladder. He stared at Alison and realized that the two of them had been exchanging a gaze not of alarm, but of cold-blooded terror. He frowned. His heart started to pump with noisy energy. The room swam. Alison stepped towards him, all the blood draining from her face. 'My daughter . . . oh my God . . .'

In that instant they were aware of it, sensing the danger, sensing the tragedy. They moved towards each other, but the room slipped away, the fire dimmed, the warmth drained away into a more primal chill.

He heard her, then, calling from outside. She was standing by the french windows, a small girl of six, fair-haired, very pretty. She was clad in a bulky anorak and boots. She looked so vulnerable. She was crying behind her tiny, round-framed glasses.

'Daddy! I'm cold!'

'MARIANNA!' he screamed.

The darkness exploded into the lounge, breaking glass, extinguishing light and fire. The girl was flung across the room. In the darkness, Brady was beaten almost senseless. But he saw his daughter carried by a dark-robed shape back out into the cold night.

'Bastards!' he screamed, and was attacked again. 'NO!'

He watched as Dominick was taken, helpless against the number and the power of the attackers. And then Alison

21

. . . Alison too was carried into the blackness, naked, abused, hanging limply over a man's shoulder.

Animal-faced men prowled the house, searching, gathering, their voices the rasping sounds of beasts.

'He's not needed. Kill him.'

Cruel words, and then a cruel assault upon his body as he lay trussed and helpless on the floor. Invisible hands wrenched at his neck, strangling the life from him. He cried with fear; he cried with pain; mostly he cried for the sight of his family being stolen from him, taken into the night, totally lost to him.

He had survived that murderous attack. His spirit had slipped from his body and grappled with the psychic force that had been working upon him. It was an ability that he could not yet consciously control; not yet . . .

From that brief, terrifying visit by the Collectors he had taken other images, other memories: a labrynthine pattern on one of their robes; a jewelled, demon-headed object, which had been disgustingly used upon his screaming wife; a face like a grinning corpse; a name that had sounded like Magondathog. What these things meant as yet he had no idea. Mostly he had memories of voices, of figures, of human creatures whom he would hunt to the ends of the earth to destroy for what they had done to him and his family that night.

With a cry something like a cry of pain, Daniel Brady snapped his mind back to reality. He sat up from his supine position on the floor, shivering and shaking like a leaf. He felt incredibly cold, and rubbed his arms vigorously, blinking hard as he focused upon the familiar surroundings of his lounge.

Climbing to his feet, he stretched, stamped, and generally worked his blood circulation back to efficiency. It was always like this when he tried to control the out-of-body experience. He woke up feeling as if he had been bed-

22

bound for a month, in a mortuary. Cold, stiff, very sore.

And he always had that waking nightmare, the visions of the night his family had been abducted. He seemed helpless to control the way his mind was determined to continually remind him of his tragedy.

As if he needed reminding!

He walked over to the curtains and pulled them back. Early morning light spilled into the chaotically untidy lounge. He looked around, scratching at the stubble on his face. Newspapers lay in discarded piles; clothes were heaped here and there; food containers, books and blankets were scattered around the room's edge. He had been away several times, and he always felt too tired to tidy up with the sort of regularity needed.

Now he grinned. He stared at the corner where he had glimpsed the spirit presence of the American woman, Ellen Bancroft.

I always think it's Alison. I'm sorry, Ellen. Nothing personal. I just always think it's her . . .

He wondered if Ellen was still there, but where would she go? Ellen Bancroft had been a research worker at the Ennean Institute of Paranormal Research, and she had come to Brady's aid at his greatest time of need. But she had died in this house, in this very room; she had died through her own carelessness, through disobedience to her own strict rules for defence against psychic attack.

But Brady felt indebted to her, not the least because she had *chosen* to haunt the place, helping Brady, advising him as best she could. Communication was the problem. Sometimes he was more aware of her than others. She could communicate through the garble of psychic writing, sometimes by dreams, sometimes through the eerie whispering sound that had accompanied his recent efforts to control the link between spirit and body . . .

'I did it,' he said to the room, still shivering slightly. His gaunt eyes surveyed the lounge. He was a drawn, thin man, now, but strong and agile. His hair was greying, but the flabbiness of the middle age he had once been approaching had been rapidly banished. He was like an animal, coiled and tensed, ready to spring. He was a hunter, and he needed all his faculties for the task ahead.

'Did you hear me?' he said, smiling slightly. 'I *did* it. Just for a few seconds, but I came *out!*'

Was that an answering gust of wind from the fire grate? Was that a congratulatory, if ghostly, touch upon his neck?

He could hear a sound, like the distant tinkling of bells . . .

Brady walked quickly to the kitchen and made himself a cup of coffee. He made it strong and sweet, sipping it appreciatively. Slowly he warmed up.

Ellen had said something to him, whispered to him as he had achieved the out-of-body trip. Something about *danger*. Something about approach.

Tinkling bells . . .

He was being targeted, he knew that. Psychic substance was again being directed at him. He was under psychic attack. An elemental, a thought form. It might have been a Watcher, a mind projection designed to gather information; it might be a Stalker, a malevolent elemental that could crush and kill . . . if it could get to him.

His house was well defended against psychic attack. Ellen Bancroft had seen to that, and from her ghostly realm, within the house, she kept an eye on the way he maintained those defences. The sound of bells was one auditory clue as to the fact that a psychic approach was being made. It didn't worry him. What concerned him was what Ellen had whispered.

Danger. Approach.

It was something more worrying than a simple attack, but he had not been able to hear her well enough.

He finished his coffee, then walked upstairs to the bathroom and peered at his weary visage in the mirror. His tongue was coated, his eyes baggy and bloodshot. He washed and shaved quickly, keeping the scraps of hair in a polythene bag. He changed his clothes, immediately washing the dirty garments.

The sensation of psychic attack grew more powerful and chilled him slightly, despite the warm early summer's day.

Check the defences. It may have been Ellen's voice in his

mind, or just his own conscience, but he hung his talisman around his neck and went out into the garden. The talisman was made of meteoric stone. It was heavy, ancient, it had been fashioned by a Norse shaman hundreds of years before, and it had the appearance of a screaming, severed head. But it was Brady's, now, and the power intrinsic in that cold stone was his power. With the talisman round his neck he felt even stronger than before.

The attack was coming from the west; that, at least, was the direction where his senses were most acutely affected. The air 'knocked', as if someone banged on wood. He stared across the garden at the first line of defences, the Talisman Wall, where the trees were beginning to come into leaf. Then he prowled around the garden, checking the herb-burning braziers of the *zona mandragora* and the complex pattern of turf mazes that surrounded the house. Only the *zona magnetica* was invisible to him, the clay and iron gargoyles, buried feet down in a line four yards or so from the wall.

The elemental, when it came, was more exploratory than aggressive. Brady was aware of it only by the way it whipped the branches of the trees like tendrils. New leaves, and bark splinters, flew like shards about the defence zones; the trees were bent and savaged, and the air howled with the dissemination of psychic energy. Brady watched closely, feeling the wind cold on his face, wary for some rock or brick shard that might be thrown at him. The smoke from the mandrake braziers formed a shimmering screen between him and the attacking force, blocking the probing fingers of the thought-form. Brady imagined he glimpsed something like a wolverine: black, gigantic and rearing up onto its hind legs as it forced its way against the invisible barriers. But the image was a flashing picture at the edge of vision, and soon the violence died away, and the garden became quiet again.

Someone, somewhere, was targeting him, feeling him out. It had been some weeks since the last attack. Brady couldn't help thinking that stronger minds were being recruited to the task of destroying him.

25

'Do your worst,' he said softly, as he walked back inside the house. 'And I'll do mine!'

He made his way to the study. He closed the curtains and the door, plunging the room into darkness, then struck a match and lit two candles. One of these was yellow, the other light blue. Each had been carefully prepared with oils, and stood in a copper holder. The yellow candle symbolized attraction, persuasion and confidence; the blue was the candle which, in this form of magic, represented tranquillity and understanding. Between the candles and illuminated by them, he placed a mirror. He positioned a second mirror behind him and sat at the desk, paper before him, a pencil held lightly in his hand. He was looking, now, at a mirror *within* a mirror, and softly he called for Ellen.

After a while he saw her reflection, a shadowy movement, then a pale oval, which resolved into her face. She was not smiling, rather, she was shaking her head.

Brady found this a very disconcerting way to contact his house-ghost. That earlier brief vision, with her voice an actuality, had been almost marvellous. To be able to talk to her so easily was what he most desired, but it was a communication that would take a long while to perfect.

'Hello Ellen,' he said, to the pale reflection in the mirror.

Almost at once his hand moved across the paper, the pencil tracing a thin scrawl that quickly resolved into Ellen's spectral handwriting.

dangdangcomingwestdangerdanger DAN DAN approach DAN seaseasea

Brady stared at the scrawl, at his own name written large, almost screaming its urgency.

Danger approaching. From the west. From the sea? Something coming from the sea?

Again his hand moved, pushed and tugged by the girl in the room, but this time it was just Ellen's continual lament, the expression of cold and alienation that told of her unhappiness.

coldcoldcoldnotimenotime. No. Time. Fading. Michael-michae Mi go over soonsoonsoon

26

Brady watched the rippling, pale reflection. Ellen seemed to fade a little, her head cocked to one side. It was like watching the moon reflected on water. More brightly then:

welldonewelldone. Possible. Control possible soontrysoonagain

'I shall,' Brady said aloud. 'It was hard, but I managed it. I was above my body for several seconds, and I saw you, Ellen, I really saw you.'

His hand wrote: *need you need need NEED* followed by the almost minutely written name *Michael*, her husband's name, the man who had been stolen from Ellen as Alison had been stolen from Brady.

'What is the danger?' Brady asked. 'Is it close? How can you see it through the defences? What is the danger? What is the danger? What is coming from the sea?'

For a moment his hand rested quiet. The image of Ellen faded from the candle-lit mirror and he thought she had gone. Then his fingers twitched, and the pencil inscribed several circles, like a child's scrawl, before writing the word *sheeeeeeee*. More doodles for a few seconds, then the word *ghosts* followed by *dange ghosts danger DAN toodark-toodark GHOS*

The incomplete word ended with the pencil being sharply drawn across the paper. The desk shook in a single, violent motion that did much to convince Brady that the message was earnestly intended. He stared at the paper, at the mirrors, at the candles. Somehow Ellen Bancroft had seen through the heavy psychic defences of the house – or perhaps she had merely tuned in to stray psychic wavelengths – and had detected the approach of something more sinister than a simple elemental.

From the west. From the sea.

Brady sat back in his chair, thoughtfully staring into the gloomy study. From *across* the sea, perhaps.

Ghosts. Danger. Approaching from across the ocean.

But what sort of ghosts exactly? And who was sending them?

Who was coming for him now?

3

As she drove up into the hills, the heat became stifling. The Cadillac had air conditioning, which she turned full on, but even then, even with the windows open, she was boiling alive.

She drove slowly. She didn't want Frankie overtaking her out of concern for her driving of his precious machine. But she had to drive the Cadillac; no one else in Ridgeville would have lent her his car. Frankie dogged her, a hundred yards behind. She could occasionally make him out through the drifting cloud of dry dust and sand that the raised rear wheels of his car threw up. The road to Blue Snake Summit was as winding as a rattler. The car lurched and bumped over the uneven surface. The sun broiled her slim flesh in the tin oven.

At last she saw the shack, tucked away below an overhang. There was a little vegetation here, and at the front of the shack was a small, fenced-off garden. She could smell a touch of water on the air, and understood, then, that there was probably a rising spring below the rocks.

Blue Snake Summit was a mound of yellow, blue rock, like the gnarled, scarred back of some slumbering monster. In the heat, the surface rippled. The shack was in the shade, but even so its metal roof couldn't have afforded much comfort at this hottest part of the day.

Mary Jane stopped the car a few hundred paces from the shack, and left it on the road. She scrambled across the hot, stony ground, into the lee of the rising hill. Behind her, Frankie parked alongside the Cadillac and spent a while checking it over, before ambling slowly along behind her. He carried a four-pack of beer, and had placed a broad-rimmed hat on his head. He was watching her solemnly, but probably had his mind on his job.

The shack had been built out of corrugated iron, wooden fencing and red brick. It was the oddest abode she had ever seen. It hardly seemed able to stand against the biting winter winds that coursed, like wild animals, around these high hills. The windows were covered with pinned hides. One of them was rolled up and she peered inside, nearly jumping out of her skin as the wizened face of the occupant stared back at her from the gloom.

'It's Mary Jane Silverlock,' she called. 'I came here before.'

Frankie sat down on a distant rock, watching her. The door to the shack opened and she stepped inside.

'Mary Jane Silverlock,' said the old man. His voice was not reedy, not high pitched like the others'. It was still strong and firm. He walked round the cluttered table and sat down, staring at her, examining her by the shaft of light that spilled from the open window. He sat in the gloom, and she could only make him out indistinctly. 'You were much smaller then. Years ago. Years ago. I remember you. I gave you a doll. What happened to that doll? I bet you threw it away.'

Mary Jane smiled and reached to her belt, to the small pouch she carried there.

The paint on the doll was faded, and one arm had been stuck back on with glue, but it was recognizable to Snake Man and he chuckled, nodding his head in an approving way.

'I knew all along,' he said. 'I've been listening to you for years. I listen to a lot of them, down there in the town. The dolls tell me everything. But your eyes went, and I could only hear . . .'

He chuckled again as Mary Jane looked slightly horrified, holding the blind doll in her hands as if it were something that might jump from her grip at any moment. 'I didn't know you were doing that,' she said.

'I have only those few heartbeats for company,' he said quietly. 'I talk to no one, I tell no secrets. You've come for

29

help, and you expect to have to pay me in some way. But you've already paid. I've listened to your dreams, to your chatter, to your games. Sometimes I've just sat here and listened to your breathing. You've been a good companion to me, and this old man's heart and blood has raced on more than a few occasions . . .'

Mary Jane flushed, knowing what he meant.

She walked to the covered window at the front of the shack and tugged up the hide. Frankie was ambling restlessly up and down, glancing at the dwelling. At any moment he would come over to investigate.

'Who's that?' asked the old man, and Mary Jane turned to look at him. She was startled by his appearance, seen clearly as light fell upon him for the first time. 'My brother,' she said, but was more than a little preoccupied by staring at her host. 'My God, you're old . . .'

He chuckled good humouredly. 'Older than you think . . .'

The lines on his face were so deep that all features seemed to have sunk into the grooves and rifts. She could only see his mouth when he opened it, and his eyes were thin gleaming lines below heavy, scarred brows. His hair was long, white and was tied about his scalp with a black band. The hands that were folded so neatly in front of him were just bones with a thin, parchment-like layer of freckled skin. It was a living corpse that sat there, its face writhing and twisting with amusement, a gruesome expression that occasionally allowed her to glimpse the pinkness of his mouth. He wore only a patterned blanket, draped about his shoulders. When he rose and walked to the small iron stove at the side of the hut, she saw that his legs had hardly enough muscle to support him. A skeleton, as white as snow, incongruously draped in a blanket.

He was fiddling with a small clay pot. The hut was filled with implements and artefacts: small tools, made of iron, of bone, of stone were scattered about the floors and slung on the walls. Pots were everywhere: storage jars, pots of paint, food containers. On one wall was a totem; and

30

everywhere, over everything, were feathers, and hides, and pieces of leather marked and grooved in strange ways. The place smelled strongly of animal skins. It was not unpleasant.

Glancing back through the window, Mary Jane could see that Frankie was on the verge of walking to the house and peering in. 'I told him to leave me alone!' she said irritably, and the old man looked at her.

'Would you like him to be distracted for a while?'

'How? He's supposed to be at work. He's bored. He'll spoil everything.'

Snake Man daubed some of the contents of his pot onto a small wood mannikin, smaller than the doll he had once given Mary Jane. He muttered something to the figurine, then tossed it into the air. To Mary Jane's astonishment the mannikin vanished, as in all the best conjuring tricks.

Frankie walked towards the hut. What the hell did Mary Jane want *here*? He had to be at work. This was ridiculous. She earned no money. She'd suffer too if he lost his job.

Time to get her back. Time to put his foot down. Time to insist! He walked quickly towards the hut.

The sound of the girl's laughter was instantly distracting. He glanced round, but could see nothing. It came again, laughter as light, as pretty as a summer breeze. It was coming from behind some rocks, over to the right. He strolled over there, and peered round.

And gaped with astonishment.

'Hi!' she said cheerfully, and went back to playing with the tiny desert rodent. It leapt about her feet, stopping occasionally to peer up at her. She sat on a rock, legs apart, skirts pulled up above perfect knees on perfect legs. Her blonde hair was long, blowing slightly in the gentle, hot breeze.

She stood up and walked over to Frankie Laine Silverlock. She was tall, full bosomed, with a touch of Indian about her eyes, which were dark brown. He looked at her and marvelled. When she shook hands his knees went weak.

'Who are you?' he asked nervously.

'Just travelling through,' she said. 'Stopped by to see the old man there. I'm heading north. Nowhere special.' She stared at him hard, then smiled sexily. 'You're a good looking boy. You're a Sioux, right? I never made it with an Indian.' Again that inviting smile. 'I'm part Indian myself,' she said. 'Grandmother married a Swedish settler . . .'

'I can hardly believe it,' murmured Frankie Laine Silverlock, as he reached for her hand and tugged her close. 'I must be dreaming.'

Her hands went to his body with a directness, and an enthusiasm, that startled him, aroused him, and made him forget all about his sister, hiding away in the ramshackle old hut.

Mary Jane watched her brother kissing and cuddling thin air, and chuckled with amusement. 'What's he seeing?'

The old man said, 'A daydream. Whatever he wants.'

'Candice Bergen,' she said. He looked so odd standing there, stroking a non-existent thigh, then holding hands with mid-air and walking slightly out of sight behind the rocks. She saw him unfastening his belt.

Screwing the air, she thought, wryly amused. *He always bragged that he could screw anything. Maybe he'll find a nice snake hole.*

She turned back to the magic man and stared at his wizened features. He seemed very gentle, very kindly. 'I've been chosen to Walk On Water.'

'I know,' he said. 'I was listening.'

'All the way to England.'

He nodded. 'That's a very great walk. It will be very hard.'

'I need a guardian,' she said, folding her arms across her chest. She didn't really know what to ask for, or how, she just knew – she'd heard people talk about it – that a

32

guardian spirit could be invaluable when making such long walks as this. Her ancestors had rarely done anything dangerous without the security of a guardian spirit.

Snake Man watched her, then shook his head. 'I could give you ten guardian spirits. They would not stay with you.'

She frowned, alarmed. 'Why?'

He shrugged. 'Because your heart is not in the great walk. Because you have been chosen but not consulted. Because you must do the bidding of the Chief against your will. Because guardian spirits do not associate with unhappiness. When our ancestors made their great walks, into the plains, into the hills, into the forests, alone and naked, to see the Magic Places, they were afraid, yes, but they went of their own accord. They were glad to go. They were pleased with the danger. Around them the spirits danced, blowing fire into the eyes of coyotes, dust into the jaws of the scuttling spiders of night. They protected. They would not protect you.'

Mary Jane became distressed, turning back to gaze out of the window. Behind the nearer rocks, Frankie Laine Silverlock humped the earth, happy in his magic.

'What am I to do? When I get there I won't come back. I don't trust Coyote, the old magic man from the west. His eyes were shady. He's trying to trick me. He says when I come back I'll have love and success, but I don't think they intend for me to return. When I get there I'll die.'

'You will be carrying something for the Great Spider,' said Snake Man, and smiled pinkly as Mary Jane glanced at him sharply.

'You know everything.'

'I listen carefully,' he said. 'Not even that old man Coyote knows. He's not expecting it. He's not listening for me. You will be carrying something very dangerous, a ghost. Why that ghost is needed in England . . .' he shrugged. 'But I know that ghost. It will consume you. You are right. You will not come back.'

Mary Jane felt her stomach turn over. Her knees began to wobble and her eyes stung with tears. She didn't want to

33

die. Ridgeville was a terrible place, somewhere to escape from, but she would have happily stayed there all her life, if she could just be left alone. Death terrified her. She read a lot, she watched TV, and there was a big world to see, a lot of places to go where things were more progressive, more exciting than Ridgeville. In time, when Frankie's savings had mounted up, they would go together, away from the shanty town, away from other Indians, to a place where their past didn't matter, where they would be people of value, not objects of curiosity, or fun.

'What am I to do?' she repeated softly. 'I must run away.'

The old man chuckled and shook his head. 'Where would you run? That old Coyote would hunt you down. I don't know why they want you, why they need *you* . . . but they do. You were chosen. There is something in you that they need. You would not get away. Old Coyote isn't listening now. But if he was, he would know where you were. He would come loping after you. A hundred miles, a thousand . . . that Coyote would come snapping at your heels.'

'Then I'm lost,' she said, and began to cry. Snake Man came over to her and put his bony arm around her shoulder. She nestled against his skeletal form, smelling the old blanket he wore, the odd aroma of an old man, not unpleasant, just . . . human.

'You have to go,' he said gently. 'You want a particular type of guardian spirit, but that wouldn't work. That doesn't mean I can't help you.'

She drew back, tugged a tissue from her jeans and wiped her eyes. 'How?'

'Follow me,' he said, and walked across the shack.

A great patterned rug hung there, marked with the symbols and totems of the days of hunting, centuries before. The rug was old and frayed. Once, perhaps, it had covered the entrance to a chief's lodge, in the great times, before the Europeans. Behind the rug was a door, and through the door the rock rose sheer and unwelcoming. Snake Man led the way around the rock to a place where the stone folded in upon itself, a shadowy place. Here, he squeezed into the body of the earth itself, and Mary Jane edged her way after him, ducking as the rock closed over her head, finally moving along the low tunnel at a crouch.

It was cold and dank. The walls were damp. This was where he got his water from.

Light flared ahead of her. He had struck light to a tallow torch using a bright gold cigarette lighter. 'So much better than flints,' he said, and beckoned her into the low-ceilinged chamber. She stepped forward, straightening up, and looked around. Immediately she gasped with horror, and covered her mouth with her hand.

'Don't be afraid,' the old man soothed. 'They're just the dead.'

They lay on thin wooden pallets around the walls. Some rested on narrow shelves carved into the rocks. Two were seated, their skulls still attached to the spines, and staring out across the chamber. Most of the dead had corroded down to bone, still swathed in the rotten fibre of their burial clothes. Some, though, were shrivelled corpses, the flesh drawn in on the cheeks, the eyes sunken, but the lids parted to show the faint glimmer of the orbs still intact. Withered hands poked from beneath the shrouds, some still clutching the edges of the cloth.

The walls of the chamber were painted with ochre. There were faces, and symbols that meant the elements of earth and fire and air. There were spirals and patterns that must have once meant something to the workers of magic in the tribes, but which to Mary Jane's eyes were just the mindless daubings of a child. Tatters of canvas and heavy jute fibre hung from the ceiling, fixed to the hard rock with iron nails. On them were colours and tiny patterns. They blew with the draught that crept in along the narrow tunnel.

Snake Man led her deeper into the chamber. There was a ledge of rock, empty and waiting. He spread the small blanket on the shelf and smiled. Mary Jane glanced around nervously. Close by lay the shrivelled body of a woman, hands crossed on her chest, eyes half open. She looked no

35

worse than the old man himself, and Mary Jane wondered how long she had been dead . . .

And as she gazed in terror, and disgust, at the recumbent relic, she screamed quickly and shrilly as she saw the corpse's chest rise and fall.

'She's alive!'

'Sleeping,' said the old man sadly. 'Soon she will be as the others, among the dead. She has slept for a long time. She is lost to me, but many times before such a sadness has not occurred.'

Mary Jane shivered as she looked at the withering body.

'You will lie here,' the old man said. 'You will have to concentrate very hard. But it won't take long.'

She watched him as he pottered about the cave of the dead. He tugged a small bone from the skeleton of a chief, examined it in the flickering torch light, then placed it in the middle of the floor. He detached a long bone from the leg of another and laid it by the first. Then he placed Mary Jane's own small doll on the floor, but first used a small crayon to colour in the features that time had faded.

She watched in silence, nervous and perplexed.

'Come here,' he said, and she walked over to him. He used a bone-handled knife to make a cut in her thumb, and absorbed the blood onto a piece of cloth. This he dropped to the floor, with the other artefacts. Finally, he snipped a lock of her hair, including a few strands of the silver, and placed it with the rest. Then, at a crouch, he drew the vague outline of a human being around the clutter of bone, wood and hair.

'We shall create something far better than a guardian spirit,' he said. 'Lie down, now.' She did as she was bidden, and he arranged her hands across her chest, the fingers curled, like a spider. He placed something on those hands, then closed her eyes with his cold, bony fingers.

Quietly, he began to chant, and the words were strange to Mary Jane. Soon she felt warm, relaxed, safe. When Snake Man instructed her in English, she was able to obey his every word.

36

Frankie Laine Silverlock was waiting for his sister by the two cars, impatient and worried.

'Where'd you get to?' he demanded irritably as she walked up to him. 'I looked in the hut and you weren't there!'

'I was walking,' Mary Jane said, and smiled sweetly.

'We've gotta get back,' the big Indian said, nervously. 'It's late. I probably got no job, thanks to you. Then what do I do? Come on Mary Jane. Let's get back.'

They returned to the town. Frankie Laine was distracted. He kept looking out of the window of their small house. He drank beer incessantly, pulling the ring from a fresh can before he'd hardly finished the first. Mary Jane sat and watched him.

'Did you see a girl up on the summit?' he asked eventually.

'Blonde?' Mary Jane said. 'A bit like Candice Bergen?'

He turned and grinned at her, his broad face full of pride, full of triumph. 'You saw her,' he said.

'You were with her,' she answered, and smiled.

'I scored,' he said. 'It's the only thing that kept me going all afternoon. I thought I was dreaming. I fell asleep and woke up and thought I'd dreamed it. But you saw her.' He swigged beer and raised the can, a toast to achievement. 'Half Indian, half what they call it . . . viking! A dream.' He looked out of the window, gazing morosely into the distance. 'She was going north. Said she might come by, but I think she was just passing through.'

'You could score with a dead lizard,' Mary Jane said.

'Yeah,' said Frankie proudly and drained the can. 'I can score with anything.' He looked round at his sister. Frowned. Stared at her for a long moment. 'You seem different.'

She shrugged. 'I'm frightened. How should I seem?'

'You don't seem as frightened as you were.' He scratched his chest. He was a bull, his dark skin glossy, his chest deep. His dark eyes shone, his broad nose twitched.

37

He watched his beautiful sister and felt the change. 'You're cold. You're distant. I can't explain it properly.'

'Stop drinking. After tonight you can drink yourself to death. I'll be a long way away.'

'Not that far. Not that long,' he said. There were tears in his almond eyes. His full lips trembled slightly. He was twenty-one, but he needed Mary Jane. He sensed, for the first time, what it would be like to be without her. He came over and picked her up by the arms, dangling her a few inches from the floor. His look was one of total affection. 'I'm gonna miss you.'

'I'll be back. You heard what that old Coyote said. I'll be back.'

'I don't understand this magic stuff. I don't understand the old men. I don't understand ghosts, gods and demons. I understand work. I understand girls. I understand cars. I feel sad, Mary Jane. I'm gonna miss you.'

'You'll lay another white girl. You'll get drunk. I'll come back. You'll say "Hi, how was it?" We'll be back to normal.'

He grasped her tightly to him. He was a bull; she was a slim girl, and her ribs felt like cracking. He cried on her shoulder, sniffling like a kid, letting the tears run free and soak through her T-shirt.

'Time to go,' she said, and stood up from the ragged sofa. Frankie Laine made to get up too, but she pushed him back down, reached down to kiss his cheek. 'You stay here.'

'I ought to come with you.'

'They want me alone. You did your job. You kept me company.'

He watched her. She was the best looking girl in Ridgeville, with that small, elfin face, the shape of her lips, those eyes and her figure, slim but so feminine. One day soon she would have left anyway. Some guy would have taken her from him. He'd have been alone eventually.

'Take care,' he said quietly, and tried to mask his tears

behind the eighth can of beer he'd drunk that evening.

'I shall,' she said, and left him. She was cold, he thought. There was something different about her. She was too calculating, too certain. Earlier, before going up to Blue Snake Summit, she'd cried, she'd shaken. Now she seemed resigned to Walking On Water. It was as if she no longer controlled her feelings. As if she watched, like remote control.

Mary Jane walked quickly through the town. It was a bright night, the moon was up. It was warm. She could see the summit against the night sky, and a light burned there, a torch, placed on one of the peaks. She smiled to think that he was still watching her. Around her, as she strolled briskly towards the centre, televisions blared, music played, children shouted. The streets were busy, young-sters, mostly, hanging out on street corners, or making plans for a midnight run to Westrock. Dogs prowled the trash cans, tugging and tipping in their search for scraps.

The Lodge was hidden from the town square behind the high façade of a drug-store. She skirted the shops, cut down the alleyway between the store and the bar, and emerged into the quiet area behind. This was a place where only the town fathers came. There was a fence, and a gate through the fence, and flowers and statues in that strange garden. The Lodge itself looked silent and dark, but there was movement inside.

She hesitated by the gate and stared at this mysterious building. She had seen it before, of course, but had never been inside. It was a tall building, with a steep roof. Objects hung from the eaves, and circles with crosses and arrows in them had been daubed on the outside walls. Above the door were the traditional artefacts of the ancestral Sioux: buffalo horns, skins, a small bow made of willow.

She walked to this door, but before she could knock, it was opened by Once-Rode-Horse, dressed bizarrely in ceremonial robes. He ushered her into the Lodge, whispering to her, 'Don't be afraid. It's just us old men and women. Always Talking is here.'

Mary Jane was glad of that. Always Talking was an old woman, and had been a good and close friend of her mother's. Mary Jane knew that the woman's real name was Shayna. Her grandfather had been Running Horse, who had been to law school and whose actions in the early part of the century had helped Ridgeville to come into being, and saved the ancestral lands beyond Blue Snake Summit from exploitation by the big corporations of white America. As a descendant of Running Horse, Shayna Always Talking was well respected, even though the trait from which she derived her name could drive sane men to distraction.

Now at last Mary Jane Silverlock saw the inside of the Lodge. It was a gloomy place, lit by four torches at the corners of the room. In the middle of the room a flameless fire burned, the smoke rising in a billowing grey cloud to a vent in the ceiling. It was cool, here. Old men sat cross-legged about the fire, staring at the ashes. They were all dressed like Once-Rode-Horse, in long ceremonial garbs, painted and patterned in the old ways. Their hair hung long, white and lank, although some wore head bands. Grey Bear, with traditional eccentricity, had placed two eagle feathers at the sides of his own red headband. He looked up as Mary Jane entered the room, and waved.

From among the circle of elders, Coyote, the stranger, rose to his feet and raised his arms. He was dressed in the skins of jackals, with the skull of a fox around his neck. He had painted every inch of his skin with brilliant reds and sombre greys. Around his eyes were stripes; on his cheeks he had daubed spirals. His hair had been plaited, and the plaits were painted black at the ends. He made a strange ululation, and chanted words that reminded Mary Jane of the alien words the old man on Snake Summit had uttered recently.

Always Talking fussed around her, soothing and reassuring her. Mary Jane was stripped naked and her body painted in various ways. She remained oblivious to all, watching Coyote, although Always Talking's hands were cold and made her shiver. After a while she was led

40

back to the main Lodge and made to kneel by the smoking ashes of the fire. There was a draught on her nude skin, and she trembled slightly, tensing her haunches, becoming aware of the gaze of the old men.

Coyote looked at her peculiarly, eyes narrowed, brow furrowed. He had sensed something about her, but could not pin it down. He lowered his arms and walked around the circle of seated elders, behind Mary Jane. The smoke from the fire billowed and swirled, making the room seem grey and cold. Old faces watched her, painted features highlighted by the flickering torches.

Would he realize, she wondered? Would he see it? Would he discover the way she was guarded against real danger?

Coyote stepped in front of her and dropped to a crouch, his eyes piercing. Mary Jane stayed still, leaning back on her haunches. The old man's hands reached out and touched her face, her shoulders, her small breasts, but this was not an intimate touch in the usual sense . . . he was feeling, seeking beyond her flesh. He murmured words that sent a chill through the girl. He rubbed his fingers together and a strange aroma assailed her nostrils, something pungent, something like the smell of a dead snake. She remained still.

Coyote, still less happy than before, stood up and moved through the grey smoke, making the fumes swirl and dance around the choking Lodge.

Always Talking brought her a clay cup and she drank the bitter liquid that it contained. The old woman brought her a plate of meat, but the meat had been prepared with sharp herbs and spices, and smelled of woodland, and fungus, something unusual for this part of the country. The food filled her, took the edge from her appetite, but also made her head spin a little. The room seemed to bend and twist. The old men receded from her vision, then loomed large, their placid expressions, their wrinkles, their gleaming eyes magnified in great detail.

Coyote raised his arms again, looked upwards and closed his eyes. He cried words in the old language, then

41

chanted several brief, sharp incantations. The skins and shields on the Lodge wall rattled and were disturbed by unfelt breezes.

'You are the little spider,' he said in English, looking at Mary Jane. 'You are the messenger. You are the carrier. You will Walk On Water to the far land, and you will take the spirits of the old people with you. This is your purpose, little spider, to weave one part of the great web, to take the magic of this land to the far land, where the Great Spider grows and feeds and makes ready.'

The room closed in upon her. Her naked flesh bristled and shivered with cold, and she felt touches on her skin, like the gentle stroking of fingers. Always Talking was standing, hidden in the shadows at the back of the Lodge. The smoke that danced before her eyes seemed to take on a shape, writhing and leaning towards her, man-like, huge, frightening. Through its tenuous wreaths she could see the dark-robed Coyote, eyes closed, hands raised from the sides of his body, head moving slightly from side to side. His voice was a dull murmur, a repetitive sound, the ritual calling up of spirits.

Outside the Lodge, a state of unnatural quiet fell across the town of Ridgeville. Televisions flickered and blurred, radios cut out, dogs stopped barking, babies ceased to cry. A wind came, then, a cold wind, blowing from the hills, from the farmlands. It swirled around the town, rattling doors and windows, sending litter blowing wildly through the deserted streets. The sound of that wind was like the distant howl of an animal pursued. And behind the wind came the darkness, a pall of gloom that blocked the stars and made the horizon fade. Ridgeville was immersed in that eerie darkness. It flowed like water up out of the earth, down across Blue Snake Summit, sweeping across the open land to the south. Shapes writhed and twisted within the spectral flood, peered through windows, rattled doorknobs, seeped into houses to pinch and probe the terrified occupants. But there was a stronger call this night, and they fled through the outskirts of the town, and loomed large above the smoky Lodge, behind the town square. The wind passed away, the darkness lifted, the shapes fell inwards, summoned by Coyote.

They were all around the walls, hovering in the shadows, crouching beneath the totems, prowling about the greyness. The fire burned high, flame suddenly licking into life. The smoke coiled and billowed. It seemed to reach out over the old men, like something alive, touching the half-glimpsed spirits. Always Talking made a shrill sound of terror and ran into the room a little, glancing nervously back over her shoulder. She dropped to her knees behind Mary Jane, crossed her arms and leaned forward, not wanting to witness the earth magic that occurred around her.

Coyote roamed among the spirits, walking the perimeter of the Lodge twice, while Mary Jane watched him apprehensively. The other old men stared at the fire, chuckling and reminiscing about the old days, when the spirits had been summoned more regularly. Coyote wandered among the gathered ghosts, selecting those who would go with the young woman from Ridgeville.

At last he seemed satisfied. 'Stand up', he told Mary Jane, and she obeyed, shivering. He stepped across the smouldering fire towards her, and in his hand he held bright slivers of bone. They were shaped like animals, or leaves, or clouds; tiny ivory-like fragments, meticulously carved. Each had a sharp edge. Coyote's dark eyes burned into hers, numbing her senses, holding her rigid. All strength went from her body, all sensation.

'Yours is a great journey, a great walk. You will take a ghost to the Great Spider, but you will be guarded on your journey, protected against all evil.'

He plucked a fragment of bone and reached to the underside of her left breast, pushing the sharp sliver into her flesh. She felt dull pain. Blood trickled down her belly. 'I will give you Enumclaw, thunder spirit, who will guard you against the sky . . .'

Something detached itself from a bright tribal shield; it blew around the room, laughing deeply; the cold smell of rain, the biting touch of a storm wind; eyes watched her, hands touched her, and Enumclaw passed into her body through the bone chip . . .

'I will give you Tieholt, a water monster, who will protect you from all demons of the deep ocean as you are Mary Jane Walks On Water . . .'

Something with immense jaws rose before her, as if out of the floor. She felt salt on her face, her body froze as if she were immersed in the icy water of a lake. The being cried once, then swam towards her. Her lungs filled with water and she choked, but it was only the illusion of drowning. The discomfort passed away. A bone chip had been embedded in her right breast and she looked down, watching the blood. In her mind she could hear the roar of an ocean, the tumbling cascade of a waterfall, the splash of salmon. Tieholt had found his niche among her grey stuff.

'I will give you Nayenez, who is the slayer of alien gods.' Coyote had moved around Mary Jane, and she felt the prick of bone being pushed into the flesh below her shoulder blade. 'This Nayenez,' Coyote said quietly, 'is a very powerful spirit, who can guide you through the rocks that crush the traveller, the reeds which cut him to pieces, the cacti that tear him to pieces; he will lead you safely across the boiling sands that overwhelm the traveller, and will destroy those people who slay with their eyes. All these things Nayenez once did. I give him to you now, but respect him . . .'

The bone chip hurt. Mary Jane stood shivering. Blood trickled down her back. Nayenez drifted down through the smoke, a tall, shadowy form, clad in furs, with a breastplate of bone. In his right hand he held two white and black feathers. His face was that of a demon, painted, broad, grinning. His body was that of a powerful warrior. He leapt from the grey smoke towards Mary Jane, who flinched as the spirit passed through her. Her skin froze. The Lodge rattled and shook with the delighted cry of this ghost as it found a new release into the mortal world. It entered her through the bone splinter in her flesh, and she felt strength in her arms and legs, and her mind filled with

44

images of subterranean passages, dark places below the earth.

'I will give you Young Grandfather, your own ancestor, who has watched you from his bones, where they lie in the high hills.'

Less pain as the bone sliver entered her flesh. She heard the thunder of hooves, smelled grass, dust, the sweat of an animal. The whole world seemed to rock and shake. The sun was bright, sharp. She realized she was seeing a vision of the hunt, of the great hunts of old. The beasts were broad-backed, powerful. The herd was like a sea of dark brown; a restless, shifting tide of flesh around which she galloped, the gutstring of her willow bow tight and hard against her finger.

Young Grandfather came out of time and passed into his daughter's grey stuff, a welcome friend among the mischievous, wailing ghosts of the other dead things that inhabited her. She felt him whispering to her. He was young, strong. He greeted her from his bones. He felt sadness at the decline of the tribe, and his family. What stories he would tell her of hunts, of pursuit, of counting coup on the tribes that hunted the same plains. He would keep her warm all across the great water. He would fight back the other spirits. He would protect her. With Young Grandfather beside her, she would come to no harm.

It was not yet finished.

Coyote said, 'These are your guardians. Now I give you Chief of Demons, who is your charge. Chief of Demons, who needs to go to England, to the Great Spider. You will carry Chief of Demons, and the others will protect you from his malice. He is not of these northern lands. Chief of Demons is from the jungle world in the far south. He is Hunhau. He is Lord of Death, and he seeks victims among the sick and dying. He is dangerous, Mary Jane Walks On Water, and he will be unpleasant company. Bear him well, and with firmness. He is needed across the water by those who are arranging for the great awakening.'

As he had spoken Coyote had smeared red stuff on Mary Jane's body, marking small symbols on her back and belly.

45

His hands had shaken as he had done this. It was a thin fragment of crystal that he introduced into her body, below her navel. His hands shook as he did this too. He was afraid of Hunhau. The Lord of Death filled him with terror. Mary Jane shook as well, with cold, with anticipation.

A putrid wind blew around the Lodge, quelling the fire, making the elders choke and hold hands to their faces. It was the smell of death, of decomposition. Laughter sounded, cackling laughter, that was lost against the ever rising wind. Something hideous flew about the Lodge, passing in front of torches, making the light dim. It swirled the ash from the fire, sent shields and spears flying from the Lodge walls. At last it moved into Mary Jane, attracted by the magic of words, paint and crystal. It was the worst thing of all, man-like, rotten, the flesh falling from its grinning face, its body opened in great rending wounds that bled darkly through its ragged clothes.

Grave spirit. Lord of Death. It danced into Mary Jane and caused her such pain that she arched backwards, sucking in breath sharply. The agony was intense. He twisted her arms, her fingers, her innards. He probed and poked her eyes, belly and backside, hurting her all the time.

Coyote closed his hands around Mary Jane's face, easing her head forward. He said words and the pain went away, and the tears ceased to flow from her eyes. Always Talking scrambled forward, her face pale and frightened, and slipped a warm shirt over Mary Jane's shoulders, tugging it down to her hips. The old men watched silently, but Once-Rode-Horse smiled at her and winked. She was handed her jeans and she tugged them on. Sensation came back to her body, and the bits of bone and crystal hurt her, but Coyote had daubed black stuff on the wounds and sealed them. He peered at her, still unhappy, aware that something was wrong, but it was too late now. Young Grandfather knew, had known the moment he had entered her. But he was keeping quiet, smiling grimly.

'Your secret, my secret,' he said to her.

'Stay close, Young Grandfather,' she said back.

46

Always Talking was kneeling by the fire, eyes closed, body swaying back and forth. Coyote watched her. The woman sang softly, humming a tune, an insistent, ritualized sound that accompanied her trance. Coyote shifted restlessly, waiting.

After a while Always Talking tensed slightly, and lifted her hands from her body, palms outwards, towards the fire. Her eyes were still closed.

'Only one,' she said softly. 'Just one. But he is strong. He is in the east.'

Coyote said, 'Is he part of the Great Spider?'

Always Talking shook her head. 'No. He is an enemy. He is already moving to the meeting place. He is strong. The girl must beware. She must strike first.'

Mary Jane listened calmly as she was told of the danger. Coyote glanced at her. She stared back.

Always Talking said, 'He is a hunter. He moves through the night. His name is Brady.'

It was well after midnight when Mary Jane Silverlock stepped out of the Lodge. The stars were brilliant, the town silent, even the dogs asleep. Coyote led her to the town square and pointed her to the east.

'May you have a good walk,' he said, as if she were going hiking in the sandstone hills.

She took a step forward and reached the edge of the square. Another step and she was through the town. Her strides were ordinary, but each time she moved she drifted across the earth, as if propelled. She walked so fast that the wind was cold on her face. She walked out across the farmland, towards the low hills. Soon she was invisible against the darkness of the land, moving faster than a bird.

4

For a while, at least, all immediate worries about a 'danger approaching from the west' had to be put from his mind. Dan Brady was becoming used to danger. Six months ago he had been an ordinary family man who would have run a mile from a threatening gang of kids. Six months ago he would have had little real idea of how to defend himself against attack or assault.

In six months the change had been devastating, and total.

He fended off attack, now, from both the mind and the body. He had pursued his family to a remote Norfolk town and found himself in the midst of the enemy: Arachne and the Collectors. They had known of his presence and sent their physical forces against him, and he had dispatched them with ease. But though he had come close to his daughter, Marianna, at the last moment Arachne had fled the area, and hope had been wrenched from his grasping fingers. He had only the amulet to show for his effort, the Nordic talisman that contained an unknown, perhaps unknowable power.

And yet he had something else. He had a knowledge that his daughter was *useful* to the evil minds behind Arachne. He had found a note to that effect: *The Brady girl's talents are unusual. We can use her before Roundelay. Tell the mammath.*

Roundelay. Mammath. Two more clues, two more strangenesses, to add to the vivid memories he still held of the night of the attack last year. But what was Roundelay? What was the mammath? And in what way could his daughter be useful to them?

As he thought of Marianna, he reached into the breast

pocket of his leather jacket and touched the other talisman he now carried, something less powerful than the Nordic stone, but far more meaningful: the remains of a pair of wire-rimmed glasses. 'Granny glasses', Dominick had called them, and Marianna had always yelled at him with annoyance when he called them that. She had needed them to correct a slight short-sightedness in her left eye. Brady had found them, crushed beneath a shoe, in a caravan near to the Norfolk town.

It brought tears to his eyes to remember the way she had looked in the glasses. They were tears he allowed, the only tears he permitted. He touched the cold frames, now, as he drove east, towards Surrey. The cold metal spoke to him, urging him to drive faster, to search harder, to get closer . . . *Find me. Find me!*

He would find them all. They were still alive, all three of them. He would find them all.

Or die trying.

Less than an hour later he had reached his destination, a drably designed six storey building, standing in elegantly maintained grounds, behind locked gates. It was on a main road, but well screened from casual view behind tall trees. Brady parked his car across the road from the gates, and sat for a while, staring at the darkened windows, and the notice board that rose just behind the fence.

The letters EIPR were prominently displayed on this board, and at first glance they were meaningless and boring. The building could have been any small-time factory, or office block, and the pedestrians who walked past the gates afforded the site no more than a casual glance.

Brady stared longer and harder, because he was half afraid to go any further towards it. What the casual glance would not show was the expansion of the letters EIPR, written so small below: The Ennean Institute of Paranormal Research.

This was the place where Ellen Bancroft had worked. It was the institute where the first clues that had led Brady to

Norfolk so recently had been found. It was the place where an almost amateur enthusiasm for researching the occult, the paranormal, the supernatural, held sway, in complete contrast to the Ministry of Defence Research Station where Brady had once worked, where a more scientific and rigorous approach to the paranormal was conducted.

The Ennean Institute was a place where essential information might be found, and where the enemy might be hiding, behind a desk, in an office, behind the innocent façade of a clerk, or junior researcher.

Two opposing needs worked within Brady, as he let the car cool down and waited for the time of his scheduled appointment to arrive. One of these was the need for that information, the need for help, the need to pick brains about Roundelay, about Arachne, about things and places with strange names, names that might seem less strange to those who had dabbled with the planes astral, neo-astral, lunar, stellar and earthly; concepts and ideas that may have been recorded, and ignored, and which might have given Brady the essential clues he needed to continue his pursuit of Arachne, his search for his family.

But against that need worked the warning he had been given by Ellen Bancroft, weeks before. *Trust no one. Trust nothing. Trust no one but yourself.*

She had taken her own advice, locking herself away in a flat in London, communicating with no one save a middle-aged man called Andrew Haddingham. *Trust no one*, she had said, but it was impossible to cut oneself off to that extent. She had partly trusted Haddingham, and had come to trust Brady. But Brady had already experienced the same tragedy as she, and they had become involved and fed off each other's strengths.

She had died, not because she had been betrayed, but because she had been careless. She had been incautious at a time when common sense bespoke the utmost care. She had paid devastatingly for her mistake, and it was a lesson that Brady had learned too. He would not repeat Ellen Bancroft's error. And he would take her advice totally to heart.

50

Trust no one!

No one except Haddingham, and him only partially. But Andrew was a friend, and a comfort, and was useful in other ways besides.

Brady crossed the road to take advantage of that usefulness now. A meeting, arranged with the Ennean, with people whose talents might further Brady's quest.

Haddingham met him in reception. The man looked pale and tired, his suit even more dishevelled than usual. He led the way through the highly polished corridors, their walls lined with pictures of great parapsychologists, to a room that overlooked the rear of the grounds. The Ennean Institute bustled with life, but had a strangely clinical feel to it. Brady always felt that it would have been more appropriately housed within an ornate, and rather cold and windy, Victorian building, in the heart of the country.

'Good to see you, Dan,' Haddingham said, unconvincingly. 'You look wrecked, though. It must have been tough.'

Brady sat down at the table, resting forward. 'Not easy,' he said. 'But I came close, Andrew. I came very close. To my daughter, at least.'

'Close, but never close enough,' Haddingham said quietly. He leaned against the windowsill, staring at his friend. 'There was killing . . .' he made it sound like a statement, but Brady guessed that it was a question.

He said, 'There's always killing, Andrew. Lives wasted, but lives saved as well.'

'How about the police? Are they hounding you?'

Brady shrugged. 'Sutherland is helpful. Sutherland understands.'

'Sutherland?'

'Local force. He's leading the official search for Alison. He's sceptical, but he at least believes what his eyes and senses tell him. He believes me, and knows that these are no ordinary abductions.'

'Sounds like a useful man,' said Haddingham, and came over to sit at the table. He was thoughtfully silent for a moment, then added, 'I'm sorry you didn't find her. It must have been agony. To come so close.'

'It was,' said Brady. 'It was, it is . . . it always will be.' He smiled quickly and reached up to take the amulet from around his neck. 'I got something, though. I got this.'

Haddingham stared at the hideous talisman, the screaming skull that communicated such pain, such agony. 'That's grotesque,' he said. 'Where was it?'

'Buried several feet down. In the ruins of an old town. Arachne was seeking it. I intend to find out why.'

'Hideous,' Haddingham said, and shook his head.

A little while later the door to the room opened and a young woman stepped inside, followed by a sallow faced man, whose arm was in a sling. Brady rose to his feet and shook hands with the woman, who was introduced as Françoise Jeury. Her accent was strongly and attractively French.

The man was not staying. He was an American, called Lee Kline, and he was on his way to London. 'Don't work her too hard,' he said pleasantly, and smiled at Brady. Then he leaned down and kissed Françoise Jeury, murmuring something to her that Brady could not hear.

He closed the door.

Brady sat down at the table again, and Françoise sat opposite him. They exchanged a long, searching stare. She was very good-looking, with her auburn hair cut quite short, framing a face that was sun-tanned, slim, yet hard, sharp. Her eyes were piercing, analytical. Brady found it quite disconcerting to be scrutinized so closely. After a moment they both smiled, and Françoise glanced at Andrew Haddingham, who was again leaning against the windowsill.

'Andrew has told me a little about you, Mister Brady,' she said, her voice a soft, lilting sound. 'How may I be of service to you?'

'You have a talent,' Brady said. 'You are psychic in an unusual way. You can touch things – objects, stones, personal things, and get feelings about them . . .'

52

She nodded. 'It's true. That is my talent, yes. At the moment I am exhausted. Quite exhausted.' She stared at Brady, her green eyes shining. She didn't look tired, but there was something about her that was, indeed, weary.

'Too tired to respond to a couple of objects?' Brady asked, and placed the skull talisman on the table. Next to it he placed the broken glasses that had belonged to Marianna. Françoise regarded the two things evenly, then shrugged. 'We'll see,' she said.

'What was your last work?' Haddingham asked from across the room, and Françoise looked at him squarely for a moment, before returning her gaze to Brady. 'A font,' she said. 'Carved and shaped from an old standing stone. There was something trapped in it, something evil. It escaped. It was returned. The man you just saw was nearly killed in the process. Me too. I had an image of what was in the stone, but it was exhausting to summon it. That's why I'm tired. I hope I can be of service.'

As she lowered her gaze to the stone talisman, Brady thought that an expression of apprehension touched her features. 'Where did that come from?' she asked.

'It's Norse,' Brady said. 'I dug it up in Norfolk. I need to get an idea of the power it contains. You may be able to sense that power.'

She shivered slightly, and crossed her hands on the table. Brady noticed that there was a thin sheen of moisture above her upper lip. She was nervous.

'I felt it . . . I sensed it . . . the moment I came into the room. It's very strong. Like a scream. I can hear the scream on that face. Ugh!' it was a sound of revulsion, and was accompanied by a violent tremor.

'Handle it,' Brady said. 'There may be stronger sensations.' He picked up the head, cradled it in his palm for a moment, then placed it close to Françoise. She reached out towards it, holding both hands above the amulet. Then she tugged back, licking her lips nervously.

She glanced up at Brady and smiled uncertainly. 'I don't like this,' she said. 'It's too strong . . . it's stronger even than . . .'

But she didn't complete the sentence. Again she reached to the viking carving, and this time her hands hovered above the talisman, shaking like leaves. A sweat broke out across her face, and her tan could not conceal the fact that she had blanched, that the blood had drained from her skin.

As Brady watched, so the woman seemed to be struggling to push her hands closer to the object. The effort was incredible. She began to tremble, and abruptly snapped her hands back into her lap and exhaled loudly.

'My God,' she said breathlessly, shaking her head. 'What in the name of all the gods *is* that?'

'Meteorite stone,' Brady said. 'Fashioned by a shaman. The face changed from benign to evil, as if by magic. There is a terrible story associated with it.'

'Pain,' Françoise agreed, and wiped her palms together, her gaze on the silent stone. 'I feel such awful pain, like a sword cutting . . . and in such a terrible place! Deep pain. But that is not what frightens me . . .'

Instead of elaborating she reached again, one hand on each side of the stone head, trying to close her fingers around it. Slowly the effort began to show, her eyes narrowing, her lips tightening, until again the breath exploded from her body and she gave up, collapsing back in her chair and shaking her head.

'What are you trying to do to me, Mister Brady?' she said, and laughed nervously.

'What's stopping you touching the stone?'

'I don't know. Something in *me*. It's far too powerful. My muscles just won't obey. I'm aware of what's in the object, but not consciously. It's a psychological phenomenon, and it's *exhausting* me!' She tried to smile, wiping a hand across her mouth, then looking down at the dampness on her palms.

'Just a moment,' she said, and left the room.

Haddingham came over in her absence and picked up the stone head, weighing it, tossing it from hand to hand. 'What d'you make of that?'

'I don't know,' Brady said.

'Funny people, these psychics.'

When Françoise Jeury returned she was in possession of two pieces of silver wire, which she shaped into loops with short handles. Holding them by the very tips she crossed the loops above the stone head. Then slowly, and with increasing difficulty, she lowered them over the talisman.

After two minutes, during which she shook and perspired and groaned with effort, the wires touched the table, around the head.

She had closed her eyes.

After a while her breathing calmed down. A few minutes later she opened her eyes, calmly raised the wires and placed them on the table, drying her hands on a cloth. She stared at the nordic carving, then leaned back in her chair and watched Brady.

'The wires diffuse the vibration,' she said. 'It's possible to get a hint of what's within, without the full, damaging effect.'

'What could you feel?'

'There is something in the stone,' she said quietly. 'I can't tell you what. I couldn't see it. All I know is . . . it's sleeping. Or resting. It's on another plane of consciousness. It's here but not here, not yet. Sleeping.'

'It, it, it,' said Brady, impatiently. 'What's *it*? Is that all you can tell me? That whatever lives within the stone is an *it*, without form, or substance, or thought, or design?'

The French woman surveyed him calmly, condemning his irritation with her own silent understanding. She smiled thinly. 'I think I can understand the way you feel,' she said. 'I wish I could tell you more.' Her face shadowed, her gaze lowered, not to the object of her recent analysis, but to some point of focus that was not so much space, as time. She was silently thoughtful, remembering, perhaps, some moment of her own tragedy. Brady felt a little embarrassed fc: his crass behaviour.

'I'm sorry,' he said. 'I didn't mean to be so sharp.'

She shook her head without looking at him. 'You are not sorry, and without your anger, without your impatience, your terrible task would be that much harder.' Now she looked at him. 'It is I who am sorry, Mister Brady. Believe me, I have been subjected to far worse abuse in my time than one man expressing frustration. I cannot get closer. I cannot see the form of . . . of whatever it is that inhabits the stone head. It lies quietly, it appears to be sleeping, biding its time. I suspect – and this is mere intuition, rather than psychic vision – I suspect that it is allied to you, now. Whatever power it possesses will be *your* power. There is a sense of agony, of murder, of betrayal from the stone . . . and there is a feeling of resolution, and a powerfully felt presence which is . . .' she frowned, thinking hard, then chuckled, as she came to a sudden understanding. 'Why . . . which is you, Mister Brady. Part of you is in the talisman. Its story has spread to involve you, in a very superficial way.'

'No other feelings, however transitory?'

Françoise Jeury sat up a little straighter, brought her head closer to the carved stone, then shrugged. 'A sensation of intense, almost impossible cold. A sense of time, of void. This is space stone, you said. I can feel that. Intense cold. Incredible time. Within that cold there is the quiet thing, the sleeping thing. Around it, a legend was built. Adepts of those old days, people with powers like my own, were able to see, to glimpse that alien thing in the stone, and to tap its power. From that came the tragedy . . . the pain . . .'

'I know about the pain,' Brady said, and reached across the table for the amulet. He placed the cord round his neck, and tucked the head into his shirt again. It nestled there, icy, protective, at once a cry of challenge to Arachne, which had striven to obtain and control the talisman, and a comforting presence, a Pandora's Box of tricks that would reveal themselves in due course.

'Could you do the same for these?' Brady asked, holding up Marianna's bent and broken spectacles. Françoise looked slightly melancholy, but nodded agreement, and reached for the glasses.

'They were your daughter's,' she said at once, and Brady

shrugged. She could have guessed that with both eyes closed.

'Her name is Marianna,' he said.

'She is young,' said Françoise, 'And so *very* angry with your son. She hates these glasses.'

Brady said nothing, neither confirmation – for Françoise was certainly correct – nor deliberate negation. He was more intrigued to note the bizarre effect that the simple personal objects were having upon the French psychic.

Françoise's first observations had been made quietly, almost as an attempt to block the sudden surge of sorrow that surfaced both inwardly and outwardly. Haddingham coughed his embarrassment, and shuffled about where he leaned against the window. Brady was more courteous. He allowed silence to envelop the room as Françoise Jeury experienced the terrible emotion that had become associated with the broken spectacles.

Slowly, ever so slowly, she raised the glasses to her chest, her head lowering, her eyes squeezing tightly shut, trying to block the tears that insistently pushed forward. Her lips became wet, her breathing became the short, racking sound that precedes crying. She closed in upon herself, and for a long minute or so, just wept.

Finally, the sorrow passed, and she was quiet. She sniffed loudly, placed the spectacles on the table, and drew out the large handkerchief she carried, wiping her eyes and mouth, then blowing her nose violently. A touch of mascara had smeared below each eye. She breathed heavily, calming herself down, then looked up at Brady and gave a half-hearted smile.

'What are you trying to do to me, Mister Brady?'

'I didn't know it would affect you so badly.'

'I'm tired. I'm very tired. The effort of . . . of *that* thing . . .' she nodded towards his chest, where the artefact hung, 'Drained me even more. I become very susceptible to a child's fear. I have a low . . . what do you say? Flash point? A low flash point for tears.'

She blew her nose again, loudly, without embarrassment. Then she flopped back in the chair, and frowned, staring at Brady. 'So much emotion,' she said. 'Confused, angry, cold . . . a jumble of feelings. But mostly . . . such fear!'

She picked up the glasses again, and cradled them gently in her right hand, rubbing her thumb over the cracked lens, the twisted metal frame.

Brady said, 'Where is she?'

Françoise hesitated before saying, 'A crowded, dark place. It's very cold. The wind rocks it. An animal walks about. Mother is . . . gone. Alone. Dark and windy. Tiny room . . .'

The caravan, Brady thought. The last, terrifying memory before the glasses were smashed and left on the floor.

'Tell me about the animal. What can you see about the animal?'

Again, that lingering, penetrating silence. Then: 'The face is the face of a beast. A mask. The body is a man. He wears an overcoat. He is very cold, very impatient. He brings food, shouts, sometimes he comforts. He is always looking, always watching. He is a dark shape, towering over me. His voice is deep and harsh. He wants to go north . . .'

'Can you sense words? Can you hear *where* in the north?'

Françoise shook her head. 'Fear. Sorrow. Loneliness. Too much of these things. Too much feeling, blocking the sounds of his words. Just . . . just something like . . .' she closed her eyes, concentrating, listening to the metal, the glass, the vibrant echoes of Brady's daughter . . . 'Just "tor". A word like "tor". Soon be at the "tor", warmer, quieter. Everything all right. "Tor". That's all.'

Haddingham said, 'That sounds like a mountain. High ground.'

Brady laughed cynically. 'Which of the thousands?'

Françoise Jeury waited patiently for a minute or so, and then smiled as she stood from the table. 'I wish I could have been of more help. I have to go now. I have a flight to Paris in two hours.'

'You've been very kind.'

★

After she had left, Haddingham and Brady strolled slowly along the dark corridor towards the library.

'I've seen the woman work before,' Haddingham said, his hands thrust lazily into the pockets of his suit trousers. 'Sometimes she's amazing. I'm sorry she couldn't be more useful to you.'

'Who knows what's useful?' Brady said. 'I've given up making judgements, Andrew. It was the same with our friend, the Medium. Angela Huxley. She saw things from the other world which meant nothing to me . . . until suddenly they did, and it turned out she had been more useful than I could have imagined.'

Haddingham grunted. It was a sound of bemusement. 'Once I was a happy man, working with electromagnetic energy. Now I'm surrounded by ghosts.'

Brady knew exactly what he meant. He himself had worked in psychic research, and this time last year had been contentedly witnessing gerbils, and other small creatures, communicating fear by no ordinary means. He had scorned the Ennean Institute's reports of objects carried through time, contacts with the dead, levitation, premonition and so forth, but that ridicule had been short-sighted and harsh. Now he took it for granted that a woman could come into his lounge – as Angela Huxley had done – close her eyes and within seconds be passing him a message from a centuries-old man; he thought nothing of his recent witnessing of a mud-drenched corpse, revived by mind power alone; he never thought to doubt that the images which Françoise Jeury had communicated to him were authentic memories of his daughter.

They were surrounded by ghosts. It was as if from the moment he had had cause to *believe* in the paranormal, he had begun to see it clearly; it had always been there, people with talent, strange phenomena, the afterlife. The only thing that had changed was his way of perceiving that universe, and now, as he paced out the stalking steps of the hunter, ghosts danced around him.

59

5

The girl was standing on the high ground to the west; a slim, dark shape against the bright blue sky. She was watching Bob Darroch across the corn field. Darroch was aware of her, but continued working on the oil filter of his old tractor, bent to the task, his grey overalls smeared with black streaks.

She had been standing up there on the ridge for five minutes. She had remained quite motionless. The day was still and hot, and until she had appeared there had been no wind. Now, a strange breeze set the immature corn into exotic rippling patterns. It was not an unwelcome wind, since it cooled his hot skin.

He glanced up at the girl again, squinting against the brightness. He didn't recognize her as anyone from the nearby town. It might have been the Gatz girl . . . no, Amy Gatz was taller, bigger built.

The corn swayed. Darroch watched as rivulets of pattern flowed towards him, as if hidden animals were scampering down the sloping land towards him. He had never seen wind behave like that before. The sky was clear; a few high, white clouds. His dog was barking, beyond the house, where his wife, Ruth, was preparing lunch.

Bob Darroch was in his late thirties, a stocky, weather-tanned man. His hair was bright yellow, tightly curled. He had farmed this land for ten years, since moving east from his father's farm in Nevada. He was a man who kept himself to himself, although he barn-danced, and church-went, and contributed to the annual school fair, and did everything a member of the community was supposed to do. But the Darrochs were childless, and the growing bitterness within him was a social barrier that grew more impenetrable with every barren year.

He wiped his hands on a filthy rag, then bolted the engine cover back into place. He wasn't fully satisfied with his work, but he was becoming increasingly distracted by the silent, watching figure of the girl.

The double doors to his new barn were open behind him and he walked towards them. He glanced back towards the high ground, and was startled to see that the girl was much nearer, standing half-way down the track at the edge of the field.

How had she moved so fast? She must have run like the wind. She stood motionless again, watching him. He put a hand on the barn door, and stared back. He could see that she was slightly dusky skinned, a touch of Indian he imagined. She was wearing jeans and a long, cotton shirt, that was belted about the waist and reached to her hips. The shirt was patterned with zigzags and spirals.

Something about her unnerved Darroch. Normally he would have wasted no time shouting out to her that she was on private land, trespassing and to get her butt off his farm, and onto the main road.

She scared him, though. The way she must have moved. The way she remained silent, staring at him. The way a wind blew around her, tugging at the corn field, but only along the closer edge.

'Who are you?' he called.

He realized that he had started to sweat. Oily moisture ran down his face and arms, and he drew his forearm across his mouth, nervous and irritated to be so disconcerted on *his* land.

I've got to get away from her!

The thought was not so much words, as intuition. The idea of escape became very powerful. Dust began to sting his eyes and the barn doors were tugged in the wind. He felt danger. It loomed towards him, making his heart beat faster.

One of the Manson lot. Some freak who'll slaughter me and Ruth, and bite the heads off the chickens. You can't trust kids

61

any more. Drugs, booze, unemployment. They go crazy.
They seduce you, they flatter you, they draw a knife on you.

He was always reading in the papers about such things. It was a crazy world, out beyond the farmlands. People shot people for no reason. Hitchhikers killed drivers, stole, raced and crashed their cars. Fathers slaughtered their families. Children ran off with Chinese mystics and got brainwashed. Girls became obsessed with religious maniacs, and killed and rampaged at their whim.

Darroch stepped into his barn, and reached for the shotgun he kept there. He kept two guns. One in the barn and one in the house. He had only ever raised one of the weapons in anger, and that was to drive off a drunk who had come careering along the narrow roadway to his house in a battered Ford and smacked the vehicle into his fence.

He broke the breech and slipped two cartridges into the barrels. He began to turn, back to the barn doors.

Something rose from the stack of loose hay in the corner . . .

The barn was wide, fresh smelling, but gloomy. It functioned as a shed, workshop and junk room, as well as a barn. There was an old television set in one corner, and the motorbike he used in preference to the truck, when going into town for anything but supplies. The generator was an ungainly, dirty machine on the other side of the barn. Farm equipment was piled up against the walls.

In the middle of this confusion were two stalls, in case he should ever acquire horses, each piled with the fresh hay that he sold to his brother. His brother lived two hundred miles away, on an almost self-sufficient small-holding. He bought hay from the family, because it was cheaper, and because it was an excuse for a family gathering. Darroch liked the money, but could have done without the strained get-togethers.

And from this hay, something like a man was rising.

At the same time the generator roared into activity, blue smoke belching out from its underside. Darroch staggered back against the wall, raising the shotgun.

62

The weapon was knocked from his hand. On the other side of the barn the television flickered into life, a peculiar white fuzz forming on the screen, its volume rising until it roared static. His motorcycle kicked into life, flew a few yards across the floor, and impacted with the wall. It lay there, moving slowly in a circle, exhaust fumes dark and smelly.

The man moved towards him through the hay, grinning.

Darroch's breath caught in his lungs, his mouth opened, but the scream did not emerge.

It was a decaying skull that leered at him. The body that supported that disgusting face was lean and rotten, bone and blue flesh showing through the tattered fragments of the burial shroud.

A low, eerie chuckle emitted from this ghastly apparition. It reached towards Darroch, and its smell was overwhelming. Darroch found his voice at last, screaming his terror. He found his legs too, and lurched awkwardly towards the door of the barn.

The girl stood there, watching him peculiarly. She seemed to be frowning. Her eyes were dark and intense. Her mouth was closed, no hint of a smile on her lips. She held no weapon.

Darroch pushed past her, and ran towards the house.

Behind him, the girl followed.

The tractor roared and puttered into life. Bob Darroch faltered in his headlong flight, and watched, open-mouthed, as the heavy old machine began to run forward, plunging into the edge of the field, through the thin wire fencing. In the still day, the rumble of its motor carried high on the air. A plume of black smoke rose from the vertical exhaust. The tractor bumped and whined its way across the field, towards the rise, turning in a wide, steady circle.

Darroch stumbled into the house, startling Ruth. She was a slightly-built woman, prematurely greying, her face drawn and harrowed. She was standing at the heavy, wood table in the kitchen trimming a piece of stewing beef.

'My God, what is it, Bob?'

Darroch could hardly speak. The tractor puttered in the distance. The generator roared.

'What's going on?'

She could sense the danger, but could not acknowledge it. Here was her husband, red-faced, terrified, unable to speak. Behind him, a figure moved, and she stared at it, frowning.

Darroch hurled himself across the kitchen, and grabbed at the second shotgun, which was propped in a corner.

'What's going on?' Ruth cried, panic rising within her. 'Who's she? Who *are* you?'

Darroch turned and saw the Indian girl standing in the back door. The girl's face showed signs of strain, of struggle. She was frowning. She looked as if she was in pain. She reached a hand towards Ruth Darroch, shaking her head.

Bob Darroch stepped forward, aiming the gun. A wind blew in his face, a great cry deafened him. Darkness seemed to swoop into the kitchen, beating and flapping around his head like some night bird.

A tall man stood before him, easing the gun from his grasp. The man smelled of desert and grease, of horses, of animals, a strong, natural scent. He was smiling broadly. His face was wide, brown, his eyes narrowed, filled with humour. He was naked but for a dirty loin-cloth. Darroch thought that he was carrying a bow . . .

It was the most fleeting of images, the man stepping out of the darkness, the gun falling from his grip . . . the light returning, the man gone.

Ruth was screaming. The girl watched silently. She was still shaking her head.

'*Who are you?*' Darroch screamed, close to tears.

The girl looked at him. 'Hungry . . .' she said, her voice soft, sounding terrified herself.

The tractor roared off the corn field, plunging back through the wire fencing, driven by invisible hands. Darroch reached to the floor and swung the shotgun up by the barrel, striking towards the girl.

The tractor smashed through the wall of the house in a

chaos of bricks, plaster and glass. Darroch screamed once as the lumbering machine struck him full on the chest, carrying him across the kitchen and crushing him against the far wall. It passed on through, its engine revving, its great rear wheels skidding as hidden forces urged it out into the daylight again.

Ruth Darroch collapsed to the floor.

The tractor slowed and stopped. The generator stopped. The noise from the motorcycle died away. Bricks fell from the smashed walls of the house, and dust billowed out into the still summer air.

The girl walked to the table and picked up the loaf of bread that was there, and the raw stewing beef. Silently, and with no second glance at the unconscious woman on the floor, she turned and walked east.

Faster than the mind could comprehend, she had vanished from sight.

6

Brady drove home in the late afternoon, tired, irritable and slightly apprehensive.

'Why don't I come with you,' Haddingham had suggested. 'I could do with some company . . . a drink or two . . .'

'Thanks. It's tempting,' Brady said pleasantly, 'But not tonight. I'm tired. I need sleep. I need to think.'

The traffic out of London was quite heavy, and slowed him down. It added to his frustration.

He had passed most of the afternoon in the Institute's reading room, searching for references to Arachne, to Roundelay, to anything that was familiar to him from his hunt. He had found nothing. Secret organizations abounded; cases of witchcraft and instances of the celebration of the Black Mass were there in quantity. He flipped through accounts of the Golden Dawn, the Red Cock, the Followers of Count St Germain, all of them modern, resurrected groups, basing themselves on medieval organizations. Those secret organizations that were new were all small, silly and dedicated to the pursuit of power and wealth through the traditional invocation of mediaeval demons which not even the Ennean truly believed in.

Brady had spoken to two young researchers who specialized in gathering information about occult practice in the British Isles. His questions were the usual ones: have you heard of a group called Arachne? Is there an occult process called Roundelay, or the 'time of change'? Does the name *mammath* mean anything? Do you have records of people being 'gathered', collected by agents of an organization perhaps more widespread than England?

Nothing. Not even the memory of the appearance of the word 'Arachne' in one of their earlier reports. It had been produced during a 'contact' between medium and afterlife, but was just one more obscure word, part of an obscure message, which Brady had understood, but which the Ennean had ignored.

What group of occult practitioners wore masks made from real animal skulls and flesh?

What Black Magic would use Norse artefacts?

Why might the gathering be selective, three in a family being taken, and one left behind?

And to all these questions, just blankness, the amateur's failure of imagination and comprehension. They could be of no help to Brady. The answers to his questions were not to be found at the Ennean Institute . . . or at least, they were not available to him from that source.

So he left Haddingham to his own devices, and drove as fast as possible back to his house, at Brook's Corner, not at all sure what he would do next.

The moment he came within eyeshot of his house, he knew that something was wrong.

He stopped the car outside the gates and stared through, along the driveway, to the silent building beyond. A light evening breeze made the trees move slightly. Everything about the scene was tranquil, unmenacing . . . and yet . . .

And yet the skin on Brady's neck crawled; his heart pounded; everything was right, and nothing was right. The house was deserted of everything but its ghost. It was peaceful, empty, welcoming . . .

And something was waiting for him! He was sure of it!

He got quietly out of the car and stood outside the iron gates of his grounds, holding them, searching the bit of garden nearest to him for a sign of movement.

If only he could speak to Ellen! If only he could reach through the defences and quickly consult her . . .

He could scent, on the breeze, the faint aroma of the herbs that smouldered in their braziers. A car drove past noisily and vanished into the distance. The whole area seemed remote, deserted. And over it all hung a pall of

67

menace, an invisible cloud of danger that tickled and nagged at him.

It was early evening. It would begin to get dark in an hour or so. He was tired; he needed food, a change of clothes. He wanted to be *inside*, where it was safe. And something was waiting for him . . .

He locked his car, then went to the boot and drew out the shotgun that had been Haddingham's gift to him. Checking that the breech was filled, he walked along the road, outside the high brick wall, until he came to the trackway through the grounds of the neighbouring house which led to the field at the bottom of his garden.

Here, the wall was lower and newer. He could just manage to see over it if he stood on tiptoe.

The garden was deserted. Fruit trees were in blossom. The remains of a builder's materials were still in evidence, including a cement mixer that his brother-in-law had left behind after the recent extension work on the garden wall.

Where the trees crowded together, to the north of the grounds, the garden was in shadow, and it was to that sinister, protected place that Brady directed his main attention.

But he could see no movement there.

Nor could he glimpse movement in the house, through any of the windows. Was it his imagination, his fatigue? Was he creating the sensation of menace himself?

He called for Ellen, but his mind-voice was lost against the drifting smoke of the mandrake barrier, sucked downwards by the iron gargoyles below the garden, twisted and turned inwards by the spiralling trap of the earth maze. And she, if she was aware of him from her presence in the house, could likewise not reach out, to warn him, to reassure him.

So he climbed over the wall, jumping down on the far side, and walking cautiously towards the house. He kept the gun pointed forward, and he kept his attention mainly on the patch of dark, where the heavy trunks of the beeches and their low foliage formed an easy hiding place for an assassin.

He moved around the whole house, checking the shed, prowling behind bushes, ruined coops, the compost heap, and even looking over into the neighbour's garden. Then, satisfied that no one was lurking in the grounds, he unlocked the front door of the house and moved inside.

Sometimes he could feel the presence of the dead woman, at other times not. At this particular moment he felt only the cool of the house, the silence of the place. There was no whispering, no rustling breeze, no hair-pricking sensation of being watched. It meant nothing, really. The ghostly existence faded and grew strong in response to energy tides beyond Brady's comprehension.

Even so, he felt unnerved by the heady silence of the house, and stalked the rooms deliberately, and pointedly, kicking open doors, using the gun to slip the latches on the wardrobes and cupboards in the bedrooms and the kitchen.

The house was empty. If it seemed unnaturally cold, for this fairly warm, early summer's evening, Brady was used to that sensation. The house was haunted; and its living occupant was a solitary, frightened man, and not the family for whom it had been designed. The house at Brook's Corner was always a chilly, unwelcoming place.

'Silly boy,' he said to himself, in a mild reprimand, and laid the gun down on the lounge table. He shrugged off his leather jacket and went upstairs to the bathroom, where he stripped, washed and tugged on fresh clothes. He looked dishevelled and drawn, and the dark lines below his eyes seemed more pronounced. He grimaced at the thick, yellow coating on his tongue, and vigorously rinsed his mouth with Listerine.

Keep fit, keep healthy. You are far more vulnerable to psychic attack if you let yourself get ill, or run down, or tired; a body in good condition contributes to the mind being in good condition, and a strong mind is the best defence against assault by elementals.

Also food, he thought.

He was hungry. He had been hungry for three days. His stomach complained, and his head spun, at times. He

69

didn't drink alcohol any more, so he was not suffering the unpleasant consequences of heavy drinking on an empty stomach; but he *was* suffering the consequences of his own laziness.

It was *essential* to eat, to keep his stomach filled. But he was effectively a single man, and had rapidly slipped back into the lazy ways of his bachelor youth: eating from cans, from junk stores which sold battery chickens cooked in seasoned flour, chicken that had been injected with water to make them juicy; more often than not he just ate chocolate, or bread, anything to take the edge off his appetite.

Tonight he decided to prepare something more substantial. He cooked, in a way, to take his mind off the sensation of danger that pervaded the house.

He boiled a chicken wing and a chicken leg, straight from the freezer, and when the fat began to scum on the water, he added salt, pepper, mixed herbs, tarragon and a splash of white wine from a bottle, months old, labelled 'For cooking'.

He played music while the meat boiled, softened and fell away from the bones. He stared through the windows at the gathering gloom, watching as night descended, feeling neither secure, nor threatened, but rather something that he could only categorize as 'uneasy'.

After an hour he picked the bones from the broth, added a handful of washed white rice, a diced stick of celery, and a splash more of the white wine. The smell was exceptionally delicious. He called this meal 'pilaff' (it probably wasn't) and when he'd pigged the lot, he felt full, satisfied, and in desperate need of a brandy.

Which he resisted.

He lounged in an armchair, his feet up on the coffee table. He held Marianna's crushed spectacles and tried at different times to cry for the loss of his family, and to control the tears that emerged in waves, rather like the emotion that could suddenly appear from nowhere, only to subside as rapidly as it had come.

He listened for Ellen, perplexed that there was no sign

70

or signal from her at all. He closed his eyes and tried to think himself from his body, but he remained rigidly attached.

Outside, the night was absolute, although he could see the glimmer of stars. Melancholy overwhelmed him, and all sense of danger passed. He closed his eyes and drifted into a light sleep.

'Daddy, I'm cold,' Marianna said. Brady shifted in his sleep, murmuring something incoherent.

'Daddy!' she said loudly. 'I'm cold. I want to come in.'

She was standing outside the french windows. She looked small, vulnerable, clad only in a thin print dress, a ragged cardigan about her shoulders. Her feet were bare. She peered at him, eyes narrowed and tired. 'Daddy. Daddy! I'm *cold.*' Her hair hung lank and unwashed about her face, fair hair parted in the middle. She looked as if she had been in the rain.

'*Daddy!*'

Brady opened his eyes and looked out into the night. He saw his daughter standing on the other side of the window. She smiled at him and raised a hand, tapping gently on the glass.

He watched her, blinking sleep from his eyes. At first she was just a white shape in the dark night. Then his brow furrowed, and he sat slowly upright in the chair. He began to recognize her.

'It's me, Daddy. It's me. Open the door. I'm cold . . .'

'Marianna . . .' he breathed, and then repeated the name more loudly, and again, 'Marianna! My God . . . *Marianna!*'

'Daddy!' she cried, and reached her arms towards Brady as he flung himself from his armchair, and ran to the windows.

An explosion of glass!

'Oh God, NO!' he screamed, as wind, rain and glass flung him backwards across the lounge. The darkness howled about the room. Fingers grabbed and punched at

71

him, the furniture shifted and overturned; the bulb in the light burst, doors slammed, curtains were shredded.

The rain saturated him, stung his flesh as he struggled up against the darkness, seeking for the figure of his daughter.

She was still there. She was watching him, her face twisted with anguish, her arms reaching. The night wind blew her flimsy clothing about her pale, thin body. Blood from Brady's lacerated face blinded him. He staggered to his feet and lurched towards her, screaming her name, desperate to reach her.

She receded from him. She seemed to drift backwards across the garden, consumed by night and darkness. He watched in horror as her frail form was dragged from his grasp. For a moment she was visible among the trees, to the north, fetched up hard against the wall. Then she vanished from sight, still silently crying her despair.

Brady rushed forward, fighting against pain and the elements.

And the bitter night faded, the pain faded, the sensation of attack . . . just passed away.

Breathing heavily, shaking like a leaf, he looked at the french windows and saw that they were intact. The dark room was undisturbed, the chairs and shelves in place, the curtains untorn. He touched his face and there was no blood, no wounding . . .

Confused, deeply anguished, he unlocked the windows and stepped out into the cool night.

'What the hell's going on?' he said, more in frustration than anger. His legs would hardly bear his weight, they were trembling so much. His heart pounded.

Part of him desperately wanted to cry.

Marianna!

Illusion only. A filthy trick of the imagination, a dream perhaps, or a projection from the mind that was attacking him.

The tears welled in his eyes, as he walked stiffly towards the part of the wall where she had last been seen. He walked through the defences, away from safety, crossing the zones into that part of the garden where psychic defence was weakest.

A night wind rustled the trees, blew the tears on his cheeks into cold streaks. He didn't care. His lips quivered and he let the sobs emerge loud and unrestrained. He cried away his bitterness, his grief.

He stood by the talisman wall and struck the brick with his fist, and this time the blood was real, as he pounded his skin and flesh against the hard wall, repeating the girl's name, letting the anxiety and disappointment drain away.

He froze suddenly, alert to a furtive movement from further down the garden. A moment later a tall figure passed between two trees, all detail invisible in the gloom.

Brady stepped towards it, his heart thundering, his mind working fast. Where was the shotgun? In the kitchen, laid across the table. Were there any tools in this area of the garden? No. But there were dead branches, some of which would be quite strong. As his mind worked, so his eyes widened, and he searched frantically for some suitable weapon.

More movement. The dark shape stepped closer, and Brady heard the sound of rasping breathing. It was a noise well familiar to him, the slavering breathing not of a beast, but of a man whose features were hidden behind a mask of dead animal flesh.

It emerged in front of him. Its eyes glittered, its jowls gleamed wetly. It was the face of a massive dog, the ears torn and ragged, the long jaws opened, the dead tongue lolling.

But it was a man. And the man raised a pistol towards Brady.

The discharge was quite shocking. At the last moment Brady flung himself to one side. The bullet smashed into the trunk of a tree, inches from his face. Wood splinters stung through the hair on the back of his neck. A second shot splintered wood from the other side of the tree. The sound was resoundingly loud and must surely have startled the neighbours.

Brady grabbed for a dead branch some four feet long.

73

He flung it, one handed, towards the dog-faced man, then ran along the edge of the garden, hugging the cover of tree and bush.

The hunter stalked him, making darting movements, breath loud, eyes searching from behind the mask.

Brady's sixth sense told him that this was not an experienced assassin. But the pistol he wielded was deadly enough at this sort of range.

'Give it up, Brady,' the hunter hissed, his accent strange; his dark shape flitted briefly through the periphery of Brady's vision. Brady found a rock, and a fragment of brick, and the next time the killer emerged from cover, he flung them both.

The rock missed, the brick struck the man's head, and the shot that was discharged went wild, the bullet striking the talisman wall.

It was a moment of confusion that allowed Brady to dart behind the woodshed. The other man pounded after him, but was less familiar with the garden.

The hunter hesitated too long behind the woodshed, listening for his prey. It gave Brady time to step quickly up to the kitchen door, to pass inside and locate his shotgun.

He kept the lights off. He moved silently through the house, and stationed himself behind the study door. If he was showing all the signs of fear, from his palpitating heart to the sweat that dripped from his face, he himself felt calm, determined, glad of this unexpected contact with Arachne.

Come and get me, he thought grimly, and tightened his grip on the heavy gun.

An eerie and total silence enveloped the house. Outside, the night was quite still. Inside, there was not even the creak of a floorboard, or the knocking of the heating system. Brady's breathing seemed to roar in his lungs, and as he tried to slow his exhalations, his head became giddy.

What had happened? Had his enemy come into the kitchen? And was he now just standing there?

Brady realized that nearly twenty minutes had passed. His legs were aching, his hands were becoming numb. He would *swear* that the hunter had not come into the house. The floor in the kitchen always made sounds. Brady would have *known*.

He was still outside, then, waiting, biding his time.

Brady would have to go after him.

He eased open the door of the study and stepped out into the gloomy hallway, peering hard along the corridor at the half-opened back door. Starlight, reflecting on the glass, enabled him to get a glimpse of his position.

But as he took a step forward, so he sensed a furtive movement on the stairs above him. He looked up, and gasped with shock.

The dog-faced man was crouched on the stairs; he seemed equally startled.

Each regarded the other for a split second, Brady stunned that his pursuer could have entered the house so silently, the dog man shocked to be caught so exposed.

It was pistol against shotgun, a frantic scrambling for position, and the discharge was a single sound from each gun. The bullet from the pistol bruised Brady's shoulder and embedded itself in the door behind him; the shot from Brady's heavier weapon shattered the banister, gouged plaster from the wall, and evoked a scream of pain from his main target. Brady was aware of the man being flung several feet up the stairs, and then the body came tumbling, with surreal slowness, down to the hallway. There it lay, twitching and emitting feeble cries, before slowly easing itself up to a standing position.

Brady switched on the hall light and stared at his attacker.

He had blond, curly hair, and narrow eyes; his lips were full and wet. His cheeks hardly showed the beard that he might have been able to grow. He seemed young, naive and terribly frightened. The mask of dog skull and flesh hung limply about his chest. His right arm was ragged with bloody, tattered clothing. The whole of his right cheek was peppered and black. He pushed himself up the wall and into a standing position, but Brady felt that at any moment he would collapse again.

Part of Brady was thundering with anger, anxious to pull the trigger a second time and add one more nail to the coffin he intended to build around Arachne. A lesser part of him – or perhaps a greater – felt compassion for this quivering, frightened youth, who had been sent to do a deed considered beneath the contempt of those who were truly in command.

'So what do I do with you now?' Brady said lightly, and stepped closer.

'*Schlachst du mich! Du bist ein töter Mann . . . !*'

Without understanding the contemptuously spoken words, Brady recognized German, and shrugged. 'French was my language, and that by the skin of my teeth. Speak in English.'

The youth spat violently, then groaned and closed his eyes briefly. Blood had flecked his mouth. He said, '*Schlachst du mich. Du wirst . . .*'

'This really won't get us anywhere –'

'Kill me!' he snapped, his accent strong, his voice still very weak. 'Or let me go. This talking is pointless. *Geringfügig!* You are a very dead man, Brady. They are going to despatch you, and within a very quick time.' He tried to smile arrogantly, but the pain of his shot-blasted shoulder was too great.

'Evidently,' said Brady quietly, in answer to the youth's angry statement. 'Twice, though, they've sent boys to do a job that really requires a little more expertise.'

'*Mein Arm zerschmettern ist,*' the hunter said, then snapped out in English, 'My arm is ruined! Are you going to shoot me again? If not. I will go. I need a doctor. Are you insane? The police will have heard the shots. I must go. Quickly. *Schnell!* They will get you, Brady. I have failed. There will be others.'

'Who sent you?' Brady asked, and raised the gun again.

The youth laughed, tried to spit again but failed. 'I'll answer no questions. You are insane if you think that! Who do you think I am? Huh? You think I'm a weak kid? Because I failed? I will succeed next time. *Glaubst du mich!*

So kill me if you don't want to see my face again, this time grinning over your corpse.'

'Tell me who sent you, and where you are from, and I'll let you go.'

'You're mad.'

But there was an anguished look in the boy's eyes. He could feel the life ebbing from his body as the blood oozed slowly from his shattered right arm. He didn't want to die. He was not that committed to the cause. And that almost certainly meant that he had had little contact with the *real* Arachne. His indoctrination was peripheral, functional. He was an expendable item in the gathered pieces of Arachne's game.

'What is Arachne's purpose?' Brady said quickly, and the youth was shocked, blinking twice, then lowering his gaze.

'I have nothing to say. If you know of Arachne, then you know their purpose . . .'

'The time of change,' Brady said, and the youth smiled evilly. 'The awakening,' he said, 'The time of change. It will be a great moment . . . for some of us. Not for you!' He laughed. But behind the cruel laughter, the arrogant defiance, there was still the shock. He was deeply unsettled, this minion of the evil game. They had said to him that Brady knew nothing, that he was just an unsuspecting and ignorant man, and the death would be easy.

'They have sent you against me,' Brady whispered, letting anger express itself in the bitterness of his tone rather than the fury of his words, 'Knowing full well that I have been expecting you. They told you nothing. They told you I would not be expecting you. But I have been waiting for you for weeks. There was one before you, and he is now a hundred feet down in a bog. They don't care whether you succeed or fail, because eventually, by pure odds alone, they think they *must* succeed in eliminating me. Do you hear what I say, young Heinrick, or Ulrich, or Adolf, or whatever your name is? You are just a piece of machinery to them, programmed, used, easily replaceable.

They knew I was waiting for you, that I would sense your coming. I have powers as they have powers. You were sent against me armed with a gun, but naked in the most important way. You are a fool, a child.'

'*Das ist nicht wahr!* I am no child. I was trained for this mission. I was given powers.'

'You caused the illusion of my daughter?'

The German youth, evidently in excruciating pain, frowned irritably, confused. 'Illusion? Illusion? Are you insane?'

He doesn't know what I'm talking about, Brady thought.

'Who trained you? Where? What was his name? Where in the world was the place of training?'

'Far away,' the youth said quietly, wincing and breathing more heavily. He began to slide down the wall, but with great effort straightened his legs again, and returned that arrogant gaze to Brady. 'Far, far away.' He grinned.

'Where?' Brady said, evenly, but the boy just shook his head.

'If you know so much, you should know all the answers.'

'Magondathog,' Brady said, quoting the strange name he had heard when his family had been abducted. The youth looked startled again, but there was a slight confusion in his gaze. It was as if . . . as if certain words, certain ideas were familiar to him, but not totally.

Brady understood at once. Much of what he would have learned about Arachne had been obliterated from his mind. He truly was the automaton that Brady had described him as.

And he was probably useless to Brady. Even if he had memories relating to Arachne, there was no telling whether they were false or not.

'What do you know of Magondathog?' Brady asked.

'Nothing. The word is meaningless.'

'When did you come to England?'

'Tomorrow . . .' that last touch of arrogance was followed by a great cry of pain, and a sudden furious lurch towards Brady, as with left hand extended, he made a grab for the shotgun.

Brady stepped back, then reached out and propelled the youth towards the front door, shoving him out into the night, then pushing and kicking him to the iron gates.

In the starlight, the youth remained defiant. He limped and staggered away down the road, but called back, 'You should have killed me. You are weak, Brady. I shall come again, and you will truly suffer before I earn my wage.'

Brady watched him until he had been swallowed by the gloom, then returned to the house.

'I'm going soft,' he said to the walls, to the lounge, to the rustling presence in the fire grate.

If you are seen to have killed someone – answered back that silence – *there will be more than a little trouble with the police. Stay cool. You did the right thing.*

'Anyway,' said Brady irritably, 'where the hell *were* you when I needed you?'

The girl. The girl, answered the house, and Brady's neck prickled as he remembered the image of Marianna that had come to the french windows.

Follow, said the house, but Brady was engaged in a question that had just occurred to him: how had such a projection of psychic substance managed to penetrate his defences? It had appeared at the house itself, having crossed the five defensive zones!

Follow, urged the house, and this time Brady sensed the urgent and eerie communication.

He quickly marked the area on the talisman wall where the apparition had vanished, and, standing by the french windows with his large compass, he determined exactly the line northwards that the projection had taken. He then moved to his maps, Ordnance Survey maps of the entire country, on a scale of one in twenty thousand.

Beginning with a detailed road and ground plan of the actual area around Brook's Corner, he methodically and carefully traced the line northwards in pencil.

This is the way she came. From somewhere along this line she projected herself home . . .

The line crossed contours, open land, the outskirts of towns and villages, rivers, railway line, roads. The journey through the maps was long and laborious, examining each tiny site which that line touched.

With each inch on the map, with each mile northwards, that line was diverging from the true path of the projection. Even by the ten-mile radius line from the house, he could have been wildly out. It was impossible to be that accurate.

Something made him determined, however. Some inner strength, or the driving passion of hope, made him work on and on, creeping up through Derbyshire, across the Pennines . . .

Towards her. Towards her. She had finally summoned enough strength to travel home! After all these months, perhaps those strange talents which she possessed had begun to develop. And she had used all her strength to transmit the savaged image of herself back to the house which she loved! She had called to him. He had to find the place from which she had shouted!

At last it was there. He slammed his hand down on the map and yelled his triumph, and only when he had allowed his excitement full expression did he laugh, straighten up and shrug. It was a long shot, longer, almost, than the distance between Brook's Corner and the high peaks of Derbyshire. And yet something within him, some voice, some intuition, would not believe that he had not found the place where Marianna was trapped. Now. At this moment. And for a while longer.

Casterigg. A town, high in the Pennine foothills, close to the Peak District. It was not the name of the town that made Brady so convinced. It was the steep rise of hill behind the town, the mountain called Maron Tor, that had caught his attention.

As he stared at the names on the map he felt himself drawn to the place, sucked downwards into the contours, powerfully attracted by the ley-line that must surely have passed through the ancient hill town.

Casterigg. Maron Tor.

Slender hope at last!

7

The old man and the girl stood below the canopy of a shoe shop. They were cold and wet. If they were miserable, it didn't show on their faces. They stood together, hand in hand, watching the summer rain.

The storm had arrived over Casterigg about half an hour before. The clouds were so low that the upper levels of Maron Tor were invisible. The great pinnacle of dark rock could hardly be seen against the black skies. The rain poured relentlessly from the heavens, almost steaming from the pavements and roads of the town, running in a great swirling river through the High Street, whose drains could not cope with this cloudburst.

The old man was in his sixties. He had deep set, blue eyes and well-groomed grey hair. He wore a long black overcoat, too hot for summer, too thin for this cold summer storm. The shoulders still gleamed with water. In one hand he held his plastic souwester. The other was wrapped firmly around the tiny hand of the girl, who was only just over half his height.

The girl's eyes were equally blue, startlingly alert. She had a solemn face, which didn't make her any the less pretty. Her fair hair was long. On each side of her face she had made two thin plaits. She wore a long transparent waterproof, from Woolworths, through which her baggy blue dungarees could be seen.

The rain thundered down, a great shining veil around the town, through which the hills were dimly perceived walls.

Across the road, a man in his late twenties stepped out of the tobacconists, and turned up the collar of his army-surplus anorak. He glanced across at the man and the girl, and briefly waved a pack of Old Holborn cigarette tobacco.

'He's not strong enough,' the little girl whispered, and the older man glancing down at her, realized she had spoken and said, 'What?'

She looked up at him. 'He's too nervous. I don't think he can get us out.'

The old man shrugged. 'I need a smoke.'

'You smoke too much.'

'It helps me think. You couldn't give up sticky buns, could you?'

She didn't smile. She stared across the road at her father. She said, 'You still smoke too much. I don't like it.'

It was the nature of Casterigg, so close to the Peaks, to be a 'hardy types' community. In their blue and red anoraks, heavy, waxed boots, gaiters, backpacks and woollen hats, those hardy types walked through the rain, chirpy and noisy, doing their own thing no matter what the climate. When the sun came out again they'd strip down to red checkered shirts, heavy-duty cord trousers, and break out the Kendal mint-cake, and brandy, as they trekked on up into the mountains.

Rain or shine, Casterigg was always busy. With the rain so heavy, there was a chance they could escape the town unnoticed. It was a slim chance. It *had* to be tried. But Uncle William was too old. Kelly was too young. And Kelly's father, Simon Fleming, was . . . was not strong enough.

'Worth a try,' Uncle William said. 'Always worth a try. They won't harm us.'

The little girl shivered. 'Not us. What about him?'

They watched as Simon Fleming darted across the street towards them, through the downpour, cursing as water went over the tops of his shoes. He gave the tobacco to Uncle William, who accepted it solemnly. He opened the pack, then fiddled with a paper from his overcoat pocket, taking his time as he rolled a thin cigarette, and lit it. Simon watched him, smiled down at his daughter, who just stared up the street, her face an expressionless mask.

Suddenly irritated, Simon turned sharply on his uncle. 'What the hell's going on? You *must* tell me!'

Uncle William just puffed on his cigarette, his face as expressionless as his great niece's, although his ice-blue eyes were narrowed, contemplative.

He said, 'Get us out of the town, Simon.'

'*Who* are these people who're stopping you? What's my daughter got to do with it? For God's sake . . .' he shivered violently, tugging his wet coat tighter around his neck. There was pain in his eyes, and confusion. 'My daughter, William. Leave her out of it!'

'Too late for that, Simon,' said Uncle William gently, and looked up and down the street.

Simon Fleming felt like hitting his uncle. He remembered the old man as having been warm, friendly, almost too friendly. A fussy old gentleman, always ready with a story or two, always ready for a game, or a walk. He was a regular visitor at Fleming's house in Luton, and more so after Kelly's birth.

He had been an ordinary relative, and a friend. Now he was cold. And Kelly was cold. And something had happened to Simon himself that had stopped him behaving normally. He watched his pretty daughter and felt alienated from her, no longer a part of her.

And he was afraid to confront it. He wanted to take her firmly by the hand and march her to the station, no argument, no nonsense. But he couldn't do it.

She was stopping him, somehow.

Or Uncle William was.

'I'm ready,' said Uncle William. He ground the cigarette out on the damp pavement.

'Come on, then,' said Simon, and with his hands in his pockets he began to walk along the High Street.

Uncle William and Kelly followed him, hand in hand, solemn-faced and saturated.

They walked past the shops, hugging the pavements, moving through the abundant tourists, trying to lose themselves in the crowds. Everything was grey. The sky was as gloomy as dusk. The stone from which the houses and shops had been built was a drab grey limestone that had become blackened with time and exhaust fumes.

Beyond the main shops the road divided, and they hurried on past the small Town Hall, the Protestant church, the Tourist Information Centre. The road sloped upwards, leading out towards the Tor.

Simon felt, more than heard, the sudden cessation of movement behind him, and he stopped and turned. Uncle William and Kelly were standing motionless, looking slightly frightened. Simon followed their gaze, ahead along the road. A solitary figure stood there, wrapped in an oilskin cape, face invisible beneath a saturated denim bush hat. It looked quite sinister through the pounding rain, but that was surely just an illusion.

'Come on,' he urged Uncle William, but the two of them hung back, the old man shaking his head.

Simon stared at the figure again. He took a few steps towards it, then hesitated. He had caught a glimpse of the darkly bearded face below the hat. The man was smiling. His gaze was almost evil. Simon felt his legs go weak, his mind begin to spin in a turmoil of indecision.

Behind him, Uncle William and Kelly had turned and were slowly walking back towards the shops. Simon ran after them, then tugged them along the other fork of the main road. They followed willingly, but without comment.

The road curved almost back upon itself. There were more shops, more of the drab stone houses, their windows blind behind white lace curtains. The hills rose steeply behind the houses, and the ruins of a Norman stronghold hugged the ridge above, a bleak and unwelcoming view.

As they weaved their way through the colourfully rainproofed climbers, ducking below umbrellas, carefully avoiding pushchairs, again Uncle William stopped. Simon had gone ahead by several paces before he realized that the other two were not with him.

They had stepped to the side of the street, and were hiding below the canopy of a craft shop, watching not him, but some point on the road further along.

Simon could see nothing sinister. He walked on through

the crowds. A man with a backpack, wearing a bright red anorak, was standing by the side of the road watching him. Simon advanced upon the man. 'Who *are* you?'

'Who are you to ask?' said the man. His accent was broad Yorkshire. His face was strong, the blond beard giving him a touch of the look of a viking.

'Why are you stopping them leaving?' Simon said, angrily.

The man looked neither puzzled nor angry. He remained totally placid as he said, 'Why am I stopping *who* leaving?'

'You're one of them.'

'One of who? I'm a climber. That's why I'm dressed like this.' No hint of humour as he spoke. The rain dripped from Simon's nose and chin, practically blinding him as he stood in the open, confronting someone who was probably exactly what he claimed to be: a mountaineer.

Simon went back to Uncle William. 'Come on. No one's going to stop us.'

Kelly shook her head, grabbed Uncle William's hand tighter. Simon practically dragged the older man onto the street, hauling the two of them after him.

But Uncle William jerked his hand away, and backed off, his face for the first time showing alarm. Simon could still distinguish nothing sinister in the street, but the other two were now walking quickly away from him, again towards the shops.

He followed them.

Thunder passed across the town in the form of two air-force jets, flying below the cloud layer, sleek silver machines streaking home to base.

They walked up back streets, which were narrow and deserted. They passed a church, two pubs and a small hotel. Simon took the lead again, directing them towards the main road to the east. This road crossed a river. On the hump-backed bridge two boys in yachting jackets fished the shallow waters, paying little attention to the occasional passing car, or hiker. Simon led the way forward, Uncle William breathing heavily behind him, Kelly hunching in her rainproof, hair lank, face saturated.

As they reached the top of the bridge a Landrover, parked fifty yards away, turned on its headlights. The wide beams were scattered through the rain, a wall of brilliant light, which was very menacing. Between Simon and the headlights, a tall, grey figure walked, silhouetted, indistinguishable in terms of facial features. The man stopped walking, letting the rain form a illuminated shroud around him.

Simon turned back. Uncle William smiled grimly and followed him. 'There's no way out.'

'They're just men,' said Simon. 'We'll go to the police. Or we'll arm ourselves. They're only men. We can push past them.'

'There's no way out,' said Uncle William again.

Simon felt his blood boiling. 'I'll kill them if they try and stop me taking my daughter.'

Why did he feel so helpless? Why couldn't he do it *now*? Why not go up to that man by the Landrover and physically assault him if he tried to prevent Kelly leaving?

His heart thundered, with rage, with frustration at the bemusement which made him so ineffectual.

She's my *daughter! Nobody tells me what to do with her!*

'Nothing's stopping you going,' said Uncle William. As they trudged back into the town, Simon glanced at him. He was a stranger. This hard-faced man was not the Uncle William who had lived here since this time last year. And what the *hell* had he done to Kelly?

They carefully avoided going anywhere near the street where Torview House silently waited for them. They had got away from the house, there was no going back again. But where to go?

Where to *go*?

'The hotel,' Simon said, answering his own question. Casterigg had several hotels, most of them small. The Castle Hotel was six storeys of the same dull grey stone. It was in the middle of the town, the tallest building in Casterigg.

They walked out of the rain and into the gloomy, rather musty foyer. Kelly took off her rainproof and discarded it casually in the corner. In her blue dungarees and soaking red boots she paced around the foyer, a self-confident child who might have drawn approving looks from middle-aged adults, but who was regarded only with anxiety by her father.

Uncle William rolled a cigarette slowly, thoughtfully. He stared out through the swing doors of the hotel.

Simon booked a room on the top floor. The hotel was only half full. Would they like Tor view, or Castle view?

Simon called to Uncle William. The old man said, 'A room in the middle of the floor, looking south.'

'Castle view, then,' said the receptionist. 'Would you like tea? Coffee? Lunch?'

'Nothing,' said Uncle William sharply. Kelly looked over. 'A bath. There'd better be hot water. I really smell.'

Coming from so small a girl, the words were startling. The girl at reception smiled uncertainly, then turned the registration card for Simon to sign. But for a moment, Simon Fleming had eyes only for his daughter. He stared at her, as shocked by the adult speech as was the receptionist, even though he had heard it before. When he turned back to the woman his face said it all: confusion, despair . . . growing panic.

They went to the sixth floor by the stairs. The hotel was cold. Stone was always cold. And the stairs were polished marble, covered by a thin layer of carpet.

The room was not much better; a bleak, square place, with two single beds. A cot bed could be put up later. The furniture was old-fashioned and dark. Pictures in awesomely bad taste hung on the walls. The wide window was filthy. It looked out over rooftops, side streets, and the steep pathway up the grassy hill to the wired-off remains of the twelfth-century fortress.

'This will do fine,' said Uncle William. He took off his coat, jacket and tie, sprawled out on one of the beds and finished his cigarette.

'Stop smoking,' said Kelly.

'Stop nagging me,' retorted Uncle William. Otherwise, they ignored each other. Kelly pottered around the room, finally going to the window and just standing there, hands in the pockets of her dungarees, staring out into the grim day.

Simon sat in the corner, next to the phone. He watched his daughter. Stop smoking, she had said, in words and tone as sharp, as hard as an adult might reprimand a child. Stop nagging, he had said, in words and tone as sharp and casual as a man addresses his partner.

It was not right. It was all wrong. The relationship was wrong. Sixty-six years and five years, yet they behaved with each other as if they were intimates.

'I'm going to get the police,' said Simon, but he made no move to pick up the phone.

Kelly ignored him. Uncle William just laughed, a humourless sound, almost sarcastic. 'They can't help,' he said. 'They'll just make things worse.'

'I want my daughter home with me,' said Simon defiantly. 'I'll get you home, Kelly. Never fear.'

The girl made no response.

'Do you hear me, Kelly?'

'I hear you.'

'You do *want* to go home, don't you?'

'I want to get out of this dump, that's for sure.'

'I'll get you out of here,' said Simon. 'I'll get you home.'

'Home!' said the girl sharply, and it was said with a tinge of cynicism, a tinge of regret.

'Mummy's getting very worried about you. She misses you. She didn't expect you to be away so long.'

Kelly sniggered. 'Life is full of little unpleasantnesses.'

'Cut it out, Kell!' sad Uncle William. He had his eyes closed and was manipulating a paper around a thin line of tobacco. His hands shook as he completed the operation.

'Cut it out yourself, Uncle *chimney*.'

Simon Fleming watched and listened in appalled, grief-stricken astonishment.

He picked up the phone and asked to be connected with his home number, two hundred miles south. When his wife answered the phone she was obviously distressed, overworked and harassed. They had a two year old boy, Richard, who was hyperactive and almost too much for

Lindsey to cope with. The strain of what she thought to be her daughter's illness, on top of trying to handle the highly demanding infant, was wearing her down rapidly.

'I think she's a little better,' Simon said, hating himself for the lie, but already too embroiled in the story to change it now. How could he have rung Lindsey two days before and said, 'She's stuck in a town in the peak district. She can't get out. Nor can Uncle William. And she's changed. She looks harder. She speaks like a girl twice her age, coarse, rough, aware.'

How could he have said that? He didn't even understand it himself. He had told Lindsey that Kelly had bronchitis, and was being well cared for, but couldn't be moved. She was in no danger. He would arrange annual leave at short notice and stay with her until she was better.

As he spoke the cold, dishonest words down the phone, he felt like screaming. He felt like shrieking to her to get help, to get the police, the army, the rest of the family, to flood Casterigg with friends and helpers, to break down the barrier – whatever it was – that was preventing two ordinary people leaving this ordinary, if wind and rain-swept mountain town.

When he placed the phone back in its cradle, he sat and stared at it for a long moment, his eyes brimming with tears.

Outside, the sound of the rain lessened, and the room brightened noticeably as the sombre clouds dispersed. Somewhere above, summer was waiting to reappear, but for the moment in the hotel room it felt like dull autumn.

'Stop staring at me, Simon,' said Uncle William. 'You did your best. It can't be helped . . .'

Simon Fleming's patience collapsed. He launched himself from the corner chair, walked silently, swiftly across the room, reached down to the old man and hauled him into a sitting position by the lapels of his shirt.

'What's going on?' he screamed. 'Tell me who's doing this to you! I'm not going to take any more of your bloody silence. What are you doing to my daughter? What's *happening*?'

He shook Uncle William in rhythm with his shouted words. Uncle William waited until the fit had passed, and an unnatural, awkward silence descended upon the two of them.

Slowly Simon let go of the man's shirt. Uncle William straightened his dress, coughed twice, then inspected his cigarette, which had been bent double with Simon's sudden violence.

Simon Fleming let the tears flow from his eyes, dropping to his haunches by the bed.

'You wouldn't understand,' said Uncle William quietly.

'Understand what?' said Simon through his tears, and with his voice rising again. 'Understand *what*? What the *hell* is happening to you? To Kelly? That's my *daughter*, damn you! Two weeks ago she was a little girl. Now she's . . . she's a *phantom*!'

He looked round at Kelly, who was standing exactly as she had been standing for the last five minutes, looking out of the window. There was the hint of a smile on her face. 'Kelly,' Simon whispered sadly.

Suddenly she reached up her hands and leant against the window, eyes closed, face twisted as if with pain. 'Moonlight on dark water,' she said. Uncle William tensed slightly, watching her. 'Moonlight. On dark water,' she repeated. 'And something else . . .'

There was a time of silence.

Kelly straightened up, then, and put her hands back into her pockets. She walked into the room again, and stood by Uncle William, the smile on her face one of mischief.

'Well?' said Uncle William.

'He's coming,' she said.

'Are you sure?'

'I just *know* it,' she said. 'He's coming. We'll get out of here . . .'

'At last,' said Uncle William. 'Yes. We'll get out of here at long, long last!'

Simon Fleming watched them. He listened to them. He submitted to helpless silence.

8

Moonlight on dark water.

It was one of those exquisite summer nights when everything is perfectly still. The Atlantic Ocean was like the proverbial mirror: calm, flat, reflective. Things moved, out on the starlit, moonlit surface: fish feeding, whales playing, night birds seeking for prey. Sometimes the eerie lights of lost Atlantis could be seen, the shimmering phosphorescence of krill.

The ocean liner cut almost soundlessly through this still night, given away only by the rushing and splashing of its bow-wave, and the distant deep throbbing of its engines. It was a great, bright machine on the vast gleaming ocean. Though it was late at night, every porthole spilled light into the darkness, the upper decks were brilliantly illuminated, and from the area of the ship's stern came the tinny sound of revelry . . .

First night out from Portsmouth: it was the first night party, and everyone, Captain included, was crowded into the vast ballroom, dancing, drinking, celebrating the passage west.

Peter Forrester, Captain of the *Maiden Castle*, had seen it all before. After a dutiful half an hour, chatting with passengers, and being very much in evidence, an 'important communication' called him, unexpectedly, to the bridge.

Normally he would have made his way first to the officer's area, to enjoy a brandy or two with his off-duty colleagues, and then retired to his cabin for some very welcome sleep. Tonight, though, he felt wide awake – if not in a particularly party-going mood – and walked slowly to the bridge.

Here, in the subdued light, three men routinely inspected monitors and scanned the ocean. A jazz tape was playing softly in the background.

'All right?' Forrester asked as he stepped on to the bridge. He crossed to the great curved window which gave the forward view into the darkness to the west. A handsome young officer, in shirt-sleeves and loosened tie, stood there, gazing forlornly into infinity. He straightened up as he realized Forrester was beside him, then smiled.

'No Russian subs so far,' he said. 'How's it going back there?'

'Same as usual,' said Forrester. 'There'll be some sore heads tomorrow.'

The younger man glanced at the Captain. 'Anything for me? If you know what I mean?' He made a vague hand gesture, that somehow insinuated the female form.

Forrester said, almost wearily, 'There's always something for you, Anthony. Isn't there always something for you? If we had a passenger list consisting solely of *geriatrics*, there'd be something for you . . .'

'But unless I look,' said Anthony Kaveney quietly, 'How will I ever find . . .' he was frowning as he spoke. He finished slowly: 'How will I ever find my true . . . my loved one . . .' He was peering hard through the window. 'What the hell *is* that?'

Forrester, who had not been paying much attention to the dark seas ahead of them, now realized that Kaveney was distracted by something. He followed the young man's direction of gaze. The other officers on the bridge joined them at the forward view position. They were pale, puzzled faces, dimly seen behind the thick glass. The liner ploughed westwards, its engines a deep, rhythmic murmur in the stillness.

Ahead, moving towards the ship on an almost parallel course, was something small and bright. It rose and fell with the wave crests. It was like a tenuous cloud, darting and writhing, coming closer.

Forrester studied the phenomenon through the binoculars. 'Anything on the radar?' he asked, and one of the officers moved to inspect the monitor.

'Nothing.'

Forrester lowered the glasses, frowning. Kaveney kept his to his eyes, peering hard at the strange object.

'Night birds?' Forrester said. 'They'd show up.'

'Not necessarily,' Kaveney said. 'Could be static electricity.'

'Surface phosphorescence?' suggested one of the others.

'It's *above* the water,' said Forrester.

Kaveney suddenly caught his breath. 'Christ Alfucking-mighty! It's a girl!'

There was an immediate moment of panic on the bridge, and then a long, stunned silence as four men watched something that should have been impossible.

A dark haired girl, surrounded by a shimmering, ghostly cloud, was walking across the ocean towards the liner.

The walk seemed endless. She had been Mary Jane Walks On Water for what seemed years. She had watched the sun rise, a blinding orb on the gleaming waters. She had seen the gloom of dusk gather, and the bright stars shine through. All these things she had seen a hundred times. Or so it felt.

She had watched the water through eyes caked with salt. She had felt the cold of night and the relative warmth of day through a skin that was like beaten leather. She had climbed the mountainous crests, and scampered down into the deep troughs, the ocean like a beach of heaving, restless whales, their great backs towering over her, their glinting eyes always watching.

Sometimes, during the nights, she had heard the sound of sea vessels passing distantly. Russian freighters, British cargo ships, ocean liners, small fishing boats. Sometimes, during the days, she had seen creatures of the abyss below, gyrating and gambolling on the surface, all smooth, black skins and threshing tentacles.

Sun rise; sun set. Moonlight on water. She walked east,

and the spirits that were bound to her played and frolicked in the vast wilderness of water.

Only Hunhau, the terrifying Lord of Death, rode in her body in silence, watching from her grey stuff as she made the magic walk across the sea.

'I'll never make it,' she said aloud. 'It's too far. This body is weakening. It's cold. Mary Jane is cold . . .'

'Not far now,' said Young Grandfather. 'I can feel the land ahead. This no-place, soft stuff, I hate.'

He had never seen an ocean like this. He had fished the edges of lakes, and followed the spoor of enemies along the soft banks of rivers. He had never seen so *much* water, in this, this no-place. He was frightened of it. He sniffed for land, and could begin to smell it.

The other spirits were restless too. Enumclaw shrieked about her head, his laughter like thunder, whipping up the calm seas around her into tiny focuses of storm; storm-seas were like brothers to the spirit, and he spiralled upwards among the thunderclouds, and streaked back to Mary Jane on the strikes of lightning.

Tieholt, the water demon, rose and fell from her grey stuff with the giant waves, and sometimes plunged down, deep down into the ocean, where he circled the sharks and the glowing fish, then swam back to the ocean's surface, snapping and crying with the pleasure of this freedom. When Tieholt played, the sea bubbled and foamed with fury, and all snapping ocean beasts stayed away. Nayenez moved through the storm winds, and the surging seas, grinning and laughing, a glowing demon, mimicking the screeching cries of sea birds and pursuing them into the thunderclouds.

Only Hunhau remained quiet. But he was hungry. He had need. Mary Jane had a hunger too. She needed rest from the walking. She needed strength.

The ocean liner loomed out of the darkness, an island of bright lights and bright sound. Mary Jane Silverlock drifted quickly across the waves towards it.

★

'She's changing direction,' Kaveney said. Forrester grunted the fact that he had already noticed that change. 'Get a boat ready for lowering,' he said.

He continued to analyse the girl through his night glasses. Her face was totally expressionless, though her eyes were open. She was white-caked with salt, and her dark hair hung lank about her shoulders. She was dressed, it would seem, in jeans and a long shirt, belted at the waist. She held her hands stiffly at her sides and walked . . . no, not so much walked as *drifted* across the sea. Sometimes her feet would touch the water. She approached rapidly, far faster than walking pace, curving her passage so that now she approached the *Maiden Castle* broadside on.

Forrester felt he had to be dreaming. All of them were dreaming, all of them on the bridge. This was a cosy sleep, and they would all abruptly awake and laugh and share that peculiar commonality.

But he was not asleep. And he didn't believe in Atlantis. And it was difficult to believe in illusion. She had started to register, if faintly, on the radar scanner. All four of them could see her, and saw an identical form of her.

But young girls didn't walk on top of the waves, hundreds of miles from land, dressed in clothes more suited to a summer's day picnic.

Don't think about it. Just get the boat down, and worry about it afterwards, when she's safely on board.

'An alien,' Kaveney said quietly. 'It's the only explanation. Her spaceship's crashed. She's not from this world . . .'

'Or hydrophobic boots?' suggested someone else, and laughed. But the sound died on his lips. No one was amused.

She walked alongside the liner, out of view of the bridge. Forrester went out onto the bridge-deck and leaned over the side. He could see her there, keeping pace with the vessel, her legs moving as if she walked, her figure covering huge distances in single strides. The shimmering mist that surrounded her seemed filled with faces, glistening forms . . .

The boat was lowered. Four seamen stood awkwardly

within it. The liner's engines whined and thumped as the speed dropped away to allow the pick-up. When the boat touched the water it cast off, started its engine and began to bob and pitch towards the girl.

She turned at the last moment, and met the gazes of the seamen who had come for her. Around her, thunder pealed and a great wind sent the little vessel pitching and swinging away, the tillerman struggling frantically.

Then the sea about them was whipped into a frenzy, and the calm night air was split by an eerie, terrifying cry. From below the waves an immense, jawed face rose, its features reptilian, its eyes demonic. Its tail lashed the ocean, struck the hull of the liner. Its mouth opened and the screech of anger grew louder. It snapped shut across the boat, severing the tiny hull in two, and one of the seamen with it.

The others dived for the water. The beast plunged after them, snapping at legs, dragging them down, sucking them into its maw where they thrashed and struggled until they drowned, and surfaced on the ocean again, as if they had never been consumed . . .

The girl rose up the side of the liner, towards the stern area. Men ran in that direction, but found no sign of her when they reached the rails. Captain Forrester's voice was almost hysterical as he issued orders over the loud-speaker . . .

The first night party drowned much of his voice, the noise of laughing and music . . .

The ballroom floor was packed. The jazz group were in full swing, and the crowds writhed and gyrated to the rhythms, almost too crowded on the dance area for comfort. The bar area was packed too, and all the tables around the floor were festooned with streamers, flowers and empty bottles of wine.

A few people might have noticed the bedraggled girl, standing at the top of the stairs to the deck, watching the festivities. None of them remarked upon her. They danced, and laughed, and chattered, and drank . . .

When the storm hit, it happened so suddenly that for a

moment there was just silence, save for the petering sound of the jazz group. The whole room had been plunged into darkness. Then the doors and portholes shattered spectacularly, spraying glass across the whole room. Tables were flung about in the sudden, icy gale, the chandelier exploded loudly, the bandstand collapsed, and rolling, booming thunder crashed through the silence, drowning the sudden hysterical screaming of the gathered throng.

Rain and wind, and a howling sound that was eerie and unnatural, the crying of a snared beast.

One woman, her face dripping blood from several glass scratches, turned to her husband for safety, and found herself staring at the grinning face of a corpse. It opened its mouth and uttered a wailing cry, as its skeletal hands closed on her neck and crushed the bones swiftly, its mouth closing on hers, sucking in the woman's thick, protruding tongue, biting into the flesh, sucking her soul-substance along with her blood.

The mayhem in the ballroom ceased, the storm passing away as suddenly as it had come. The crowds wailed and cried, stumbling around in the darkness, calling for help. But the sound had gone, and the wind, and the rain.

It passed downwards, deeper into the ship.

Don't harm them! Please don't harm them!

The girl walked along a silent corridor, looking for a place to rest. She was shaking. Young Grandfather remained close, frightened for her. He was not as strong as he had thought. He tried to hold the other spirits in order, but he was just an old Indian, and the others were forces of nature. All he could do was stand between them and Mary Jane, protecting her.

Can't you stop them?

They are too strong. They must have their fun. Find a place to sleep.

She opened a door and found a dark room, and lay down on the floor, curled up like a child. Young Grandfather rose above her, a broad, strong man, his chest deep, the muscles of his arms hard and knotted. In his kirtle, his

97

body daubed with paint, his eyes gleaming as he watched the door, he looked magnificent.

He watched his sleeping daughter. She was beautiful. In his day, she would have been a prize among prizes, and hunters would have sought her for their wife, and brought much pride to his family.

Young Grandfather crouched beside his daughter and stroked her hair. The others were beyond, passing through the corridors and rooms, feeding and replenishing upon the unsuspecting passengers of the great iron boat.

It was possible to hear the screams.

A young couple in one of the cabins were abruptly disturbed in their pursuit of physical love. The door to their cabin burst open and a screaming gale blew the thin sheet from their bodies. They cried out, twisted upright on the bed, naked bodies suddenly icy cold as the wind froze the sweat on their skins. Eyes wide, terrified, they watched as the room was filled with a swirling dark fog, through which a glowing shape approached. When it reached them it leaned towards them. Decayed flesh fell from its bones, its eyes hypnotized them, its hands crushed the life from their bodies. It drank them, holding their limp bodies in its arms, head bent to their faces as it picked out their eyes and greystuff through the cavities of their skulls.

Something darted into the cabin of a businessman. He was propped up in bed, reading a sheaf of reports. That invisible something ran around the room and snatched the papers from his hands, scattering them. He stepped from the bed, confused, slightly angry. He was wearing only pyjama bottoms, and these were torn from him as he stooped to gather up the sheets. He yelled out in pain and surprise. A man-thing had darted through his field of view, like an Indian, its body daubed with paint, its dark hair stuck through with feathers.

His bare buttocks were slapped and he turned quickly. He was painfully prodded from behind again, and yelled, and the prodding became more severe, drawing blood. There was nothing behind him, and he turned and twisted, holding his backside. The abuse continued, and was

98

accompanied by malevolent laughter. He ran out into the corridor, genitals flopping painfully, still trying to protect his flabby buttocks from the increasingly severe attack. He was driven up on to the deck, screaming with pain, wincing and leaping as each blow struck him. He plunged through the confused, hysterical crowds of the party-goers, who were spilling out onto the decks at last.

He ran straight for the side rails. With a sound like a shot he was slapped so hard that his body flew, like a flapping night bird, over the side and into the cold waters below.

He was seen and a boat was lowered.

The storm winds that howled through the lower decks at last died away. Cabin doors stopped banging open and shut. Beds ceased to fly into the air, the sheets and blankets behaving as if with a life of their own. Trolleys stopped rattling mindlessly through the corridors. Faces ceased to leer, grinning and terrifying, from lavatory basins, cupboards and portholes.

In eight cabins, the dead lay in their own blood, crushed and drained to satiate a terrible appetite.

Mary Jane had slept enough.

She awoke, stood up, and felt the reassuring presence of Young Grandfather. Hunhau was a sleeping, satiated presence in her greystuff. The others crowded around, laughing and contented that they had indulged themselves in a little bit of mortal teasing.

'The land is close,' said Young Grandfather.

'Time to walk,' said Mary Jane. She rose up through the levels, and walked quickly out to the stern deck. It was a bright, fresh dawn. The ship seemed shrouded in shocked silence. A man, ashen faced and frightened, was watching her. He wore a uniform. He was the ship's Captain. In his right hand he held a black, metal pistol.

'You . . .' he said, and raised the gun. Young Grandfather swooped upon him and knocked the weapon aside. The ashen-faced man collapsed to the deck.

Mary Jane walked down the hull of the ship and onto the water. In a few minutes she had been swallowed up by the bright, rising sun.

9

Moonlight on dark water.

He's coming. He's coming. I'm sure. At last. We'll get out of here at last.

Moonlight on dark water.

He's coming. He's coming . . .

With each step Dan Brady took up the steep, slippery path to the summit of Maron Tor, a feeling of sadness grew . . . and a feeling of being watched. It was a much warmer and brighter day than yesterday, although a brisk wind blew around the upper slopes of the peak, and Brady felt chilled.

He stopped several times, to get his breath, and turned to look back along the valley. The town of Casterigg, built out of local grey stone, was in sunshine. It seemed to gleam, still damp from the previous day's downpour.

It had been an early summer much like this, rainy and cool, when Brady had honeymooned with Alison, in the Lake District. It was this rising memory, of a time more than ten years before, that caused his sadness.

She had been a great walker. It was typical of Alison that, whereas most newly-wed couples would have sought sun, beaches and a lazy time to enjoy their new marriage, she had insisted on fell-walking in the Lake District. Most evenings, Brady had been too tired to enjoy his honeymoon in the traditional way. But it had been an exhilarating week, and they had talked and loved almost every hour of the day, enjoying the closeness, the shared activity.

He could still see her: she had had short hair, and worn a red woolly hat and red anorak. Her legs were so thin that her huge walking boots had looked almost comical. They had taken it in turns to hang onto the tags on each other's rucksacks, being dragged along by their partner . . .

He shook the memories away quickly. The Lakes were a long way away, both in space and time.

He was here for a purpose. He was making this climb for a reason.

His consciousness of being watched stayed with him as he came onto the summit of the Tor itself. A solitary hiker occupied the top of the mountain. He was sitting against the concrete monolith that marked the summit, chewing a sandwich and gazing thoughtfully out across the wide, glacial valley. Brady glanced at him quickly, noticed that he was young, and dressed in all the right equipment: heavy boots, gaiters and a chunky white jumper. His backpack was on the ground beside him. He didn't look at Brady as the breathless, sweating man came on to the level ground nearby.

Maron Tor was a huge peak, dark and uninviting. It was accessible from south and north by ridge paths that hugged the sheer, eastern face. The mountain had been quarried in Victorian times, and looked as if it had been chopped down the middle. On that daunting, vertical face, two climbers swung precariously from bright orange ropes. About a quarter of a mile away, several holiday-makers were gasping their way up the muddy path.

Brady walked forward to the drop, standing a cautious few yards from the edge itself, and surveying the surrounding land. Casterigg nestled at the bottom of the valley, a wider town than he had thought, with a complex of back streets and narrow alleys that seemed almost to disappear into the steep hill that rose on its southern side.

That hill, much lower than Maron Tor, was topped by a spectacular ruined castle. It had guarded this valley in Norman times; it had controlled the only pass through these particular peaks. The hills were gouged out by water into sheer gulleys and narrow dales, and the fortress had been built with cliffs on three sides, and the steep ascent from Casterigg on its fourth.

Exceptionally strategic placing.

Other towns gleamed in the far distance. Farmland lay peaceful in the valley bottom. High ridges bounded that farmland.

Somewhere here . . . somewhere close by . . . Marianna. She was here, she *had* to be. Perhaps they were all here, Dominick, Alison and Marianna bound and afraid, aware that Brady was close, sensing him . . .

The wind tugged at him and Brady stepped backwards, away from the cliff. As he moved he was aware that the sitting man had been regarding him, and had quickly looked away.

Brady walked over to him, and the man rose to his feet, aware of Brady's approach, and apparently discomforted by it.

'Quite a climb up,' Brady said.

The man nodded, not meeting Brady's gaze. 'Hard on the legs. Harder going down.'

His voice was soft. When at last he glanced at Brady, his eyes were narrowed, gleaming, searching.

'May I ask you a question?' Brady said. The man shrugged. 'How long have you been in Casterigg? How long have you been staying here?'

'A few days . . .'

Brady produced a photograph of Marianna. 'Have you seen this girl? She's quite small. Six years old.'

The man favoured the photograph with the briefest of glances, then shook his head. 'Sorry. Can't help.'

Brady shrugged. 'Thanks anyway.' He turned away and began to retrace his steps towards the path.

The man called out. 'What are you, a private detective?'

Brady looked round. 'I'm her father,' he said. There was no change of expression on the young man's face. After a second or two, Brady chose to ignore him again.

He glanced for the last time at the town of Casterigg, as seen from this major vantage point. It was an organic place, and yet curiously it seemed to grow from the land, like an amorphous grey rock, a limestone fungus, sprouting from the earth. Brady had hoped to sense his daughter. He had come to the Tor hoping that, as he had looked down

102

upon the houses, he would have seen, or glimpsed, or *felt* the girl. He had failed to do that, and yet the trip had not been wasted. He had looked at Casterigg from the sky, seen its angles, its nooks, its crannies; he had seen it in relation to the hills around. He already felt an expert on the place.

He descended the Tor, picking his way carefully along the cliff edge, watching where he put his feet on the slippery mud and grass. He passed the ascending group, and smiled at them. They all bade him cheery good afternoons. They were middle-aged and panting badly, but were clearly enjoying the exercise.

A sensation of danger rapidly grew in Brady, and he glanced back up the slope. There was no sign of anyone on the summit of the Tor. He had suddenly felt very cold, a chill that had risen from the inside, rather than coming from the cold wind.

Cloud shadows chased across the scree, hundreds of feet below him, and he could see the bright shapes of walkers there.

The ground below him moved!

For a second he thought he must have been over-balancing, and he flung his arms out to the sides, looking down and around. Again, the earth beneath him jerked, and a great split suddenly appeared behind him. He realized that the section of path on which he had been standing had come away from the hillside, and was crashing down the cliff.

He leapt from the edge, slipping and scrabbling at the ground as his purchase went and he began to tumble. He was suddenly lying across the new cliff edge, clinging onto a heavy tuft of grass, feet dangling in mid-air. He quickly wormed his way back to safety, then turned round, still crouching, his heart racing, his mind not yet in tune with the fact that he had almost fallen several hundred feet to his certain death.

High on the Tor, a tall man-shape watched him. It might have been the same man he had just spoken to, but it was hard to tell. As Brady stared upwards, so the shape turned and vanished.

★

Brady had left Berkshire in mid-morning and had arrived in Casterigg, in the Peaks, in the early afternoon. He was thirsty, now, after the strenuous climb, but English public houses weren't open until five-thirty at the earliest. Despite the danger of consuming alcohol (it made a man susceptible to psychic attack) he could have contentedly polished off a pint of good, real ale.

He was shaken by what had just happened to him. If his legs had felt stronger he might have chased back up to the summit. But even if he had done that, what then? Accuse some innocent hiker of affecting the earth of Maron Tor with his mind?

It was not worth it. If that had *not* been an accident, then it meant only one thing: someone in Casterigg was very unhappy with his presence here.

And that could only be for the good.

He began the laborious process of searching for Marianna. He was convinced that she was here . . . or had been. The town was small. Someone – surely to God *someone* – would have noticed her!

He showed the photographs of his family in shops, cafés, Tourist Information Centres, and private houses. He worked through the High Street first. He asked in the two banks. He asked in the tiny Building Society branch. No one had seen the girl, or the boy, or the woman. No one recognized the faces.

The pubs were all closed, but he went round to the rear entrances and consulted the publicans privately. Still no joy. As he came out of the town again, back towards the distant Tor, he saw a church, standing back from the road. It was locked, but inside someone was practising the organ. He could hear the stopping and starting of a single, complex passage, worked over repeatedly.

He finally gained entrance to the gloomy, stone interior by way of the sacristy. He stood at the side of the church, for a moment, and watched the young priest as he practised. Two coffins stood in the transept, covered with

104

floral wreaths. Light, filtering through a stained glass window above the altar, bathed the silent boxes with colour.

'May I have a word?' Brady called, when the priest ceased playing for a moment and the reverberation of the organ had died away. The man seemed startled, but got up and climbed down the steps from the instrument.

He walked quietly across the church, and spoke in a hushed, reverent whisper. 'I didn't see you here. How did you get in?'

'Through the side,' said Brady. 'I apologize for the intrusion.'

The priest smiled politely. He was young, fair-haired, and spoke with a mild Scottish accent. 'I have to lock the church on occasions like this . . .' he indicated the coffins. 'In a small town there's too much morbid curiosity for the dead. And the motorcycle gangs are a nuisance. They come from the big towns, and will happily open coffins as part of their . . . fun, if you understand me. I have to be cautious. The side door should have been locked.'

As he spoke he guided Brady gently back to the sacristy. The small room reeked of stale incense, and church garments. A row of white surplices occupied most of the space in this minuscule changing room.

'Now what can I do for you?'

Brady showed him the photographs, and explained the circumstances of his search. He explained that he was convinced that at least the *girl* was here, in the town.

The priest stared at Marianna's photograph long and hard. Then shook his head. But he was frowning. Brady's heart increased its beat rate . . .

Dear God, let him have seen her!

But the priest said, 'I'm sorry. I can't help. For a moment . . . For a moment I thought I knew her. But it's not the same child. There *is* a distressed child in Casterigg. I saw her yesterday. I've seen her on two or three occasions. There is a certain familiarity . . .' again he shook his head and passed the photograph back to Brady. 'I'm very sorry.'

'So am I,' said Brady pleasantly.

The priest searched Brady's face for a moment. 'You're a very sad man. It's written, if you'll forgive me, all over you.'

Brady laughed sourly. 'You're quite right. These three people are my whole life, my family.'

The priest frowned. 'Your *family*! And they're lost to you! Now I understand . . . I hardly know what to say.' He seemed genuinely distressed. 'I had thought you to be an investigator . . . but your family! My dear man, I shall pray for you. And I shall pray for them. God help you to find them!'

Brady bowed slightly. 'I'd appreciate help from *any* quarter.'

As he walked to the door, the priest said, 'This is a sad town.' He said it hesitantly, almost nervously. Brady glanced back at him. The priest said, 'Go carefully. Casterigg is in the grip of a malaise which I hope to God will pass . . .'

'What sort of malaise?' Brady asked quietly.

The priest just shook his head. 'I wish I could answer that question. Go carefully.'

Perhaps because of the priest's strangely depressed manner, Brady walked back through the town and noticed how *oppressive* the place was. The day was fairly bright, although the clouds were building again as the afternoon drew to a close, but everyone walked about in sombre silence, and the buildings themselves seemed miserable, soulless places.

It was probably just his imagination.

He began to work his way slowly through one of the wider side streets, showing the photographs, watching people's faces for any sort of reaction at all.

He was surprised, after ten minutes, to see a small, grey and bleak looking police station. He had not realized that there was a police building in Casterigg, otherwise he would have gone there first of all.

To describe the place as a 'station' was an exaggeration. It consisted of a single room, with a counter, a television, two phones, two desks, and two surly looking constables, sitting reading the national newspapers.

When Brady entered the shop, one of them sighed and came over to the counter, pulling a white note-pad across the surface.

'Good afternoon, sir,' he said loudly, wearily. 'What can we do for you?'

'I'm looking for three people,' Brady said, and spread the photographs out on the counter top. After both policemen had glanced cursorily at the portraits, and shaken their heads, Brady briefly explained his reasons for looking, and his suspicion that at least the girl was in Casterigg, or had been until recently. The picture still meant nothing to the men.

But Brady had suddenly begun to interest them. He was aware that their scrutiny had changed from simple indifference to thoughtful assessment. As he returned the pictures to his inside pocket, he watched the policemen.

One of them said, 'Would you be familiar, at all, with a Simon Fleming? A man of about your own age. Shorter, a little better kept.'

Ignoring that last observation, Brady said, 'I've never heard of him. Why do you ask?'

Neither man spoke for a second, perhaps weighing up the wisdom or otherwise of continuing the conversation. Then one of them returned to the desk. The other leaned on the counter, chewing at the inside of his lip, eyes narrowed.

'Very odd Mister . . . what was your name, sir?'

'Brady. Daniel Brady.'

'Well, Mister Brady. As I say, it's very odd indeed. You come in here looking for your family, who you say were abducted from you. And you have reason to believe that they're being held in Casterigg. This is a small, Peak District town, full of tourists, full of old people, and full of locals, who avoid those tourists. It's not a wealthy place despite the mines and the income from the jewellery stones

107

they dig out of them. It's an unremarkable place. But in the space of five days we have three remarkable events. You're one of them. Yesterday a man was in here with the opposite problem to yours . . .'

'I don't understand.'

'His family are being *held* here, in Casterigg, against their will. He came in here and that's exactly what he told us. They're trapped in the hotel, the . . . which one was it, John?'

'The Castle.'

'Right. The Castle. There they are, *he* says. Trapped in their room. Somebody here won't let them out of the town. *Who* won't let you out of the town, I ask. People, he says. They look like hikers, tourists. But they're evil. It's his word. Evil. His car won't work. Nobody will rent him a car. When they try to run, they can't get past these . . . guardians!'

The policeman smiled, straightening up. 'One can't get out. One's trying to get in. This coincidence is very odd, Mister Brady.'

Brady suddenly realized that despite the deliberate, almost patronizing tone of the young officer's voice, he was deadly serious! He was genuinely perturbed by that coincidence.

But who the hell was Simon Fleming? The name meant nothing to him. And yet . . . and yet, maybe Fleming's *experience* did. His family, hounded and trapped by unseen men . . . yes, that had a familiar feel to it.

Fleming would be important to contact.

'Three odd things, you said,' Brady reminded the policeman.

'First murders in Casterigg for as long as *I* can remember,' the man said. 'Perhaps that's not so interesting to you, Mister Brady, but they say odd things come in threes.'

'The coffins in the church,' Brady said quietly.

'Service is the day after tomorrow. That's Mary and little Tommy Bryson in the boxes. Jack Bryson was quite well known round here. There was quite a hunt going on

108

for him up until three days ago. Killed himself, out on the moors. A family, wiped out in two days, and no one the wiser for why he did it. Then comes Mister Fleming with his invisible cage. Now you.' The policeman leaned closer. 'Just what makes you so *sure* your daughter is in the town? Did she get a message out to you?'

'Sort of,' said Brady. 'It's hard to explain . . .'

'Try me.'

'I've been consulting psychics in my search. Mediums. People with strange talents. A psychic woman gave me the clue to Casterigg.'

Whatever response Brady had expected, he was surprised. The policeman looked at first amused, then quite impressed. It was as if he had half expected that answer. He nodded slowly, thoughtfully examining the counter. 'I'll not say a word against that, Mister Brady. I've seen them in action. Do you remember the Ross boy, John?' He glanced round at his colleague, who nodded as he read his paper, without looking up. 'That was a lad,' the policeman went on, 'who got lost in one of the disused mines. We had pot-holers, engineers, the lot, trying to find him. A psychic lady, I forget her name, reckoned she could "feel" the boy three miles away, near the Emmett farm. And that's where he was, in the rising pool. Turned out there was an underground river, that rose on the farmland, and his body had been carried there when he'd slipped into a sink hole. Very impressive. So if you say you've been told your daughter is here . . . well,' he smiled thinly at Brady, 'we'll do our best to find her.'

'Thank you,' said Brady.

The Castle Hotel, the policeman had said, and Brady quickly located the place, and walked around it. It was a tall building, but an otherwise unremarkable structure, looking as dismal and grey as the rest of Casterigg.

From the back streets, Brady surveyed the windows that looked up to the hill where the Norman fortress stood. He glimpsed movement in one of the top windows only, a

109

man, who had been standing, staring out into the gathering dusk, and had only given himself away to Brady when he had turned back into the room.

Brady went to reception and asked for Simon Fleming.

The girl smiled sweetly as she called the room, but there was no answer. 'Mister Fleming is out,' she said. 'I don't *think* he came back. But the other two are in. Unless they slipped out without my noticing.' She tried the room again. Still no answer.

'May I go up?' he asked, and the attractive girl shrugged.

'I don't see why not. Room 26.'

Brady took the stairs. He noticed that his palms were sweating slightly, and that his awareness was sharpened, a result of adrenalin activity in his body. He hesitated in the cold stairwell and listened to the silent hotel, listened *beyond* the silence, for the tell-tale auditory hallucinations that accompanied psychic attack.

A clicking sound, like a creaky box being opened. A deep, distant booming, like thunder . . .

Psychic energy was building around him, or near him, and yet he felt distinctly that it was not being targeted *at* him. He was entering a psychic field. The target was above him . . .

Cautiously, he continued his ascent. The prickling of his skin increased, and his mouth went dry. The air about him seemed to shimmer slightly, and the temperature dropped so alarmingly that his breath misted. He touched the Norse amulet round his neck, and it was warm, reassuring.

On the top landing he stopped and looked about him. Although there were windows at either end of the corridor, the passage was dark. The air seemed to move sluggishly. The mist from his own lungs spiralled away from him, a slow, eerie vortex of fog in this gloomy, haunted place.

He scented something sharp, acrid. It was a smell with which he was well familiar. Scanning the walls of the corridor he soon saw it, a thumb-sized smear of dark unguent.

Psychic defences! Simple, often very effective. He had

110

been similarly defended whilst he had languished in hospital, recovering from the near fatal attack on him at Christmas. Herbs, chemicals, body exudates, and the power of mind: an almost invisible barrier to the ghouls and ghosties of the night, and to the more malevolent elementals that could be created by the savage mind of a psychic adept.

What Brady could feel was a wall of psychic energy, a ghost, struggling to break those effective defences.

He walked slowly along the corridor, touching the cold walls with his hands, keeping himself well away from that frigid stone and plaster. The darkness was a sinister illusion. He glanced at the numbers on each door as he passed them, and hesitated, breathing hard, outside Room 26. Looking back towards the stairwell he could see the tormented outline of the elemental. He glimpsed eyes, gaping jaws, glistening nostrils. He heard the clack and scrape of keratinized substance, perhaps as claws, or scales, on the plaster walls. The ghost made a sudden rush towards him, uttering a wailing cry of unnatural quality, then receded, unable to move after Brady.

Brady stood and watched the phenomenon. He recognized it as weak. It was terrifying to behold, certainly, but that was its whole point. It was a haunting designed to *scare*, to remind the target that he, or she, was under surveillance.

Brady knocked on the door. He called his name through, identified himself, and his purpose. He knocked again, and then a third time, standing to one side of the door in case the occupants should decide to use a little more force than his body could tolerate.

But there was no answer from within. And he heard no sound of movement. He risked a glance through the keyhole, but it had been blocked from the other side.

'I'm not a part of them,' he called. 'I can help you. You can help me. We're on the same side. Please let me in.'

Silence.

It was the sort of silence that screamed the presence of two people, breathlessly waiting behind the door, listening

111

to every movement outside. Terror. An apprehension that bordered on the hysterical. They were there. He could *feel* them. But he could also understand that debilitating fear that drained all reason, all ability to act and react in a sane and ordered way.

'I'll come back,' he called through the door. 'Look out of your window and you'll see me . . .'

He passed back through the zone of haunting, shivering violently as the ice cold air penetrated his clothes, and descended the stone stairs. He left the hotel and walked back to the side street, standing for a while, watching the upper level of the building. For a moment he thought a face glanced out at him from one of the windows, but it was hard to be sure.

He walked back to the High Street. It was after dusk. Somewhere in Casterigg, Simon Fleming was hiding. He was not in his room, or at least, it seemed likely that he was not in the room. So where would he have gone?

Brady asked the receptionist in the Castle Hotel for an approximate description of the man. Armed with that simple information he began to work his way through the town, checking the public houses above all.

It was an obvious place to look. Simon Fleming would not, yet, know the dangers of alcohol on his psychic vulnerability.

10

Land at last! They would soon be there. High, sea-scoured cliffs and bleak, stony farmland; scattered hamlets, silent towns . . . it made Young Grandfather hunger for the plains, and the hunt. It brought out the worst of the capricious Nayenez, who would violently haunt a farmstead at one moment, and the next would clear the stones from a field with a single breath, leaving a bemused farmer staring at the boulder pile and frantically pinching himself.

Land at last. There at last. A few hours more. A little more walking and Mary Jane's mission would be finished.

He was sitting in the far corner of the lounge bar. The pub was the Lion and Lamb, and was clearly the most popular place in Casterigg. The whole lounge reeked of leather, sweat and that peculiar odour associated with water-proofing chemicals. The bar area was crowded with chunky hikers, mostly men, who grinned through full, straggly beards, well spattered with froth from their pints of ale, and discussed the relative merits of different climbs and hikes.

Brady worked his way through them to the bar and spoke to the landlord, whom he had seen earlier in the afternoon in connection with Marianna. The man didn't know Simon Fleming by name, but there *was* a man who sounded like him, and Brady followed the direction of the pointing finger.

The man was seated glumly behind a small table, staring out across a half consumed pint of beer. He was curled up inside his anorak almost foetally. He looked to be about thirty years old, greying, receding, rather soft. There was little personality in his face, save for the spectacularly bad temper that was obviously afflicting him now.

As Brady walked over to him, he looked up. His eyes were grey, ice cold, sharp. He frowned slightly.

Brady said, 'Are you Simon Fleming?'

'Christ!' the man screamed, his face registering a sudden panic. He literally threw the table at Brady. The beer glass smacked against Brady's chest, spilling its contents down his jacket. The impact of the heavy wood table sent Brady reeling backwards, struggling for balance.

Fleming shot from the bar, barging his way through the crowds, elbowing people aside and screaming, 'Let me through. For Christ's sake, let me out!'

As Brady went in pursuit, two burly climbers reached out brawny hands and grabbed him. 'Just a second, sunshine,' one of them said, sipping his beer arrogantly as he held Brady still.

'Just let go of me,' said Brady angrily.

'He seemed frightened of you . . .'

'He's a frightened man. I need to talk to him and he's getting away. Let *go*!'

The two youths exchanged a semi-amused look, not playing Brady's game at all. 'Seems to me,' said the taller, 'That this gentleman isn't enjoying our conversation.'

'That's right,' said the other. He didn't look at Brady, but his grip on Brady's arm grew more powerful. 'People always in a rush, always in a –'

He got no more words out. He was spluttering blood after Brady's swift, accurate and powerful punch. The other man turned quickly to retaliate and met a blow in the stomach that doubled him up.

Brady jerked him up again by his shetland jumper. 'Don't fuck about with me . . . *sunshine*!'

Before either of them could go for Brady – which was clearly their intention – the barman had grabbed one, and two locals the other, and their struggling, abuse-shouting forms were restrained as Brady left the pub.

Damn! he thought. *Damn people for not minding their own business.*

114

He looked both ways along the dark, nearly empty street.

Fleming was racing away on the Castle side, his hunched figure loping along in the shadows of the shops. He cast a quick, frightened look backwards, saw Brady starting to run after him, and darted out of sight.

He had gone down an alleyway between shops, Brady discovered. It was dark, uninviting. He walked cautiously through and emerged unchallenged into one of Casterigg's backstreets.

Distantly, he could hear the sound of a running man. The echoing thud of footsteps seemed to come from all around, but he moved quickly through the gloom, towards the line of houses that sat along the base of the rising hill, where the ruins perched.

The moonlight was quite full, and the houses seemed to gleam. 'Fleming!' he called. 'Simon! I'm not going to hurt you. I want to talk. That's all. Just talk.'

The night was silent. Brady hesitated, standing on a corner, touching the grey, cold stone of a house. He looked ahead, behind. He listened.

Someone moved stealthily, some way ahead. He walked quickly in that direction. It was an alley, leading back to the main road, but it curved and wiggled its way, and Brady could not see the end.

He picked his steps cautiously through the narrow passage, stopping every few paces to listen, to glance behind him.

Fleming must have found a niche in the alley, a hiding place. Brady would have walked right past his crouched, breathless body. A moment later Brady heard the sound of the man running back the way they had come. He turned and ran in pursuit, and as he came out into the back street again, something struck him forcibly in the chest, winding him.

'Leave me alone!' the man screamed. 'And let my daughter *go*, damn you!'

He struck again with the weapon he held, a jagged piece of old fencing that he had presumably found in the alley. Brady fended off the blow, then made a grab for the wood.

115

'I'm nothing to do with them!' he tried to say, but Fleming was intent on committing murder. He staggered backwards, like a beast at bay, lips drawn back, eyes wide, breath sharply drawn and angry.

And then it happened. The unexpected. The shocking . . .

One moment Brady had been facing a murderous young man, and was struggling to find the breath and the words to calm that wild spirit.

The next, his name had been screamed from somewhere to the right, and turning he had seen her, just briefly . . .

And his heart threatened to burst from his chest, his legs threatened to collapse beneath his weight . . .

'ALISON!' he screamed. 'ALISON!'

'DAN! Oh my God, Dan! For pity's sake –'

She had been raggedly dressed, deathly pale, her hands tied behind her back. A towering, dark shape had bundled her into a nondescript car, something like a Ford, he thought, and the vehicle had screeched away.

'ALISON!'

At last he found his legs. He raced so fast after the car that when he reached the main street he collapsed on the road, striking his face hard on the tarmac. He struggled upright, unaware that he was bleeding from a huge graze on his nose. He could just see the car streaking away into the darkness towards the Tor.

Tears came then. He ran to the rear of the shops where he had parked his own car. He was vaguely aware of Simon Fleming walking unsteadily after him, watching him peculiarly, but he had no time to worry about the man now. As he raced for his vehicle, the tears flooded down his face. His sobs were loud in the night, and he cried her name over and over.

He *couldn't* lose her now! He *mustn't*! Oh God, to get so close only to have her taken from him again. She had been here. All the time he had explored the shops and the pubs and the streets she had been *here*, perhaps aware of him, unable to call to him. And Arachne had known he had come, and had tried to smuggle her away again. And by pure fortune, and the grace of Alison's powerful lungs, screaming through the night to him, he had seen her.

'Start! Damn it, *start!*'

Crying, shaking, he fumbled with the keys in the ignition, jammed his foot repeatedly on the accelerator, and finally roared away in a great cloud of exhaust fumes and flying gravel.

At more than eighty miles an hour he streaked out of the town, up the road to the Tor. He could see no tail-lights ahead. Other cars veered to avoid him as he tore along the narrow roadway, his headlights on full beam. He touched ninety and when the road curved to the right, he went over the grass verge, smashed through a wood and barbed wire fence, and bumped and lurched across the cow field beyond.

Cursing loudly, he spun the wheel and drove angrily back, frantically searching for the area of impact and passing back to the road through the break in the fence. A strand of barbed wire was caught in the gap between bonnet and chassis. It dragged along the road beside him.

Twenty minutes later he stopped the car on the dark road, half way up the Tor, where the beginning of the real walking was marked with a small tea shop. He wept loudly, shaking like a leaf, as he stared back towards the bright lights of Casterigg. The moon, behind clouds, eerily illuminated the towering keep of the ruined fortress.

She had gone. She had been within a hundred yards of him, and she had gone. So close. So bloody *close!*

Fists clenched, he let the agony and the pain cry itself out of his system. His voice was an animal's howling, raised against the stillness of night. The cry he uttered was the repeated, melancholy calling of her name.

At last he grew chilly. The tears dried, and his body shook with night's cold, not grief. He climbed back into his car and drove back to Casterigg. By the time he got there, he was charged up again, his mind alert, his resolve returned.

Where had he seen her? In the confusion, in his panic,

he realized that he had not properly located the house from which she had been bundled. He retraced his pursuit of Fleming, and eventually found the alleyway where Fleming had attacked him. From here he could identify the row of tall, dark houses where the car had been. He walked to them. They were all apparently unoccupied, although in one he could see a light through the back. Each house was on three storeys, backing, it seemed, onto the steep hillside. He found an alleyway through and struggled, in the darkness, to make out details of the garden areas, and rear windows. There were more lights on here. Each house, in fact, seemed to be occupied. The gardens were narrow and not very long, and the lower slopes of the hill were less steep, and densely wooded. Somewhere, water was running from a cleft in the rock.

Which house had it been? He stood before their darkened fronts and stared up at them. One of three, he was sure, and he tried the front doors of each of them, and checked the windows.

Then, taking his nerve firmly by the hand, he rang the doorbell of the house that was equipped with such modernity, and hammered on the heavy iron knockers of the other two.

No one answered at any of them.

Behind him, a voice said, 'Number Twelve is what you want.'

Brady turned. Simon Fleming was standing a few feet away. He still carried the broken piece of fencing. He looked dishevelled, but in the moonlight his pale eyes gleamed with interest, with curiosity. 'Who are you?'

'Dan Brady. I'd have introduced myself earlier, but you didn't give me much opportunity.'

'Who was the woman?' Fleming asked, ignoring what Brady had said. He kept his distance. The tension in his body was almost tangible. Brady made no move towards him.

'My wife, Alison,' he said.

Fleming looked up at the front of the house. 'I've been in there once,' he said. 'There's nothing inside. Not now.

118

Not since . . .' again he gave Brady that searching, inquisitive look.

'Not since . . . ?' Brady prompted.

'Not since I helped my daughter and Uncle William to get away.'

'Were they being kept there? Against their will?'

'I had thought so,' Fleming said quietly. 'Escaping was far too easy. Except that . . .'

Infuriatingly, he trailed off again. He was still unsure of Brady. He closed the distance between them, though. 'You want to look inside?'

'That's my intention,' said Brady.

'Round the back, then,' Fleming said, and led the way quickly back to the alley.

They jumped over fences, and padded silently across the gardens, disturbing nothing but one solitary cat, which followed them friskily, balancing on fences, watching them, glad of these unexpected playmates. It purred loudly, and brushed up against their legs when they stopped, and try as he might, Brady could not discourage its company.

There was a single light on at number 12, on the first floor. Fleming forced the back door. He did it noisily, the wood splintering around the lock. Inside, the smell was overpowering: rotting food, drains, and that lingering aroma of tomcat. The walls and surfaces were covered with a thin, tacky sheen of grease.

The kitchen light didn't work, but the light in the hall showed Brady that the kitchen was effectively functionless. No stove, no cupboards, no sink, just a single tap on the wall, and a battered table, on which the offending food remains could still be seen.

The rooms were all deserted. The light was on in a bathroom, where a single sink hung perilously from its holding on the wall. The lavatory bowl was grimed with dark faecal matter, however, and the flush worked.

Someone had been here. Someone had used the house.

Uncle William and Fleming's daughter, of course. But someone else too?

119

The plaster walls were decaying. The wooden slats of the plasterboard ceilings were showing through where the plaster had fallen away. Mice infested the place. Empty tins of beans, tomatoes and ravioli were piled neatly in the corner of a room on the second floor. Here also were two piles of filthy clothing, very old, fashions from the fifties.

But the most interesting thing to Brady was the 'unofficial' decoration of the walls, here.

On every wall there were markings. They had been made, as far as he could see, in blood, but a few were scratchings in the plaster, made with a stone that was still in evidence.

Strange symbols, some of them conforming to the classical occult pattern of spiral and labrynth; others less familiar, some vaguely animalistic, others representations of the elements. In straggling letters, words had been scratched on the walls: AOTH on the wall facing more or less north; THAAO, on that facing south; OMAG, to the west, and on the eastern wall a word that might have been CHGOM.

'Does that mean anything to you?' Fleming asked, as he saw Brady's interest. Brady straightened up, shaking his head. 'Not in that form,' he said.

'In what form, then?'

'Maybe no form. Maybe as Uriel, Gabriel, Michael and Raphael.'

Fleming frowned slightly. 'I've heard of them,' he said.

Brady smiled thinly. 'I should sincerely hope so.'

They went through the rest of the house. It was as deserted as the ground floor. The smell pervaded every room.

Had Alison really been kept here, under these appalling conditions? It made his blood boil to think of it.

But where were the others? Where was little Marianna; where was shy Dominick? Had they been here too? From where had Marianna reached to him, if not from this house?

The obvious answer was that she, and Alison, and others too, perhaps, had all been here until recently, and had been

120

taken away when outside forces – in the form of Brady, perhaps Fleming too – had come a little too close for comfort.

'Lights in every room except the kitchen,' he said to Fleming. 'The place has been used.'

'Of course,' Fleming said. 'I could have told you that.'

'Then let's talk about it,' said Brady.

They went downstairs again. For a minute or two, Brady stamped around on the floorboards, and opened the understairs cupboard, carefully searching for a possible passageway, concealed below.

'I don't think the house has a cellar,' Fleming said, and Brady shrugged and accepted that. As they stepped out into the night, however, he stopped, staring at the moonlit trees, the rising hill before him. Again, he heard the sound of water running over rocks. The garden was unkempt, untended. The fence at its far end was broken and overgrown. The nearer trees seemed almost to tower over the private land, as if hugging it. House and hill, connected by rough nature.

Brady was sure that there was an underground passage between the house and the system of caves which must surely run through to the hill. But it was too dark, and too dangerous, to search for that system now.

'Let me tell you what I already know,' said Brady, as they sat in the rather bleak bar of the Castle Hotel. 'You're in Room 26, with an old man and a young girl. She's your daughter. I'm not sure who he is. You claim that they're trapped in Casterigg, and you have come here to try and get them out. You've failed. They're haunted, and perhaps you are too. The upper floor of this hotel certainly has a strong psychic presence, a ghost. Your old man has set up defences against attack. They can't get out, but nothing evil can get in.'

Despite Brady's strong assurances that it was dangerous to do so, Simon Fleming was sipping his second double scotch of the last few minutes. Brady had coffee. His hands shook violently as he tried to raise the cup to his lips, and he placed it down in the saucer again, and sat there, staring at it. Thoughts of Alison induced surges of panic in him. He could hardly bear to realize that she was so close, but that with every passing second she might be getting further away from him, trussed and helpless in that speeding car.

'I don't understand what's going on,' Fleming said sadly. He seemed helpless, and young. There were scant years between the two men, but Fleming had no power, no authority. He was a wretched, frightened man, a beaten man.

He said, 'All I can tell you is what has happened, what I've seen. From the beginning, then . . .' He drained his glass, choked slightly, then sat back in his chair and fixed his gaze somewhere beyond Daniel Brady.

'Kelly is five years old. You wouldn't think it to hear her talking, now – she's wild, coarse, like an immature adult.' He trailed off, then snapped his mind back to the moment. 'I've got a son, Richard, who's two. He's one of these hyperactive children, you know? Very hard to handle, very demanding. We live in a small house in Luton. Kelly goes to school there. Anyway, there was a fire at the school, and everyone was sent home for a week. Can you imagine having Kelly *and* Richard to look after? I couldn't take time off work. I had to eventually, but at the time the easiest thing was to send Kelly to Uncle William.

'Uncle William is a relative on Lindsey's side. That's my wife. He has a smallholding about ten miles from here, near Sheffield. It's a lovely place, and Kelly loves Uncle William very much. He's an old bachelor, but not fussy, if you know what I mean. Very warm, very good with kids. Very good to Lindsey and me. A real friend. Or so he was, once.' Fleming's face darkened and he leaned forward to toy with his empty whisky glass.

'I rang up William. He sounded very distracted, not at all his usual self. He wasn't sure about letting Kelly come to stay. He said things weren't too good for him at that moment, and perhaps Kelly should go somewhere else. I wish I'd taken note of what he said. But I was too worried about Lindsey, too selfish. I ignored William's uncertainty, promised him that Kelly would be no trouble, I talked him into having her. He wasn't happy about it.

'We put her on the coach to Sheffield. She's made the trip before. She called that evening to say she was safely there. Fine, we thought. We heard nothing for two days. I rang a couple of times. No answer. I wasn't worried. They were probably out touring. By the third day I was slightly worried. Still no word from Kelly. Still no answer from the phone. On the fourth day . . . well, on the fourth day I woke up and just *knew* that something was wrong. I had that feeling you can get, very painful, very scary. I tried to find the neighbour's number, but couldn't get any joy. There was nothing for it . . . I drove to the house . . .'

Where had they *gone*?

The small stone house was quite empty. It was cool, fresh. There were no food smells, no sense of anybody having been here in recent days. In the small guest bedroom Fleming found Kelly's small travelling case, and several of her clothes still inside it. But Uncle William's shaving things were missing, as was his big overcoat.

If they had gone out for a day trip, why would he have taken his shaving mug and brush? If they had gone to stay overnight somewhere, wouldn't Kelly have taken her case?

Perhaps they had packed one bag between them . . .

But Fleming felt unnerved. And in the kitchen, on the table, he found what he took to be a communication from Uncle William: a postcard, with a message in felt-tip written over the tiny biro scrawl of the original greeting.

The postcard showed Maron Tor, seen from Casterigg, a town only a few miles away. The message read simply: *we've gone here.*

Fleming pocketed the card. He felt slightly sick, he couldn't think why. Perhaps it was the nature of that message. It had been written in haste, almost frantically. Everything about it communicated fear . . .

He walked round the acre and a half of grounds,

123

searching for something, anything that might put his mind at rest. Then he went to the house next door.

The old couple who lived there looked pale and frightened. Yes, they'd seen William and the girl. William had been away for a long time.

'Away? Away where?'

'I really couldn't tell you,' said Mrs Chalmers. 'But he's been gone for several weeks. He came back about a week ago, looking very peculiar. Ill, we thought, didn't we Bill?'

'Ill,' said Bill Chalmers, nodding his head sagely. 'Definitely ill. Very pale. Very unfriendly.'

'Then your girl came. We saw them walking down the lane, and she was happy enough, though not him. Then the men came. That would have been . . . when would that have been, Bill?'

'The other day or so,' said Bill Chalmers. Again he nodded.

'That would be it,' said Mrs Chalmers helpfully. 'The other day or so. About four of them. Very late at night. Two cars, and they kept their engines running, but didn't have any lights on. Anyways, that was that. Next day Bill went round to see William, and they were both gone.'

More and more perturbed, Fleming went back to the house. This time he looked for evidence of Uncle William's travels, and found it in the top drawer of his chest. It was in the form of hotel receipts, restaurant receipts, half-used railway tickets. He realized that he'd had no contact with William for about four months. The receipts covered the spring period, and showed that William had been in Durham, in Scotland, in Dublin, of all places, then back to Cornwall, and Portsmouth. He had even been in London.

Simon Fleming had known none of this. And it was an activity so unlike Uncle William that it was hard to believe these receipts did not belong to someone else.

Strange behaviour. Strange men. Midnight cars. Scrawled messages on postcards . . .

What the *hell* was going on?

He drove quickly to Casterigg and parked in the centre

124

of the town. He searched half-heartedly among the cafés, pubs and shops. He walked the back streets and front streets. He found no sign of them. Frustrated, increasingly anguished, he slept the night in his car. At crack of dawn he was up, and retracing his steps of the previous day, calling out Kelly's name, hoping that his voice would carry to her, hoping that the early morning silence would favour him.

At midday he was lounging disconsolately against a wall, weary and hungry, close to tears.

He heard a distant rapping sound, someone knocking on glass.

Looking up, looking round, he finally saw her. Kelly!

She was standing in the window of a house, tapping on the glass, waving at him. He ran quickly over to her, smiled, and called to her. Then he knocked on the door, repeating the action loudly, irritably.

Finally, it was Uncle William who opened the door, admitting Fleming before he got so distraught that he actually barged in through the wood.

The house was in a similar condition to that which would greet the search of Daniel Brady, a few days later. Filthy, cold, smelly . . . wretched.

Kelly sat in the corner of a room on the first floor. She seemed subdued, frightened. She wouldn't speak to Fleming, her own father, and this bizarre state continued during the day.

Neither of them would leave the house. They were terrified. Uncle William sat on the floor, smoking endlessly, staring into the middle distance. He answered Fleming's increasingly angry questions with monosyllables, shrugs, the occasional brief phrase.

'We can't get out,' he said at one point. 'They're keeping us here.'

'Who are? Who are keeping you here?'

He learned that there had been others, trapped in the house, but that they had been taken away a day or two before. But 'they', the unspecified oppressors, did not want William and Kelly to leave, and somehow that simple fact was enough to keep them bound in the house.

125

'But they can't do anything to us,' Uncle William said smugly. He smiled thinly at Simon Fleming. 'Because I'm too strong, now. They didn't expect it. They didn't foresee it. That's a laugh. That's a joke. They didn't realize what would happen. I can't get out. But they can't get close. Not close enough!'

'I want my daughter back. I want her out of here . . .'

Fleming tried to drag the girl bodily from the house. She screamed and struggled, and when he came to the front door, opened it and tried to carry her through, she was practically hysterical. She stared out into the street, and the look on her face was one of appalling terror.

Fleming fetched take-away food, and the two of them ate so hungrily that he guessed this was the first good food they had had for days. He called Lindsey. He lied to her. He said that Kelly was ill, but safe, and would be back in a few days.

'You've driven them away from the house,' Uncle William said. 'That's one good thing. But they won't let us out of the town.'

Fleming could see nothing threatening; he could see no one who represented danger. He sat with them through the long day following, watching them, listening to their silence, and occasionally to their brief expressions of hope.

Rain built up from the west. Early on the following morning they rose, dressed, and Uncle William said, 'Get us out of here, Simon.'

They left the house, nervously looking around them. The rain was literally sheeting from the overcast skies. Casterigg was awash. 'I need tobacco,' said Uncle William. He and Kelly sheltered beneath the canopy of a shoe shop.

Later, they tried to leave the town and failed.

Uncle William was right. Whoever 'they' were, they couldn't get close to them. But they were stopping William and Kelly leaving.

'I don't expect you to understand,' Uncle William said, as they sat miserably in the room in the Castle Hotel, 'But something is coming for me. I'm helpless against it, of that I'm sure. I've got to get out of here before it comes. Or

126

we're all lost. They can't get close to me, but they've trapped me here. Kelly too. She's what you might call their insurance. But I've got to get out of here, Simon. The thing that's coming for me . . .'

Fleming had never seen such genuine fear in the old man's eyes.

They sat and stared at each other in silence.

'Where's it coming from?' Fleming asked eventually.

Uncle William said, 'The west. It's coming from the west. And it's nearly here . . .'

11

The boy was dreaming of Red Indians. They whooped and screamed through his unconscious mind. Their horses thundered. Their guns roared as they chased across the idyllic green lands of the dream state.

He awoke abruptly, shaking and sweaty. He was startled by movement in the darkness, and after a moment he sat up in bed, staring into the gloom.

He was a boy of seven years of age. His tonsils had been removed two days before, and he remained in the hospital ward because of a slight infection. It was a children's ward, boys and girls mixed together. They slept peacefully, some noisily. Only the boy was awake.

He watched the Indian who stood in the middle of the aisle between the rows of beds. In the slight moonlight that filtered between cracks in the curtaining, his eyes were wide, startled, and yet delighted.

The Indian was tall and almost naked. He was very handsome. He had the face of a chief. His hair was long and dark, his shoulders broad and strong. He carried a bow and arrows in his left hand. After a moment he looked around, not seeming to see the boy. He walked slowly from the ward, padding silently as only Indians know how to do.

The boy flung back the covers of his bed, swung his legs out and fumbled for his slippers. He didn't bother with his dressing gown, but followed the Indian, wearing just his rumpled pyjamas.

When the Indian stopped, the boy stopped. He stared fascinated at the tall man. It seemed to the boy that the hospital wards were filled with the smell of grass and animals, not that cloying chemical smell that made him so homesick. It was the smell of fields in summer, when the air was hot and still, and everything – trees, plants, animals – were sleepy.

Suddenly the Indian had gone. The boy hesitated, staring along the corridor, then pushing open the door to a ward. Everything was so quiet, there were not even noises coming from the nurse's stations.

He stepped into the ward, then turned quickly and looked up. The Indian was standing in the corner of the room, staring down at him. Boy and ghost exchanged a long, silent gaze. Then the Indian reached down and the boy felt himself lifted from his feet, swung high into the air.

The Indian had a good, strong face, a kindly face. His eyes were narrowed and they searched the boy's, but his lips were stretched into an amused smile. The boy dangled there, high in the air, and then the Indian lowered him to the floor again, turned him around and pushed him out into the corridor.

When the boy turned back there was no sign of his ghostly friend at all.

But he was lost, now. He had walked up stairs, round corridors, through long, wide wards where old men snored. He didn't know the way back to his own bed.

He was a small, baggily dressed shape, padding quietly through the hospital, pushing open doors and peering into the darkness. And at last he came to a set of swing doors through which he could hear a peculiar sound.

It was a sickly, rasping sound, like an animal slobbering as it chewed on a piece of tough meat. He could hear the sound of its breathing, breath sucked through a full mouth as the jaws chomped and chewed.

Was it a dog? On the ward?

He pushed the doors open and peered in. There was a terrible smell, a really awful smell . . .

And something like a huge grasshopper stood over one of the beds, holding a limp body, its glistening insect jaws tearing and sucking at its prey . . .

★

A nurse, just beginning her ward round, heard the sound of running. She turned and saw the small boy tearing towards her. He was running blind, and collided with her before he noticed her. He immediately started to scream, waking up the whole ward.

She grasped him by the shoulders and tried to shake some sense into him.

'Where are *you* from? What are you doing out of bed?'

The boy sobbed. And through the sobs she began to make out the words: 'It's eating them! It's eating them!'

'What's eating what?' she said, and dropped to a crouch. The boy's skin was icy cold. He was shaking violently. His screams and crying grew louder, more uncontrolled.

'Eating them! It's eating them! An insect . . . an insect . . . !'

The nurse stood quickly, realizing that, whatever the garbled speech meant, something was wrong, somewhere. She ran back along his path, pushing through into the ward at the end of the corridor. This was a ward where old men came to cope with simple illnesses, that might nevertheless prove fatal. She knew all of them, rich, ripe old characters, many of them destined to make their goodbyes to her from the beds they now lay in.

Nurse Prichard walked quietly into that ward, afraid of disturbing the sleeping occupants. There was a smell like the operating theatres after a heavy operation. It didn't make her gag. She was used to it.

But not here, not where the old men slept.

Her legs turned to jelly. She walked a few paces between the beds. Moonlight glistened on strange draperies, hanging from the curtain rails around each cot.

Suddenly, coldly panicked she went back to the entrance and switched on the lights . . .

'Oh my GOD!'

They lay where they had been tossed; slumped, chewed bodies, scattered about the floor. Intestines had been drawn from them and tossed over the rails and bedsteads.

In the middle of the floor a neat pile of heads had accumulated, their eyes picked out, their mouths gaping in silent screams.

There was not a living man on the ward. They had all been butchered in this grotesque way.

Mary Jane Silverlock rose to her feet in the darkness of the hospital laundry room. She was still tired. As the great walk reached its end, so her fatique was growing. She needed to rest with increasing frequency. Energy was draining. Not even her guardian spirits could keep the decay from her body.

She should not have chosen a hospital to rest in. She had forgotten that Hunhau preyed on the sick and ailing.

'Chief of Demons is not with me,' she said quietly. The others were there, snug in her grey stuff. Young Grandfather said, 'He was the locust. He has fed upon the sick. I saw him. He is bloated with their soul stuff. He has caused great destruction of life.'

'He is so evil,' Mary Jane said. 'And yet he is so important. Why is he so important?'

'He is Chief of Demons,' Young Grandfather said. 'I am just an old Indian. In my time I had heard of this Lord of Death. He has great knowledge, great power, magic power from those lands far in the south. I am just an old Indian. I don't understand these magic things.'

She stood in the darkness. Enumclaw and Tieholt slept. She could feel the strand of life between herself and Hunhau. He was not far away. He could never be far away. The crystal chip in her belly flesh was sore. It seemed to twist around, snagged and tugged by the Chief of Demons, who would love to have escaped the girl's control, to have gone wild, free, in this new land.

At last he came back through the darkness.

He was like a corpse with the grey, narrow head of an insect. His eyes glittered, his jaws clacked. He laughed and the apparition changed. The skull grinned. The evil eyes winked at her from the paper-fleshed sockets.

He stepped towards her and tugged at her stomach, moving back into her grey-stuff.

Mary Jane opened the door of the laundry room and stepped out into the darkened corridor. All around her she could hear a strange sound, the sound of running, of clattering activity. There were raised voices. It sounded like confusion. On a nearby wall, blue light was reflected.

She walked over to a window and peered out into the street. There were police everywhere. The street was blocked off by cars. Uniformed men prowled up and down, looking eerie in the half light.

Hunhau chuckled to himself as he snuggled inside his carrier.

The sound of voices came nearer.

'How do I get out of here?'

Nayenez stirred for the first time in days. He had played mischievous tricks on the ocean liner. Now it was time to work.

He was a tall, lean shape, running lightly and at a stoop ahead of Mary Jane, guiding the way. He blew darkness into the eyes of the nurses and doctors they passed. Mary Jane stood still in the centre of the corridor and the hospital staff walked by her without noticing. She stood against a wall and three police officers stood right by her, not aware of her. Nayenez blew softly at them. They brushed at their faces, but were blind to the girl.

The Navajo spirit ran softly on ahead, taking Mary Jane down stairs, through doors, through galleries, and at last out into the back courtyard of the hospital.

Enumclaw surfaced again. He was a thunder cloud, ripping through the parked cars and the ranks of men who were watching and waiting for the assassin to escape the hospital premises. Mary Jane walked stiffly through the mayhem. Cars rose sedately into the air, spinning and twisting away, to suddenly fall with great, crashing explosions, onto the roadway.

The crowds scattered. It was early in the morning, and the chaotic police activity had drawn the sightseers out of their beds by the hundreds. The hospital was under siege,

132

but through its eastern entrance, the killer escaped.

Nayenez created the illusion of running men, and the police chased shadows for long minutes, until Mary Jane was safely away.

12

Everything that Simon Fleming said convinced Brady that
Fleming's family were also under attack by the killers
known as Arachne. It was attack of a slightly different
nature to that which had been perpetrated on Brady.
Uncle William and Kelly were clearly of use to them, and
were being kept here until . . .

Until something came for them 'from the west'.

Brady remembered Ellen Bancroft's garbled warning.
Danger from the west. She. Danger.

Casterigg was a focus, then. The same danger that
threatened Brady, threatened Uncle William.

What were Arachne up to?

There was one thing that Brady needed to do before
confronting the old man and the girl. It was his simple way
of confirming that Arachne *had* been operating in Casterigg.
He had seen illusion, strange marking, and he had seen
Alison . . . or had that been illusion too? He couldn't
believe that it had been.

But there were two bodies in coffins in the church. He
felt he wanted to see those bodies, to see the manner of
their deaths . . .

Fleming was desperately uncomfortable at the thought
of such 'body inspecting'. Brady led the way through the
night to the small house where the priest lived. The man
was sleepy, but got dressed and came down to the front
door.

Brady said, 'I can't tell you why, father, but I need to see
those poor people in the church. It may help me find my
daughter. I swear to respect the dead.'

The priest was perturbed for a moment, then nodded his
agreement. 'If it will help . . . very well.'

He let them into the church and stood by as Brady lifted the coffin lids, one after another. Fleming gasped his horror at the sights revealed within, and even the priest balked.

'I had no idea . . .' he whispered in the cold silence.

Brady stared at the woman's face, the bulging eyes, the hideously protruding tongue. Her hands were fixed together at the wrists, the fingers curled outwards, as if she had fought against ropes. No ropes bound her, and Brady suspected that no ropes ever had.

She had been tied by psychic forces, and strangled by a Stalker, a malicious and deadly elemental. The boy, her son, was similarly trussed, and had been similarly dispatched.

To the police it had looked like the mad attack of a crazed husband. But Brady recognized the certain mark of Arachne. He closed the coffin lids, and led the shaking Fleming out of the church again.

The girl was huddled in the corner of the room, knees drawn up, eyes wide, face solemn. As Brady followed Simon Fleming into Room 26 of the Castle Hotel, he almost gasped with surprise. He could see at once why the priest had hesitated on being shown the photograph of Marianna. The resemblance was very close.

But Marianna's hair was shorter, curlier, perhaps a shade or two lighter. And she was a happy, jolly looking girl, not sour like Kelly Fleming.

The old man whom Simon referred to as Uncle William was walking distractedly up and down the floor, smoking a thin cigarette, and blowing a voluminous cloud of smoke from his nostrils after every deep draw.

As Brady entered the room, he turned and stared hard at the stranger, then shrugged and went to sit on the edge of the bed. The atmosphere in the place was hostile and very tense.

Fleming said, 'This is Daniel Brady. He may be able to help us.'

Brady thought that the girl smiled slightly, but when he glanced at her she was staring at nothing in particular, as straight-faced and unhappy as before. It was, indeed, very cold in the room, that unnatural cold that Brady had come to associate with psychic forces. The haunting presence outside in the corridor was perhaps draining the heat from the space beyond the door. That presence had still been there, seconds before, as Fleming had led Brady from the stairwell, but the younger man had not seemed to notice it.

'I hope that you can help me too,' Brady said, watching the old man. William said nothing. He regarded his cigarette almost curiously, then stubbed it out in an ash tray. Brady went over to the window and sat down on the ledge.

Fleming looked helplessly at his new-found colleague. He seemed to be saying, 'See what I mean? Impossible.'

Brady said, 'I've heard about your difficulties.'

'Have you indeed,' said William softly, disagreeably. He didn't meet Brady's gaze.

'What does the name "Arachne" mean to you?' Brady went on. The old man responded with a thin smile, then glanced up, his eyes twinkling.

'Spiders,' said the girl, and shivered. 'Hate spiders.'

William said, 'What does Arachne mean to *you*, Brady?'

'It means a lot,' he answered, 'and it means very little.' He took the photographs of his family from his pocket and tossed them to William, who picked them up and looked at each in turn. 'It means finding those three people. They have names. Marianna Brady. Dominick Brady. Alison Brady. It means finding the "Roundelay" before the "Roundelay" can *use* those three people. The trouble is: I don't even know what the Roundelay is. Or Magondathog. That's a place, I think. But who can tell? And the mammath. Perhaps the mammath is female. It sounds female. Perhaps she lives at Magondathog. Who can tell? Perhaps she runs Arachne. So many funny names, Uncle William. One horrendous purpose: they kill, they maim, they abduct. They are "awakening" something. They are gathering. They are, at least in part . . . vulnerable. They are not invincible. But they are clever. They slip out of my grasp each time my fingers close upon them. They have my family, Uncle William. And I want my family back. I shall hunt them until I achieve that end. I shall fight them with every weapon at my disposal. *That's* what Arachne means to me.'

Kelly was staring at him, now. So was William. The girl struggled to her feet and walked over to the bed, picking up the photographs. Uncle William tapped one of the pictures, and the two of them exchanged a significant glance. Simon Fleming stood in the far corner of the room, just watching.

When Kelly turned round again, to speak to Brady, there were tears in her eyes. She held the picture of Marianna.

'We saw her,' she said. Her hands were shaking. 'She was in the house. She was so sad . . .'

The tears rolled down her cheeks. She walked over to Brady and stood there, half crying, clutching the photograph of his daughter as if it was something precious to her.

The sadness got to Brady, and he felt his own eyes sting. He reached out and hugged little Kelly to him, squeezing his eyes tight shut, trying to hold back the surge of grief that threatened to overwhelm him.

He began to shake. At last! At last, he was close.

Alison had been here. And Marianna. Dominick would not be far away. *Oh God*, he thought, *they've* got *to be somewhere about. They* mustn't *have been taken far away again* . . .

'When did you see her?' he asked.

William began the laborious process of rolling a new cigarette. He said, 'A couple of days ago.'

'She was in that awful house,' said Kelly. 'Where we were trapped.'

'She was in one of the upper rooms,' William continued. 'I think she was tied up for a while. She was crying a lot. We were locked downstairs, but the lock wasn't strong, and I managed to break the door open. I went upstairs and comforted her. She was very distressed.'

'I stayed with her for a while,' said Kelly. 'Her wrists were all cut where they'd tied her up. We didn't talk. We just sat and played. She said her name was Marianna. This is the girl . . .'

The words were like shots. Each of them burst loud in Brady's mind. He wanted Kelly and Uncle William to say over and over again that they'd seen his daughter. Tell me again. And again. Say her name. Describe her . . . Great God in Heaven, these people have talked to her, they've *touched* her!

'What happened to her?' Brady asked, his voice slightly tremulous. 'Did you see what happened to her?'

Kelly shook her head. Uncle William said, 'In the morning we heard the sound of voices. There was a car outside, which drove off. The girl was gone.'

'And my wife? Alison? She was in the house too. I saw her last night . . .'

William shook his head. His grey eyes seemed cold, but Brady thought there was concern there, compassion. 'I'm afraid not. Perhaps they were keeping her somewhere else.'

'I heard a woman talking,' said Kelly, and she and William exchanged a glance. Kelly looked back at Brady, her lips quivering. 'I heard a lot of people talking. A lot of sad people. But I only saw Marianna.'

Brady took the photograph from the girl's fingers.

Where had they *taken* her? If this couple, this old man and his niece, were still being trapped in Casterigg by Arachne, then there was a chance that Alison and Marianna were still in the area, moved out of immediate harm's way.

'Now you know what Arachne means to me,' Brady repeated. 'But what the hell are they? Satanists? Black magicians? That's Hollywood stuff, isn't it? What are they doing? What's their purpose?'

Uncle William stood up and crossed to the window, standing right by Brady as he peered out into the night. 'Are you thinking aloud, or asking me?'

'I'm asking you what you know . . .'

'If anything,' said William. And shrugged. 'Like you, Mister Brady, I struggle to make sense of the incomprehensible.'

'Tell me anyway.'

The old man's breath misted in the cold, bleak room.

'A year ago my house began to be haunted. Presences, apparitions, strange manifestations. Every night I was watched from the darkness. Even in a town, even walking in a street, someone, or some *thing*, followed me. I was frightened at first, especially of the ghosts. They were like animal men, figures with animal faces, but the bodies of human beings. They were shadowy, grey presences, and they did me no harm. They just watched.

'One night, very early in the morning, I woke to find my room full of men. Real men this time, most of them masked. One of them, he was about sixty I suppose, was sitting on the bed. He said only that I could be very useful to them. I had a particular talent that was rare, and necessary to them. I was not to be afraid. Only good could come of my co-operation.

'I'm sure I went through the ritual objections: who are you, what do you want, how dare you enter my house like this. Get out. Leave me alone. All of that useless verbiage. They wanted me, and they were not going to settle for anything less than me.'

'Did they tell you what your talent was?' Brady asked. Kelly had walked over to her father and was standing, holding his hand as he sat on a chair in the corner. Both of them listened intently. What Uncle William had to say concerned them both, and concerned them greatly.

Uncle William smiled, glanced at Brady and his grey eyes briefly twinkled with amusement. 'As if it were not already obvious, apparently I'm quite primitive.' He tapped his skull. 'In here. My hind brain. Which I suppose,' he smiled again, 'is behind my be*fore* brain. I don't understand the anatomy of these things. This part of my brain is more ancient than most people's. It has bits and pieces left over from more primitive life forms.' He shrugged and winked at Kelly. 'I can't say that I'd ever

139

noticed any such thing. I mean, I didn't paint myself with woad, and do midnight dances to the Moon Goddess.'

Neither Kelly nor Simon Fleming smiled. Fleming looked appalled, listening to Uncle William's story and holding tighter to his daughter. 'What do they want Kelly for?' he breathed, and the anger in his voice came from his confusion. He was frightened by the images from William's story.

William said sharply, 'I didn't want her to come and stay. You will remember that, Simon. But you were too anxious to get rid of her for a while. But I didn't want her here. I knew there was danger . . .'

He looked back at Brady. His face was drawn, and deeply lined, but he looked strong. 'They put something in me. They implanted something in that primitive bit of mind. I became its carrier. I was only vaguely aware of it. It doesn't interact with me, and I don't interact with it . . .'

He's lying, Brady thought. *He's lying. He learned psychic defence from somewhere.*

'Then, towards the end of the year, the hauntings started again. I guessed that these people – you call them Arachne, though it's not a name I've heard – I supposed that they were coming back. I started to move about the country. Running. Hiding. They followed me, and now I think about it, I don't suppose they were ever very far away. One day I came home. I had decided to give up. In whatever way they were using me, the most troublesome effect upon me was my own anxiety. If they wanted to put something else in me, then why not let them? But I had a sense of danger. A strong sense of danger. When Simon rang up and asked me to take Kelly, I was indecisive, but I let her come. That was a bad mistake.

'The men came back and took us. They didn't want me running around any more. They threatened to kill Kelly if I didn't stay put and do what they said. They put us in that house. They also showed me two corpses . . .'

Brady nodded. 'I've seen them.'

Uncle William glanced at him sharply, and repeated, 'You've seen them.' He digested that piece of information swiftly, adding, 'Then you've seen what these people are capable of.'

'Too many times,' Brady said. 'They tried to do it to me.'

William looked haunted, harrowed, as he said, 'I couldn't contemplate them doing it to . . .' he broke off before saying Kelly's name, inclined his head very slightly towards the girl.

And *again* Brady had the strongest sense that the man was not telling the truth.

The look between them was almost a duel, eye to eye, mind to mind: Uncle William challenging Brady to believe what he was saying. And Brady listened implacably, digesting the story word by word. It was true, he felt, but not the whole truth.

Uncle William knew more than he was saying!

William went on, 'We were locked in the house. There were men there, guarding us, guarding the others. There were psychic forms as well, ghosts, sometimes just an overwhelming feeling of fear, of terror. We literally couldn't get out.

'Then Simon came. He interfered. Good for him. Suddenly the house was free. But now the *town* was our prison. We tried to get out, but it was clear that there was a defensive wall around Casterigg. I think that if we'd tried to run, they would have killed . . . Kelly . . . immediately.'

Simon Fleming rose to his feet, and tugged Kelly closer to him. 'I'll kill them first,' he said defiantly. 'This is my daughter. I'll do everything I can to stop them . . .'

Brady was sympathetic. He knew exactly how Fleming felt. He could also see that Kelly's father might be more of a threat to the girl's safety than anything.

'They want to keep you where they can see you,' he said to William, 'because they have further use for you.'

'So I imagine. A further addition to my little storehouse. That's what I am, isn't it? A storehouse. That's my talent. I'm a carrier. They refer to me as an "accumulator". I accumulate spirits, ghosts, psychic substance. I can't feel it. I'm perfectly normal in most ways. But I am now aware that the spirit which is to be "stored" within me . . . it's terrifying. It's a killer. It will control me totally . . .'

There was something quite genuine about his harrowed look, now. He frowned, his hands shook slightly. The thought of the 'arrival from the west' was quite genuinely frightening.

'What's more,' he said quietly, staring out into the darkness, 'They don't intend for their insurance to survive. Nor her father.' His voice had dropped to a whisper.

'How can you be sure?'

'I can't *feel* the spirit that I'm carrying, but I now sense things more strongly. I've developed a sort of premonition ability. I imagine it's the effect of carrying something supernatural. I'll be honest with you, Mister Brady. I had a strong idea that you were coming to Casterigg. I think you *can* help me. And little Kelly there. I think you're the man who can help us get out of Casterigg without endangering the girl's life.'

'And afterwards?' Brady said quietly. 'Who will protect them afterwards?'

Uncle William had taken the point and was well aware of the problem. 'It will have to be me, Mister Brady. Quite how I really don't know . . .'

'Except that you do,' Brady said sharply. 'You've already blocked off this floor of the hotel to psychic attack. I saw the elemental that has been trying to get to you. I also saw your organic barrier. What did you use? Mandrake? Henbane?'

'Many things,' William said. He regarded Brady curiously. 'A barrier, yes. But is it strong enough to stand against a full attack? When the girl arrives from the west, Arachne will stop playing with me, humouring me. They'll reach through that barrier and snatch me out with all the ease in the world.'

'If that's the case,' said Brady, 'How do you feel that I can help you?'

'You can get us out,' William said. 'The moment you walked through the door I felt your power. Your story about your family, the hint that you survived attack by this Arachne . . . everything about you is power, Mister Brady. You are a hunter. You are very strong. The immediate danger is Casterigg. Once we are beyond Casterigg, we will fend for ourselves. But they are all around us. They are out there, among the tourists, waiting in pubs, in shops, in houses, waiting in cars. Waiting. I am too old, the girl is too young, Simon is too confused. You, though, you can lead us out of here . . . before she comes.'

From the west. Danger. She. Danger.

'Please . . .' said Kelly. 'Please help us.'

A strange mixture of emotions played through Daniel Brady. He acknowledged selfishness, but found it difficult to resolve the moral dilemma in which he found himself.

To regard Kelly, a sad and worried little girl, so like Marianna, to think of her in danger, to think of her in need of him . . . how could he refuse her?

But Marianna herself might have been close by. He had come here to find those who were precious to *him*, not to help strangers.

And yet how could his arrival here be anything more than fortuitous? Casterigg was a focus, a gathering point. He had been drawn here, as Uncle William had been dragged here, and the mysterious girl from the west was arriving. The whole town was a magic place, central to all three participants in the bizarre ghost dance. In a way, Brady had no right to refuse to help William. He, Brady, was William's salvation.

Brady stared at the older man. For whatever reason, Uncle William was keeping something back. But Kelly Fleming was more important than anything. She was a child, and innocent of what was passing in Casterigg.

For her sake . . . as he would have wanted another to have done for Marianna . . . he had to abandon his own night hunt.

For the moment, he had to help two people escape Arachne.

Casterigg would not go away, and nor would the girl from the west. He could come back quickly. He could return to the focal point.

'What happened to your car?' Brady said to Fleming. Fleming shrugged.

'Completely dead.'

'We can try mine,' Brady said, 'But I suspect the same thing will have happened. I'm not parked far away. Wait here, watch out the back window. When you see me, come down the stairs as fast as you can. I'll go round to the front, and we'll try and barge our way through.'

'Be careful,' said Uncle William.

'Please come back,' said Kelly quietly.

'I'll be back,' replied Brady, and shuddered, as if he had a presentiment of the swiftness with which he would abandon that promise.

He left the hotel room, and passed quickly through the zone of psychic energy, which was now much reduced. He ran down the stairs and out through the reception area. There were a few tourists still busy in the main streets, and he was glad of the ordinary activity to cover his own cautious, rather melodramatic movements through Casterigg.

Something was going to happen! His heart was racing. He had a strong sense of impending change . . .

He stopped in a shop doorway and looked around. No one took any notice of him. Out on the Tor, lights glowed, and he frowned as he stared at them. A car or two droned past. There was laughter from a pub.

He walked on, briskly pacing out the distance from the hotel to the public car park where he had put his vehicle. At each corner he hesitated, looked back, looked ahead, then moved on.

Something was going to happen . . .

The car park was behind the main street, a wide area, dimly lit from lampposts at each corner. There were a few cars parked there, and one coach. Brady's own vehicle was somewhere in the middle. He made his way through the darkness, then stopped in shock.

Someone was standing by his car. A woman. She looked round as Brady approached, then cried out.

'Dan!'

For a second Brady was too stunned to react. She had cried his name, and begun to stagger towards him. She was crying. She was ragged. She was in a state of such terror that as her voice rose to a keening cry, a wail of fear, of cold, of relief, Brady could hardly recognize the sound of her, or the sight of her.

But she came towards him, running faster and faster, her arms stretched out towards him. Again she cried his name. And this time he responded.

'Alison! Christ Almighty, *Alison*!'

When they reached each other they collided so hard that Brady was almost winded. He swept her into his arms, and began to cry. All he could find to say to her was her name, over and over. He hugged her, kissed the side of her head, ran his fingers through her hair.

No illusion this: there was solid, substantial flesh in his arms.

'My God Dan, I've been so afraid . . .' she sobbed. Her hands clutched at his back. She kissed his neck. She shook like a leaf. She was filthy, her clothes ragged, her hair lank. She had been in a better state than this, earlier, when he had glimpsed her. She had seen him. She had escaped from them, had come crawling and running through the night, across fields, through fences . . . she had come back to Casterigg, back to her husband.

She was deathly white. In the darkness, her features lit only by a touch of moon, and the dim lights from the car park edge, she looked haunted, almost deathlike. Her eyes were dark. She looked bruised. She was chubbier than he remembered her. Her lips were thinner, and she looked tired, haggard to an extreme.

He could understand that well enough.

They held hands and stood back, just looking at each other. Alison began to cry. 'I thought . . . I thought

145

you were dead . . . they told me you were dead . . .'

'They nearly managed it,' Brady said, his own voice wavering as he fought to control his tears. 'God, Alison, it's good to find you again . . . oh God . . . it's been so long . . .'

Again they hugged. Again they wept. This time Alison managed to get out the names of her children. 'Marianna was here . . . she was here . . . I heard her.'

'I'll find her,' Brady said. 'First we've got to get you to safety.'

Appalling realization!

Where was safe? He couldn't leave her now. Not now. Not ever again. And he couldn't take her with him, helping the Flemings to escape Casterigg.

This was a deadly town. He had to get her out of here as soon as possible. But Marianna might still have been around . . .

His head began to spin. What to do? What to do?

Alison was trembling as he held her. 'Don't worry,' he whispered. 'Everything will be all right now. Now I have you, I shan't let you go.'

She pulled back from him, urgency darkening her features. 'The children, Dan. We've got to find the children.'

'Easy,' Brady said. 'Easy. Everything in its time. First we have to get you to somewhere warm, somewhere safe . . .'

'But Marianna was here. She may be here!' Her voice was beginning to rise hysterically. She sounded hoarse, as if she was ill. 'Dan! It doesn't matter about me. It's them. Dom. Marianna. We've got to do something!' She began to cry again. She fought against her husband as Brady urged her towards the car.

Suddenly she stiffened. Her tears vanished. Her grip on his arm became powerful, agonizing. Her fingers dug into his flesh.

She said, 'The farm. They'll have taken her to the farm.'

'What farm?'

'Christ! Dan! She'll be there. The farm!'

146

'*Which* farm?'

'Leave the car. Quickly!'

She dragged at his hand, and he began to run after her, across the car park, into the darker land beyond. A stream ran close by the park; it was a gentle rushing sound in the still night. Alison led him along its winding course, skirting the edge of the town. She slipped twice, but was driven onwards by her own frantic concern for Marianna.

The moon was dropping towards the high hills to the west. The castle ruins stood out in the eerie half-light. Maron Tor was in total darkness behind him.

'*Which* farm?' he breathed again, as he picked his way carefully between trees, and over a wire-topped fence.

'*That* farm,' Alison said, and pointed at a single lighted window, ahead of them. The light reflected from the still surface of a wide pond. 'The house was only one hide-out. They kept us in that farm for a few days. Separated, but I could hear her crying.'

They stopped at the edge of the field closest to the farm building itself. They were breathless after the run. Alison's hand in his was ice cold, and he squeezed her fingers to try to get some warmth into them.

'I tried to get away from here too,' she said quietly, her voice still strangely hoarse. 'There are too many of them around. I got as far as the High Street. I think there's a way to the back of the house, by the pond.'

She tugged at him again, and they crouched low and scampered across the field and into the cover of a dense stand of young silver birch. The ground here was muddy after the rain of the day before. The air smelled freshly of pond water, and the pool lapped gently at its edges, stirred by a slight night wind.

Brady wanted to say to her, 'Wait here. I'll go in alone.' But he dared not leave her. The thought of coming back to this sheltered place and finding her gone again sent sickening shock waves through him. He fought that terror down . . .

'We'll have to go together,' he whispered, and began to stand up. He was instantly alert, instantly on edge.

'Quiet!' he hissed to Alison, as she began to speak to him. 'What is it?'

He raised a finger to his lips. In the darkness around them there was movement. It was slow, stealthy, deliberate. It was the sound of someone approaching.

'Get ready to run like hell,' he said, then gasped. 'Jesus!'

There were two of them. They stepped out of the night, out of the darkness, hesitated, then closed in upon the couple by the pool. Their faces were the pallid faces of pigs, dead-eyed, slavering jaws, that same hissing breath that had haunted him since the attack at Christmas.

Brady grabbed for Alison's hand, and turned to run. Her hand was cold, pudgy. He hesitated, his heart racing. 'Come on!' he cried at her, then pulled back in horror.

He let the fat hand go, raised his own hand to stifle the scream of anguish, of disappointment that surfaced immediately.

'Alison!' he cried, and watched as the features of his pale, frightened wife thickened and changed, the flesh oozing across the bones of the skull, dripping from the brow to the cheeks, the mouth stretching into a wide, dead grin, the eyes becoming puffy, narrowed, pig-like.

'I've been so scared without you, Dan,' came Alison's voice from the mouth of this horror. It was hoarse, unreal. He should have realized that the moment she had spoken. 'Oh Dan, Danny, Dandandan. Oh come to my arms, oh Danny boy!'

The taunting in Alison's voice was followed by loud, harsh laughter. The shapechanger twisted, writhed, thickened and shortened. The features became blank; the ragged clothing split as the body became fat. Soon, Brady was staring at the corpse-like face of the hideous creature that had invaded his house, last December.

He had lurched towards one of the shapes and torn back the hood, screaming, 'Stop this! Bastards! Bastards!' A fat, white face had stared at him, the head bald, the eyes tiny and piggish. The lipless mouth had stretched into a quick smile, while the flared, almost flat nostrils snorted in breath, a sound that was not laughter, but was intended to be. The face was

148

the real face of a man, no mask, but its awful appearance shocked Brady, and though he reached out to scratch and beat at the pallid jowls, his blows were tempered.

Now, as the full realization of the way he had been tricked sunk into his stunned mind, Brady screamed his wife's name one last time and ran at the amorphous horror before him, striking violently about the creature's head and face.

It flung him aside with contemptuous ease, and he staggered at the edge of the pond, just managing to stay upright. The shapechanger reached for him, clutched his neck and dragged him round, flinging him heavily towards the other two men. One of them caught him, struck him in the stomach, then on the face. Brady fended off the third blow, drove backwards with his elbow, and heard the grunting of a winded man.

He fought back frantically. The grinning thing that had so recently taken on the form of Alison, came towards him menacingly. Moonlight glinted on a steel blade.

'What a nuisance you are, Brady,' this creature hissed. As it stabbed at him, Brady jerked backwards, flinging one of the others round so that the man's body came between him and the knife.

But a blow to the back of his head sent him reeling forward, staggering in the muddy edge of the pool. As he turned back to dry land, the shapechanger slashed the knife at him, and the cold blade cut into his wrist. He felt no pain, just the sudden warmth of spilled blood, and an immediate weakness in his left arm. He tripped, fell, and cold water closed over his head.

He struggled to find a grip on the slippery pool bottom. As he came up above the water again, powerful, killing hands grasped him by the head and neck, and began to shake him. Dimly, through water and darkness, he could see the rotting face of a pig.

He was pushed down again. Other hands grasped at his flailing limbs and restrained them. He kicked and twisted, but there was no way up for him, now.

As his body drowned, his spirit slipped upwards from

149

the dying flesh. It was a splendid sensation of release. He came up into the darkness, rising stiffly above the threshing corpse below. The shapechanger saw him, and its grotesque features became more blank than ever, the sign of its shock.

And then, around this nightmare scene, something even stranger began to occur. The darkness of night became interspersed with shifting, darting brightness. The trees stood out in eerie silhouettes all around the pond, as glowing forms approached the scene of the murder.

Brady's soul was sucked back into the body, and he felt himself rise above the cold pond, gasping for breath, spitting the foul water from his mouth. The killing grips upon him were gone, and he splashed and struggled to find a footing.

Someone was crying out. The shapechanger babbled and spluttered and seemed unable to move.

Through the trees came four gigantic wolf-like shapes, running on their hindlegs, their upper torsos bulging with dark fur, their forelimbs glinting at the tip where immense claws were opened, ready for the kill. The faces were broad, the snouts long. They growled deeply, and leapt upon the three screaming men so fast that Brady hardly had time to grasp the movement.

There was the sound of slashing and rending. Blood splashed across Brady's frozen face. He saw the shape-changer twist and dissolve, struggling to adopt a more fleet-footed animal form, but one of the ghostly wolves bit at his throat, and tore that throat away, a ragged, bloody mess.

The corpses were flung into the pond. The wolves lifted muzzles to the dark night skies and howled, towering above the crouched form of Daniel Brady, surrounding him. He could smell them, rank and animal; one of them peered down at him, then leaned close, breathing its foetid breath upon his face, licking its lips.

The glowing forms turned and dispersed into the woodland, darting shapes among the trees, finally lost to sight.

150

Brady staggered to his feet and began to make his way back towards the town. He was shivering, damp and frozen in the cool night. Disappointment was a gnawing pain in his stomach. And yet there were no tears. As swiftly as he had found Alison, he had lost her. He should have been stricken with grief, distressed to the point of incapacity.

He felt disappointment. Too many shocks in too short a time had numbed him to greater feeling.

What had they been, those wolves?

He found a rough trackway and followed it by moonlight, scrambling over a closed gate. He used the moonlit castle for his 'compass', because the farmland here was tree-bordered and confusing and he could easily have got lost.

A nice trick. A good trick. Arachne have some clever weapons in their arsenal. A shapechanger!

There was someone walking ahead of him. He was sure of it. The man was walking in the same direction as he, hastening his step slightly, as if not wanting to be seen. Brady rubbed warmth into his arms, tried to forget the pain in his neck muscles, the soreness of his face where he had been punched, the throbbing ache in his wrist where the knife had struck him . . .

He needed his wits about him.

The wolves! What were the wolves?

At the outskirts of town he lost the 'sensation' of the man moving ahead of him. He walked cautiously between the outlying houses, jumping a stile to get to the narrow street.

Uncle William was standing in the darkness of an alleyway. Brady heard him breathing. He stopped and turned. Uncle William stepped forward, looking slightly apprehensive.

'We got worried about you,' the old man said.

'I had a little difficulty,' Brady responded quietly. He said nothing more for a moment, just stared at the other man. In the cold night, they were a strange pair of duellists.

You! It was you!

'Are you hurt?' asked William.

'Cut and bruised. They still underestimate me.'

'You must develop your powers,' said Uncle William. Moonlight shone on his grey eyes. He watched Brady with an intensity that was almost petrifying.

'I'm trying,' Brady said. 'They tricked me. I thought I found my wife. I wasn't expecting such a trick.'

'The tuilak. I should have warned you about it.'

'The what?'

'The shapechanger. A most unpleasant creature. Artificial, of course.'

'And now very dead . . .' Brady stepped towards Uncle William. The old man's breath was strong with the scent of stale tobacco. He stood his ground as Brady came very close. 'A wolf killed it. Four wolves . . . four *un*-wolves. Ghosts. Tangible. Gigantic. Where the hell did *they* come from, Uncle William?'

The old man didn't reply. He suddenly frowned, glanced beyond Brady, upwards, westwards . . .

'Perhaps we can finish the discussion later,' he said. 'I think events are beginning to approach a climax.'

Reflected in Uncle William's eyes, something bright burned. Thunder rolled across the town, and Brady glanced round, to see what had attracted the old man's attention.

A storm was approaching, over the high ground close to the ruined castle. Clouds swirled around a focus of intense brightness, that moved rapidly through the night.

At its centre was the dark shape of a girl.

The long walk was over.

13

She crouched on the hill behind Casterigg, in the lee of an outcrop of wind-scoured limestone. In the darkness below, a few lights showed her the location of the town. A line of dull yellow beacons showed the main street. The wind tugged at her and she shivered. Against a patch of bright cloud, the great Tor was a dark god, silently watching her from the earth.

He's down there.

She shivered with something that was not the night's chill. She said the name to herself again.

Brady. Brady.

Hunhau, Lord of Death, mocked her from within her grey stuff. *I shall consume him. I shall suck him dry.* Chief of Demons danced through her nerve cells, the ancient war dance of his Mayan tribesfolk. *I shall suck out his soul, pick out his grey stuff, lap him up, lap him up . . .*

Mary Jane Silverlock shuddered at the image of the bloated corpse that filled her mind's eye; Hunhau was truly awful to regard, a disgusting sight, calculated to inspire pure terror in the hearts of his victims. Young Grandfather watched him too, and whispered reassuringly to Mary Jane.

Bone and crystal pricked at her body. She was sore where the spirit-keys were pressed into the flesh of her body.

Brady. Brady.

He was waiting for her, down there in the darkness. Why was she so afraid?

She remembered the words of Always Talking. *He is a hunter. He moves through the night.*

Wind stirred the grass on the steep hill. A rabbit darted

153

from its warren. Her heart stopped with shock and she looked anxiously into the gloom. Was it him? Was he coming towards her even now? What manner of terrible enemy was he?

He is strong. The girl must strike first.

'I shall nibble on his rotting innards,' sang Hunhau, Chief of Demons.

'I shall strike through his eyes with lightning,' thundered Enumclaw, storm god.

'I shall make water bubble in his lungs, so that he spouts like the whale creatures of legend,' cried Tieholt, water god.

'I will walk him into cliffs and crush the rock about his skull,' echoed Nayenez, slayer of alien gods, demon eyes gleaming as he watched the silent dales through the eyes of the girl.

'I will watch over you,' whispered Young Grandfather. 'I shall strike this Brady first. I shall hold his wrists. I shall trip him. You should not fear Brady. Against you and I, little daughter, he has no chance.'

'We must kill him quickly,' she said silently. 'We must do the deed at once.'

She was thinking of Frankie Laine Silverlock, waiting at home for her, so helpless for all his strength. She was thinking of Ridgeville, missing it very greatly. She thought of Snake Man, and the shack on Blue Snake Summit. She thought of the secret that he kept for her, now; her secret, and Young Grandfather's. The others had not seen, had not noticed.

She had to go back. She *had* to survive the Walk On Water, and go back to her home.

'Let's go,' she said, and rose from her crouching position.

The demons in her grey stuff whooped and howled their pleasure, and struck forward from her, stretching themselves to the very limits of their attachment to her, by the chips of bone and crystal.

She walked down the hills towards the dead-of-night lights of the town. Around her the air glowed and boomed as thunder and water and earth exploded and chased, went seeking mischief.

The thunder woke an old man who lived with his wife at the edge of Casterigg. His name was Graham Charnock, but everyone called him Grey. He sat up in bed and listened to the wind. He glimpsed that eerie light up on the hills through the chink in the curtaining.

Pat stirred, half asleep, half awake. 'What is it, Grey?'

'Storm coming. Thunder.'

'Go to sleep. It'll pass over.'

He got out of bed and went to the window, opening the curtains and staring out into the pitch black night. He frowned. This was no storm with which he was familiar. It was like a whirlwind of light. He could see the outcrops of rock on the hill, west of Castle Ridge. He could see the lightning-shattered mountain ash that topped the steep hill, its branches spreading horizontally, wind-twisted and skeletal. The light was moving towards him. The wind seemed to whirl about its centre. Lightning struck outwards, like sparks from a spinning firework.

Thunder rolled across the silent town. Something like a gigantic fish seemed to form itself, cloud-like and tenuous, at the edge of the brightness.

Charnock rubbed his eyes, frowning even more. Was he dreaming? Was this some waking nightmare? He peered harder at the storm.

'Come back to bed,' said his wife, Pat. The room was almost lit up by the brightness that approached.

The house shook with the next thunderclap, and even Pat stirred, sat up and peered sleepily across the room.

'Never seen anything like this,' Charnock whispered. He was suddenly afraid, terribly afraid. 'Someone out there,' he said. 'Someone walking out there.'

His face was glowing with the light from outside. His unshaven cheeks were dark, his skin pale. His eyes were bright points of light as he watched the strange storm.

'Mother of God!' he screamed suddenly, and staggered

back from the window. Pat looked up and screamed too.

The face of a gigantic spider was staring in at them, its chelicerae moving slowly, dripping juices. The bright, black eyes swivelled to stare at each of them . . .

It came through the window, into the room. It was immense. It had the partial body of a man, its flesh rotting and blue, the belly distended and split; the limbs were thin and covered with fine bristles, spider-like, clacking gently as it scuttled about the floor. The eyes watched. The jaws moved. The head moved jerkily, surveying the two old people.

Suddenly it rushed across the room. Pat screamed once, shrill and short. It had snatched her up from the bed like a rag doll, and held her in two of its quivering limbs as it chewed quickly into her face. She hung there, totally limp, as the jaws worked on her, and for a few minutes there was stillness and silence as the juices were sucked from her body. The spider's limbs seemed to swell slightly. The woman's corpse whitened and shrivelled. Graham Charnock stood frozen, petrified, against the far wall.

When the creature dropped the drained body of his wife and turned to stare at him with its eight, gleaming black eyes, he hadn't even the strength to scream.

The spider was on him in seconds, holding him up to its face, swaying slightly as it considered where to bite . . .

Others, sleeping quietly in Casterigg, were awoken by the sound of thunder.

Kath Mitchell, the local schoolteacher, always slept very heavily. She roused with a start, puzzled by the distant sound of a storm, and by a high-pitched keening sound.

She turned over in her narrow bed and her heart leapt.

Standing in the corner of her small bedroom was a tall, swaying form, a man . . . an Indian.

'Ayeee, ayay, eeeyaya . . .' sang the spirit in its strange, reedy voice.

'Ay, ay, ay,' gasped Kath, feeling the blood drain from

156

her face and limbs. She started to shake violently. 'Oh my God . . .' she said aloud.

She started to get out of bed, ever so slowly, ever so easily. The spirit began to dance, stepping slightly forward then back, then turning round, swaying from the waist.

'Ayeee, arayaaaa, ayeearara . . .' sang Nayenez as he danced towards the girl.

She stood trembling by the bed, arms hanging limply by her sides, clutching slightly at the bottom of the baggy shirt she wore at night.

Nayenez looked up at her, and her legs turned to jelly.

His bright eyes burned deeply into her. But this was no romantic look; it was evil, debilitating, lustful.

She stared back. He towered above her. His body smelled of sweat and grease. The feathers in his hair shifted as his long hair shook. His mouth stretched wide into a handsome smile, and bright white teeth glistened from his mouth. His eyes were evil . . . but they were beautiful.

Kath shook and felt cold. But she couldn't take her eyes from the tall, muscular man before her.

He sang to her. He chanted his love chant. Her skin was pale, but light illuminated her features. She was a pretty girl, dark haired, pale-eyed. The shirt dropped from her body. Naked, she reached for the tall Indian, and though she was petrified, shaking with fear, she felt his strong embrace.

'Ayeee, ayeee,' chanted the tall Indian, as he laid the girl gently on the bed.

She sang too. She sang in her tremulous, high-pitched voice as she welcomed her ghostly lover. She sang as they moved together, locked in the deathly embrace of haunted love. She sang until the spirit passed from her body, like a fleeting, vanishing wind . . .

The storm swept through Casterigg, terrifying, tormenting, destroying. The spirits walked abroad with abandon. Mary Jane stood at the edge of the town and watched as the

157

shimmering ghosts darted and cried and whooped their joy, fleeing from house to house, running and stalking through the rooms, rattling doors and windows, waking the occupants, manifesting themselves in terrifying ways.

Hunhau, Lord of Death, was the most terrifying of all. He stalked the streets, darting into houses here and there, to feed upon the defenceless soul-stuff within. He was a bloated corpse. He dangled from ceilings, rose from between sleeping husbands and wives, peered suddenly out of cupboards, skull grinning, sockets empty, entrails dangling disgustingly from the rends in his decaying belly.

Sometimes he was an insect, sometimes a spider, sometimes he appeared as a jackal, and barked loudly as he pounced.

The storm settled on the town. Mary Jane watched.

Somewhere . . . somewhere two men ran for their lives . . .

Around the town, dark figures arose from the earth. They rose from fields, from streams, from the dark places below fallen trees. They stepped out of the crevices in rock, lifted their heads from the ditches where they had lain. They stood. They smelled the air. They listened to the sound of thunder. They saw the distant storm.

They began to walk towards Casterigg, entering the outskirts through the main roadways, and the alleys, moving silently and cautiously towards the centre of the town.

Abruptly, then, the storm died, and Casterigg became quiet again. Those who had been woken by the chaos crawled gratefully back to bed. Lights went out. Security was found in darkness, blankets and warmth.

'Quickly! There's no time to lose!' William Farmer's voice was loud and sharp in the night.

Brady obeyed him without thinking, and the two men raced headlong through the streets, back to the Castle Hotel.

They hesitated on the steps at the front. William looked quickly along the road.

A figure walked slowly towards them, passing at the edge of the circle of light thrown onto the pavement by a lamp.

'Who is it?' Brady asked.

William said quietly, 'One of the dead.'

Brady stared at the figure again. 'What dead?'

'Never mind. There are many others. They're part of the cage that has trapped me in Casterigg.' He pushed through the hotel doors, and waved at the night porter, who recognized him and smiled thinly.

As William raced up the stairs, he said, 'They've broken the cage bars. There may be a chance to get out, now . . .'

Brady shook his head, watching the sprightly old man curiously. William ran like an athlete, all sign of age gone from his movements.

He was a focus of power, both physical and spiritual. And he had not told Brady the whole truth about himself.

In the hotel room they found Kelly Fleming sitting pale as death, and very solemn, on the bed. Her father, Simon, paced the floor restlessly.

'You took your time,' he said irritably, then noticed the blood on Brady's wrist. 'What happened?'

'I got tricked,' Brady said. 'I wasn't careful enough.'

Fleming ignored that. He asked anxiously, 'The car?'

'I still don't know. Get some water, will you?'

Uncle William had sat next to Kelly, and was slowly rolling a cigarette as he watched Brady. Brady took off his jacket, rolled up his sleeve, and cleaned the gash in his flesh with the water that Simon Fleming brought. He tied the wound with a strip of sheeting. The wrist was sore, but remained reasonably flexible.

The temperature in the room suddenly dropped sharply. Simon Fleming gasped, more with shock than discomfort. Kelly shivered where she sat on the bed, and glanced anxiously at Uncle William. Brady noticed that the old man's eyes were half closed, and that he was concentrating

159

hard. A moment later he seemed to become aware of Brady's fixed stare, and looked away.

Fleming said, 'What's causing the cold?'

'Attack,' said Brady. 'Or defence.' He shrugged his jacket back on. His breath frosted. He walked over to Uncle William and said, 'You're doing this. Aren't you.'

'We've got to get out of here,' William said. 'I'm measuring their strength.'

'What the hell are we going to do?' Fleming asked angrily. He shuddered and shook with the cold, arms wrapped around his body. 'I'm not sitting around here waiting for a bunch of thugs to come for my daughter. If I can't get her out, then you must. Brady! You *must*.'

He walked over to Brady, and his face was angry, his lips drawn back with cold and bitterness. But his eyes implored Brady to help. 'They said I wasn't strong enough to do it. These two. I heard them talking. He's done something to Kelly. But she's still my daughter. You've got to get her out of here, back to Lindsey . . .'

'I'm going to try,' Brady said. 'I'll go for the car again.'

He fumbled in his saturated clothes for his keys. They were still in his trousers pocket. But as he made for the door, Fleming reached out and tugged him viciously back.

'No you don't!'

He grabbed for the keys, then pushed Brady towards his daughter. Stabbing a finger at the girl, his face twisted with desperation, he said, 'You get *her* out! You stay with her. I can't take the chance of these . . . *people* getting you, killing you. They're not after me. I'll go . . .'

Brady said, 'It's far too dangerous. You don't know what you're up against.'

'*I'm* not up against *anything*!' Fleming shouted. There were tears in his eyes, which he brushed aside. His breath misted heavily in the freezing air. 'Look after *her*, damn you! Get her out no matter what happens. I'll get the car . . . if I can. I've got more chance than you . . .'

He looked at Kelly, and he was crying. Kelly stared back at him blankly, neither sympathetic, nor embarrassed.

160

'I'm going to get you home, Kelly,' Fleming said softly. 'I swear to God I will . . .'

Brady told him where the car was. He was unhappy with the thought of Fleming going out into that haunted night alone, but perhaps he had a point. Perhaps Arachne would not recognize him, would let him pass.

Fleming left the room. Uncle William said, 'The cage is open, but not that open. He hasn't got a chance.'

Brady turned sharply, hesitated briefly, then reached down and jerked Uncle William to his feet by the collars of his coat. He shook the old man violently, just once, then dragged him close. Old man and young, they stared into each others' eyes like young lovers; but there was nothing like love passing between them. It was a searching, knowing look, each man aware of the power of the other, nervous of that opposed power, but determined to prove himself the stronger.

Brady felt electricity tingle in the air around him, making the hairs on his arms and neck stand up on end. Psychic discharge, the summoning of terrible destructive energy from Uncle William.

But the old man held back. His face flushed with anger, with effort, as Brady's hold on him cut off his breathing slightly, and made him stretch uncomfortably to Brady's height.

'So who the hell *are* you, *Uncle* William? And why don't you let loose the dogs that you keep up there?' He nodded at William's head.

William just smiled. Then frowned. He was aware of something. Brady loosened his grip slightly, and Uncle William straightened up.

A moment later Kelly screamed. The room seemed to explode. The shockwave was deafening, and Brady twisted round, and was knocked flying by an impact of some sort. The air was sucked from his lungs. The light shattered, but the darkness was illuminated by a glowing shape by the door, that reached out boney arms, and opened its mouth and wailed hideously.

Brady glimpsed the apparition only briefly. The room

was suddenly filled with a greenish haze that swirled about the corpse-like spectre, flowing from the ceiling to the floor, and billowing about Brady, like smoke.

In that haze, slender, screeching beast-shapes swirled and flew, prodding at the spectre, rushing at it and overwhelming it.

Above the wailing of the ghost came another sound, an ululating, primitive chanting, whose words sent thrills of terror through Brady, even though he could not recognize the alien sounds . . .

He recognized where they came from, however.

Uncle William was standing, facing the spectral form that hovered by the doorway. His arms were stretched towards it, his mouth was open, his eyes were just white orbs. The smoke billowed from his mouth. His skin oozed slime. His hair was standing directly on end, as if he were being subjected to an immense electrical charge.

Around his head, tiny elementals clustered, smoky grey forms in the green haze, that clung to him, and seemed to be absorbed into him, only to worm their way out of his pores and sockets again.

There were three powerful thumps. Plaster fell from the ceiling. The room smelled of scorched flesh. Whirling shapes, like fireworks, charged at the vanishing spectre and exploded with shrill, briefly lived buzzing-sounds. More thumping. Brady's body reacted to immense shock-waves, his stomach feeling winded, the breath dragged from his lungs again.

And he glimpsed something like a horned wolf leap across the room, on its hind legs, its back raised in spiky fur, its limbs reaching out towards the ghost. It was the briefest of visions.

Suddenly the room was in total darkness, and total stillness. Uncle William struck a match and walked into the adjoining bathroom, where he unscrewed the light bulb and replaced the shattered bulb in the lounge.

He smoothed down his startlingly spiky hair. The bulb was only forty watts, and it was dim. It made the hotel room seem claustrophobic.

Brady hesitated before speaking. Uncle William watched him, half amused. Kelly was curled up on the bed, like a foetus.

'What attacked us?' Brady said.

'Hunhau,' said Uncle William. 'It has come for me. Arachne will place it in me, with the others. I will accumulate it. Or so they would like.'

'What's Hunhau?' Brady asked.

'A demon. A Mayan spirit, very old, very powerful. The gatherer of the dead and the sick and dying. A magical spirit, with many talents. It has been carried a long way to be added to me, to be stored in me, ready for use.'

The bulb swung slightly in a breeze. The dim light made the features of Uncle William's face shift as the shadows moved. The two men stared at each other, uncompromisingly.

Brady said, 'There is more than one spirit already in you.'

William nodded, his gaze unwavering. 'It's true. I have three. Their names and natures don't matter. One is from the far gone age of stone, from before life in this land. From the earliest of times. Its magic is very strong, very primitive. One is from the time of bronze. You saw the wolf. That is its main manifestation. The third is from the far north, the ice wastes, from a time perhaps two thousand years before the present. Their names don't matter. Nor their natures. Each was a shaman, a demon-god, a magic thing, with magic powers. The magic is different for them all. I have accumulated them. I have stored them.' He stepped towards Brady. His breath was sour, cold, crisp. The men were only inches apart. Their breath frosted and the clouds mixed in the pale light.

Kelly moaned softly as she lay on the bed. William ignored her.

'I was trapped,' he said. 'They found out my talent and trapped me, used me. I was to carry the resurrected spirits until the Roundelay. A part of my brain is very primitive. Back here,' he tapped the back of his skull. 'Cerebellum. The place from which the gods came in days of old; the

163

place to which they return. There are many of us. Accumulators. We are part of the final plan.'

Brady started to speak, but William raised a hand and pressed one icy cold finger against Brady's lips.

He went on, 'Arachne overlooked something. The fact that magic does not just accumulate. It grows. With one god within my skull I was powerless. With two I felt the stirrings of control. When they placed the third into me I had learned more than enough. The magic within me is greater than the sum of my parts, Brady. Not great enough. Not yet. But enough to defend myself against them, to keep them at bay. But that Hunhau.' He shook his head. 'I will not be able to resist it again. That was a weak attack. In time my defences will break down. It will come again, and it will join me. And Hunhau is Lord of Demons, Lord of Death. I will have no hope at all of controlling my own destiny. They trapped me here while the girl carried Hunhau from America. They couldn't get in, but I couldn't get out. They could have killed Kelly so easily. She was their insurance that I would stay put. Simon was not strong enough to get us out. You may be. Your spirit is strong. Your own powers are remarkable. You can lead us through the cage.'

'My daughter may still be here,' said Brady stiffly. 'You must remember that! My daughter Marianna reached to me from this place. You yourselves saw her. How can I leave Casterigg knowing that I'm leaving my daughter? If my mind is not totally attuned to the task at hand, then I'm no more strong than Simon.'

'Your daughter is not here any more,' said William softly.

Brady felt his heart start to race. 'How can you know that?'

'I *do* know,' said Uncle William. His pale eyes were emotionless, like steel.

'She called to me,' Brady said, helplessly. 'I can't have come all this way for nothing.'

'*I* called to you,' said William, and waited for the implication to sink into the other man's mind.

164

He called? *He* called me? What in God's name . . . ?

'I don't understand,' Brady said weakly.

'She was here. I discovered her story, I discovered all about you. I knew you were the one to get Kelly and myself out of this place. I enhanced your daughter's own powers, using her grief, her desperation, her loneliness. I caused her to project to you, to reach to you. I needed you, Mister Brady, and that was the only way I could get you to come to Casterigg. In time I would have sent Simon looking for you. You arrived fast. And thank the fates. For *she* arrived fast too. A few days searching further south for you, and I would have been consumed by the Chief of Demons, and would have become a powerful, but mindless, magic machine to Arachne . . .'

Brady felt faint. His head spun. He could not believe what he was hearing, and yet he had to. He was confused. It was not as if Marianna had *not* been here. She had, and Uncle William had used her to his own ends. But again, Marianna was gone. Alison and Dominick had probably not been here at all.

Out of his fingers . . . slipping . . . slipped. He always came so close. He always ended up so far!

He felt tears rise to his eyes. He was trembling. 'I've *got* to find her,' he said quietly. 'You used her to get to me. Now I'll use you to get to her!'

His fury made him reach out and grab Uncle William. The old man detached Brady's fingers from his lapels with astonishing ease, his own fingers feeling like steel.

'Of course,' he said. 'I know where she is. She is not in Casterigg. But I know where she is. I know where they all are. Alison, Dominick. And your daughter. I know . . .'

'Then tell me where!' screamed Brady.

Could it really be true! It *had* to be true.

'They are close by. About twenty miles away.'

'*Where*?'

But Uncle William just smiled and shook his head. 'You have a chance to get out of here, Mister Brady. I don't intend to let you go alone. Once we're beyond the cage. Once we're out of the clutches of . . . of Hunhau especially. *Then*, Mister Brady, we'll go together.' He grinned. 'I have a few scores to settle myself.'

Brady turned from the old man and went to the window. A stiff, dark shape stood on the street below, staring up at the hotel.

'We'll give Simon five minutes,' Brady said. 'Then we'll run. Then we'll see whether I'm as powerful as you think.'

'On your own, no,' said Uncle William. 'The two of us together . . . then we have a chance.'

'Five minutes,' said Brady. 'I hope to God the car starts.'

Simon Fleming crouched behind the wall around the car park, then cautiously peered over. It was very dark. He could make out the gleam of distant lamplight on a chrome bumper, and gradually distinguished the shape of Brady's car.

The was no one nearby. A moving shadow that caused him to jump turned out to be just a small tree, blowing in the night breeze.

Further across the town, strange light flickered in the sky, and thunder rolled. Fleming glanced that way and watched the electric storm, as it rippled above the town centre. He had seen several people on his way here. They had been standing in doorways, or against the walls of houses, and as he had run past they had made no response.

What they were doing out at this time of the morning he couldn't imagine. His own ignorance had thus probably saved him so far.

He jumped the wall and fumbled in his coat pocket for the car keys. He raced across the empty compound, feet slapping noisily against the tarmac surface. At the car he flung himself to a crouch, on the far side, then slowly rose and peered all around him, through the windows, round the back, searching the darkness for movement.

No movement.

His heart thundered in his chest. His breathing was hoarse and painful. He allowed himself a few seconds to

166

calm down, then cautiously opened the door on the passenger side. He peered into the car, opened the back door and checked to make sure that no one was hiding on the floor. Then he opened the trunk and inspected the equipment and boxes that Brady kept there.

Nothing lurked amongst that equipment. Fleming closed the trunk and climbed into the car.

First he tried the lights. They were dead. With sinking heart he put the key into the ignition and turned it.

There was a dull click. No engine response at all. He tried again, several times.

Dead. Completely dead.

Tugging the key from the ignition he sat in the darkness and the silence, staring through the windscreen, wondering what the hell to do next.

And the car started!

His eyes popped wide as the engine roared into life, the chassis shaking with the vibration. He put his foot onto the accelerator and revved up. He put the car into gear, reached for the handbrake.

And found only a cold, clammy hand . . .

With a scream of shock he jumped from the car.

The engine died. The car was silent. He walked back to the vehicle and leaned inside, peering between the seats at the horrible object that was stuck there, impaled on the handbrake.

Severed at the wrist, its fingers curled, it seemed to twitch and feel in the darkness.

'Oh my God . . .' he breathed.

Behind him, there was movement. He spun round, his heart missing several beats with the shock of it. 'Who are you?'

Shapes moved towards him through the darkness. There were several of them, and they ringed him, pinning him to the car. They stood off from him by several yards, and in the night's gloom he could make out nothing save for the fact that they were human shapes.

And that one of them was a girl.

She was smaller than the men who stood around her.

She wore a pale shirt, down to her hips, and jeans. She was slim. Her eyes gleamed with stray light. Fleming found himself fixated by the hints he could get of her.

The others were tall, broad men. Their breathing was curiously hoarse, as if they sucked breath through masks.

He heard a voice say, 'That's not Brady.'

Another voice, also male, and deeper, said, 'Are you sure?'

'Quite sure. This is the old man's nephew.'

'Good enough. This one needed to be killed.'

'But Brady. We need to get Brady before –'

'Everything in its time. There are several hours before dawn. The girl has only just arrived.'

Several of the shapes faded from view, walking away from the trembling figure of Simon Fleming.

The younger voice said, 'So we kill this one?'

'Incapacitate it, at least.'

'Mightn't it be useful?'

There was a thoughtful silence. Then the older voice said, 'No. We have to be out of this place before sunrise. There isn't time to elaborate already complicated plans. Destroy it.'

Two shapes remained in the darkness. One man, and the girl. The man shape walked forward. Fleming prepared to fight it, but as he glimpsed the face he felt his knees go weak, and he collapsed to the ground. The man laughed. The decomposing features of a goat peered down at him. Stinking saliva dripped into his mouth from the creature's mask. Fleming gagged, but felt helpless. He could see the girl still watching. Abruptly, she turned away and vanished into the night.

The goat-faced man raised what looked like a sliver of bone and pressed it against Fleming's throat. Then he laughed quietly, reached down and tugged Fleming's shirt from his trousers. Cold air struck his skin; cold fingers pinched his flesh. The sliver of bone was a sharp pain as it was stabbed into his stomach muscles.

The goat-faced man laughed. 'Hope you like westerns . . .' he said, and slipped away into the darkness.

168

A Red Indian stood above him, peering down. The Indian started to dance. Fleming struggled to his feet and watched. The bone sliver in his flesh was sore.

The Indian was huge. His arms bulged with muscles. Feathers were stuck in his hair. His body was naked but for a loin cloth. His legs rippled with power as he danced.

'I am Nayenez,' the Indian said. 'You are my special hawk. Dance, my little hawk. Dance . . .'

'I don't want to dance . . .' Fleming said feebly, and the Indian laughed. He moved around the smaller man, dancing without music, dancing in that curious slow-stepping, twisting way that Fleming had seen in early Hollywood films.

'Dance!' said Nayenez, and Fleming's legs were powered against his will. He felt his feet move on the tarmacked car park. He stepped forward, then back, then slowly turned round.

'Good,' said Nayenez. 'Good, my little hawk. Dance. Dance with me to the high places. You are my special hawk. You will fly like a bird. You will fly swift as a stone. Dance . . .'

The Indian twirled and ducked and shifted from foot to foot, and it was as if a drum rhythm sounded to which his movements responded. But the night was silent, save for the chanting of the ghost, and the soft slap of his moccasins on the hard ground.

'Dance,' chanted Nayenez, and Fleming followed him, and together they moved through the town, to the west and north, towards the Tor.

'You will fly like my own special bird,' sang Nayenez, and Fleming sang, 'I shall fly. Ayeee, akaaa, I shall fly, I shall fly . . .'

'Swift as stone,' sang the Indian, as he danced towards the high ground, twirling and stepping out the beat.

'Hard, swift stone,' sang Fleming, entranced and obsessed, now, with the ghost dance that was leading him to his doom.

Through the long night they danced. Across the wet fields they danced. Across ditches and streams, through

169

copses and across outcrops of hard rock. They touched the earth, they kissed the trees, they danced towards the moon, towards the high skull of the Tor.

'Aeyeeeia. Akaaayaaaei . . .' sang Simon Fleming, and Nayenez chanted, 'Dance, dance, my brave young hawk. Swift as stone, wings spread wide, what a flight you will make before the sun rises. Dance, my hawk, dance for your Nayenez . . .'

And Fleming twirled, and stomped the ground, and followed the Indian up the steep slopes of the Tor. It would be the dance of his life, the longest dance, the greatest dance.

The sky was brightening as they reached the summit of Maron Tor, and the two were a single silhouette against the horizon, for only the spinning, chanting form of Fleming could be seen by mortal eye.

At last he stood atop the mountain and embraced the dawn.

'Fly like a bird!' sang Nayenez.

'A bird . . . a bird,' echoed Simon Fleming.

'Fly as swift as stone!' sang Nayenez.

'Stone . . .' echoed Simon Fleming. 'Stone.'

He flew from the summit of Maron Tor. Swift as a hawk. Swift as stone.

He flew like a stone bird.

He did not utter a cry.

14

'He's not coming back,' said Uncle William suddenly.

'We said we'd give him five minutes,' Brady responded, frowning. He turned from the window. Kelly was sitting up on the bed. She had just whispered something to her uncle. Brady had heard the faint murmur of her voice. William was standing, now, and buttoning up his long, black overcoat.

'We'll go now,' William said. 'Dress warmly. Hurry.'

Brady was confused. 'We can't just desert him. He's the girl's father . . .'

'He's not coming back,' William repeated, a touch testily. 'Please don't argue with me, Mister Brady. We have a chance. What do the space people call it? A window. We have a small window for escape. I should have realized . . .'

As he spoke he helped Kelly on with a thick jumper, over which she buttoned on a transparent rainproof.

'Realized what?'

'That they might think Simon was you. They're distracted. Now in the name of more gods than you've ever conceived of . . . come on!'

Brady followed. He could do nothing else. He felt so helpless, his heart aching, his stomach churning. William Farmer claimed to know where his family had been taken! It had to be true. It had to be more than a simple, cruel ruse to gain Brady's support.

Brady was frozen. His clothes were damp, and even though he had put one of Uncle William's vests on underneath his cotton shirt, he felt chilled to the marrow.

A few minutes running would warm him up. His wrist ached and throbbed. But it was his heart that caused him the greatest concern.

He felt weakened by need. He was a man who needed to be in control at all times, and now Uncle William was leading the party. And Brady was jumping to the old man's command . . .

For the sake of his family!

There were so many questions still to ask. *What* did William know about Arachne? What was Roundelay? What was the mammath, where was Magondathog, how would accumulators be used?

What special talent did Marianna have that was going to be so useful to them? How long . . . he choked at the thought . . . how long would his family survive? What was the usual fate of the victims of Arachne's bands of abduction agents?

But he could not ask these questions now. William was leading the way out into the hotel corridor, through the weak psychic barriers, towards the more potent cage that existed around the hotel itself.

In the dark hotel foyer they stopped. There was a dim light on in the porter's lodge, a tiny room behind the reception desk. While Uncle William and Kelly hesitated in the total darkness of a corner of the foyer, Brady ran at a crouch behind the desk, peered in through the window and nearly gagged at the sight of the old man's remains.

Brady hurried back to the others, and they stood by the glass doors, watching the dark, deserted street outside. 'How the hell are we going to get out?' Brady said. 'If there are so many of them, with spirits that can do *that*!' He jerked a thumb back towards the tiny, lighted room.

'As I said before,' murmured Uncle William. 'Me alone, no. You alone, certainly not. But together! There will be a certain division of labour on their part, with two foci for their psychic energies. That's their weakness, and our hope. Trust me, Mister Brady.'

'Reassure me,' said Brady.

Uncle William smiled thinly, glancing at the younger man. Around him, a moment later, that same green haze began to form. Brady sensed movement behind him, and turned, startled to see four tall, swaying shapes in the gloom. He could make out no features, save the essential power of the beasts, and a certain gleaming about the eye region. Their breathing was hoarse, but faint.

Uncle William murmured alien words. Sweat formed on his face, ran down his neck and cheeks. Brady listened to the ancient language, but could make no sense of it. And yet it was clearly a demonstration of magic abilities, learned from the guests who lodged within his head . . .

There was the feel of an icy wind. The four demonic shapes had leapt past Brady, through the material barrier of the hotel door, and fled into the night, leading the way for the mortals who followed them.

'I have many guardians,' said William. 'They would always have been able to take me out through the *inner* cage that your Arachne erected to keep me here . . . but not the outer . . .'

'Then why even try?'

'Come on,' said William, and he reached for Kelly's hand. The girl obeyed wordlessly. The three of them pushed through the doors and out into the early morning. A few stars gleamed above them, but dark clouds against the dark sky made the night feel slightly oppressive.

They ran lightly along the street, and Brady realized they were heading towards the high cliff, where the castle ruins stood. That was deeper in the town than seemed sensible, and he slowed his pace. William glanced back, then stopped.

'Keep moving, Mister Brady.'

'There's no escape this way.'

'There's a way up to the castle. If they've drawn the net in tighter, they've almost certainly abandoned the ruins. It's a stiff climb on the other side, but we can do it . . .'

William started to run again, clutching Kelly's tiny hand in his. Brady sprinted after him. 'How the hell do we get up to the ruins in the first place?'

'Just run!' said William, reaching out to urge Brady along.

They passed three human figures, each standing motionless and clawing at its neck. Brady frowned as he stared at them, then ran on past. Against one he could see the vague outline of one of William's hounds. His guardians had attacked the opposition, and made possible this first part of the escape.

They came to the house where Marianna had been kept prisoner, and went straight in. A single light burned, through the back, in the untidy and rat-infested kitchen area.

'There's someone here,' Brady whispered, and kicked suddenly through into the stark room. The smell was as bad as before, but now there was the unmistakable odour of a human presence in the place. Brady rushed into the kitchen, twisting round in time to strike and defend himself against the man who had been hiding behind the door.

Two blows were exchanged, and Brady backed off.

Uncle William came into the kitchen with Kelly, holding hands. They watched the stranger coldly. He was middle aged, but well-built, dressed in hiking clothes. His face was badly scarred. He was like a cornered animal, taken by surprise, rapidly assessing the odds. He had clearly not expected Arachne's triple prey to come back to the house.

The air crackled with static, and Brady glanced nervously at Uncle William. He realized that a different sort of attack was in progress. The atmosphere in the kitchen became sour with the smell of scorching. Brady stepped back, noticing that a grey haze was forming about each of the other men. They were staring at each other across the room. There were two dull thumps and a series of tiny balls of light suddenly flashed between Uncle William and the guardian. They vanished with slight crackling sounds, then the guardian was flung backwards, striking the wall very hard.

'Damn you!' he screamed, and made a rush for the door. He jerked backwards, clutching his throat, then flung out his hands, fingers spread, and Uncle William doubled up, clutching his stomach . . .

Again, the kitchen had shaken to a blow, the feeling of an

174

earthquake. The guardian moved rapidly towards his opponent, intending to escape.

Kelly fell forward, beneath the man's legs, and he tripped, sprawling noisily on the ground. As he fell, Uncle William raised his right hand, and a thin, stiletto blade gleamed there.

The man screamed briefly and shrilly as he saw where he was falling. Uncle William's hand seemed almost to caress the other's throat, and a snag-nail of bloody steel probed from the back of the man's neck.

In two swift movements the job was finished. Uncle William stood, brushed himself down, and helped Kelly to her feet. Brady watched them, slightly horrified, quite stunned.

It had all been so fast. A psychic duel, and then a cold-blooded ending to the matter. And Kelly had helped!

'Don't just stand there,' said William abruptly. 'Come and help.'

He was tugging at the lino, which came away in a large section. Below it the floor was of stone, and the stone had a handle in it. Uncle William tugged. Brady reached down and helped. It was a heavy slab, and it moved sluggishly.

'Use some of that stored power,' said Brady, as he sweated and strained.

'Don't be so damned lazy.'

The slab rose, and they let it fall heavily to the floor. A musty, stony smell rose from the well that was revealed. Brady peered into the darkness below his feet. He could hear the sound of water, echoing in a cavernous space.

Uncle William reached into his pocket and drew out what looked like a fountain pen; it was a torch. He shone it down into the gloom, and Brady could see that, some four feet below the kitchen floor level, there were rusting iron rings. The actual well was about twelve feet deep.

William went first, and Brady helped Kelly down after. As he himself fumbled with his feet for the dubious security of the iron ladder, he cast a last glance at the corpse in the kitchen.

It was too easy. It was all too easy . . . Uncle William had

175

been trapped in Casterigg, and needed Brady to help him out. And yet here they were, passing through Arachne's cage with a minimum of harassment . . .

'Come on Brady! Come on!'

He dropped to a crouch at the bottom of the well and peered along the narrow passage that led horizontally towards the high cliff. Kelly was already easing her way along the damp-walled tunnel, and William began to follow her as soon as he saw that Brady was safely down.

The passage was cramped and low for about twenty yards, then became narrower and higher. The torchlight flickered off the wet walls. Water trickled abundantly, making the floor slippery and dangerous. They edged their ways sidewise along the crack, towards the sound of the underground river.

Stopping for a moment, Brady said, 'Why the hell didn't you use this escape route before? Why wait until now?'

'I only found it at the end of our imprisonment,' said William. 'It was guarded. It was guarded at its farther end too. I'm hoping that they've brought that guard down into the town, now.' He edged his way along the passage, then glanced back, shining the torch at Brady. 'And I repeat . . . you weren't with us, then.'

Too easy, Brady thought. *Something's not right.*

More lies from Uncle William? More half-truths? The man had used Brady's daughter, in order to use Brady . . . he had even used his own nephew, callously leaving him to his fate. It was not unthinkable that he planned to use Brady even more than Brady was expecting.

He was uncomfortable with the thought. He was uncomfortable with everything about this escape. He was especially uncomfortable with the darkness, the heavy smell of rock, the claustrophobic pressing of rock against his body.

At last they emerged into a vertical well, and Brady teetered on the edge of the underground stream. It was wide, but shallow, the rocks around slick with green slime. The stream came out of the solid limestone, and vanished similarly, through a low arch. The cave was wide and low, and the natural well rose hundreds of feet to a grating, in the grounds of the castle. There was another much-corroded ladder here, and when Brady reached up to touch it, it shook, ringing slightly, somewhere further up where it was loose against the rock.

'This won't hold our weights,' Brady said.

'It'll have to,' said Uncle William, staring up towards the night. There was no movement up there, no sign of brightness, save for a single, faint star.

'You knew about this tunnel all the time.'

William smiled. 'If you say so, Mister Brady. The point is: I couldn't use it. I couldn't take the chance of using it. I sensed the place as soon as I was brought to the house. I don't think my captors realized that I would discover their emergency exit. It's been here for hundreds of years; a natural well, extended to a number of different exits and hidey-holes below the town.'

'The ladder is the original, by the looks of it,' Brady added, and shook it again. The frail structure clanged and shuddered. He shook his head. 'There's no way up that!'

'Trust in my guardians,' said William, adding, 'And pray for a convenient handhold if something *does* give way.'

Uncle William went first. He reached up, took a grip on the rusting metal, and Brady shoved him the last few feet. The ladder moved; the old man's body swayed. Rock fragments tumbled and struck the water below. 'It'll hold,' William said, and around him green mist played, and the cavern turned even colder than the ice cold of the underground stream.

The long ascent began.

They've taken Nayenez from me! One of my guardian spirits . . . taken, with no warning, no word!

She walked swiftly through the dead streets of Casterigg, through a gate, and onto the steep hill towards the castle. She followed the two men who had been waiting for her, the two who would control the taking of Hunhau from her grey stuff, and give it to the old man. Hunhau they could have with pleasure. But Nayenez!

He was one of my guardians! They can't take my guardians. Without them I'm too vulnerable!

She realized immediately what she had known all along. They did not intend to let her live. Brady and she would face each other and destroy each other. Whoever he was, these children of the Great Spider did not want him; they were afraid of him. They would play him off against her, and eliminate two inconveniences at once.

Young Grandfather watched the ground through her eyes. It was a hard, steep climb.

'Hurry!' said one of the men ahead of her. 'They're bound to be coming this way.'

Enumclaw and Tieholt remained fast in her mind. They had had their fun, played their games, and now they rested. Nayenez was dancing towards the dark mountain, taken from her as abruptly as the bone had been pincered from her body.

The wound bled and ached. But the greatest ache was in her belly, where Hunhau waited, excitedly, for his release from the carrier. He grimaced and wailed within her greystuff, promising the terrible things that he would do to her when he was free.

Young Grandfather whispered to her. 'I am ready for any and all treachery. Trust in me. I may be only an old Indian, but these others do not know the extent of my power. Trust in me. I shall destroy Brady before he can destroy you. We shall make the walk home together.'

On and on, up the slippery hillside, towards the imposing ruins above. She no longer walked in the old way, and her legs ached, her breath came harsh and short.

Below her feet, beyond her awareness, three people climbed through the rock.

At the top of the ladder Uncle William fumbled in his overcoat pocket and produced a tungsten steel rod. Brady stood precariously below him, watching by the feeble

178

starlight. Two rungs had broken beneath his feet as he had ascended, but miraculously – or more probably, by magic – the rusting fixture had remained in place on the cold, rock wall of the shaft.

The padlock, holding down the well's grating, snapped after three strenuous applications of the iron bar. The broken lock tumbled down the well, and splashed noisily into the water below.

William put his shoulders to the grating and heaved, pulling himself up the ladder at the same time. The well cover creaked, then gave, and swung open. Kelly scrambled up the ladder beside her great-uncle, and wormed out into the cold night. Brady was able to push the older man's feet, and give him that extra momentum upwards, and soon Brady himself was being hauled out into the grounds of Casterigg Castle.

He looked around him quickly, obtaining fleeting images of the ruins: they were in the lee of the great keep, which rose sheer and dark behind them. Its windows and doorways were blind cavities in the paler stone of the starlit walls. Wind made deep whining sounds as it passed through the long-deserted structure. The outer walls stretched away on both sides, surrounded by tall trees, and topped by barbed wire. What had been the courtyards were now lawns and banks, neatly maintained for the tourist. Once they had been muddy, animal-infested thoroughfares through the castle grounds. Now they were gardens.

All this he took in at a glance. A glance was all there was time for.

Arachne struck!

They came swooping out of the night, screaming like banshees, hovering above Brady, William Farmer and the cowering form of little Kelly. She screamed and flung up her hands to her ears, to block the terrifying sound of the elementals that were swiftly moving to attack them.

William immediately flung up his own defences, drawing on the ancient power that he stored. His eyes rolled up so that just the whites showed, his skin almost

179

burst into sweat, and around the three of them formed a shimmering, hazy veil of multi-hued light. The veil seemed to fade, but Brady could distinguish a swirling, restless form surrounding them, as if they stood in a fish bowl, staring out through water.

The air imploded. Dark shapes leapt out through the psychic wall, giant wolves, that snatched and locked with the enemy. As the strands of psychic energy entwined, they seemed to vanish, but the ground bubbled and burned where they fought.

The banshee screaming was superseded by the perpetual howling of wind. A storm raced around the inner barrier, and Uncle William turned blindly to follow the writhing, hostile shape within it. Brady glimpsed a strange face, saw lightning crackle and strike towards him. A gigantic fish opened its jaws, making him jump out of his skin as it seemed to snap straight at him, and then was gone . . .

Of all things, a tall, powerful-looking Red Indian ran around the castle grounds, watching him coldly, finally walking right up to the edge of the psychic barrier and staring through.

The images formed and vanished. They puzzled Brady totally. Uncle William began to shake. There were more air explosions, and other elementals emerged from his mind, formed, coalesced, and darted away through the wall, to join the affray.

Through the atmospheric chaos, through the flickering psychic light, which lit up the castle grounds in eerie flashes, three human figures walked. Two were men. They wore masks on their faces, the sickeningly rotten heads of animals, hollowed and split to fit over the human heads below. One was a pig, the other a goat, the tongues lolling disgustingly, the dead eyes sparkling with magic life.

Between them walked a girl. Brady focused upon her, fixed upon her, and knew instantly!

She. From the west. Danger. This was the girl, this was the danger that Ellen Bancroft had sensed, peering from her ghostly realm through the weakened psychic defences around his house.

180

She. From the west. A beautiful young girl, who watched him as curiously and as fixedly as he watched her. She was slim. She was quite devastatingly attractive, her hair long and dark, with a streak of silver, highlighted by stars and the psychic discharge around her. She walked through the confusion, slowly and confidently, her arms hanging limp by her sides.

The storm seemed to focus around her. The Indian walked behind her, watching Brady over her shoulder. Through the howling gale, Brady heard William cry out. 'I'm weakening,' he said. Brady saw that he was holding Kelly's hand. His face gleamed with the sweat that poured from him.

Sound rose from the earth, from the well, a deep moaning, that rose and fell in volume and pitch. Below, in the valley, the town of Casterigg began to come awake for the second time, lights going on in houses as the strange phenomenon on the castle ridge awoke the sleepy, frightened occupants. The girl remained motionless, the tall Indian watching from behind her.

'How the hell do we get out of *here*?' Brady demanded of the old man. He had not expected anything as powerful as this.

William Farmer just shook his head. 'The girl . . .' he said with difficulty. 'The girl . . . look closely . . .'

Brady stepped forward . . .

That's him! That's Brady. The hunter. The enemy. The threat!

Young Grandfather danced and whooped out his war cry. He strung an arrow in his bow, ready to shoot the enemy.

Mary Jane stared at the youthful looking man. Around her, the spirits she had carried across the water mixed with the strange forces that had guarded the town for the last few days. Spirit forms alien to Enumclaw and Tieholt, spirit forms from the dark life of *this* land. They jostled and fought for position, sensing that there was danger,

181

knowing that their prey were the three weak-looking mortals standing before them.

Hunhau, Lord of Death, Chief of Demons, emerged from her grey stuff, rose to his full height, towering over the cowering forms of Brady, the girl, and the old man.

'I want him now,' crooned Hunhau. 'I want this Brady.'

'Brady is the concern of others,' whispered the mind voice of the man in the goat mask. 'Your destiny is to enter the old man, to join with the others, to become all-powerful.'

'Brady,' cried Hunhau. 'I want to chew at his grey stuff!'

Chief of Demons surged forward, attacked the psychic wall, and drove Brady backwards, his face twisted with shock.

'You have not been brought here to indulge in petty revenge,' came the voice of Arachne.

Mary Jane watched the tussle, listened to the storm noise, heard the wailing of demons and the clap of thunder, the crackle of static electricity, the groaning of the earth.

She stepped forward, staring at the man she had feared for all of her long walk over water. He was nice to look at, but his eyes were hard, fierce. She would have liked to have known him, to speak to him, to ask him why and how he was a danger to her.

'Mister Farmer,' called the man in the goat-mask. 'You must give up this pointless reluctance. You have an agreement with us. You must admit this shaman, accumulate him. Mister Farmer, cease to resist . . .'

His reply was a bolt of blue energy in the form of a cat, that leapt through the psychic wall and sent him flying. The energy dissipated.

Mary Jane heard all this, and saw all this, but was mostly aware of Brady, who stared at her, then stepped towards her . . .

'Beware,' whispered Young Grandfather.

'He's as afraid as I am,' she said. 'And he's behind the barrier . . .'

'*Beware!*' cried Young Grandfather, and Mary Jane suddenly reacted with terrible shock –

182

For suddenly Brady was *outside* the barrier, in front of her, reaching to her, rushing towards her!

Brady's cry of shock and surprise was lost against the screaming of the elementals that swooped towards him suddenly. One second he had been approaching the girl, peering at her, protected by Uncle William's mind-defences . . .

The next, he was outside, unprotected, and something like a hand in his back had propelled him towards the girl.

She stepped towards him, her face twisting into a mask of pure hate. The air hissed, the tall Indian drew back his bow and let loose an arrow which Brady avoided with an ease, and a swiftness, that did not come from his own skills.

The talisman on his chest burned his skin. He touched it, felt it hot, and drew his hand away, recognizing, without really thinking about it, that the Norse artefact was beginning to function, defending its wearer . . .

A man with the face of a pig struck at him with a knife. He reached out his arm and struck back, and the body flew across the castle grounds, striking the wall above the cliffs, and vanishing; the man with the face of a goat discharged a pistol at him; the bullets sped into the night. Brady walked to him, flung him to the well, and the body disappeared into the gaping depths of the earth. The girl screamed, her mouth wide, her eyes closed. The Indian ran at him, but was driven back, shielding his eyes against some unseen brightness. The girl was scratching at her stomach. She opened the flesh and something bright glittered in her bloody fingers, and she tossed this object at Brady, who was sent reeling backwards . . .

Something like a rotting corpse ran at him, grinning, reaching.

His chest burned. Fire leapt towards the hideous figure, enveloped it, but was shrugged aside. Brady chased the running girl. An arrow grazed his shoulder. He was impelled to run by forces beyond his control. She was screaming, she turned, she faced him . . .

Against his will he reached for her and flung her hard against the walls of the keep. She flew like a stone, striking the ruins fifty feet from the ground, and tumbling to the earth, a sadly broken shape. A storm broke around her, wind and rain driving at Brady. The figure of the corpse came back to him, and it seemed to be stuck, unable to approach, unable to depart . . .

Through the gale, through the swirling haze, through the driving rain, Brady saw Uncle William and Kelly, hand in hand, running to the farther wall of the castle. They clambered over the wall, and vanished from sight . . .

Betrayed! Bastards! Betrayed, left to die, left like a rat in a trap!

Suddenly the storm drained skywards, the rain visibly curving upwards and speeding into the night; the wind, the light, the shimmering psychic forces all followed, as if sucked up by a whirlwind. The threshing, corpse-like figure tried one last time to approach Brady, then wailed in a high-pitched, terrifying way, reached up to the heavens, and followed the other elementals.

Brady was drenched, with rain and sweat. He was shaking. The sudden stillness was almost as shocking as the previous mayhem. He looked nervously around for the Indian, but saw only a fleet-footed shape, running in the night's shadow, against the keep, towards the crushed body of the girl.

Bastards! he thought again, and went after Uncle William.

He reached the edge of the castle grounds, stretched to look over the wall, and heard rather than saw the two of them, scrambling down a steep path on the cliff face.

He jumped across the wall, cutting himself badly on the barbed wire, and slipped and staggered after them. The wind blew against him, dangerously threatening to blow him from the steep drop. He clung to rocks, to grass, to the twisting roots of wind-blasted trees. He slipped and sprawled in pursuit of the other two, and eventually reached the bottom of the cliff.

His mind was filled with thoughts of his family; his head

echoed with the words which Uncle William had spoken – the fact that he *knew* where Brady's family were being held. Twenty miles from here. All of them. All of them together. Twenty miles away only!

'William Farmer!' he called through the night. 'For Christ's sake stop! I shan't hurt you! For pity's sake . . . *Farmer! William!* Stop!'

He was vaguely aware that the old man had stopped, glanced back, and sworn at him.

He knew where Marianna was! He *had* to stop, to tell Brady. He couldn't just rush away into the night, into darkness, into oblivion!

It no longer mattered that Brady had been betrayed. It was no longer of importance that Uncle William had brought Brady to Casterigg specifically to aid his escape, at the expense of Brady's life.

The two of us together, William had said, and what he had meant was, *With you, Brady, to attract and hold the killing psychic forces, Kelly and I can get away . . .*

'Uncle William!'

And suddenly he was there – and yet not there!

One moment he and Kelly had been running along the dale, between high cliffs, away from the great pinnacle of rock where the castle stood. Brady had been doggedly pursuing them through the darkness, skidding on the slippery grass and stones of this well-trodden trackway up into the hills.

One moment they had been ahead of him, the next . . . they were above him! An impossible climb above him. He could see their shapes, faintly visible against the clouds and stars of the sky. Wind blew their coats. They still held hands, the old man and the little girl.

'You promised to tell me where my family are!' Brady shouted up at them. 'You owe me that. You owe me at least that!'

'We owe you nothing,' shouted back the girl.

'William!' shouted Brady. 'You owe me that information. For God's sake!'

'Don't waste your breath, Brady,' shouted Uncle

William. 'I owe nothing to anyone! Any means to an end . . .'

Brady stared up at them, through the darkness, through the pain.

'You said you knew . . .'

'I said many things,' said Uncle William, and laughed. 'But I always *was* a terrible liar, Mister Brady.'

'Who are you?' he shouted, all hope draining into the earth, into the cold night. But they had abruptly vanished. 'Who are you?' Brady screamed. As if from a great distance he heard a girl's laughter. The sound mocked him, infuriated him.

He found a terrible strength. He flung himself at the rising wall of wet, slick rock, and scrabbled and hauled himself upwards. Sometimes his feet slipped on the smooth rock, unable to find a purchase. His fingers curled on tiny crevices and ledges, and dragged him up the cliff. The wind tugged at him. His body ached. Blood oozed from his fingertips and cheeks where the hard rock scratched and wounded him.

And he dragged himself above the dale, onto the rising land beyond. He straightened, and shouted, his voice a shriek of anger, fury . . . a sound that might have stilled even the most aggressive of beasts. He cried for Uncle William and Kelly to stop, and distantly a light flickered.

He ran towards that light. It was in a sheltered place, beneath a tree, beside a small crag of dark limestone. The branches of the tree whipped against the stone, the leaves rustling loud in the night.

Uncle William held a small torch, pointing it towards Brady. Kelly stood beside him, huddled in her coat. Brady could just make out the gleam of her eyes, the impassiveness of her gaze.

'Don't come too close, Mister Brady. You've seen what we can do.'

Brady stopped. He was frozen, despite his efforts at climbing. The sweat on his body was cool and uncomfortable.

'I shan't hurt you,' Brady gasped, trying to recover his breath.

'Certainly, you shan't,' said Kelly, coldly.

186

'I can't let you go. Not without . . . not without telling me *something*.'

'So it would seem,' said William Farmer. 'That was a very determined climb. You are a very determined, very *dangerous* man.'

Brady was confused. 'Dangerous? Dangerous to whom?'

'To us,' said Kelly. 'To the others like us.'

'I don't understand. Who are you? *What* are you? Where's my family? You said you knew . . .'

'Alas,' said Uncle William, almost apologetically. 'All I can tell you is that your daughter was in Casterigg, and they have taken her west. Perhaps to Wales. She had gone from Casterigg before you arrived. She was a means to an end, to get you here.'

'So you can't help me at all,' said Brady, and he felt the last vestiges of hope drain from his drenched, dispirited corpse.

'We are helping far more than you,' said Kelly quietly, and Brady frowned.

'Who *are* you?' he asked again, after a moment.

'We're an accumulator,' she said. 'You know that already.'

'I thought . . .' Brady looked at William Farmer. The two of them, Farmer and the girl, held hands. In the darkness, despite the thin pencil beam of light, Brady thought that the expressions on their faces were identical. They could have been one and the same person, a bizarre fusion of features, one young, one old, but the same . . . identical!

'We're the strongest of them,' William Farmer said, 'because we are *two*. We've accumulated the most.'

'That's why we've broken away,' the girl continued, her voice calm, deep, like an adult's. 'Uncle William was good. He was a good accumulator, useful to them. But when *I* joined him . . .' she smiled. 'Unexpectedly, I am an accumulator too. And the two of us together, fusing minds, sharing minds, sharing space . . .' her voice was like a feral growl, filled with pleasure, with triumph. 'We are *tremendously* strong. They didn't expect it.'

187

William added, 'That's what is so nice about them,' he used the word 'nice' mockingly. 'They have their purpose, they have their plan, but it is early days for them, and they are spread thin. They are vulnerable, vulnerable to the powers they have raised and stored,' he tapped his skull meaningfully. 'Mostly, they are vulnerable to their own arrogance . . .'

'Arachne,' Brady breathed. He recognized what William was saying. He had experienced that vulnerability himself, on more than one occasion.

'Arachne,' William repeated. 'They are spread wide and thin, but they are numerous. They are strong. They are *growing*.'

'To what end?' said Brady. 'What is their purpose?'

'The summoning of great power,' breathed William. 'The control of futures. The changing of the world . . .'

'What power? To what end?'

'I cannot tell you what I do not know. That is our task, now, with the others, those few like us who have broken loose . . .'

Kelly's voice was sudden and shrill, as if she laughed as she spoke. 'You got us out. If thanks is what you want, then thank you. But we hoped you would die. We *expected* you to die . . .'

'Well, I didn't,' Brady said back, defiantly. The torch waved through the night. The tree whipped against the crag of rock, blown by a cold night wind that chilled Brady even more.

'No, you didn't,' said the girl. 'You're a nuisance to them, Brady. To Arachne. You're now a nuisance to us. We're fighting the same battle. The destruction of this growing power is our mutual purpose. Same battle, but . . . we're better at it than you. We're from the *inside*. All across England, across the world, there are those of us, once recruited, who have broken away, who have turned their powers *against* Arachne . . .' she stepped forwards, away from Uncle William, and Brady thought there was something in her face that pleaded for his understanding and common sense. 'You *must* see that. There is a war beginning, a war that will be fought silently, in the mind, in secret places, away from the public eye. We are well equipped to battle with Arachne. You are just . . . what are you? Blind violence! Desperate quest! You blunder your way about England, seeking not to destroy an evil power, but to rescue your family. You are not dedicated to the *higher* aim, and therefore you are a nuisance. You will only get in the way.'

William said, 'Give it up, Brady. For our sakes, for everyone's sake. Don't be the unknown factor that can destroy all our work, even as you try to destroy Arachne's. Go home. Leave the battle to those who have the power . . .'

'Yes,' said Brady coldly. 'And leave my family to their fates.' He shook his head. 'I may not be as strong as you . . . psychically. But *nothing* will make me stop the search. Destroy me if you will. But while I'm alive, while my family is alive, I'll not give up.'

Kelly pleaded with him again. 'We'll find them for you, Brady. We'll release them. We'll keep you informed. *Trust* us to help you, if that's what we must do to keep you out of the way. But go home. *Please* go home.'

Brady was cold; he was furious; he was desperate. He trusted no one. He trusted nothing. The two figures before him were as evil, as threatening, as Arachne. He could not take any notice of them.

He stepped quickly forward, his blood boiling, intending to grab the girl and confront her face to face about what she knew. He felt he could overwhelm the both of them, together.

For his trouble he felt a violent blow to his forehead, and was sent reeling backwards. For a second he thought they had attacked him psychically, but by the meagre light of cloud covered moon and stars, he could see Uncle William shaking his hand, to ease pain.

Brady felt stunned. His legs were quite weak. He sat on the cold ground and watched the two figures begin to walk swiftly into the darkness.

'Come back!' he yelled, and scrabbled to his feet. His

189

legs gave out and he realized that whatever William Farmer had done to him, it had been very effective.

On all fours he screamed into the darkness, 'Wait!'

'No time, Mister Brady. No time,' called back Uncle William.

Panic rose suddenly in Brady. His tenuous link with Arachne was again slipping away. 'What will they do with my family?' he screamed. 'Tell me! What is their purpose?'

Kelly's voice was faint. 'They will use what was placed within them. And then they will cast them aside. But there is still time. Leave it to us, Brady. Go home, and leave the hunting to those who are beginning to know the prey . . .'

'Come back! Come back!'

His screams were long, loud and desperate. They fled into the windy night and were blown away.

He scrabbled on the ground, and at last strength returned to his limbs. He stood up and weakly made his way back to the rock face. There was no safe way down that he could see, and slowly he began to walk along the cliff tops, until again he fell, this time bruising himself badly.

An hour later he was still huddled by the dropaway, staring towards the dark shape of the castle on the crag. He was sobbing, racked with grief, shaking with cold.

The last sound he uttered, before falling into a long, deep sleep, was the name of his daughter.

Marianna.

For a while, Young Grandfather crouched in the shadows of the castle wall. What a cold, hard place this was. His arrows had missed. He had always been the best warrior with bow and arrow, but he had missed, and the body of Mary Jane was shattered.

He chanted a song of regret. The bone fragment that held him was still in the corpse. The others had gone, rising up into the wind, into the sky, deserting the dead girl.

But Young Grandfather had made a promise, and he would keep that promise. He had thought himself to be

190

strong. He could kill a buffalo with his bare hands. He had counted coup more than a thousand times. He had ridden the plains for twenty days and nights without stopping. He had thought himself strong, powerful.

It was a cold time, a hard time. There were creatures in this alien world who were far more powerful than he. It had been a shock, a humiliation, to realize that he could not protect his daughter properly.

But more important, now, was his honour.

He rose from the shadows, a shadow himself. He was drawn towards the decaying flesh and bone of the false-thing that contained his daughter. He stood above her and reached for her, and their minds touched . . .

Images of an earlier time, a time in the Blue Snake Hills, the time of protection . . .

You will lie here, the old man, Snake Man, had said.

She watched him as he pottered about the cave of the dead. He tugged a small bone from the skeleton of a chief. He detached a long bone from the leg of another. He took Mary Jane's small painted doll from her and placed it on the floor.

'Come here,' he had said, and he used a bone-handled knife to make a cut in her thumb. He snipped her hair. Around the little pile of relics he drew the shape of a human female.

He had made her lie down and close her eyes, but just once, as he chanted, she had glanced from the rock ledge where she rested and seen what was taking shape in the middle of the cave. The flesh had grown about the bone and hair and doll. It had become firm, it had expanded, frightening her. She saw the features moulded on the life-size figure, saw her own face, blank and staring. When the artificial creature had stood it was so like her that she thought it must have been her.

Snake Man clothed the false-thing in her clothes, and at last her mind drifted from the sleeping body to the false-thing, and she had walked about the cave, and seen her own body, naked, protected by the hideous, quivering shape of a spider on its breast.

In this way, herself, but not herself, she had Walked On Water. Now, the false-thing was dead, decayed . . . she lay sleeping four thousand miles away, living flesh, without mind.

That mind now rose from the painted doll that lay among the rotting fragments of the false-thing. Mary Jane Silverlock was a shivering, naked spirit, the silver streak gone from her hair.

She stared down at the corpse. Young Grandfather watched too. The elements reclaimed the bits and pieces, flesh dissolving, bone crumbling.

Soon, all that remained were the bones of a chief, and the longer bone of another man, and a small doll, its face painted brightly, and swathed in a lock of dark hair, with two strands of silver.

Across a great sea, across a vast land, Mary Jane lay sleeping, hands crossed on her breast, like a spider, guarding her mortal flesh.

Young Grandfather said, 'I was not strong enough. That Brady was stronger. I'm sorry.'

'Don't be sorry,' she said, and reached for her Young Grandfather, holding his hand, smiling. 'You did your best.'

'It's a long walk home,' he said. 'In the spirit world, everything is slow. It will be a slow walk.'

'Then we'd better start walking. I'm too young to give up now. I want to be back in Ridgeville. I want lovers and sons. I want the land of my ancestors. I will not give up until I'm home.'

'It's such a long way,' sighed Young Grandfather.

They turned to the west. They drifted across the land, without food, without sleep, without rest. They were ghosts, drawn back to the place of their dreams.

They walked for many years.

CODA

At dawn, Brady made his way back to the castle grounds, and there he found the bizarre remains of the girl. Shivering with a chill, his arms wrapped around his body, he walked away from the scene of that strange confrontation, picking his way carefully back to the town.

He went to his car, wondering how he would get the vehicle started without keys, but the keys were in the ignition, the car unlocked.

A human hand was impaled upon the handbrake, and with hardly a thought, Brady removed the offending object and wiped the brake with a tissue.

There was no sign of Simon Fleming.

As he climbed into his car, a police vehicle streaked past along the road towards Maron Tor. Brady watched it go. It gleamed bright in the early morning sun. Minutes later, an ambulance followed it.

He drove slowly after the police, keeping his distance, and pulled off the road some way away, peering down the steep slopes to the scree that littered the bottom of the great drop from the summit of Maron Tor.

He couldn't see clearly, but he knew that the sprawled shape down there, around which uniformed figures fussed, was the body of Simon Fleming.

He waited around no longer. He drove from the town of Casterigg, towards Sheffield, until at last he joined the motorway south, and sped back to London.

He had failed again. Again, he had come close, but at the last moment his family had been twisted away from him, jerked from his grasp.

William Farmer's words burned at him. *Give it up. Go home. Leave it to us. Trust us. Give it up. Give it up.*

193

As if he could!

'Never!' he said aloud, to passing traffic. He wound down the window and shouted out into the bright day, *'Never! I'll never give it up!'*

No one heard. The cars roared past, all sound lost against the wind.

'Give it up . . .' he murmured to himself, and smiled grimly.

No chance of that, Uncle Williams. I'll trust no one to do my business for me. I'll find them on my own, with or without your help. And if you get in my way . . .

If you get in my way then I'll kill you, too. I shall have no choice in the matter. My family are nobody's business but my own, and I intend to find them, and bring them back with me, safe, alive . . . secure!

He felt very angry. He drove back towards his home with his right foot pressed hard against the floor. The car vibrated violently as he forced it to a speed close to ninety miles an hour. He hardly saw the traffic on the motorway – but he saw the land around, the wide land, with its hills and forests . . . it seemed to him to be an *endless* land, and his despair began to grow again.

At home, in the cold house, he found a letter from Françoise Jeury. It was a kind note, saying that she would always be willing to help him again, and would be back in England before too long. There was a postcard from someone else he knew, a girl called Anita Herbert, the daughter of a man whom Brady had seen killed in Norfolk, just a few weeks ago. She would like to visit, and Brady wondered whether or not that was a good idea; but memories of his previous encounter with her were warm, reassuring . . .

Yes, he thought. By all means come and visit.

But mostly there was the silence in the house, even the ghost huddling and lurking in some remote corner of the building. Brady spread out a map of Britain. He leaned on the table, staring at it. He moved his finger from the coast of Norfolk, where he had had one encounter with Arachne, to the high peaks of Derbyshire. Then he ran his finger in an enormous cross, from the highlands of Scotland to the ragged south coast of Dorset, and from the marshlands of Suffolk, in the east, to the remote mountains of Wales – and again his spirits sank.

So many places . . . such a wide land . . . a thousand towns, a million hidden places, in valleys, behind hills, behind the walls of farms . . .

How could he possibly ever hope to find three small people in such a vast sprawl of country?

He banged his fist against the table, frustrated and almost tearful.

Somewhere there, somewhere on the map, his family were to be found. But where? Where were Arachne now? Where would the next contact be?

He sat down at the table and closed the map.

He had no choice, really, but to wait for time to tell . . .

THE SHRINE

For Anne Holdstock, a little devil in her own right.

THE SHRINE

But from which earth, and grave, and dust,
The Lord shall raise me up, I trust.

Sir Walter Raleigh

PROLOGUE

Six people sat around a candle-lit table, in a low-ceilinged, oak-beamed room. They talked loudly and happily as the fourth bottle of wine gave up the ghost. Between them, on the table, lay the remnants of an enormous salmon trout, white-boned and picked clean. They were ebullient, because the Savilles always did things in style.

It was the sort of evening that Colin Saville welcomed. He sat quietly at the top of the table and listened to gossipy chatter about the City, about banking, and about commercial law. It was fascinating.

He himself was an archaeologist, and not given to enlarging on the details of his work. He invited acquaintances to supper because they were company he enjoyed, and their conversation was stimulating.

He was a tall, slimly built man in his mid-thirties, fair-haired and weather-tanned from the elements. He was active on the legal side of archaeology, but still enjoyed a simple dig.

Of course, in recent years there had been the deeper, more prevailing interest, which not even his wife knew about . . .

Janine smiled at him down the table. He smiled thinly back. She glanced down at the empty bottle of white wine (from their favourite vineyards in the Burgundy town of Meursault) but he shook his head. Four in one evening was quite enough.

Almost in the same motion he turned his head to glance at the open french windows. Janine was frowning too.

'That's Jessie . . .'

Conversation round the table stopped abruptly and the sound of the Saville's Border collie, Jessie, became instantly audible. The dog was barking quite furiously. She was somewhere near the swimming pool.

'An intruder?' one of the guests suggested.

Saville said, 'Jessie wouldn't bark at an intruder. She'd probably play with them.'

'A fox,' Janine said. 'Probably a fox.'

The sound of the dog stopped. Saville smiled and nodded. 'Almost certainly. I lost two chickens to a fox last year. Did I tell you?'

'Ah, the joys of country life,' the banker said. 'I can never understand –'

'*Daddy!*'

Saville nearly jumped out of his seat as the cry from his daughter cut the banker's sentence in two. Rachel was standing at the top of the stairs, peering through the bannisters at the supper-party below.

'What is it, darling?'

'It's cold. I'm freezing.'

'But it's a summer's night, sweetheart.'

'If she's cold, she's cold,' Janine said, patiently, and Saville frowned. An extravagant man in certain ways, he hated to turn on the central heating prematurely, which seemed to be what was being suggested.

'It's *freezing*, daddy!'

'All right, darling. I'll come up.'

Saville excused himself from the table. Janine said, 'There's a duvet in her top wardrobe.'

Saville climbed the stairs, and the conversation blossomed again below. As he turned on to the upper landing he suddenly stopped and frowned.

The girl had not been dreaming. It was distinctly chilly here. His cheeks felt it, and the tip of his nose. Downstairs, the chatter was noisy and unbothered. But now Saville felt a distinct iciness that was not physical, and his heart started to flutter with alarm.

'Daddy!'

He walked into Rachel's room and looked coldly at his daughter. She was tucked up in bed, the summer duvet tugged to her chin. His breath frosted as he stood in the doorway and looked at her. 'Hurry up,' the girl said.

He reached for the thick winter covering and spread it over the bed. 'Better?'

'A bit.'

'Try and sleep.' He kissed Rachel's head (her hair was frozen!) then checked the windows of her room, reaching up to feel for something at the corners. At the doorway he again ran his fingers lightly along the wood and sniffed.

Everything was in order.

Back on the landing he walked slowly towards his study. The landing was narrow and formed three quarters of a square. Below was an open-plan games-room, with doorways open to both the lounge and the small dining-area. It had been so hot earlier! A cool draught from the whole house had been very welcome.

'Hurry up, Colin,' Janine called.

'I think we may have a burst pipe,' he called back. 'I'm going to check it.'

He heard her grumble, but then the dinner-table chatter continued. He approached his study and stopped. White frost formed in the air before him. A drop of moisture in his nose felt stingingly cold. The brass door-handle was almost impossible to touch, but he twisted it and stepped into the small, book-filled room. Here he kept his private papers, his desk and a couch for afternoon snoozing.

He closed the door behind him, murmuring words to himself, making a peculiar sign in the air. He held his fingers in a special way.

The entire room was frosted white. His teeth chattered slightly as the intense, supernatural cold began to penetrate his summer clothing. Two cobwebs sparkled in eerie blue light. It was dark outside, but the whole room

205

was illuminated by the chill glow from its walls, floor and ceiling. He could make out the shape of every object in his study by its strange glow.

Stretched out on the couch, arms by his sides, eyes closed, chest rising almost imperceptibly, was the figure of a naked man. Because of the whiteness of the features, from hair to toes, it took Saville a moment to recognize the nature of the intruder, and his identity.

Then he gasped with shock, and felt a second, but more meaningful thrill of fear.

As he stared at the figure it began to sit up. It turned on the couch and stood. It stared at Saville, but there was a blind look about the eyes. The breathing was regular, but no frost formed in the air. The hands clenched and unclenched.

'Daniel Brady,' Saville murmured, shaking his head. 'Well I'm damned. I'd thought . . .' He broke off, smiling slightly. 'Well I'm damned,' he repeated, then asked more loudly, 'How the hell did you find me?'

The figure said nothing, made no move.

'I'm defended,' Saville said. 'You can't hurt me. You can hurt my family, but you can't hurt me.'

Still the apparition was silent.

'You're powerful. I give you that,' Saville smiled cruelly. 'But you'll never be powerful enough. This sort of trickery is all right for ordinary people. But we're used to it. You can't hurt us. You'll never hurt us. It's just a matter of time before we destroy you.'

The apparition took a step towards Saville, and Saville jerked with shock, moving backwards until the door was against his back. Then he laughed. He was jumpy. This was just a psychic projection. It couldn't see or hear. It was just a warning.

Then, on the apparition's chest, a face began to glow, a small, skull-featured head, about the size of a child's palm. Saville recognized it at once. The Viking talisman from Uffricshame, in Norfolk. He had spent weeks – earlier in

206

the year – excavating at the old Anglo-Saxon town for that particular object of Viking power. Brady had thwarted him. It had not occurred to Saville, as he had escaped Dan Brady's fury, that the man would actually find the talisman for himself.*

Clearly, Brady had succeeded where weeks of patient excavation had failed. Saville knew well what sort of power the screaming-skull amulet would confer upon its wearer . . .

Certainly power enough to account for Brady's penetration of the psychic defences around the house.

'I've found you,' the apparition breathed, the voice a coarse hiss, utterly unlike a human voice. Saville shook with fright. But perhaps the voice, too, was just a static illusion, a programmed part of the projection. The figure had no consciousness.

It stepped forward again, and this time seemed to bend and wave, as if struggling.

Saville smiled and glanced down at the floor, where the trapping-circle was hidden. His entire house was defended, and riddled with psychic traps. The only nagging thought was how such an elemental could have entered this room at all.

Saville walked around the apparition, slapping his arms and shoulders to try and keep some warmth in his rapidly chilling body. Facing the blank-featured figure again, he smiled. 'Well, Mr Brady,' he said softly. 'You've rather overstepped the mark this time.' He chuckled at his own joke, glancing down at the circle's edge. 'If you're going to play supernatural tricks on people, you really ought to get proper training first. We'll be one jump ahead of you all the time.'

As if in reply, the whole room reverberated to a sudden blow. The air was split by a shocking crack. Every bookshelf trembled, every loose object in the room shifted

* See *Nighthunter 2: The Talisman*.

by a few inches. The windows rattled, the light fixture in the ceiling swung violently.

Saville was taken by surprise and stepped back again. As he turned to face his desk, so a glowing shape appeared there.

'What the devil . . .?'

Rapidly, the blur of glowing white coalesced into a girl's face, and it was a face he recognized very well. Long hair, sparkling eyes, a mischievous grin. The face came towards him, towering above him.

'Remember . . .' the apparition of Daniel Brady hissed. 'Remember Marianna . . . my daughter . . . my daughter . . . where is she? Where is she kept?'

How the hell was Brady doing this? Saville backed away, but the child's face followed, looming over him. He could almost hear the girl's laughter, and then the sound of her sobbing.

Another face formed, this time a boy's, shy and nervous. The hair was dark, the features sensitive. The apparition of Brady pointed towards Saville. 'Remember . . . remember Dominick . . . my son. My son. Where have you taken him?'

'I don't know,' Saville stammered. He was frozen. He could see the phone on his desk. He wondered if Janine and the guests had heard the sound of the shock. But he had designed this room to be utterly soundproof. He had to get help. Brady was close by. He *had* to be close by. How else could he project not two but three apparitions? He was almost certainly in the grounds. But that damned amulet. What help was it giving him? What extra power?

'Damn you, Brady. Damn you . . .'

But how could he damn a man who had almost literally come back from the dead to pursue those who had abducted his family?

Saville had been there on that winter's night. He had followed the rest of the group of collectors into the darkened lounge. The place had been half-decorated for

208

Christmas, a pathetic sight that had amused him. He had watched the rape of Brady's wife, Alison, and it had meant nothing to him, a cold act, coldly witnessed. These people meant nothing beyond the sacrifice they would make to the greater cause. He himself had carried the inert body of the boy out into the cold night, knocking him senseless when he had begun to struggle again. The boy would be taken north. The girl to the east. The woman . . . there were plans for the woman.

Saville's own daughter, Rachel, would soon herself be a part of that same plan. He had offered her to Arachne as his gift. In a year or so, when the call would come, he would dispose of Janine and lead his daughter to the secret place called *Magondathog*.

Her life for his own immortality.

He would leave his own house as they had left Brady's that night: burning.

He remembered the flames. He remembered the sight of Daniel Brady himself, trussed up like a Christmas turkey and dead by strangulation, lying by the side of the burning sofa.

It had gone wrong. It had gone badly wrong. It had gone wrong in a way that could not be explained. For the house had survived, and Dan Brady had stepped back from the grave . . .

To become a hunter. A death-hunter.

And he was powerful.

A third face formed in the room, an older woman, narrow-featured, beautiful, her face smiling, eyes twinkling.

'Alison . . .' hissed the ghostly figure of Brady himself. 'Remember Alison. I can't forget her. Where is she? Where is she? My wife . . . my wife . . .'

Saville said nothing. The ghost of the man watched him blindly, pointing its finger towards him. But it was trapped in the circle. The faces were merely secondary echoes.

Saville stepped quickly through the shimmering images.

His heart nearly shot from his chest with fear, but he reached the desk and snatched the phone from its cradle. The faces were still watching him, the reminders of Brady's family, the three people that Arachne had taken months before.

He dialled a number.

Damn Brady! Damn him for following! Damn him for surviving the attack.

A voice answered on the other end of the phone.

Saville said, 'Never mind that. Just listen. I'm at home and Brady is attacking me, Daniel Brady, remember? He's here . . .

'Right. *Brady.* How the hell can this keep happening. . . ?

'I don't care about that, I thought we'd dispensed with him . . .

'Well he's here now . . .

'Yes, an elemental . . .

'Yes . . .

'How the hell do I know? He's here, he's manifesting . . .

'Not physical, no, but that damned amulet is the problem . . .

'God only knows . . .

'Close by, yes, that's what I thought . . .

'Monitor my house, that's all I ask . . .

'Yes, just get a guardian out here, quickly, quickly!'

He slammed down the receiver then reached out to a glass cabinet and drew down a shotgun.

Walking around the apparition he cast it a last, angry glance. 'I'll get you now, Brady. I'll finish the job that should have been finished months ago.'

As he spoke the words, so the ghost vanished and the faces faded. The coldness in the room dissipated in a second, and the eerie glow disappeared. Saville ran out onto the landing and raced downstairs.

'We've got an intruder!' he shouted to his guests, and

210

everyone stood from the table and began to talk all at once.

Janine was terrified. 'Rachel . . .?'

'She's fine. But there was a man in her room.'

'Oh my God!'

'Leave her!' Saville shouted, as his wife tried to run upstairs. 'He's still in the grounds. We've got to find him.'

The two male guests needed no further prompting, nor did the banker's wife, who shrugged on her cardigan and picked up the short-bladed salmon knife.

Outside it was dark. The moon was half full and low over the giant chestnut tree that stood in the middle of the wide lawn.

'We need torches,' the banker said.

'We've got them. Fire torches for later.' Saville had been intending to invite the guests to go nude swimming in the pool by firelight. They had done it before, and it was always a popular way to end the evening. The torches he had made were brands of dried grass and creeper and wood chips, tightly wound around hazelwood hafts, then drenched in paraffin. He stuck them alight with a match. The torches flared furiously in the dark night. Each of the guests then ran in different directions carrying sticks to act as cudgels.

Saville himself ran towards the main gates, to the cluster of oaks that stood there. The gates were locked and the wall was high. Brady might still be trying to get out of the grounds.

As Saville ran, the fire from his torch streamed behind him, sparks flying up into the night.

After the effort of projecting his elemental image he'll be weak, he thought.

He'll be weak. Drained. He won't be able to get out of the grounds!

Weak. Helpless . . .

Jessie, the dog, barked and scampered about the garden, following each bright streamer of fire in turn. The voices of the guests were shrill and loud in the night,

211

calling to each other, shouting that they'd found nothing.

Saville reached the wrought-iron gates and rattled them, ensuring that they were still locked. The cars were parked just inside. His torch threw the crowded oaks into eerie yellow relief.

'Where the hell are you?' Saville growled as he ran around the wall, keeping the fire away from the trees, holding the heavy shotgun with difficulty.

He turned back towards the gate, and a thin bright light flashed out of the darkness just in front of his face. The movement of the cold metal was so fast that he hardly had time to register its presence and cry out for help . . .

The oak tree by the main gate was burning. Janine saw it, screamed and ran towards it. 'The cars!' she cried, and from around the garden the others came running, dropping their firebrands, suddenly panicking as they saw the flames reaching closer to their precious vehicles.

The whole tree was flaring. It was like an immense November bonfire, licking high into the night. Branches fell; fire crackled. Janine walked towards the dying tree and stared through the wall of brilliant yellow flame.

Something like a Guy Fawkes dummy was wedged in the branches, slumped forward as it crisped and burned, its arms dangling loosely by its sides.

After a while it slipped from the tree and fell heavily, still alight, to the ground below.

PART ONE
The Shrine

1

Another day, another lay, Geoff Cochrane thought to himself as he walked with his daughter, Nancy, along Anerley Avenue to the gates of her school. He smiled thinly to himself, but said aloud, 'Ah well, another day, another textbook.'

Nancy hardly acknowledged the attempted humour. She made a sort of *huh* sound, and sank even deeper into the black mood that had possessed her since the day before. Cochrane sighed. Nancy was ten years old, a very small, very pretty girl, with bright yellow hair imperfectly brushed. Without thinking, Cochrane reached out and smoothed down the wild locks. Nancy glanced at him angrily.

'Here we are,' Cochrane said. They were by the gates to St Mary's primary. The children had already gone into the school hall from the playground. A single female figure stood on the steps, distantly watching. Nancy stared at the teacher and sighed irritably.

'Who's that?' Cochrane asked.

'Miss Bowman. She's awful.'

'Your teacher?'

'All the time. I don't like her. She's cold. We never laugh.'

Nancy turned to her father and stared up at him, and Cochrane crouched down, smiling. The girl's eyes were rimmed with dark lines. There were little lines too, above her nose, where she frowned too often. Her pale eyes seemed slightly moist, and Cochrane felt very uncomfortable.

'Sandwiches,' he said, passing her the paper parcel.

She accepted the lunch without comment, then said, 'Have you got yours?'

Cochrane patted his jacket pocket. 'Egg and cress.'

'Yuk,' said the girl, deliberately.

'You've got ham and marmalade.'

'That's better.'

'Are you warm enough?'

'Are you?'

'I'll be all right,' he said. The day was crisp, although it was still early September; it was as if, overnight, autumn had edged summer aside. His breath had frosted slightly that morning when, at six-thirty, the two of them had crawled reluctantly from their sleeping-bags (in Mrs Buxton's boarding-house) to make breakfast.

The woman on the steps blew her whistle, two short, almost reluctant sounds, a gentle reminder that assembly was already underway and the school gates would soon be locked. Cochrane raised a hand and the teacher waved back, then turned into the building.

'Off you go,' said Cochrane, straightening up. Nancy stared up at him. Her father said, 'Give 'em hell.'

Nancy said, 'Be careful.'

'I'm always careful.'

'No you're not. You're never careful. Remember –'

'Manston Manor!' he said loudly and in unison with his daughter. They both smiled. Nancy always brought up Manston Manor. Repeatedly. Endlessly. She would never let him forget.

'Well you just *do* that!' she said sternly, tapping him at hip level. 'I don't like it when you do things without me.'

'Good God, girl, you're only ten years old. You sound so like June sometimes . . .'

'Don't invoke the dead. It's dangerous.'

'Sorry.'

'Anyway, mummy wasn't firm enough with you.'

'How would you know?'

She gasped with exasperation. 'I do *remember* her, you know. I'm not thick.'

'Of course you're not. I remember her too,' he said softly. 'All the time.'

Nancy wasn't going to allow him a moment's maudlin sentiment. 'Well you've got *me* now. I just wish . . .' She stared at the red-brick school.

'What do you wish?'

'I wish I didn't have to go in there, for a start. It's so boring.' She looked up at him. 'And I wish I could come with you today.'

'I'll be fine. It's a routine lay, I'm sure of it.'

'With those farmers . . .'

'They know what the ghost looks like. They know the land.'

'I don't trust them.'

'What d'you mean?'

'That old one . . .'

'What, Ed Blanford? I can't think why.'

'He carries a shotgun.'

'Farmers often do.'

Nancy was manifestly irritated with her father. Her face was quite pale, and her features were lined with concern. 'He's clumsy. He carries the gun as if he's nervous. He'll use it.'

Cochrane shrugged. 'What does that matter? He'll shoot an apparition. If that's what cheers him up . . .'

'That's what I mean! He'll fire at the ghost. Where does the shot go? *Somewhere*. Knowing you, you'll be on the other side . . .'

'*That's* not fair,' Cochrane said loudly, put out by the insinuation.

Nancy said loudly, 'Manston Manor, daddy.'

'That was different, for heaven's sake.'

'Stupidity by any other name, *for heaven's sake*.'

'That's what June used to say.'

'I know. I remember.'

217

Abruptly, Cochrane reached out and swivelled his daughter round, propelling her firmly towards the school. 'Too damned cocky by half,' he said after her. Without looking round, Nancy shouted back, 'You just be careful.'

'I'll try,' he called after her. 'But you know me.'

'Manston Manor,' she called as she walked aggressively to the school steps. And added, 'Highbrook Field. Minster Lovell. Watch out for jumpy farmers.'

When she had gone, Cochrane smiled. He noticed that he was shaking slightly; memories of June had been brought to the fore by seeing this miniaturized version of his wife in full, angry swing. There were tears in his eyes and he quickly wiped them away. Foolish, he thought. It was five years since June had been taken from him. A long time to get over the grief. But with little Nancy as a constant reminder, somehow that last ten per cent of a shadow of sadness would never go away. This time he let the tears well up in his eyes, walking slowly back along the lane to the bus stop.

'Dammit, I'm late. No time for dawdling.'

He shrugged his heavy backpack on to his shoulders and walked more briskly, thinking ahead to his rendezvous on Pitthurst Hill.

It's no life for the girl. I ought to settle her somewhere, in a proper school. She's growing up too fast, but without a proper education . . .

Cochrane sat on the upper deck of the bus, watching as the town of Anerley was left behind and the land opened out into a hilly spread of farms, the ridges tree-capped, the fields a mix of late summer colours. He should have been thinking about the haunted wood, and how he might set about the laying of the ghostly presences that had been terrorizing the farms around. But as usual he was obsessed with feelings of guilt about the way his profession was affecting his daughter.

218

Cochrane was a ghost-hunter. He was a small, stocky man with a shock of fair hair that he combed back; it fell lank and unkempt about his shoulders. His face was weather-tanned and hard, much lined. He had lived with grief and anger for five years. He had lived rough, sleeping in tents or on floors for more weeks than he had lived in comfort. All of these things were marked upon him, and were becoming marked upon Nancy.

He should have put his daughter into a boarding-school, he knew well enough. But his work was erratically paid, and his private funds limited. So he had taken the girl with him, since June's death. He played fair with the Social Services and did his utmost to give them no real cause for concern. Nancy had attended schools all over the country, never staying longer than half a term at any one. He could work it quite easily while she was young, but soon she would be at the age for secondary education. What would happen then? She would have to settle.

And he would lose her. And in that way he would lose the ghostly presence of June, his support, his strength.

The bus pulled up close to the old water-mill, a ruined shell of a building that still straddled the shallow flow of the River Dour. Cochrane jumped down and shivered in the cold air. The land was very slightly misty, and up on the ridge that led to Pitthurst Hill a veil of grey made the trees dark and uninviting. Somewhere up there the farmers would be waiting for him, and he didn't hesitate, climbing the roadside fence and trudging up across the corn stubble of the nearest field.

Another day another lay. Or so he hoped. The farmers had offered him good money to come and put an end to their haunting. Often he was offered a pittance. Occasionally his employer would renege on payment and that always proved difficult. How could he say, 'But I got rid of your ghost' when there was no tangible evidence to back him up. The best payment came from mildly eccentric landed gentry. Cochrane's inner sight, and

219

Nancy's heightened perception, were two tools that could more often than not tell where there *was* spiritual energy about, and frequently the house was psychically 'cold'.

But, of course, Cochrane could always manufacture a ghost, and then get rid of it. His most spectacular exorcisms were sham, trickery. And they paid well. He could manage a better-than-average wage, but often found it difficult to advertise his talents, and whole seasons might pass while he waited, on the poverty line, for a letter to come.

'Dear Cochrane. My home, at Manston Manor, is infested with ghosts, most clearly from Cromwellian times, and I understand you are in the business of getting rid of them. Come at once. I shall expect you tomorrow afternoon, and can accommodate you in the house. We will discuss fees later. Sincerely, Lord Edwin Angus de Wells.'

Arrogant letters; empty houses; two weeks' luxury bed and board; a theatrical night; a fee of five hundred pounds.

It didn't always work as easily. At Manston Manor he had failed to detect the raw psychic energy of the adolescent gardener's assistant, a lad who was mentally retarded and even more deeply disturbed by one of the daughters of the house. Cochrane had almost been impaled on a garden fork, which the boy, without being aware of it, had flung twenty yards!

I'll be careful, Nancy, he murmured as he crossed the gate into a field of bright yellow rape.

Over the ridge he found the track that led between hills to the Blanford farm and on, then, to the smaller farm owned by the Kitting family. Distantly, through the dewy haze, he could see the darkly wooded ridge where the farmers would be waiting. Pitthurst Wood was broader and wider than the usual beechwood stands round about, probably because it covered an unusual and dangerous archae-ological site. No doubt Blanford would have loved to have cleared the beech and set the high ground to crop, but he wasn't allowed to by law, and so far he had respected that law.

But something in that wood had little or no respect for Blanford and the other farmers around, and when Cochrane had first arrived he had found three quite shaken families, desperate for an end to be put to the terrifying apparitions which were infesting the surrounding landscape.

They had not associated the ghosts with Pitthurst Wood. Cochrane had done that, from the name, from the ancient tin mines that the wood covered, and from plotting the sites of several apparitions, as reported to him (he had seen no ghosts himself) and finding a common centre.

It had taken him two weeks to fix upon Pitthurst Hill. Today he was going to try and find the precise source of the haunting.

He soon saw the three farmers and waved to them as he climbed slowly up the hill towards them. They were all dressed in heavy-duty jackets, with caps or woollen hats perched above their ruddy faces. Blanford had his shotgun crooked in his arm, broken at the breech. He was the only one who wore wellington boots. The other two, Ben Kitting and Jack Goddard, carried small knapsacks and staffs. A pick-axe and two shovels were propped up against a tree.

Jack Goddard, who was years younger than the other two men, waved as Cochrane approached. Blanford and Kitting merely watched him, scowling.

'Chilly day,' Cochrane called as he approached.

'Aye,' said Blanford sourly. 'Especially if you're standing doing nothing for an hour or more.'

'Sorry I'm late. Had to get my daughter to school.'

Goddard shook hands with him. He was shorter than the others and was a pleasant enough man, not from the area. Blanford's and Kitting's families had owned the farms here for generations, and the land was in their blood.

As is too often the way with country folk, they were narrow and unwelcoming, and did not think highly of Jack Goddard.

'Let's get started, shall we?' Blanford said, still grumpy.

'There's no hurry,' Cochrane replied.

'That may be so for you, Mr Cochrane. But there's some of us got animals to tend, and fertilizer to spread.'

'I said I wanted you for a day. I assumed you would make arrangements.'

'Easier said than done,' murmured Kitting, shivering inside his dark jacket. 'But we'll stay as long as it takes.'

'What shall we do, Mr Cochrane?' asked Jack Goddard. 'Spread out and beat the brush?' He laughed and Cochrane smiled too, imagining ghosts fleeing from cover in the fashion of pheasants.

'First things first.' He looked at Blanford. 'What do you intend doing with the gun, Mr Blanford?'

'Well, I'm not going to play a jig on it, Mr Cochrane.'

Ignoring the man's abrasive tone, Cochrane drew out his pipe and began to tamp tobacco into it. 'You can't shoot ghosts.'

'I feel happier with it.'

'I'd feel happier without it. If elemental energy *does* form, and startles you, I'd rather not end up as peppered steak.'

'I know how to use a gun, Mr Cochrane,' Blanford informed him acidly. 'I'm fifty-two years old and I've carried a gun since age five. I haven't yet shot a man by mistake, exceptin' a skinhead this time last year, and that hardly counts.'

Cochrane could see that he was fighting a losing battle. 'Very well. Let's go inside the aura . . .'

'The what?' Goddard asked as the four of them stepped forward to the woods.

'Inside the shadow of the wood,' Cochrane said. 'If the ghost, or ghosts, are tied to the woodland I'll begin to sense them inside the actual edge. A woodland is an entity, Mr

222

Goddard. Its root-system and canopy form a cyclic whole. The individual trees are just like separate cells.'

'Don't understand that,' Ben Kitting said gruffly. 'Wood is wood. This one's out of bounds to my children. Too many pits.'

Pitthurst Wood was not dense. The canopy formed incomplete cover, and the underbrush was a tangle of briar, bramble and browning fern. The ground was not even, but thrown up into humps and barrows, between which were deep craters, the rubble spill within them overgrown and compacted. These were the remaining signs of the once feverish activity on the summit of Pitthurst Hill because of its wealth of tin so close to the surface. Two thousand years removed or more, burrowings into the hill had formed shafts and tunnels that had long since been filled in, although Jack Goddard had said that local lore told of people occasionally vanishing through a field into a collapsed mine-hole. The tunnels were said to extend for miles around, like a network of subterranean passages, some reaching as far as Anerley. It sounded very unlikely to Cochrane. He had also established that no one in living memory had suffered the 'subsidence' fate, and surveying the surrounding land the day before he had seen no obvious depressions in the stable farmland which would testify to such a collapse.

Nevertheless, the fact that Pitthurst Hill was associated with such legends told Cochrane that the site had power.

A few yards inside the woodland edge was a clearing among the slender beech trunks, and here Cochrane shrugged off his heavy pack and began to unload it. The farmers stood around him, watching.

'What happens now?' Blanford insisted, and Cochrane felt a great surge of irritation.

He passed Blanford a pair of infra-red-sensitive goggles. To Kitting he gave a pair of goggles whose glass eyes reflected in flashing blue. 'First, I'd like you to circuit the wood. Walk around a few yards inside, wearing these, and

223

look about you. Let me know if you see anything strange at all.'

Blanford put the goggles on and laughed. 'Night glasses.'

'You'll be observing in the infra-red range of light, and there is often an echo in that frequency.'

Kitting said, 'What have I got?'

'K-lenses. Kirlian aura. You're more likely to see an echo than Mr Blanford.'

'Good God,' Kitting said as he put the goggles on. 'Why, Mr Cochrane, you're glowing.'

'Everything should be glowing slightly. Search among it for anything humanoid or unusual. Mr Kitting, you circle to the east. Mr Blanford, to the west. Don't walk too fast.'

As the two farmers stepped away from the clearing, Goddard said, 'What about me?'

'We're going to plot the magnetic flux in the area,' Cochrane said. He had unpacked the sack and the clearing was full of gadgets and gauges. Goddard picked up one of them. 'A geiger counter. Are ghosts radioactive, then?'

'I've come across a radiation source shaped into an elemental form, yes. It's rare.'

Goddard looked around at the equipment. 'Magneto-meter. Ah yes. What's this?'

'Radio scanner. Looking for unusual radio emission. This' – Cochrane placed what looked like a wristwatch on his arm – 'is skin-reactive. The same principle as a lie-detector. It flashes brightly when my skin temperature or bio-electric field changes, and that can happen if I'm subconsciously monitoring a presence.'

'Well I'm damned. You've got everything here except a bottle to put the ghost in.'

Cochrane laughed. He held up a small green box which the astonished farmer was able to see was glass painted with a thin covering. 'You're kidding!'

'Not at all,' said Cochrane. 'Some forms of psychic energy can cause electrons to shift in their atomic orbit. In

224

some simple inorganic molecules this can cause a colour change. It shows up as spots of colour.'

A few yards away Blanford tripped and swore loudly, distracting Cochrane for a moment. Then he picked up one of the magnetic-flux monitors and passed it to Goddard. The farmer held it, staring at it as if uncertain and scared.

'All right,' Cochrane said. 'Watch for the needle to do strange things, then call me.'

Goddard stared at him. 'That's what I don't understand, you know . . .'

'What's that?'

'This "psychic energy" stuff. The other night you started to say about ghosts not always being ghosts.' The farmer was shaking his head, puzzled and rather distracted.

The four of them had been talking in the kitchen of Blanford's farm. Cochrane had been about to explain the basic nature of psychic manifestation, when a new arrival had broken up the evening.

'It's very simple,' he said, as they began to walk into the heart of the small woodland. 'There are two types of *ghost*, which is to say *echo*. Passive echo, which is your traditional haunting. The echo is in the stonework, or the ground, or trapped in the aura of the house, or landscape. It triggers itself, by natural means: magnetic-flux change, high wind, underground river flooding. A natural event gives rise to the sighting of the ghost, which can appear to *anyone*. Then there's active echo. You know how some people see ghosts habitually, others don't. The active echo is a stored memory – same as before – which is triggered by an active mind. Psychic stimulus to dead psychic echo. So the ghost appears only to certain people.

'But what some people call ghosts are actually elementals . . .'

Cochrane stopped talking, staring down at the instrument in his hand. Slowly he showed it to Goddard, who nodded as if he understood the meaning of the

225

swivelling needle. The wristlet on Cochrane's arm remained 'cold'.

'Elementals . . .' Goddard prompted.

'Yes. An elemental is a fabricated ghost. It's made by an active mind, sometimes without the active mind being aware of it. Poltergeist activity is the transference of mind power, objects being thrown about; but that mind power can be shaped into human form. Sometimes it can be invested with the consciousness of the shaper incorporated into the "ghost". It's called a *watcher*, and what it sees and hears is known to the mind *creating* that ghost. If that mind is strong, the elemental can be made very destructive indeed. A psychic attacker. Several minds together – and I've only heard of this, never witnessed it – can give the elemental real human form and texture. It's called a *stock*. A man thing, solid, conscious, living and breathing. Only it has no heart, no compassion, and is mindlessly destructive.'

Goddard chuckled. 'If I hadn't known Ed Blanford for ten years or more I'd say you'd witnessed your first of these things at last.'

'Well,' Cochrane said with a smile. 'You never know.'

Much though he liked Jack Goddard, Cochrane was glad when the farmer stopped talking and took off on his own, walking slowly about the inner wood, watching for magnetic anomalies. It gave Cochrane time to think carefully about Pitthurst Wood, and about the Roman mines . . . and most particularly about the peculiar nature of the local haunting.

Keeping the farmers busy, and well away from him, Cochrane had soon mapped the site, and explored most of its craters and hillocks. He had felt no psychic interaction, and the guide on his left arm had remained coldly grey. But the readings from his magnetic flux monitors were anomalous and exciting.

226

He went back to the small clearing and crouched down, using a spare set of K-glasses to study the thin, rather fluctuating aura of the surrounding woodland.

There was certainly no doubt in his mind that Pitthurst Wood was the source of a genuine haunting. Despite his failure to detect the spiritual presence, this was no hysterical or sham invention by the crusty, pragmatic landowners. It was also, if their combined reports were accurate, a most bizarre haunting.

Blanford had suffered the most. He had repeatedly woken in the night to the sight of a ragged, terrified boy standing in his bedroom. The ghostly presence had screamed in a shrill, unhuman way, and vanished from the room. He had seen the same apparition in his farm grounds, and walking by dusk or dawn out across the fields. The ghost left positive signs of its presence – foul-smelling exudates where it had walked, impressions of its feet. This phenomenon was not unknown to Cochrane, although it roused the suspicion that the youthful apparition was either a *stock*, or no psychic manifestation at all.

Goddard, too, had seen the boy-ghost, but only once, and from a considerable distance. He had shared with Ben Kitting an experience of what they had termed 'stoneworld'. Goddard had described it best. He had been working in the yard, reshaping a ploughshare that had buckled on a piece of rock. It had been in the middle of the summer, an overcast, rather humid day. He had suddenly felt dizzy. The persistent sound of the hens, and the hammering of one of the farm-hands repairing the barn roof, had suddenly slipped away. Looking up he had found himself standing in a bleak, ice-grey landscape, between savaged pinnacles of stone and twisted, blackened thorns. The sky had been almost black, and the landscape glowing with a cold, white light. A freezing wind had been blowing, and distantly he had heard the sea. Somewhere, too, an animal had howled, like a hound, but deeper and more prolonged.

After a few seconds of shock he had started to run, and the ghostly landscape had twisted and writhed around him, sending him sprawling, clutching at the nearest thorn tree for support. And at the moment the apparition had faded he had found himself sprawled on the ground clutching at his wife's leg, shouting hysterically.

The same vision had taken him over a few weeks later, when he had been in the house, late at night. Stepping out of the back door he had been back in stoneworld, and some immense dark shape was swooping towards him from the shadowy rocks.

Kitting had described the land in almost exactly the same detail. He had glimpsed something more of the shape that had hovered among the rocks and he had called it a 'trog'. His encounter with the troglodyte had shaken him deeply. He had seen it twice more, always at night, always when he was alone, beyond the farmhouse. It had moved slowly across the dark fields, a grey, towering shape walking at an unreal speed towards the town.

It was Ben Kitting, in fact, who had been put on to Geoff Cochrane by a family friend. The three farmers were offering a fee of six hundred pounds for Cochrane's services. None of them had offered accommodation, but they had agreed to his basic living expenses. He had been here for more than two weeks now, staying at Mrs Buxton's lodging-house and spending his time between the library and the land.

'It's here,' Cochrane said. It was after midday, and he was standing in the bottom of one of the deeper depressions of the overgrown mines.

The farmers stood above him, Jack Goddard kicking around at a pile of ancient rubble.

Blanford said, 'Below the ground?'

'Below the ground.'

The farmer looked uneasily about, his grip on the stock of

228

the shotgun becoming more firm. Kitting shuffled restlessly, arms folded, face furrowed. 'How can you be sure?'

'It's my job to be sure.'

'Anyway. What is this *it* you keep talking about?'

Cochrane sighed with fatigue. 'The source of the ghost,
Mr Kitting.'

'A body, you mean.'

'Or an object. Something buried here. Probably a long
way down.'

Blanford at last placed the shotgun on the ground.
'Better get the shovels, then: get digging.'

'I hate to sound a contradictory note,' Jack Goddard
called suddenly, 'but I think what you're after is over here.'

What Goddard had found was clearly of recent design.
Turf had been removed from a wide area and meticulously
replaced. The cuts were almost completely stitched
together, but Goddard tugged at one and the fresh earth
and clear signs of digging were revealed below.

'Well, well, well,' Cochrane murmured.

'Do we dig?'

'We dig,' Cochrane agreed, and Kitting fetched the
spades.

Two feet below the surface, Goddard's blade scraped on
stone. They cleared the earth away to expose a grey slab of
rock. Cochrane crouched and traced out the pattern that
had been etched on the grey surface. He said nothing for a
moment, but when Blanford murmured, 'Like one of those
paper mazes . . .' he said quietly, 'It's a labyrinth.
Thousands of years old. You see them in the tombs of the
ancient Greeks. The maze where the Minotaur hid was like
this. It's an occult symbol that survived across millennia . . .'

'This is recent,' Goddard said.

'I know.' Cochrane rang a shovel against the stone.
'And there's space below it.'

Goddard ran his own shovel around the edge of the slab,
and together the four men heaved it upright. Dust and a

229

foul smell billowed from the gaping shaft which they thus exposed, and when the rock-covering had fallen heavily to one side they stood around the pit and stared into the darkness.

The shaft was not of recent manufacture. It was almost perfectly round, and had been driven through the bedrock. It had been blocked by rubble and earth until recently, and Cochrane could see the signs of the clearing. The shaft wall was freshly scratched. Blanford dropped a match into the gloom. It flickered and burned out about twenty feet below the surface. By dropping four matches together, Cochrane glimpsed the wide chamber which stretched out from the vertical shaft.

Here, then, was an access pit to the old workings. But none of the farmers could recall seeing any excavation on the ridge in the last few years. Blanford's farm came right up to the woodland itself. To get access to Pitthurst Hill a man, or men – with trucks – would have had to come along the dirt roadway that Cochrane had earlier followed, taking them right past the farm buildings themselves. It was impossible to believe that such activity could have passed unnoticed.

And yet someone had cleared hundreds of tons of rubble out of the mines, laid a slab of covering stone . . . and then *disposed* of the waste!

Kitting went off to fetch torches and rope. He returned within the hour, and Blanford made a firm and fast rope-ladder which he dropped into the shaft. Cochrane led the way down, holding one of the torches and slipping carefully down to the bottom of the pit. He crouched there nervously, shining his torch in all directions.

There was still much debris in the tunnels and a strong smell of decay. The walls were cold to the touch and in places quite slippery, as if moisture was oozing through. The dank surface made him shiver. The cold stone,

230

closing over his head as he stooped and began to edge along one of the passages, gave him an intensely claustrophobic feeling.

Behind him, Jack Goddard slid to the bottom of the shaft and began to follow. Cochrane heard a mighty oath as Blanford hit the ragged ground a little too hard. Kitting stayed on the surface, watching alternately through the infra-red goggles and the Kirlian lenses.

'There's always been local talk about tunnels below the ground,' Blanford said in an awed whisper. 'I never believed them . . .'

'These have been unblocked,' Cochrane said as he edged along the dark passage, throwing a beam of bright light into the gloomy distance.

'What for, I wonder?'

'We'll find out.'

They dropped down a second shaft. The smell of stone and dank grew overpowering, and Jack Goddard began to suffer from dizziness. 'I've heard that some old places have a bug, or fungus or something, that can kill you.'

Cochrane reassured him as he slid down the rope, held by the muscular Blanford. 'That's in enclosed chambers that have not been totally blocked. Places like tombs. These were mineshafts.'

They were now about forty feet below the hill, and the mine-workings opened out into tall, ragged passages, where a more ancient wall-marking could be seen – the scratches and dents of Roman pickaxes that had torn out the ore. Several galleries led off from the main shaft, but most were half-blocked where the roof had slowly crumbled over the centuries.

In the stifling stillness a sudden breeze ruffled Cochrane's long hair and made him start with shock. Instantly, on his arm, the grey dial glowed bright yellow, and the glow did not change as the moment's fright went away. Goddard frantically waved his torch about, illuminating one dark tunnel mouth after another. Above their heads Blanford peered through the darkness and called, 'What's down there?'

'More tunnels,' called Cochrane. 'Get Kitting down, if he's secured the first rope. I need him down here too.'

'Why not me?'

'You're too big.'

Minutes later the agile figure of Kitting slid into the lower vault. The man was pale and frightened. The strange breeze still blew around them, stirring dust on the floor. There was the hint of a smell that was all too familiar to Cochrane, the slightly musty odour he associated with both death and an elemental. He began to question the wisdom of exposing the three farmers to the possibility of psychic attack. They wouldn't have a clue how to cope with such a thing and would be fatally vulnerable to a stalker or some worse manifestation of refined psychic energy.

'I think you'd be wise to leave this to me,' Cochrane said. But Kitting shook his head.

'We've come this far with you, Mr Cochrane. We'll see it through.'

'It's not a ghost,' Cochrane said quietly, and the two men with him looked startled. In the yellow torchlight their features were shadowy and frightened.

'Not a ghost?'

'Something malevolent. I can smell it. I'm aware of it, although it's invisible.' He held up the glowing bracelet. 'Listen, I've had a lot of experience of these things and it's no ghost you've got down here. Go up the rope.'

Goddard hesitated for just a moment before saying, 'If that's what you advise, then that's what I'll do.'

'You too, Mr Kitting.'

But Ben Kitting shrugged. 'You've warned me. I take responsibility. But you'll never search this warren alone. I'll stay down.'

'Very well, but if you see anything, or hear anything, get back here fast and get into this circle . . .'

232

As he spoke, Cochrane was smearing a circle on the ground with water and a more pungent liquid. He marked four crosses on the outside and by each made a symbol. 'I have to tell you,' he said as he finished, 'that protection is as much in the mind of the attacked as in the circle, and this will only hold against the simplest psychic attack if you're inside it.'

'I've got faith,' said Kitting. 'The Lord is my shepherd, and my children's guardian. I have no fear of the dark.'

'If your faith *is* strong, that will help. But it would be a mistake to assume a psychic presence to be a religious manifestation. Concentrate the mind on your God, and your own mind strengthens.'

'Life itself is strengthened by belief in Christ,' Kitting averred solemnly, and Cochrane smiled. He had not thought of this abrasive farmer as a staunch Christian, and the dogma emerging from the man seemed incongruous.

They separated, then, and explored the tunnels, clambering over the loose rubble, rock and dirt that had slowly collapsed from the ceilings. In places Cochrane found cleared vaults, deep pits and small piles of bones. He began to feel disorientated and dizzy, jumping as the echo and murmur of Kittings's passage through other chambers came to him.

And then suddenly it was there, and Cochrane gasped with shocked surprise. He called urgently for Ben Kitting and guided the man to him by repeated whispers. When he saw Kitting's torchbeam flashing behind him he signalled back. Kitting arrived, grey with dirt and quite breathless.

The entrance to a vault had been blocked. The whole tunnel was closed off by a smooth wall of plaster which was hard and solid to the touch. Deeply inscribed on the wall was a symbol that Cochrane had come across once before: the ancient labyrinth, but this time with the shape of a spider superimposed upon it.

The blood drained from his face and his hands shook so

badly that the torchlight wavered dramatically. 'Oh my dear God . . .' he breathed, and Kitting said, 'What is it?'

'I don't know. Except that . . .'

'Except that what? Come on, man, you're the expert.'

Cochrane traced the spider shape, his finger trembling like a leaf. He licked his lips nervously. 'We should leave this alone . . .'

'Is this the source of the ghost?'

'Without a doubt. It's the source of a lot more.'

'Then we'll break through and destroy it. I'll go and get the axe.'

'No!' Cochrane's voice sounded hysterical and shrill in the enclosed place. 'Don't touch it. Leave well enough alone.'

'Why? Good God, man, we've not done all this to leave well enough alone. You're frightened to death. I'm not. There's a ghost in there. We hired you to destroy it. And that's what you'll do.'

'It's not a ghost. It's Arachne. Kitting, you don't understand. Your good Lord won't help you if you release what's beyond that wall.'

'What *is* beyond the wall?' Kitting asked menacingly, and Cochrane almost groaned with frustration.

'I don't *know* . . .'

'Then you're talking nonsense, Mr Cochrane.'

Kitting turned on his heel, still bent over in the cramped tunnel, and began to walk back to the lower vault. Cochrane glanced once more at the seal and the symbol and felt such cold, such bone-chilling fear, that he could hardly move. The breeze, he realized, was coming from the seal itself! A physical impossibility yes, but this was no physical breeze.

Cold sweat dripped from him. The spider symbol seemed to twitch and move a little. He had no idea what was beyond the seal. But he knew that to break the wall would be to invoke a terrible fate.

And yet, a bizarre compulsion kept him standing there.

An irrational curiosity kept his eyes fixed to the symbol, thinking about what he knew, what he had heard, the hints and fragments of the story he was building in his own mind about Arachne, about the roundelay.

What *was* beyond the wall?

'No!' he said aloud, and tried to block the sound of his inner voice urging him to explore further. 'We *mustn't* break in.'

But what *was* beyond the wall?

And as he stood, transfixed and terrified, Blanford and Kitting came edging along the passageway, sweating and grunting with effort and claustrophobia. They carried an axe and two shovels between them.

'Out of the way, Mr Cochrane,' Blanford said haughtily. 'Be ready to trap your ghost, but otherwise don't interfere.'

Cochrane edged back along the tunnel. Every ounce of sense in him told him to run, to get up to the surface as quickly as possible. And yet he stayed, watching with terrified eyes, his body drenched with cold sweat, as Blanford started to hack through the seal.

The farmer gouged out a wide hole. Dust, wind and a mournful sound, like a distant wolf crying in the night, emerged from the darkness beyond. The smell of must was stronger. Blanford shone a torch into the interior and said, 'Christ Almighty! It's full of corpses!'

He stepped back from the broken seal, shaken and horrified. He looked at Cochrane aghast. 'Bodies everywhere. We'll have to get the police.'

Kitting had taken up the axe and was smashing away to enlarge the hole. Suddenly the whole seal separated from the rock wall and collapsed inwards. Ben Kitting stepped over the rubble and shone his torch around the small chamber beyond. Cochrane, against his better judgement, edged forward and by torchlight could see the horror that lay there. He noticed too, that two other tunnels from the chamber had been sealed off, and that around the walls there was a great deal of loose rock and earth.

'What the devil have we got here?' Blanford whispered, still shaking.

'It's a shrine,' Cochrane said, and wondered where the idea came from. He stepped forward and stood up straight, looking down at the floor where the dead humans lay.

There were eight of them. They were on their backs and their hands were folded on their chests. They were all fully clothed. They had been arranged like the legs of a spider around a central body, but the body was not human. It was a gleaming jewelled shaft, about eighteen inches long and the thickness of a wrist. Its head was a hideous demonic face, horned and narrow-eyed. The precious stones were pressed into the intricate design on the gold body. It had about it the sense of immense richness, and Ben Kitting reached for it.

'Don't!' snapped Cochrane, and the farmer drew back.

'Why not? Looks precious to me. Worth a fortune . . .'

'It's a totem. It's the centre of the shrine. It mustn't be touched, not before it's been made safe.'

'A totem?' Blanford whispered.

Before Cochrane could answer, Kitting said, 'Are they all dead?'

Cochrane edged around the shrine. The furthest corpse from the entrance was a boy, in ragged, filthy clothes. Blanford said, 'That's him. That's the ghost.'

The boy's face was grey, but there was no sign of decomposition. One corpse, that of a woman, had shrivelled to a flesh-coated skeleton. One, that of a man, could be seen to be just breathing. Three men, three women and two children, one of each sex.

'Three dead, I make it. Five still alive . . . just.' Kitting was flashing his torch from body to body. The beam came to rest on the jewelled totem, and the farmer just stood and stared at the strange object. He seemed almost to have been hypnotized by the grinning, staring face of the demon.

Ed Blanford looked about nervously, flashing his torch

236

on the walls and the ceilings as if afraid that something would drop upon him. 'Look at that,' he breathed.

Cochrane glanced round to survey the patterns and symbols that had been painted in red and green on the wall. Some he recognized; there were Egyptian hieroglyphs, Greek letters, Norse runes, more of the peculiar labyrinth patterns, representations of leaves and human skulls. Others were alien to his knowledge, unfamiliar symbols with obscure powers.

He turned back to the bodies, intending to leave the shrine immediately. And as he did so, Ben Kitting reached down to pick up the totem . . .

'Don't touch it!' Cochrane screamed.

Too late.

Kitting had the object in his fingers and was lifting it from its position.

Cochrane ran for the tunnel, barging past Blanford, who yelled, winded and startled by the other man's panic. There was a sound like an implosion and a great searing blast of heat. The air was cut by a shriek of tremendous and terrifying volume and the tunnel through which Cochrane blindly staggered was illuminated by a harsh, cold light.

He glanced round. Ed Blanford was stumbling after him. Beyond the bulky farmer's body Cochrane could see the malevolent shape that was rising from where Kitting had dropped the gleaming totem.

It was grey and manlike, but its face, which Cochrane briefly glimpsed, was a hideous parody of a human face, all bulging folds of flesh, tiny gleaming eyes and long, bright teeth. As it straightened, it cracked and rustled, as if leathery wings were opening. Its shrill scream rose to its highest pitch as it struck out at Kitting. All Cochrane heard was the man's death-groan and the appalling sound of flesh being split by claws.

Cochrane reached the lower rope and began to haul himself up. Blanford stumbled from the tunnel, tears of

237

pure terror running from his eyes. 'What's happened?' called Jack Goddard from the gallery above.

'A guardian!' Cochrane grunted as he used all his strength to ascend to safety. 'Kitting released the bloody guardian . . .'

'Where is he?'

'Dead.'

'Oh God!' Goddard reached down and helped Cochrane haul himself up. Below him, Blanford puffed and blew, his face rigid with fear, his eyes bulging from his face.

'Come on, Ed!' Jack Goddard called. Below the struggling farmer the vault was illuminated by the eerie grey light. 'Come *on*!'

'My grip's going,' Blanford grunted. He twitched and jerked on the rope and tried to look down below.

'Keep looking up here!' Cochrane shouted at him, and the terrified gaze swung up again. Below Blanford a shape stepped into the light and peered up. Goddard gasped and again Blanford tried to look down.

'Haul him up,' Cochrane breathed, and they took the strain on the rope and jerked the farmer to the upper level. Cochrane could hardly bear to look down at the grinning face of Ben Kitting. Kitting reached for the end of the rope and caught it. His face had been split open to the nasal bridge and red brains glistened in the grey light. The guardian had disembowelled him and slashed his throat, and the farmer's dark coat was a bright hue of scarlet.

'It's possessed the corpse,' Cochrane said. He reached down and grabbed for Blanford and hauled the heavy farmer into safety. But the rope was held by the dead man below and there was no time to wrench it loose, or detach it from the metal pin that held it secure in the upper gallery.

'Come on!'

They ran and stumbled through the warren of tunnels. Goddard smacked his head against the rock ceiling and nearly knocked himself out. He staggered heavily, with Cochrane helping him. When they got to the rope leading

238

up to the surface and the woodland Goddard straightened up, clutching his head and smiling.

'Are you all right?' Cochrane asked.

Goddard showed the blood on his hand. 'I'm fine. I just feel a little . . .'

He stopped talking and slowly, almost theatrically, collapsed.

'Leave him,' snapped Blanford, taking a grip on the rope.

'He's out cold. You'll have to help me.'

'Leave him.'

Blanford was already panting and straining to haul himself up the rope to safety. Cochrane frantically slapped Goddard's face, trying to bring the man round, but Goddard remained dead to the world, his skin as cold as ice.

In the distance, through the tunnel, the grey light began to appear. The wind grew strong, the smell stronger. Cochrane could hear the regular, slow footfall of the body of Ben Kitting, and knew that with the guardian controlling the muscles of the corpse, Kitting was both invulnerable and deadly. Quite why the guardian had not pursued them in its own form Cochrane didn't know, except that . . . except that it meant the guardian was not as strong as it looked, and was a particular form of elemental that Cochrane had encountered before . . .

'Wake up, damn you! Goddard!'

Cochrane frantically shook and slapped the limp body of the young farmer. His ministrations had no effect at all. Goddard was out for the count. Blanford had reached the surface and there was no way that Cochrane could manage to get up the rope carrying the other man's body. There just wasn't the physical space in the shaft and there wasn't enough rope for Cochrane to tie the end round the body and haul it up physically.

Kitting's possessed corpse lurched closer. Cochrane hardly thought about the implications of the possession –

239

intuition told him that the guardian was an elemental composed of stored, and powerfully released, psychic energy; enough to kill one man, it would need the physical shape of an animal to continue to exist, and clearly Kitting's corpse was unfavourable. Nevertheless, it could easily destroy Cochrane and Blanford, and Jack Goddard too.

If it possessed Goddard it would be unthinkably strong. But as a weak spiritual essence, the simple protective circle should keep it at bay.

'I'm sorry, Jack,' Cochrane whispered as, seconds after his moment's confused thinking, he dragged Goddard's body into the circle he had drawn earlier. He folded the man's limbs so that Goddard looked like a sleeping embryo. Quickly he drew a second circle outside the first, hoping that it was wide enough to contain Goddard's waking body. On waking he would stretch, and if one inch of his flesh extended beyond the circle . . .

Then Cochrane covered the farmer's body with incense and protective chemicals. He drenched the body with holy water and scrawled further symbols at the four corners. A moment later he glanced up to see the dripping, destroyed body of Ben Kitting come into the vault and stop. The thing's mouth opened and emitted the guardian's shrill screech.

'I'm pulling the rope up!' Blanford yelled, as the scream reached his ears.

'Wait!' Cochrane shouted. He leapt for the end of the rope ladder. He felt Blanford tug it and almost lost his grip. He scrabbled and struggled and got his back arched against the wall, his knees braced across the shaft. Blanford tugged and twisted.

'Stop tugging!' Cochrane yelled.

'Too late, Cochrane. I'm not letting that thing out!'

Blanford vanished from the clear circle of light above. Cochrane could hear him grunting and straining to lift the slab of rock back across the shaft. He reacted like an animal at bay, clawing his way up the rope, breaking nails, splitting skin, banging and bruising his body on the sharp rock sides.

As Cochrane reached the entrance to the shaft and poked his head into the daylight, Blanford had just got the slab of enclosing rock into a vertical position. A moment after Cochrane scrambled free, the slab fell down, cutting the rope on its razor edge, sealing off the shrine.

Blanford was as white as a sheet. Cochrane caught his breath, looked down at his hands that were shaking like leaves in a storm, then said, 'You bastard.'

'Every man for himself,' Blanford said,

'We could have got Goddard up, if you'd helped.'

'Bugger Goddard,' Blanford said coldly. 'I'm not throwing my life away for the likes of him, kids or no kids.'

Cochrane stepped quickly across the slab of stone and kicked Blanford between the legs. The farmer screeched with pain and buckled at the knees. Cochrane kicked out again, fetching Blanford a stunning, strangling blow to the throat.

As the farmer lay gagging and gasping at his feet, Cochrane looked about him at the haunted wood.

'With a bit of luck,' he said, to no one in particular, 'the guardian won't get out for a while. And with a bit more luck, they won't know the shrine has been broken. That'll give us a little time to work out what in God's name to do next.'

He turned from Blanford and walked back towards the road, gathering up his equipment as he went.

But there was a watcher in the town of Anerley.

The guardian's cry of warning was a loud and startling echo in its mind. It looked up from where it worked and stared towards Pitthurst Hill. After a moment or two it rose from where it had been sitting and left the room. It walked for a while and found a phone. Picking up the receiver, the watcher dialled a number.

The number rang for a long time before it was answered.

'What do you want?'

'I am the watcher at Anerley. Send help. The shrine has been disturbed.'

PART TWO
The Summoning

2

As quietly as possible, the girl eased herself out of Dan Brady's uncomfortable double bed. She tugged her baggy rugby shirt over her head and stood for a moment staring down at the heavenly sleeping man. She glanced at the digital clock and saw that it was three in the morning. It was cold in the room but she had other, more pressing concerns.

Whenever she indulged in excessive alcohol, she would wake up in the early hours dehydrated and desperate for liquid; whenever she enjoyed a long bout of sex, she would wake ravenous, desperate for bread, or biscuits, or anything. The evening before, Anita Herbert had fed both of her consuming passions, despite Brady's advice that she should stick to soft drinks. Now she was suffering. Half asleep, and feeling the beginnings of a hangover in the dull ache above her eyes, she eased her way downstairs to the kitchen.

'Bless you, Mr Brady,' she said, as she found cold roast pork, a granary loaf and a jug of ice-cold grapefruit juice. She ate and drank with almost choking speed. When thirst and hunger were satisfied she drained the last of a bottle of wine, then went to the downstairs toilet.

Wide awake by now she glanced guiltily up the stairs, then crept into the lounge closing the door quietly behind her and turning on the light. This is where it had all happened, she thought to herself again; somehow, at night, the room seemed more eerie than when she had sat here during the afternoon. The horrible events that had led to Brady's family being stolen from him were closer to her, like ghosts looking over her shoulder.

Here was where it had begun for Brady. For Anita herself it had begun in a Norfolk village, when her father had died by the blade of an axe and only Brady had been able to help her. She had recovered almost completely from the tragedy now and, during the months since that brutal winter, Brady had kept in touch with her, and on occasion seen her. But this was the first time he had invited her to visit him at home.

Dan Brady's house was a big, rambling, detached property surrounded by high walls and, in places, a dense stand of trees. He had defended the building – and the grounds – against psychic attack: there was a peculiarly patterned maze immediately around the house itself; braziers of pungent herbs and chemicals smouldered all round the garden. He had buried clay and iron gargoyles, hideous objects of the supernatural, to judge by the descriptions he had given her.

Inside the house were ghost-traps, chemical defences against elementals, and all manner of symbols and seals to ward off destructive influences from either mind or otherworld. The house smelled faintly of vinegar, strongly of garlic, and occasionally of dank woodland, an aroma she could never pin down to its source.

The lounge was cold. Anita tugged the rugby shirt as far down her legs as it would reach and did up the buttons at the collar. She was a small girl, and the shirt – which belonged to a boyfriend – almost swamped her. Walking around the room she came to the bureau with its collection of framed photographs. She had seen them during the previous afternoon, but Brady had not explained who they showed. It didn't take much to guess. Anita picked up the picture of Marianna; the girl wore small-framed glasses and had two gaps in her teeth, but she was grinning with such humour that Anita almost laughed in sympathy with the long-forgotten joke.

Dominick was more solemn, but she thought him a very handsome lad. He was beginning to take after his father –

246

the same deep-set eyes, with their hard, searching stare, the same softness around the mouth, just the hint of a nervous smile.

And the photograph of Alison Brady was just gorgeous. Anita sighed quickly and put the picture down, reluctant to gaze too long at the woman who had once lived with the man upstairs; so sexy, so confident, so all-round beautiful. It made Anita irritated with herself to recognize the touch of jealousy in her own behaviour. For a second she felt as if she had been an intruder in Brady's bed, used by the man in the absence of his wife. The feeling passed. Brady and she had used each other, and there was nothing wrong with that at all.

She opened the bureau and stood there, staring at the contents, wondering whether to snoop further.

The hair on her neck pricked suddenly, and her skin reacted to a cool breeze. Slowly, she closed the bureau. Out of the corner of her eye she could see something . . .

It floated towards her . . .

The lights went out and she almost screamed with shock!

In the darkened room the figure was like a wraith of mist, an eerily glowing form that drifted towards the terrified girl. The ghost was that of a women. She was tall and dark-haired, her face drawn, almost skeletal, patches of dark shadow in the pale skin. She was quite naked. Her spectral form rippled and moved like smoke in a bottle, and she began to reach towards Anita.

'Who are you?' the girl whispered, but as she spoke the ghastly shape began to fade into darkness, dissolving into the foggy texture and drifting upwards to the ceiling.

The french doors rattled violently, shaken by a sudden wind. In the room, the curtains started to blow in a gale, flapping almost horizontally; papers swirled up from the sofa, their pages of newsprint opening out and fluttering and flapping about Anita's head like hideous paper birds. She ran about the lounge, beating at the rustling sheets,

247

stumbling against furniture which was abruptly dragged away from her by unseen hands.

'Leave me alone!' she cried out suddenly, as a low, moaning whine came from the fire, and ash and dust blew at her, stinging her eyes. Her eyes watered and she blinked, and as she glanced through the tears at the french windows, she saw the woman again, her face stretched in a terrible smile showing bright white teeth, her eyes staring, her skeletal hands reaching as she drifted towards the petrified intruder . . . Anita Herbert.

Anita turned and ran frantically towards the door. As she ran she managed to stifle her scream, but couldn't help sobbing aloud with fear.

A second before she reached the edge of the lounge, the door opened and the lights came on. She stopped, blinking both with astonishment and the sudden glare. All she felt, as she shook with cold and terror, was Brady's arm around her shoulder. All she heard was his gentle, reassuring whisper.

'It's okay. It's okay.'

'Oh God, Dan . . .'

He led her back into the room. There was a pungent smell in the air, the strong smell of an animal. Brady was wearing an old anorak over his bare flesh, and he was shivering too, his pale legs goose-pimpled and comical. But he made Anita feel so secure, as she nestled deeper into his embrace. He would be angry with her, she was sure of that, but his anger didn't matter anywhere near as much as the fact that he supported her. He was on her side. She needed that very much indeed.

'Looks to me as if you've been snooping,' he said mildly.

'I *have* been snooping,' she agreed in her best lost-little-girl voice. 'Please don't be angry.'

'I'm not angry,' he said matter-of-factly. He pushed her gently away and stood staring around the room, his hands in the pockets of the anorak. 'And don't come the little girl,' he said, almost as an afterthought.

248

'Sorry.'

'Why were you snooping?'

She shrugged. 'I was interested. I wanted to ask you so much this afternoon . . . I mean yesterday afternoon . . . but . . .' She shrugged again. 'Well, I didn't like to, really. It seemed nosy.'

He looked at her and smiled. 'I have few enough secrets in the world, Annie. My life is an open book. I'm the bait in a cage for death and I gave up all rights to privacy a long time ago. You only have to ask.'

'Thank you. And I'm still sorry.'

Dan Brady stood before her, and his presence was more reassuring than an army. He was dishevelled, his hair sticking up in odd spikes and waves. His eyes were dark-rimmed and bleary, his cheeks darkly stubbled. And yet there was an aura of power about him that was quite tangible. As she tried to move towards him, that same power pushed her back. She hesitated, arms wrapped around her body, trembling despite the voluminous night-shirt she wore. He didn't want her near for the moment, so she was unable to step close. His eyes gleamed. He looked at her, at the room, at the photographs. He was like an animal, standing in silence, scenting and sensing some prey that he knew was in the area, but couldn't yet see.

'Is it still here?' he asked.

'I don't know. I don't think so. Oh God, Dan, I was frightened. She was so *hideous*!'

Brady looked startled for a second, then frowned. 'She?'

'The woman, the ghost. Like a skeleton, grinning and reaching and . . .' She broke off, at once perturbed and angry by the sight of Dan Brady standing before her, rocking with laughter.

'What's so damned *funny*?' she shouted, indignant to the last.

He opened his anorak and drew her into the warm interior, rubbing his hands up and down her back to try to ease the chill. He still chuckled. 'What's so damned funny?' she repeated, more softly.

'The jealousy of the female sex,' he said. Then, more seriously, 'There was, and is, nothing to be afraid of. You've made the acquaintance of an old friend of mine, that's all.'

'An old friend!'

'A very old friend,' he repeated, 'And a very courageous one. Her name is Ellen. Ellen Bancroft. Come on, we'll try and bury the hatchet with her.'

What astonished Brady more than anything was that Anita Herbert had *seen* the ghost with whom he shared the house. In all the months that he had maintained his relationship with the girl, she had not once hinted, or given a sign, that she was psychic to such an advanced extent. To see a ghost was rare; Brady, despite many talents, both latent and developing, had seen his old friend only once, and that when he had first achieved a successful 'out-of-body' journey to the ceiling and back.

The ghost of the American woman communicated mostly by psychic writing, although she made dream appearances, and was an occasional blurred image in Brady's special mirror. Ellen guarded the house while he was away. She was also his link with the nearer reaches of the so-called hinterland, the otherworld which was so often referred to as the 'astral plane'.

'Let's call her back,' Brady said, as he sat down at the table with Anita. The girl was still very pale, very shaken. He pulled a pad of paper towards him, and picked up a pencil, inspecting the tip. 'This is how I chat to Ellen. It's clumsy, but effective . . .'

'But who *is* she, Dan?'

Briefly, Brady outlined Ellen Bancroft's tragic history.

Three months before the attack on Brady's own family, the same group of collectors, hideously clad in masks made

250

from animal skulls, had come to Ellen's flat in Surrey. They had tried to kill her, after taking her husband, Michael, and ten-year-old son, Justin. The memories of that night had almost destroyed her: the sight of her son being carried away by a dark figure, the sounds of the beasts who had crowded into the darkened room, the rain sweeping in through the shattered windows. She had escaped the nightmare pursued by something invisible, a stalker, the product of an evil mind.

For six months she had hidden, terrified, in a flat in London. Three months after Brady's family had been stolen, to suit the necromantic ends of the group he had come to know as Arachne, Ellen Bancroft had found him, and joined forces with him. A mutual friend had been the go-between.

Together they had defended the house with circles of iron and clay, talismans, mazes and chemical barriers to the passage of elemental psychic life-forms. Brooks Corner, the name of the house, was a fortress. Men could come and go, but psychic attack was easily repulsed.

In defending the house, Ellen Bancroft had died. She had been incautious in her excitement at actually *trapping* one of Arachne's spirit forces in this very lounge. The creature's death-throes had killed her. But Ellen had decided to remain around the house, helping Brady . . . and hoping that, as he searched for his own family, he would come across Michael and Justin, and release them to normality. Sadness, yes; but a life that could be started over, free of Arachne. Free of the occult.

'Why did she try and frighten me like that?' Anita asked.

Brady smiled. 'We'll find out.' *A jealous ghost*, he was thinking. *I could write a paper on the subject.*

All tiredness had gone from Brady. It was a trick he had learned over the long, hard months: to snatch sleep when he could, always keeping a sort of 'psychic-eye' open, to emerge from sleep in an instant and be ready to fight or flee. Metabolically, he was changing fast. God alone knew what damage he was doing to his body. He seemed to have almost total control over his adrenalin surge now, and could control his heart-rate with ease. He could slip from his body without difficulty, although he could not travel far from the flesh matrix. He could play tricks with his own spirit-stuff . . .

His hand, resting on the blank paper pad, began to twitch. The tip of the pencil made random marks for a few seconds, then zig-zagged wildly across the sheet.

'Psychic art?' Anita asked, a twinkle in her eyes.

Brady was slightly puzzled. The first contact was usually a long stream of letters forming his name: *Dandandandan*, He had never experienced such violence before.

The hair on his neck prickled. Something was wrong.

Anita continued to watch expectantly.

Then his fingers moved and the pencil wrote his name. He smiled, then frowned. It *wasn't* his name. It was the word *damn*. Without a break his hand was guided to write the word *you*.

Damn you.

Then it all poured out, a continuous scrawl about the page, that made Anita's eyes pop, and Brady's arm ache:

DamnyoudamndamnDAMNyouyouBradyDAMNherher herridridOUTOUT . . .

Followed by a streak of anger that broke the pencil point and gouged a shallow furrow in the wooden table surface. Brady's arm felt bruised. The room seemed very cold.

'Ellen,' he said aloud, placing a new pencil on a new page of the pad. 'What's the matter with you? Why are you angry?'

'It's me,' Anita Herbert whispered, horrified. 'You're right. She's jealous. She's terribly jealous of me . . .'

'It's more than that . . .' he said quietly. 'She's angry and she's taking it out on you. I can see that. But *why* is she angry?'

Now that he thought about it, Ellen had been very quiet

for several weeks. He had been conscious of her presence for some days, without noticing the usual signs of her activity. It was not unusual, certainly, for Ellen to go into decline. She was caught midway between *terra-firma* and the otherworld, and she had often complained of feeling cold, and of the need to move on soon. It was – in its way – a form of pain to be caught in the house, even though she had chosen the house as a prison. She could vaguely glimpse the otherworld, and could sense it more clearly when Brady broke the defences around the building. Something 'beyond' was drawing her closer, dragging her slowly from the fabric of the stone towards the wide, bright place that was the hinterland, the first plane of the otherworld.

His hand remained motionless on the table. His skin temperature dropped even lower. Which meant Ellen was close by. He noticed that Anita's breath was frosting slightly. The girl watched him anxiously.

'Tell her I'll go,' she said. 'I don't mind. I don't want to upset her.'

Brady's hand moved. Although the words were all run together, he could make out the message clearly enough:

Sad. Sad. Sad. So cold. Oh Dan. Oh cold Dan. Sorry. Sorry. Lost so lost so cold. Love him. Loved him. Too late too late. Oh Dan oh Dan oh Dan.

'Ellen, what is it? Communicate to me, Ellen. I don't understand what you're saying. What's too late? What is too late? Ellen! Don't go!'

But she had gone. He felt it with senses that he could not identify. It was a gut feeling that told him she had drawn back from his mind, from his hand. His skin warmed slightly.

'What's happened?' Anita asked.

'She doesn't want to talk. She's gone back into the stone. Something's happened. She's distressed . . .'

'Look!'

Brady turned, following the direction of Anita's

253

suddenly frightened gaze. In the middle of the bright room a shadowy, human shape rippled and blurred, a tall figure, female. Brady could hardly make out any details of the body, but he could see long hair, broad shoulders, an overall slimness.

Suddenly the bulbs in the lounge lights shattered explosively, plunging the room again into darkness. Glass tinkled on the parquet flooring around the carpet. A sudden wind blew through the chimney and the edges of door and windows. The curtains billowed, the furniture shifted, the carpet rippled as if animals crawled below it. The haunting activity died away slowly then, and Brady rose to his feet and reached towards the bureau for his small flashlight.

He hesitated, listening.

'Can you hear that?' he asked Anita.

'Yes. Yes, I can.'

Somewhere in the room, and yet nowhere in the room, a woman was crying softly, a bitter sound, anguish and anger combined.

3

At the gates to the school, Geoff Cochrane swung his daughter up onto the wall so that she was standing at his height. He held her against the green railings.

'Let's go through it once more –'

'We've been through it a *hundred times*!' Nancy protested.

Almost angrily, Cochrane shook her. She was as pale as him, her eyes narrowed with anxiety. In the playground a few children played tag. Most of the school would arrive in about twenty minutes. They were very early, and the restless night they'd spent did not help humours.

'You don't leave the school premises until this evening. You stay with other kids all day, every minute that you're not in the classroom.'

'They'll run away,' Nancy said sullenly. 'I told you. They don't like me.'

'Then stay *close* to a group. A group who don't know you. Just follow them about and sit down where they sit down, and read a book or something. What I don't want you doing is wandering off, sulkily, into some remote corner.'

'I shan't. I've promised you that.'

'And no sneaking out to the sweetshop.'

'I've got no money,' she retorted angrily.

'When school finishes, go straight to Mrs Buxton's. Sit in her lounge and watch TV. Wait for me. Do not come looking for me. Do not take a walk . . .'

'Do not pass GO or collect two hundred pounds.'

'I'm *serious*, Nancy.'

'I *know*. You've been serious for hours. I'm not stupid! You only have to tell me once!'

Remorselessly, Cochrane nagged at his daughter. 'I don't even want you to go into her garden. You can stay in our room, or in the lounge. I'll fetch you when I can.'

A sudden silence, the steady exchange of irritated stares. Then a softening, and brief smiles. Cochrane hugged his daughter, then helped her down from the wall.

She sighed, almost in exasperation, staring up at her father. 'I knew you'd muck it up.'

'Nothing was mucked up. We found more than we expected.'

'You bit off more than you could chew.'

'I didn't even nibble. I ran like hell.'

She continued to watch him, her lips pursed, her frown making her look older than she was. And then she said, suddenly, almost accusingly, 'You've found *them* again, haven't you? It's them.'

Cochrane dropped to a crouch, his stomach suddenly churning.

'What makes you say that?'

'You. Your face. Your everything. I've seen you frightened, daddy. But I've only see you terrified once before.'

He felt his eyes sting with tears. He was utterly confused. The girl was a child, and yet she was so aware. Every day it grew more difficult to judge what sort of a role she should play, and how he should treat her. He drew her to him and hugged her again, whispering. 'Yes, darling. It's them again. And that's why I'm so anxious for your safety.'

'Tell me about it,' she said.

'I need to get my thoughts in order. Tonight we'll talk. Tonight we're moving to one of the farmhouses. We'll talk there. Everything. But for today, just go and get wise.'

'Okay,' she said, touching one cold finger to the tip of his nose. Then, without a smile, without any warmth at all, she turned on her heel and walked stiffly into the playground, her lunch-box clasped firmly in her right hand.

Cochrane made his way straight to Pitthurst Hill. He carried a heavy backpack, the main load of which was a pick-axe. By the time he reached the deserted wood, his shoulders were aching from the effort of carrying his equipment.

He felt nervous as he stood alone in the silent beechwood. There was no sound of traffic, or of voices, and his imagination began to play tricks with him; each rustle of wind on leaf was a footfall that startled him; each cloud shadow was Kitting's corpse, lurching horribly towards him.

His heart beating rapidly, Cochrane shrugged off first his fears and then his pack. He stood by the exposed stone slab, then walked around it, wondering whether he dared raise the lid to expose the tunnels below.

Behind him the breech of a shotgun was loudly slammed shut. Cochrane straightened up and slowly turned round, not really knowing how Blanford would be feeling today. The red-faced farmer stood there in his long, heavy anorak, smiling thinly from under his green bush-hat.

'I ought to blow your frigging brains out, Cochrane,' he said in a low growl.

Cochrane only rose slightly to the bait. 'If I'd known where you wear yours, I wouldn't have kicked you,' he said. Blanford's smile vanished abruptly. The young man standing with him sniggered.

'What's so damned funny?' Blanford snapped, and the youth shrugged. This was Blanford's eldest son, a sallow-faced adolescent, who carried himself with what Cochrane could only describe as social indifference. He slouched, looked sullen, shrugged a lot. His hair was a flop of blond over the right side of his face. He wore a single earring.

'Good morning, Derek,' Cochrane said, and the youth nodded.

Blanford walked up to Cochrane and let the barrel of his gun prod the ghost-hunter in the stomach. Cochrane stood his ground, staring at the farmer's livid face, watching the turmoil of anger and confusion that registered in the other man's eyes.

'I don't like guns, Blanford,' he said. 'Put it down.'

Blanford nudged the shotgun, almost toppling Cochrane. 'For your information, Mr Ghost-hunter, the next time you try a trick like yesterday it'll be the last thing you do. Are you listening to me?'

'I'm listening,' Cochrane said, as he was again violently prodded backwards by the loaded gun.

'I swear by my maker, Cochrane, that I'll answer to the law for your death. No man does twice to me what you did. If it weren't for the fact –'

'You've made your point, Blanford,' Cochrane snapped, and quickly moved the barrel of the gun from his stomach. 'Derek, we're going to need your help.'

'I ain't going down,' the boy said, taking a step backwards in sudden alarm.

'To lift the stone,' Cochrane replied.

'You must be out of your mind!' Blanford said loudly, his own irritation suddenly forgotten. He stared at Cochrane as if he thought the ghost-hunter was mad. 'Lift up the bloody stone again! And let out that . . . that *thing*?'

'Jack Goddard's down there. Remember?'

'Goddard's dead. Keep the place sealed.'

'I'm tired of you arguing, Blanford. Just do as I say for the moment, will you? Derek, come and help with the slab. Blanford, you stand five feet back and watch as we lift it; and if anything, *anything* moves, you just shout like hell. But don't go firing that bloody gun!'

Blanford blinked twice, glanced at his son, then stepped back, dropping to a crouch on the far side of the sealing-stone.

Cochrane dug the blade of the pick-axe under the stone's edge and levered it for a moment until the slab moved. He hesitated, glancing at the youth, 'Ready?'

'Yeah. Ready.'

And then looking at the crouching farmer. 'Here goes . . .'

The two of them hauled with all their strength and the stone shifted. They opened a gap of six inches, and Blanford strained to stare into the darkness. Another foot and Blanford stood up, peering at the exposed space.

'Some dust . . . no movement.'

'Good,' said Cochrane. The stone slab shifted to the vertical. 'Hold it there,' Cochrane said to Derek Blanford, but then looked at the farmer and changed his mind. 'Let it fall.'

Using his torch, he peered down the shaft, his heart racing with anticipation. Without emotion, Blanford said, 'There you are. It's taken him. Killed him.'

'We don't know that just yet,' Cochrane said tiredly. But he had to face the fact of his disappointment. There was no sign, below, of Jack Goddard. Only the coil of rope lying across the barely visible circle which Cochrane had inscribed the day before.

'Well, that's that,' Blanford said. 'Seal it off and have done with it.'

'Not yet,' said Cochrane. 'I've got to erase that circle.'

He tied a new length of rope to the nearest tree and tossed the free end down the shaft. Blanford was almost beside himself with disapproval. 'You're never going down! You're crazy. You're a crazy man, Cochrane. You'll bring that damned corpse out into the farmland!'

'Listen, Blanford,' Cochrane almost shouted. 'I've got enough problems of my own. All I need you to do is . . . do what I say. Watch when I say watch, pull when I say pull, and run when I say run.'

'But that thing . . .' the farmer stuttered, his normally ruddy face quite pale. His son stood above the pit, peering

259

down, as if unbothered by the thought of the nightmare below.

'That *thing* is just a guardian,' Cochrane explained patiently. 'It had – and certainly still *has* – power, yes. But it was just a simple elemental. It was a watchdog. Think of it as a sort of spirit machine, programmed to kill, to possess, and to drive intruders away. I don't imagine it could actually *see* Goddard inside the circle. It probably came after us until we closed the shaft, and then stopped. Goddard probably crawled down one of the passages and is still down there. With a bit of luck he's still alive . . .'

'Then call to him,' Blanford said. 'It's too risky going down.'

'I'm going to erase that circle. The guardian was bad enough, but let me tell you, Mr Blanford, you've seen nothing yet. When we broke that shrine we did something very foolish. People will be coming here to see what happened. I do not want to meet those people. If they see a protective circle on the access tunnel to their shrine they'll know that I'm here, a man of talent, a man who threatens them. They'll come looking for me. That circle is like a fingerprint, and I'm going to smudge it out as best I can. They won't be *looking* for a circle, so perhaps they won't see it. Now, enough talk. If you hear me shout 'HAUL', you haul me up like your life depends upon it. Because it very well might . . . Is that clear?'

Blanford nodded his head slowly in astonishment, then said, 'Perfectly clear.'

'Good. Don't forget.'

As Cochrane swung himself on to the rope he smiled. He had pepped up his nerve with his outburst to Blandford, gaining courage to drop back into the realm of Arachne.

Cochrane slid slowly down the rope, shining the torch down, listening constantly. He almost slipped off the rope as he squeezed his body round to peer into the chamber before actually entering it. But the area, with its three tunnels, was deserted. Cochrane touched the ground, shone the torch into each of the three maws, then back at the circle . . .

He jumped out of his skin, and returned the beam of light to the last passageway.

'Oh God . . .'

There was a body, curled up against the wall, about twenty paces along from the chamber. It was difficult to make out the man's identity, but after a moment Cochrane could see the split skull, and recognized the clothing. It was Kitting. The spirit of the guardian had abandoned the feeble flesh.

The presence, so close, of the farmer's savaged body made Cochrane increasingly jumpy. As he smudged out the circle he continually flashed his torch around, terrified that something would creep up behind him. He could feel the same eerie breeze on his face.

Quickly, he scattered dust over the floor of the chamber, then sprinkled an odourless ash, which would mask the slight pungence of the herbs he had incorporated into the protective wall. That would have to do. As he had said to Blanford, when the visitors came to inspect the damage they would not be looking for such a circle, and might well miss the traces.

He didn't even know when they would come, but he felt it would be soon. They would come and go as invisibly and as discreetly as when they had constructed the shrine itself. Three farmers had failed to notice them, though the work must have taken days.

When he had finished with the circle, Cochrane gathered up the rope and wound it round his shoulders. Blanford tugged on the rope that connected him to the surface, and Cochrane peered up the shaft at the small circle of daylight above. As he expected, Blanford's message was simply, 'Hurry up.'

Going back to the passageway where Kitting's body was slumped, Cochrane called softly for Jack Goddard. His

261

voice seemed to echo into the distance, then whisper to him from the other tunnels. He called more loudly. Dust fell from above, startling him. He flashed the torch about, terrified that the grey, leathery form of the elemental would come stalking rapidly out of the darkness, but the passages were empty and silent.

Where could Goddard have gone? The possibilities were hardly endless . . . He might have regained consciousness, kept calm, and crawled away into the tunnels, looking for the source of the uncanny breeze that blew in the subterranean realm. He might have come to and gone quite berserk with panic, with claustrophobia, and in a state of complete madness gone walking blindly through the stygian maze. Then again, the guardian might have taken him back to the shrine, a healthy, living body with which it would escape the tunnels to stalk those who had disturbed the hallowed pláce.

The remotest possibly of all was that Goddard, searching in the darkness, had found a way out; that they would return to the farm and find him, angry, but understanding; and his wife Kathy would have snapped out of the state of shock caused by the news about her husband's loss . . .

'Pull me up,' Cochrane called, and felt his body jerked violently from the ground. As he swung and bumped his way upwards he found himself thinking with increasing sympathy about Kathy Goddard, and the terrible evening that he and Blanford had gone through after re-sealing the shrine . . .

Cochrane had gone first to Kitting's farm, practically dragging Blanford to begin with, as the farmer (not surprisingly) had only one thing on his mind: blowing Cochrane's brains out. But the ghost-hunter had known well that Blanford's presence at the farm was essential. Keeping the shotgun well out of the farmer's reach, he had led the way to the small cluster of ramshackle buildings and outhouses that was the Kitting farmstead.

Dorothy Kitting had died ten years before. Ben lived with his eldest son, John, and John's family. They ran the farm together, but relations between father and son were strained not quite to the point of open hostility, but not far from it.

When Cochrane entered the kitchen, Blanford following reluctantly behind, the family had been eating. Mary Kitting greeted them at the door, but John remained seated, and continued to eat, making it very difficult for Cochrane to initiate the difficult subject.

'Could we talk for a minute, Mr Kitting?'

The younger man looked up. 'I'm eatin' me supper. This is supper. It's suppertime.' He waved a hand at the broth and bread on the table. Next to him his two children spooned soup into their mouths, ignoring the visitors totally.

'It's important,' Cochrane said, his voice shaking, and Blanford said, 'Very important, John.'

'Bloody well wait, then. In the front room. When I've finished me supper I'll come through.'

And with that he went back to his dish, and turned to his son, making a quiet comment that induced laughter in the lad.

Like father like son, Cochrane thought, as he went through into the dingy sitting-room. It smelled of polish and furniture. It was obviously rarely used.

'What's all this about?' John Kitting asked as he joined them, minutes later. 'Where's Ben?'

'Your father's dead,' Cochrane said, almost coldly. 'An accident. I'm terribly sorry to have to tell you this, but he fell. In the tin mines. Blanford and I came straight here to tell you. We're both very shaken up too . . .'

While he was speaking John Kitting stared at him in disbelief. 'Ben dead?' he said quietly, looking at Blanford for affirmation.

263

'I'm sorry, John. As this man says, it was an accident.'

'What the hell was he doing up at the mines?'

'He was helping me,' Cochrane said. 'We were looking for the ghost that's been –'

'That bloody haunting!' John Kitting shouted, interrupting Cochrane. 'I knew it! I knew it'd end up bad for the man.' He stepped towards Cochrane, his face red, his eyes wild. 'You're the bloody expert, aren't you? I know you, now . . .'

'I'm the ghost-hunter,' Cochrane said carefully. Kitting took him by the shirt-front and lifted him off his heels.

'My father was a careful man. He wouldn't have fallen down a shaft. You're not telling me the truth.' As he held Cochrane in this painful and awkward position he turned to look at Blanford. 'What happened, Ed?'

Cochrane said, 'It couldn't be –'

'Shut up!' Kitting roared, smashing Cochrane back against the marble fireplace. Cochrane thought his back was broken. He reached a hand up to try and ease Kitting's grip on his shirt and collar. He began to feel strangled. As his fingers touched Kitting's hand the young man pushed him so hard against the jutting marble ledge that his lungs felt winded, and he went weak.

'I asked you a question, Ed.'

Blanford was watching Cochrane peculiarly. Part of him, no doubt, was enjoying the spectacle of the ghost-hunter being put into the position of the inferior. Blanford wanted revenge. But it wasn't the time for revenge, now. There was innocent tragedy to come through. There was responsibility.

'Let the man go, John,' Blanford said, and Kitting released his grip, staring hard and cold at Cochrane.

'What happened, Ed?' Kitting asked again, and Blanford shrugged.

'We were down the old mines. Someone has cleared them out, made passages, chambers, things like that. That's where the ghost came from . . .'

264

'You all saw the ghost. I never saw the ghost. Ghosts are story stuff.' He still stared at Cochrane.

Blanford said, 'There was a ghost, all right. It killed Ben.'

'How can a ghost kill a man? Ghosts are . . . nothing. Flimsy. Cloudlike. How can a ghost kill a man, Ed?'

'It ripped him open,' Blanford said after a moment, and Cochrane saw the shock register in Kitting's mind as a sudden widening of the pupils and paling of the face. Kitting began to look like a hunted animal. His breath grew heavy and loud. He came closer to Cochrane, and there was a glow in his eyes that was perhaps madness, but more likely murder.

'Animals rip animals open, Ed. Ghosts don't do that. What are you telling me?'

'I don't understand it, John. I wish to God I did. Ask him. Ask Cochrane.'

There was a moment's pause. Kitting's breathing was getting louder with every second; his eyes were reddening. Tears were coming. Grief would save the moment.

Cochrane said gently, 'I warned him there was danger. He didn't listen.'

'It's true, John,' Blanford said.

'Just like Ben,' John Kitting said bitterly. 'Always was an awkward fucker. Never listened . . .'

He turned from Cochrane and walked to the musty sofa, sitting down on its arm. Seconds later he was crying, his back to the two men, his head dropped forward on his chest. He made no sound. He just shook.

When he had recovered his composure he went to a darkly varnished cupboard, unlocked the door and drew out a cracked decanter of a tawny-coloured spirit which Cochrane took to be brandy. He swigged from the decanter, but didn't offer it to his guests.

Without looking round, he said, 'What happens now? We contact the police, I suppose?'

Cochrane glanced anxiously at Blanford, then addressed Kitting: 'I want to ask you not to do that. Not yet.'

265

Blanford said, 'I'll arrange for a couple of men to come over and help, John.'

Kitting turned round again, puzzled but no longer angry, and his grief faded. He watched Cochrane suspiciously. 'Where's Ben's body?'

'Still down the shaft.'

'You mean you left it there?' Anger began to surface again.

'We had to,' Cochrane said. 'There were only the two of us. And Ed, here, was hurt as well. We'll be able to fetch him up tomorrow, I promise you.'

'I'll keep you to that promise, ghost-hunter,' Kitting said, almost in a snarl. Then: 'Why no police? You been breaking the law?'

Blanford stepped in quickly. 'John, the fact is, Jack Goddard's still trapped in the mines. Probably alive. He came down with us after the ghost and got lost . . .'

Kitting shrugged. 'We can get a search party . . .'

'It's not that easy, Mr Kitting,' Cochrane cut in. 'The mines are dangerous. They *are* haunted. What happened to your father could happen again. That's why I would request you *not* to contact the police just yet. And why I'd like you to get your children away from here.'

'My kids? Why?'

'Because of what we found in the mine . . . If the ghost escapes, they could be in danger. Not just them, of course. Everyone. I'd rather have children out of harm's way while I try to seal up the mines forever. Could you manage that for me? Is there somewhere for them to go?'

Kitting thought hard for a moment, then slowly nodded. 'I suppose so. Mary's sister won't mind.'

'Good,' said Cochrane.

The first hurdle was over.

The meeting with Kathy Goddard was shorter, but far more dramatic. She saw Cochrane and Ed Blanford

266

approaching the back door, through the kitchen garden, and by the time the two men were ready to knock she was standing, composed and ashen-faced, behind one of the pine chairs. Her two sons, both in the their early teens, were reluctantly leaving the kitchen on their mother's instruction.

'Where's Jack?' she asked in a shaking voice, her eyes flickering from one man to the other. A half-smile touched her lips, and curls of greying brown hair fell over her eyes. She swept them back. She looked older than Jack Goddard; she was a very handsome woman, in a refined, rather slender way.

Cochrane told her what had happened. He told her gently, without reference to Ben Kitting's awful mutilation, but he had to tell her that Kitting was dead. And at that moment she started to scream.

Ed Blanford went round to her and caught her just as she slumped backwards in a dead faint, the scream dying on her lips. The two boys burst into the kitchen and stood there, helpless, almost in tears themselves.

When she recovered consciousness she was in a state of shock, alternately crying loudly, then plunging into a melancholy silence. Cochrane had never encountered this condition before. He had assumed farm people to be sturdy, pragmatic and level-headed. He now faced a combination of grief and panic that was totally incapacitating the woman.

Kathy Goddard clearly needed supervision and care. Blanford helped her to her own car. The two boys brought blankets, clothes and school books. They drove slowly to Blanford's farmhouse, where Susan Blanford would be able to sit with the distraught woman.

A long and restless night had begun.

Cochrane stood among the trees on Pitthurst Hill and surveyed the rolling farmland, with its tight knots of trees and little clusters of dark farm-buildings. The terrain was peaceful. It had an undisturbed feel to it, even though there was hardly a square foot that had not been ploughed and planted for a thousand years. The bulky figure of Ed Blanford was a plodding silhouette, making its way slowly up a dirt-track and over a hill. His skinny son ambled along behind him. Soon they had vanished from sight.

Blanford's anger with the ghost-hunter had abated considerably, but the relationship between the two men was brittle and edgy. Cochrane was uncertain exactly how much support he might command from Blanford in a crisis. He had a suspicion that some residual resentment remained in the crusty old farmer, ready to transform into bitterness at the slightest prompting.

And that damned shotgun!

He put such concerns from his mind, walked twice around the considerable expanse of the wooded knoll, then came back to the sealing-stone, where he sat down.

Where could Goddard be? They would have to go back down. And he would have to lead them, protecting them as much as possible against the ferocity of the spirit guardian. It was only fair to Goddard that they should try to find him, but who knew how far the tunnels went? If the man was alive and *compos mentis* he might already have walked for miles, only to collapse of asphyxiation.

How much air was there in the mines? The shrine, he realized now he thought about it, had been well aerated. It had been cool and fresh, despite the smell of the human offerings.

Perhaps there were inlets from the upper world to the lower all over the landscape. In which case, Goddard had a chance of survival and escape.

Always assuming he was not, now, carrying a passenger . . .

Cochrane remained where he was for some hours, listening and watching for either ghosts or men.

How long would it take Arachne to come, he wondered?

How long before he would have to face them again?

Late in the afternoon, just as Cochrane was thinking of returning to the town, the figure of a man appeared on the far horizon, and stood there. There was no doubt at all in Cochrane's mind that the new arrival was watching Pitthurst Hill.

4

Dan Brady remained in the darkened lounge, wrapped in a blanket, for the rest of the night. The sound of Ellen's grief, the distant, ghostly sobbing, died away after an hour or so and Brady was able to sleep. He had hoped to be able to sleep until he woke naturally, but the disturbances of the night were to continue.

At five-thirty that morning the phone rang.

He stumbled blearily across the lounge and snatched the receiver from its cradle. Outside, the dawn was grey and misty, looking uninvitingly chilly.

'Sorry to wake you,' came the voice. 'It's Sutherland . . .'

'Morning,' Brady mumbled through a mouth that felt dry and sharp. 'How can I help?'

'There's been another attack. I'd like you here as soon as possible. Can you manage that?'

Brady rapidly woke up to full alertness, rubbing his eyes, straightening, letting the blanket fall from his shoulders.

'Are you sure it's Arachne?'

'All the signs of it being so, Mr Brady,' said the other man 'But this attack is unusual.'

Minutes later Brady was in his car and driving smoothly through his gates and out onto the road west. He had left Anita Herbert sleeping soundly in his bed. He hadn't bothered to shave or wash, and he brushed his teeth as he drove along. The sudden excitement he felt was quite irrational, a combination of anticipation and terror and anxiety at what he would see: the remnants of a family after a brutal attack by the followers of the evil and violent movement which he called Arachne.

The man who had called him was Andrew Sutherland, a police superintendent who had investigated the attack on Brady's family and pledged support to Brady, in return for Brady's own co-operation in finding the abductors . . . and murderers.

Sutherland met him at the gate to a small detached cottage, fifteen miles from Brady's home. The policeman was tall and ruddy-faced, a large-built man dressed in a long black raincoat. His grey hair was tousled and unkempt, and he looked very tired.

An ambulance and half a dozen police cars were parked on the roadside by the house, and as Brady walked with Sutherland towards the open front door of the cottage, he could see over twenty uniformed men walking slowly about the grounds, examining every inch of garden, vegetable patch and lawn. It was a chilly morning, and the remains of the mist hung heavy and damp about them.

'Arachne for sure?' Brady asked.

Sutherland nodded. 'Without doubt, I'd say. It could be a copy-cat attack, but we've kept the details of these abductions out of the papers. The family is called Turner. The target seems to have been the seventeen-year-old daughter, and perhaps the wife. Daughter Christine. Wife called Beth. There are rope marks on Norman Turner's throat, which suggests he was to be killed and left . . .'

At the door, Brady stopped, frowning. 'I'm beginning to understand,' he said. 'They're all still here.'

'Precisely. That's why I thought you should come out here. For some reason the attackers didn't go through with it. They abandoned the abduction and left suddenly. They set fire to the lounge, but there was a sprinkler system that doused the flames. Turner called us out at four this morning.'

'What time was the attack?'

'This is difficult to know. Some hours before. Turner is

holding a lot back. He says "last evening". I don't know why he waited so long to call us. But he isn't talking. It's probably shock, but with your shared experience perhaps you can get through to him . . .'

'I'll try.'

The lounge of the cottage was long and brightly decorated, although now it was streaked with lines and patches of charring. The carpet was burned, and the sofa was totally blackened and covered by a polythene sheet. A policeman was sitting at the table, writing a report. Two policewomen were standing outside sipping coffee. The whole house had that still, strained air of a place that has been invaded and is somehow open to the elements.

'The two women have been sedated,' Sutherland said, as he ushered Brady into the lounge. 'That's Norman Turner.'

Brady stared for a moment at the tall, dishevelled man who stood by the far window, staring out into the new day. He was wearing jeans and a heavy Shetland jumper. His hands were in his pockets, and he stooped slightly. Even from across the lounge Brady could see that the man was trembling.

Memories came back to Brady so powerfully and so fast that for a moment his knees went weak, his head spinning.

The lounge was his lounge; the place was bright with paperchains and Christmas lights. The snow was a brightness in the night, piled on window-ledge and against the french windows. The fire was a cheery crackle, making the winter night seem warm and cosy. He was on the ladder by the decorative tree. Dominick was a sulky figure, curled up by the fire, Alison was sitting, peeling chestnuts. Marianna . . . Where was Marianna?

'Daddy . . . Daddy, I'm cold . . .
She was outside the french windows, standing in the snow, all wrapped up against the cold, and looking frightened behind her funny little spectacles.

272

'Daddy . . .'

'MARIANNA! OH GOD NO!'

He screamed and jumped from the ladder, running towards his daughter. The windows imploded. The lounge plunged into darkness, glass raining down around him. Marianna was thrown at him, screaming. The wind roared in from outside. Above the howling of that supernatural gale, he heard the terrified shrieking of his family. Alison, Marianna, Dominick, carried from him, stolen, taken into the winter land outside . . .

In the blackness, shapes moved about. Dark men in dark robes, their faces like hideous animals, a leering goat, the dull features of a cow, the grinning obscenity of a pig . . .

'He's still alive,' the pig had said.

'Then kill him. Bring the fetch to kill him.'

He had been lifted by invisible hands. Invisible fingers, like thick rods of steel, had crushed the life from him.

Almost . . .

The haunting terror of his own near-death and the foul abuse of his precious family faded away. Norman Turner was looking at him from across the room, frowning slightly. Brady tried to smile, but he couldn't. He glanced slowly around the lounge noting the certain signs that the visitors to this house had been the group he himself was pursuing.

Two patterned candles lay on the floor, each circled with police markers. The colouring was black, the patterning gold. The walls of the room were marked with scratches made by a knife. Brady could see the ill-formed shape of a labyrinth and the half-formed symbols that almost certainly denoted an entity of power. Although the room smelled of charring, there was just the hint of something more pungent, a herb, probably smeared somewhere in the room as a later attractant for an elemental – an elemental that would arrive invisibly, to guard the premises against snoopers.

273

But the real evidence that this was the work of Arachne lay with Norman Turner, and Brady walked over to him slowly.

'My name's Dan Brady.'

Turner stared at him blankly for a moment; he was still visibly shaking. 'Scotland Yard?' he asked abruptly, and Brady frowned.

'I'm nothing to do with the police . . .'

'Then why're you here? Who let you in?'

'I was asked to come. To talk to you about what happened.'

Turner scowled. His eyes were black-rimmed; he looked drawn and half-dead, a good-looking man wrecked by terror. 'I've told everything I know. There's nothing more to tell.'

'Tell me.'

Turner sighed irritably and walked back to the wide window, where he leaned on the sill and stared out into the grey day.

'A gang of kids burst in on us. Tried to . . . muck around with my wife and daughter. They beat me up, and set light to the place. Then they left. God knows what they wanted. God knows why they chose us. Bastards. If I ever . . .'

He looked round at Brady. The fact that he was lying was all too transparent. Brady asked, 'When did this happen?'

'Last night. We were watching TV.'

'And they came bursting in, smashed all the lights and set about you and your family?'

'That's right.'

'What about the candles?'

Turner shrugged. 'I think they were mucking about with, you know . . . black magic.'

'Did they wear masks?'

'Yes. Animals. I already told the police that . . .'

For whatever reason, Turner was unwilling to recount the truth of what had happened. Perhaps he hoped the

274

nightmare would go away. He wanted the police gone as quickly as possible, and was not going to go into detail.

But Brady knew that Turner had seen a lot more than he was letting on. He came up close by the man, smelling his sweat, his fear, noticing how he shook more violently. Their eyes met. Brady let his gaze rest easily and uncompromisingly on the flickering, nervous eyes of the other man.

Softly, Brady said, 'Let me tell *you* what you saw. The door burst open. The lights went out. Candles were lit. The men wore dark robes. Their masks were the dead heads of animals, split to make helmets. There was a goat, a pig, a cow, maybe a dog . . .'

As he spoke, Norman Turner went even paler than before, licking his lips nervously, staring at Brady.

Brady went on, 'They tied you up. Let me see your wrists . . .'

He lifted Turner's arm, and saw the red marks of the ropes.

'. . . but you couldn't see the rope that bound you. Something strangled you, but you couldn't see what it was . . .'

'How do you know?' Turner breathed, almost silently. Tears welled up in his eyes. 'How do you know?'

Brady went on relentlessly. 'By some faint light you saw your wife stripped –'

'Shut up!' Turner said, but so quietly it was almost inaudible. He looked as if he was about to burst into tears, to sob uncontrollably. Brady reached out and gently touched his shoulder.

'One of the beasts had a long jewelled shaft. A piece of metal. It had a demon's head on the end. Did they use it on her? Where you trussed and helpless, watching them abuse your wife?'

Turner said nothing. He stared and stared, the tears rolling down his cheeks, and very slowly he started to shudder, letting the grief come.

'Bastards . . .' he whispered. 'Bloody bastards . . . They did . . . they savaged them both . . . Beth. Christine. They screamed so horribly . . . oh God, their screams . . .'

He stopped talking and cried loudly. Brady stood, hand resting on Turner's shoulder, and after a minute or so the man regained his composure. He stared out of the window. 'What will they be like . . . How will, you know . . . how will they be . . . here . . .' He tapped his head. 'When they come round. When they have to remember. I don't think they'll ever be the same again. It was so hideous. So violent.'

'I know,' Brady said.

Turner looked at him. 'Who are you?'

'I'm a man like you,' Brady said. 'My wife was taken from me as well. Raped. Stolen. And not just her. My family too.'

Turner could hardly take it all in. He shook his head slowly, as if in disbelief. 'Who were they?'

'I wish I knew.'

'Why? I mean . . . what was their purpose? Why assault a family so savagely?'

'Black magic,' Brady said simply. 'This will sound a hard and cruel thing to say, but you've been lucky. Very lucky.'

'Lucky? Are you crazy?' Turner laughed sourly, rubbing his neck.

'You're alive,' Brady said. 'They meant to kill you. They meant to kill me, too, but I survived. We're rarities, you and I. We're the lucky ones. But your wife and daughter are still with you. That makes you luckiest of all. Something went wrong, last night. And I must find out what . . .'

'Lucky,' Turner repeated, still smiling and shaking his head. Then he glanced sharply at Brady. 'How often has this happened before?'

'Many times.'

'Families broken? Killed?'

'Some killed, some abducted. Gangs of these men are

276

roaming the countryside *collecting*. I have to find out why, and where the people they steal are taken.'

Turner sat down on the arm of a chair. He leaned forward, folding in on himself, as if trying to become invisible. Brady sat down on the other arm.

'You *must* tell me what you remember. Anything you heard, or saw. Tell me everything. Especially . . . especially at the moment they left. How did that happen?'

Turner shrugged. 'They just left. I was trussed up and helpless. There were hands at my throat. God, the pain. That was terrible. The room was full of smoke and black shapes. I could see one candle burning. There was a lot of laughter, and a bit of an argument. Two of the men were tussling. Beth was screaming her head off, and they kept slapping her. Christine was . . . Christine was naked and they were . . . Oh *God*!' He broke down, hands to his face. Brady soothed and reassured him.

'I understand. I understand. Don't speak about things that are too personal.'

'She just lay there,' Turner said weakly. 'Unmoving, letting them use that . . . that *thing*. Beth was screaming enough for the two of them, but the sight of her, of Christine, so dead, and yet I know she was conscious. I know she was. And all that laughter, as if it were some sort of wild party.'

'And then?'

Turner sighed deeply. 'And then it stopped. Sudden silence. Beth stopped screaming. Someone put the candles out. The argument stopped, and there was just a sort of heavy, rasping breathing. It was as frightening as before. They all just stood there, quite motionless, animals in the shape of men. Christine started to cry, and one of them leaned down and did something, I don't know what, and she was silent. I tried to shout, but my mouth wouldn't open.'

'And they left without saying anything else?'

'No not quite. One of them murmured something about

277

a shrine. He said, "Which shrine?" And one of the others said something like "Pitthurst". Then a deep voice said "Who controls the fetch?" I don't know what that is. Another one said, "I do". I heard the deep voice say, "Kill them and burn the house". There was a woman among them because she said, "Why is it *us*". The deep voice said something like, "We're closest to the border". The woman made a fuss. There was a lot to do, she said. And then they all moved out of the house, quite silently. Flames began to leap up around me and the fingers on my neck pressed again. And Beth was picked up bodily and swung about. I couldn't see by what. It was a nightmare . . . I must have dreamt that bit, because she was . . . she was in *mid-air*, but nothing holding her. I started to shout at last, and then the sprinkler system came on. Beth was thrown to the ground. Whoever was strangling me went away. But I couldn't move for hours. My hands were tied. The girls were tied . . . only . . .' He looked hauntedly at Brady.

Brady said. 'No ropes.'

'No ropes,' Turner agreed, raising his wrists and showing the vicious red weals. 'Hypnosis, I suppose; the suggestion of ropes.'

'Something like that,' Brady said, remembering how his own body had been trussed and bound by invisible thongs. Not hypnosis, but the creation of rope by a violent mind. A type of psychic attack, invisible, yet manifesting as bruises, cuts and weals as deep and as painful as those on Turner's wrists.

'From what you tell me,' Brady said, 'You've not just been lucky. You've had two or three gods on your side. Something disturbed them in the middle of their collection.'

'The shrine,' Turner said. 'They were called to the shrine.'

'You heard the name Pitthurst. Nothing else?'

'Just that. I've looked on my road atlas. I spent hours

278

searching for the place. I was going to go after them . . .'
He shook his head. 'Not there.'

So that's why you were so long calling the police, Brady thought. The man, in anger, had plotted revenge. Frustrated by the name not appearing in his atlas, soon his grief and terror had come back, and he had become vulnerable again.

Pitthurst. A wood, almost certainly. A wood near to a town, on the borders. That could mean the Welsh borders. A long enough stretch of land to search. Brady nevertheless had maps which would show the details. If Pitthurst was shown on any large-scale Ordnance Survey map, he would find it.

Brady said, 'Thank you for being so frank with me, Mr Turner. I appreciate it. You've helped me a lot. You may not realize it, but you've helped many people, people like you and me, and like Beth and Christine, but people who weren't so lucky.'

Turner looked at Brady with an expression of almost childish desperation. '*Have* we been lucky? For all of this, have we . . . have we got away lightly?'

Brady reached out to squeeze the other man's arm. 'By God, you have. When you feel anguish, or despair, think of the others. And trust in me, Mr Turner. On behalf of us all I intend to exact revenge. I swear to let you know. For the moment, I ask just one thing of you.'

'Which is?'

'Say nothing to the police. They mean well, but they are formal and legal and book-bound. We shall never revenge ourselves if we let the police dictate what is to happen. All I ask –'

To his surprise, Turner reached up a hand and pressed his fingers against Brady's mouth. 'Don't say anything,' he said. 'It's what I felt. I know exactly what you mean. I couldn't tell them about what happened here, because I wanted to take it upon myself. But I'm neither strong enough nor aware enough.' He smiled at Brady, and for the

279

first time the smile was genuine, a gesture of the hope he felt.

'Thank you,' said Brady, and began to rise to go. Turner reached out and stopped him.

'For the rape of my daughter . . . for the assault on my wife . . . kill someone, Brady. Kill them in a way they deserve.'

Brady lifted the damp, trembling hand that held him and kissed the fingers. 'I shall be glad to.'

Outside the lounge, Sutherland was sipping tea and talking to another plain-clothes man. 'Any luck?' he asked Brady.

'He's terrified,' Brady said. 'But it *was* Arachne . . .'

'He admitted to the animal masks?'

'It happened just as it happened to me. They were going to take the two women. The girl . . .' Brady hesitated, unsure whether or not he should say anything; if Turner wished the fact kept secret he might mention *Pitthurst* in a moment's pique with Brady if he knew Brady had betrayed the trust. And Brady wanted that name kept quiet.

But Sutherland said, 'The girl was raped, we know that.'

'He thinks you don't. For his pride . . .'

'I understand. What I don't understand is –'

'Why they survived,' Brady cut in. 'The attack stopped. Suddenly and without warning, the whole attack stopped. They listened, they talked, one of them mentioned "the borders", they tried to kill the Turners with fire, and went away. From the way he describes it, they were called off somewhere. This is one lucky family.'

Sutherland watched him carefully, then sipped from his china cup. 'Not very helpful,' he said after a moment.

'Unfinished business,' Brady said quietly. 'They may be back.'

Sutherland considered that, frowning, then nodded. 'I

280

take your point. This family might well become the bait in a trap for these creatures.'

'You may have to wait a while to spring that trap, but you have everything to gain and nothing to lose but men from traffic duty.'

Sutherland smiled thinly, and Brady went into the kitchen to give a statement to a waiting constable. When that was done he went home. An hour before, he had been dog-tired. Now he had a straw grasped firmly in his hand, and he did not intend to let it go.

A hundred or so miles away, in the town of Anerley, a girl sat in the middle of her classroom and watched, with a growing sense of unease, as her teacher spoke to the class about life on the farm. It was a simple enough lesson, a basic study of how a farmer used his land, sold his crops, and how those crops would be distributed on the open market.

Miss Bowman was a very good teacher. Her voice rose and fell in an interesting way, she smiled, she made little jokes, she had no hesitation in walloping Sarah Biggs for talking (and Sarah Biggs was *always* talking, or mucking about) and all in all, class with Miss Bowman was something to be looked forward to.

To everyone except Nancy Cochrane.

Nancy had not been comfortable in the class since the very first day. Although the children were her own age, she felt much older, and they seemed *horribly* young to her. It made her father laugh when she tried to express her irritation, a ten-year-old bitterly complaining about her classmates being 'childish'. She sat next to a girl called Faith Brooker, who was *always* writing rude notes to the boys in the class, and getting them back. Her desk was a museum of love-notes, hate-notes and crude drawings accumulated over many terms. And she hadn't got a good word to say to Nancy. The boy behind her was the class

281

hard man, a sallow-faced, rather spotty youth called John Borsnan. He had painted a filthy design on her back during art class and when she found it she hit him so hard on the nose that she drew blood. Ridiculed in front of his cronies, the boy maintained an undercover war of kicks, ink-splashes and whispered threats which were driving Nancy to distraction.

But these were the things she was used to, as a girl on the road, always snatching lessons in out-of-the-way schools, growing up faster than her peers because of the responsibilities that had been forced upon her. Sometimes, as the other children played, she would go to the toilets, lock a door and just cry. It was wonderfully cathartic. She cried for the memory of her mother; she cried for the sadness she could feel in her father; she cried with frustration. Afterwards, she always felt revitalized, and ready to survive another day.

But at this school she had not yet shed a single tear. She accepted the ostracism with a shrug: some classes you won, some you lost. What concerned her was the chill she felt whenever Miss Bowman looked at her.

If the rest of the class adored their brash and beautiful young teacher, Nancy Cochrane was terrified of her. It was a feeling that had been growing since her first day at school, an anguish that had registered on the very first occasion, when Miss Bowman had introduced her to the class, holding her hand. Girl and woman had glanced at each other, and the gaze had held. The woman frowned slightly. The girl had broken into a sudden, cold sweat. Nancy had sat down at her desk, trembling. For an hour or more Miss Bowman had seemed distracted, continually glancing at the new girl.

Then the atmosphere had relaxed, and Nancy Cochrane had gone into her simple class-survival mode.

Today, though, that state of agitation had clearly returned to Miss Bowman. The woman was dressed in a light summer skirt and blouse. Her long dark hair was combed out, hiding her face when she stared through the classroom window, and she was spending a lot of time at the window.

Her behaviour was the cause of some amusement. She was stopping in mid-sentence, staring out into the day, then abruptly remembering where she was and what she was doing.

'Where was I, Sarah?' she asked at one point, having been talking about the seasonal slaughter of lambs. And the girl replied, 'Eggs, miss.' Miss Bowman began to ramble on about the grading of eggs, a complete change of subject that reduced the class to fits of hysterical laughter.

The teacher stared at them darkly. The laughter died away. The woman's face was hard and white, her eyes glittered. For a second her lips drew back, exposing her teeth, and during the moment of what seemed to be almost manifest anger, her gaze had fixed on Nancy Cochrane.

Nancy's body went quite cold. A voice seemed to whisper in her head, a nonsense voice, a gabble of foul sounds.

Then the sensations went away. Miss Bowman turned to the blackboard and began to write something. A title. The title of an essay. For the rest of the period the class wrote in silence, while their teacher sat and stared at them, her eyes like glass, her lips trembling slightly.

When school ended, Nancy grabbed her satchel and coat and walked quickly into the playground with all the other children. She followed close behind a group of girls from her own class. Sarah Biggs was still the star of the day and the 'lamb and egg' incident was being re-told and elaborated, with much mimicking, eliciting great gales of laughter. Nancy walked behind the group, but Sarah saw her.

'Watch out. It's Cocky.'

They giggled and ran off, and Nancy heard her nickname called in derisory fashion. She hastened after the group and reached the gates of the school. Why she glanced back she didn't know, she hadn't intended to. But a tug at her mind made her stop and turn.

Miss Bowman was standing on the steps, beckoning to her.

5

It took Dan Brady just ten minutes to locate Pitthurst. He chewed a bacon sandwich and sipped coffee as his newly-acquired computer went through its search. Anita Herbert stood in the doorway to his tiny 'computer room' and watched the shifting columns on the screen.

The information that he was scanning was the Ordnance Survey Index, or rather, an illegally obtained copy of that index. It contained the name of every wood, church, tumulus, castle, field and track that was shown on the largest-scale map they produced. Each name was grid-referenced. When Brady had acquired the disc, he had bought the VDU to match. Now, slowly, he was building up a file on Arachne, programming his new toy with everything he knew and every location that he knew to be important to the other side.

One day, perhaps, a pattern would emerge . . . new technology against the occult. The idea appealed to him.

There were only two Pitthursts on the file, one in Devon, the other close to the Welsh borders, and it was there that Brady concentrated his efforts. The closest town was Anerley. Pitthurst was a wood, marked as extending over 'Roman mines'.

He arrived in Anerley quite late in the afternoon. It had taken him a few hours to get ready for the trip, and to check the house. It had taken him fractionally longer to convince Anita Herbert that she should stay behind. They had argued bitterly. But Brady won the point.

He did not tell her where he was going.

He drove through the town several times, looking at it,

getting to know its layout, its shops, its back streets. He checked out the places where the streets ran into farmland, or bordered streams. He looked for deserted buildings, warehouses, junkyards, the sort of places where a man – or men – might hide. Anerley turned out to be a very ordinary place, just two churches of historical interest and a scattering of old buildings. It had a new school, a new hospital and a small, new-looking police station. Brady went into the police station and asked directions to another wood in the vicinity. No one knew. The policemen were not locals. The tiny station had an air of boredom about it, which told Brady something important: nothing was going on in Anerley yet.

He drove out of the town, parked by the roadside and followed the marked track over the nearer fields and ridges to the location of the mines. He had no idea what he expected to find there. The landscape was deserted and bleak. A brisk, rather autumnish wind blew. He carried a shoulder-bag with all his supplies, including a pistol and a torch, but he knew that he was naked against the power of Arachne if they were here already.

Something told him that he was here first. It was the same sixth sense that made him quietly confident about this wood being the destination of the group whose work had been interrupted.

Arachne was coming to Anerley. And Brady was here, waiting for them.

But what was the shrine that Turner had referred to? In his mind's eye Brady had an image of a Holy Virgin shrine, a statue in a grotto by the side of the road. So as he approached the distant woodland he half expected to see some statue or idol, something vile and evil-looking, a grotesque face out of pre-history watching him from a crudely constructed shelter.

But the first thing he saw, when he came in sight of Pitthurst Hill, was a man, standing among the trees, watching him.

286

By the time Brady reached the line of the woods, the man had vanished. Exercising the utmost caution, Brady walked around the knoll, then began to explore among the stand of trees. He could see the signs of the old mine-workings. In places the trees grew out of slips of rubble and land, the trunks angled, the roots rising above the ground and exposing narrow holes in the substrata. From one of these came a foul smell, and Brady shone his torch into the crevice, wondering if this was just a badger hole, or a deeper shaft. He could see nothing but a tangle of thin root and a wide, earthy tunnel.

The wind stirred the branches above him. He listened beyond the sounds of nature for any sign of the man who had been standing here. He looked out across the open farmland, but could see only one indication of human life in the form of a tractor, moving slowly between two fields, about a mile distant.

But eventually he found the slab of stone that covered the shaft into the mines.

Brady walked about the exposed stone, breathing heavily. He had no idea what lay below, but the carving of the labyrinth on its rough surface was familiar to him. He stooped to run his fingers round the pattern. It was incomplete and inaccurate, but it set his heart pounding in his chest . . .

'He's still alive,' the pig-faced man had said, *and another of them had leaned down to where he lay, trussed up and close to death. On the dark robe of the second man had been marked the same labyrinth, and the ancient image had become, for Brady, the symbol of Arachne.*

'They've been here,' he whispered to himself, glancing anxiously around. But the stone slab had been recently uncovered. Fresh dirt was scattered around. He doubted very much if Arachne themselves had defiled their own shrine, and began to understand that someone, locally, had been interfering . . .

An interference which had summoned the collectors.

Who had been standing in the woods? Brady rose to his feet and called loudly. Birds shifted restlessly in the tree-tops, but no man stepped forward.

Then the whole world turned grey.

For a moment Brady was too startled to react. A freezing wind blew around him, driving swirls of mist across a ghostly, shimmering landscape. Great pinnacles of wind-scoured stone rose about him; twisted thorns, as grey as ash, moved in the silent, spectral storm like sentient creatures . . .

Brady turned around. Something dark and sinister hovered beyond the swirling fog. He dropped his body to the ground in a defensive crouch and rose above the fleshy cage, a spirit released into the haunted land. Below him, his corpse trembled and became coated with a fine white layer. He could see, now, how the illusion was imposed upon the woodland. It seemed to emanate from a part of the hill where a large tree grew.

And as he watched, so the strange landscape vanished. He returned to his body and stood up straight, slightly shaken, very confused.

Behind him there was a sound like stone being struck very forcibly. He turned. The noise came again, and he stepped back in shocked surprise as the heavy stone slab jumped an inch or two from its setting. Someone – or some *thing* –was trying to get out. A moment later the stone was struck again from below, rising inches into the air before thudding back to the ground. An eerie wailing sounded from the dark place beneath, and Brady glimpsed an ashen face. He reached for his pack and drew out the police revolver that he now carried with him . . .

For a few seconds there was silence. He took a step forward, glancing apprehensively around.

The stone slab flew up into the air, struck with tremendous force. Two bleeding, broken hands clutched at the ground, and the skull-like features of a man, ghastly white and grinning, stared at Brady from the pit. The stone slab toppled back, striking the hideous apparition, but the corpse remained where it was, wailing loudly, struggling to escape the burden.

The fingers scrabbled at the soil. The eyes remained fixed on Brady. Glistening saliva dripped from the parted lips.

The 'life' suddenly went from the body. The eyes glazed and the whole struggle ceased. The face vanished below the stone, which fell almost back into position, catching the ragged hands and holding them in the daylight. Brady heard a leathery rustling sound – like wings, he thought – and then there was just stillness.

He stepped cautiously forward and reached to touch the cold, stiff fingers, half expecting them to twitch. On one of the fingers was a thin gold wedding ring.

'What the devil were you?' Brady said aloud.

Behind him, a voice said, 'Devil is right.'

Brady started with surprise, every nerve quivering; but he turned slowly, sensing the menace in the voice.

The man who stood there was in his thirties, Brady guessed, a short man, stockily built. He had long fair hair, combed back from a face that was lined by weather and hard living. He watched Brady through bright, pale eyes. He was standing sideways on, his right arm extended. The small pistol that he held didn't waver from its target: Brady's forehead.

Dan Brady slowly straightened up, but kept his arm limp, his own pistol loose in the grip.

The other man inclined his head slightly. 'Drop the armoury.'

Brady obeyed.

'Move away from it.'

Brady stepped sideways. The other man reached for the

289

revolver and hefted it in his hand. 'A Webley. Police weapon. Are you police?'

'No,' said Brady.

'Then who are you?'

'Daniel Brady. Esquire. Who are you?'

'What are you doing here?' the other man asked, ignoring Brady's question.

'Waiting for someone.'

Still the small pistol pointed at his face. Pale eyes scanned him from head to toe. The other man was puzzled by the new arrival. 'You seem nervous, Mr Brady.'

'You're standing by the reason for that. And I don't like guns when they're pointed at me.'

'Is that right?' He looked down at the dead hands, crushed by the stone. 'A farmer. Called Kitting. What happened to him almost defies understanding. What I don't understand, though, is what *you're* doing here.'

'I told you,' Brady said. 'I'm waiting for someone . . .'

'Waiting for me, perhaps?'

'I don't know. I don't know who you are.'

'Cochrane,' the man said. 'Geoffrey Cochrane. Does that ring the proverbial bell?'

Brady said No. Cochrane was nervous. The hand that held the pistol had started to tremble, slightly. This man was not a part of Arachne, Brady was certain of that. But who the hell was he? He certainly knew about the corpse. And if Pitthurst Hill was the location of an Arachnian shrine . . . then perhaps Cochrane was the man who had disturbed that sanctuary.

'Come over here,' Cochrane said. He stepped back round the stone, then nodded down towards it. 'What does that pattern mean to you?'

'A labyrinth,' Brady said. 'A Greek symbol. More than Greek, a widespread symbol. The maze of life. Theseus and the Minotaur. Eleusian rites, worship of Diana and Hecate. It has a more sinister meaning, these days . . .'

He saw the flicker of confusion on Cochrane's face. That

290

last reference had meant something. The pale eyes narrowed suspiciously.

Cochrane said, 'What if I showed you a symbol that looked like a spider. What would that mean to you?'

So here we are, Brady thought. Now we come to it. Cochrane isn't Arachne. No member of the cult would be so gross. But Cochrane was suspicious of Brady himself. They were waiting for the same group, but Cochrane thought Brady was a front runner. Suddenly the small pistol looked like a cannon and Brady became aware of every bead of moisture on Cochrane's face, every raised hair on the finger that curled around the trigger.

'It would mean Arachne,' Brady said. 'A goddess. Greek, I suppose. Oh what a tangled web they weave. But this little fly keeps well out of Mother Spider's clutches.'

Cochrane frowned with the recognition of it, with a growing confusion. At last it occurred to him that Brady was a man like himself. He said softly, 'What did they take?'

'My wife, my daughter, my son,' Brady said coldly. The pistol lowered slightly.

'What were their names?'

Brady felt a chill of irritation. This had gone on long enough. But he managed to say the names to Cochrane, though it made him shake to do so. 'Alison. Marianna. Dominick.'

'Do you carry their pictures?' Cochrane asked, and held out his hand. Brady bit his lip, watched the other man steadily, then reached into his pocket for the precious photographs he always kept with him. Cochrane approached, took the pictures and glanced at each in turn.

He held up the photograph of Dominick. 'There are eight dead people in a shrine below where we stand. This boy is one of them . . .'

The words, spoken rapidly and coldly, were like hammer blows to Brady. The blood drained from his face. The world slipped away from him. He shouted, 'NO!' and reached out to grab Cochrane's jacket, feeling the tears suddenly well up in his eyes.

Slowly the moment of crisis passed. Cochrane stared at him impassively. His gun arm was limp. Brady frowned and let the man go. Cochrane straightened his jacket, then pocketed his pistol, passing the Webley back to Brady. 'I had to be sure. I'm sorry.'

'Yes,' said Brady weakly, shaking his head, rubbing his hands together to get the circulation back. 'Yes, I understand.'

'How did you know where to come?'

Brady shrugged. The effects of the shock had not yet worn off. 'A family. A survivor . . . heard the name Pitthurst . . .'

'And from that you found the very place. Well done.'

'Well done . . .' Brady repeated softly. He stared hard at the other man. Part of him was angry; a part still shook with anguish. There was something unfinished between the two men. Something important to Brady.

'Dominick . . .' he whispered, and looked at the stone.

'I had to be sure,' Cochrane repeated. 'It was a mean trick. I'm sorry.'

Brady smiled, a gesture without humour. 'It *was* a trick. . . ?' he asked insistently.

Cochrane frowned. 'I don't . . .'

Frustration made Brady shout the words: 'Just tell me! Let me hear it from you!'

Cochrane suddenly understood. He shook his head. 'There *is* a boy's body. Below us. But it's not your son. None of your family is down there.'

Brady said nothing. He just nodded, then turned from Cochrane, taking a deep breath.

'Right. Tell me what's going on here.'

'I'm in a hurry, Miss Bowman,' Nancy called. The teacher remained motionless on the steps of the school. Slowly her arm lowered. There was no expression on the woman's face.

Nancy Cochrane shrugged her satchel further on to her shoulder, then turned down the street, away from the school gates. As she walked so she picked up the pace, until she was almost running. She hardly dared look back; she didn't want to look through the railings at the steps.

But at the last moment, before she would have been out of sight of the playground, she cast a quick glance through the fence.

Miss Bowman was nowhere to be seen.

The girl stopped walking, then took a pace or two back, peering through the iron railings at the deserted tarmac playing area. Her heart slowed down, and she felt a strong sense of relief.

Something was wrong. Something was very wrong.

With Miss Bowman.

Geoff Cochrane reached down and grabbed the cold, grey hands of the dead farmer. 'He was a pain in the backside, but I wouldn't have wished this upon him.'

Brady heaved at the stone slab and managed to shift it slightly. Cochrane tugged and the corpse's arms came into view. The stone collapsed. Brady wheezed with the effort.

'Jesus! I can't hold this.'

'Just one more try,' Cochrane urged. 'We need to get the body out.'

Brady smiled. 'Why?'

'For decency's sake,' said Cochrane. 'His son isn't going to co-operate too much longer.'

'But this increases the risk to your friend Goddard. If he *is* alive down there, maybe he's alive because the guardian had Kitting's body to play with.'

Cochrane stared at him, then looked down at the curled fingers of the two exposed hands. He shook his head. 'I haven't really thought this through, have I?'

'No,' said Brady. 'You haven't.' He went on, 'Let the body drop. It's an easy vehicle for the elemental, but it's weak. It's weak *because* it's easy. Goddard may be down there. He can outrun the corpse. He can survive . . .'

'Lift the stone,' Cochrane said, and reached to help. Together they managed to raise the slab almost vertically. Kitting's grotesque remains tumbled noisily into the darkness. Dust and the stench of decay swirled into the late afternoon air. Brady stared down into the darkness. Geoff Cochrane called 'Jack', but no voice answered him.

They let the stone fall back.

That evening, a sort of council meeting was held around the large square table in the kitchen of the Blanford farmhouse. Ed Blanford sat opposite Dan Brady, the shotgun, broken at the breach, on the table before him. His round, ruddy face seemed always to be smiling without humour; small dull eyes watched Brady with great suspicion.

Next to Ed Blanford, Susan Blanford was a small, pale-faced woman, with bright sympathetic eyes. She sat, holding a mug of tea, and hardly spoke. But she had spent the day looking after Kathy Goddard, whose distress had taken the form of helpless silence. The Blanfords' eldest daughter, Sophie, was coming home from the private nursing home where she worked. Brady had suggested having a nurse at the farm, not just for Kathy Goddard, but for those of the shrine victims who were still alive.

Mary and John Kitting also sat at the table. Their two children were now safely established with an aunt, several miles away. The Goddard boys would be going to stay with relatives the day after. John Kitting looked as if he had been crying again for the loss of a father he had never really loved. He was both sad and angry. This whole tragic situation had arisen because of Cochrane's interference with natural order, he said, tampering with things that were better left alone. But his anger never exploded; it was spoken in a bitter undertone, and Mary held his hand and comforted him.

Brady and Cochrane sat facing the farmers. It was time to explain what had happened, what was likely to happen as a consequence, and to propose protective, and defensive, measures. The whole situation had to be handled carefully. John Kitting in particular was likely to upset Brady's plan, by insisting on calling in the police. And every so often, Susan Blanford murmured, 'This is wrong. We shouldn't be taking things into our own hands. Ed, dear, we *must* send for the police . . .'

Geoff Cochrane said, 'Listen. Everybody, listen to me' He spoke slowly and carefully, trying to involve all five people at the table. 'These are the facts. They are unpleasant. They are frightening. They are now irrevocable. Firstly, against our better judgement we have disturbed the shrine of a powerful and bloody group of killers. They are known as Arachne . . .'

'That means spider,' Ed Blanford said. 'There was a spider drawn down on the sealed doorway.'

'That's right. Their sign, without doubt. When we breached that shrine we did something very foolish. They will be coming to Anerley to repair the damage. They may already be here . . .'

'You should have *left it alone*,' John Kitting rasped bitterly. 'You had no right to go interfering with devil stuff. Look what you've bloody done, now. Damn you, Cochrane!'

As his voice started to rise, so Mary Kitting squeezed his hand. But Cochrane silenced him by slapping his own hand onto the table. Brady watched the performance and was impressed. Kitting went red, but shut up instantly.

Hurry up, Geoff, Brady willed silently. He glanced out into the gathering dusk. He could see stark trees on a distant ridge. His hair pricked, his skin itched. They were coming closer. There was so little time. He had to see the shrine, and he had to see it now. But there was no point in going back twice. What had to be done had to be done that night, and they would need all the help they could get. They were certainly going to need the two men's physical strength. Even then, the dismantling of the shrine was going to take some hours . . .

Cochrane spoke firmly and deliberately in the silence that followed his dramatic gesture.

'Now let me get one thing absolutely clear. And Ed . . .' It was the first time he had used Blanford's Christian name, and the farmer scowled, looking uncomfortable. 'Ed, I expect you to back me up on this. No nonsense, right?' He looked hard at the younger Kitting. 'It was your father who brought all this down on our heads. I'll take my share of the responsibility, so will Ed. So must Jack Goddard. You were haunted by ghostly figures and you called me in to exorcise your farms. The moment I saw the source of those ghosts I wanted to leave it alone. When I saw the spider symbol I said *distinctly*: Don't touch it. Am I right, Ed?'

Blanford shrugged, then added. 'It was Ben who broke through the seal. You told us not to.'

'And inside the shrine I recognized it at once for what it was. And I said, Don't touch anything. I said it *distinctly*. But your father couldn't keep his hands off the totem. *He* released the guardian. The guardian killed him. Am I right, Ed?'

'We've been through this before. You're right. Why the hell don't you listen, John? It was Ben did the interfering . . .'

John Kitting was looking sour. Cochrane now said, turning to Ed Blanford. 'But let's not get away from the fact that we *all* had a part to play in what has happened. And we all have a part to play in repairing the damage. Firstly, to involve the police will be disaster. Please trust us on that. Secondly, whether we like it or not we're all in very great danger. We have to protect ourselves. We have to get ourselves into a defensible position. This is even more important when I say that thirdly, there are people in that shrine who are still *alive*. Two are dead. I think that was very apparent. Two, maybe three. But five or six of the victims were breathing. We have to get them out and into safety. We have to protect them. That's why we must all help. John, Ed, we're going to have to lift them bodily from the shrine, and that's going to take time.'

'And take them where?' John Kitting asked.

Brady said, tapping the table. 'Right here, John. To this farm.'

Ed Blanford spluttered. 'My farm! Who the hell said. . . ?'

'Come on, Ed,' Brady said tiredly. 'Don't make a fuss now. You've got Kathy Goddard here. You've got a daughter who's a nurse. I've looked at the farm buildings – they're compact, they'd be defensible with guns and they're the best group of buildings to defend against psychic attack. You've got some big rooms, here. We can set up a hospital ward for the shrine victims.'

Ed Blanford was redder than usual. Brady could see panic in his eyes. 'But these . . . these people, this Arachne. They'll come *here*. They'll attack my farm . . .'

'Yes, they will,' Brady said. 'But Cochrane and I have a few tricks up our sleeves to keep them at bay.'

'Maybe it's just the totem they want,' Susan Blanford said. 'If we left that in the mines, perhaps they wouldn't bother us.'

Cochrane said, 'You're right, Susan. It *is* the totem they'll be after. But we can't leave it in the mines. It's too powerful. We have to destroy it. And that means bringing it to the farm too.'

'Why can't we destroy it in the mines?' asked Mary Kitting quietly. She looked from Cochrane to Brady, and her pretty face was etched with suspicion. Brady felt a tingle of discomfort as the woman's innocence confronted the less-than-innocent design of Brady's true plan. He glanced at Cochrane, who merely shrugged.

The farmers would have to be told the *whole* truth of what Brady intended.

'I don't know *how* to destroy it,' Cochrane said. 'I know what it is. I know what it contains. But exactly how to destroy it is beyond me, at the moment . . .'

As he spoke Brady felt a cold shiver. Cochrane knew what it was? He knew what it *contained*? That was more than he had told Brady himself. But Brady kept quiet, his face impassive.

Susan Blanford said, 'Then we'd be mad to bring it to the farm. You'll be placing all our lives in danger!'

'We have to make them come here,' Brady said. 'If they're a group like the group which attacked my family last Christmas, then there will be five or six of them, with a supernatural element in tow; a creature like the guardian that killed Ben Kitting. They'll soon sense the totem. They'll close in on the farm . . . And we'll have them.'

Mary Kitting laughed sourly. 'I thought as much. You're setting us up as the bait in a trap.'

Without blinking, without embarrassment, Brady said, 'That's right. The bait in a trap for Arachne. They'll come here to retrieve the totem and destroy everyone on the farm. They'll play right into our hands, because Geoff and I will be waiting for them'

There was a shocked hush in the room. Ed Blanford's breathing was a distant wheezing sound. Susan Blanford stared at her cup, while the Kittings exchanged hostile, terrified glances with the ghost-hunters.

'You're playing with our lives,' said Mary Kitting quietly, 'You're playing with our families . . . for your own ends. I can't believe you're not both as evil as these Arachne people themselves.'

Brady shook his head. 'I'm cold. I'm hardened against loss. That I'll grant you. But not evil, Mary. At the back of

298

my mind is a single thought: that the collectors who are coming to Anerley to repair this shrine are the same group of killers who stole my wife and my two children. I've killed three of them. But to *capture* one, to have one of them in my grasp . . . Not for revenge, Mary. Not to kill him or her slowly and agonizingly. I'm beyond that, now. I want my family back. I need to know what Arachne *is*, what their purpose is. The only way I shall ever be able to do that, to *really* help people like myself, and a woman called Ellen Bancroft, and families like the Turners – so many families that you may never have heard of, but who are living, now, in a shadowland of grief and loss – to help them, to destroy this evil thing, we *have* to capture one of those who knows the greater purpose . . .'

'A cage for death,' Cochrane said emptily. His face was white. He was staring into the middle distance. 'The farm will be the cage. The totem will be the bait. We will risk our lives, yes. But we will all be protected. When they come, we will close the cage . . .' He suddenly focussed on John Kitting. 'Please help us.'

Kitting stared back. Mary Kitting was frowning, uncertain, yet disturbed by what Brady had said.

'A cage for death,' she repeated.

'A hope for the living,' Brady added. 'Arachne is a rot that has penetrated the world. A beginning must be made to cut that rot out of the land around us.'

'Please help us,' Cochrane repeated.

Susan Blanford said, 'Do you swear to us that you will do everything possible to protect us from danger?'

'Yes, I do,' Cochrane said, and Brady added, 'If you obey us, if you do what we say, when we say it, we should avoid any danger to anyone in this room.'

Susan said, 'We will place our faith in God, and our trust in you.' But as she spoke so she picked up her husband's shotgun and snapped it shut. The noise was loud and startling in the stillness. 'Our trust, Mr Brady. Our *trust*, Mr Cochrane.' Her eyes, once so warm and sympathetic, glittered with cold hatred now. 'I swear to you both that the moment I feel you have betrayed that trust I shall treat you as Ed treats a fox. I shall not hesitate before shooting you to death.'

6

At seven o'clock, Nancy Cochrane lost her temper. She almost screeched her frustration, throwing her book across the room and standing up. As she walked to the landing, Mrs Buxton appeared at the bottom of the stairs, frowning.

'Is everything all right, dear?'

'No!' Nancy proclaimed loudly. 'Where's daddy? He was supposed to have picked me up by now.'

'I'm sure I don't know,' Mrs Buxton said soothingly. 'If I were you I'd just do my homework and wait for him to call.'

'May I call him? Please?'

'Of course you may, my dear. You know how to work the phone, I expect.'

Mrs Buxton vanished, which was just as well. As Nancy walked down the stairs her face was white and her blood boiling. *You know how to work the phone, I expect* . . . What an insult! What did Mrs Buxton think she was, for heaven's sake? A *child*? She would happily have kicked the old woman's knees and slapped the cup of tea from her hands.

Standing by the phone, fuming, Nancy could see the flicker of the TV set in her landlady's lounge. She stuck out her tongue and waggled it about.

'May the evil eye get a good look at your knickers,' she said as she dialled the number her father had given her. She giggled at the thought.

The phone was answered.

'The Blanford farm.'

'Is daddy there, please?'

The woman on the other end said, 'Is that Nancy?'

'Yes. Hurry, please.'

A moment later her father came on the phone. 'What's the matter, Nancy? Are you all right?'

'Where *are* you?'

'Where d'you think I am?' he said. 'Have you done your homework?'

She came close to tears. 'My *homework*! Daddy! You said you'd pick me up from here. You said you'd come and collect me. Where *are* you? I've been waiting for *hours*.'

'I'm sorry, sweetheart. Something turned up and I've been a bit preoccupied. Are you hungry?'

'Of course I'm not hungry,' Nancy snapped back. Her father infuriated her sometimes. Mrs Buxton always gave her tea.

'Well. I suggest you watch the television for a while, then have an early night. I'll pick you up from school tomorrow.'

For a second she was too stunned to speak. Then, almost in tears, she began to object. 'I *can't* stay here on my own . . .'

'Of course you can. Why ever not?'

'I want to be with you. You said you'd pick me up later!'

'Well, I've changed my mind. I'm going to be doing something very difficult tonight. Not dangerous, just difficult. You can't do it with me, and I don't want you alone at the farm. I'll be far happier knowing you're safely in bed at Mrs Buxton's. Nobody knows you're there. In the morning Mrs Buxton will take you to school –'

'No! I'm *not* going back to school. Daddy, come and get me *now*.'

Mrs Buxton appeared in the doorway of her lounge, looking quizzically at the girl whose raised voice had disturbed her. Nancy turned her back on the woman.

Cochrane was saying, 'I'm not going to come and fetch you now and you *will* go to school tomorrow. Is that clearly understood?'

302

'I'm frightened, daddy,' she said softly.

'Nonsense. Frightened of what?'

'Miss Bowman.'

'Who's she?'

'You *know* who she is. My teacher. There's something funny about her. Something not right. Daddy, I'm scared. I want you to go and see her. She was watching me today. She followed me out of school. I don't like her . . .'

'I didn't like my teachers either,' Cochrane said, his voice almost callous, infuriatingly distracted. She could hear someone talking in the background. He had ceased to take her phone call seriously.

'Are you listening to me, daddy? Are you *listening*?'

'Of course I am, love. Listen, I've got to go.'

'But Miss Bowman! She's strange. I'm frightened of her.'

'I've got to go, Nancy. I'll come and sort Miss Bowman out tomorrow. Watch some TV then get a good sleep. You're safe. That's all that matters. You're safe there.'

'Daddy! Don't go . . .'

'Do what I *say*, Nancy. Goodnight now.'

There was a dull click. Geoff Cochrane had put the receiver down on his daughter. Slowly she placed her own receiver down. Ashen-faced, hardly able to restrain her tears, she walked upstairs to her room, ignoring Mrs Buxton's questions.

'Sorry about that,' Cochrane said, as he came back into the kitchen. 'Daughter trouble. She'd rather be here, with me.'

'Is she safe?' Brady asked, and Cochrane nodded distractingly. 'Safer there than here, that's for sure.'

In the kitchen, John and Mary Kitting and Ed Blanford were wrapped against the cold and loaded down with lengths of rope, torches and bags containing Cochrane's supernatural defence equipment. Brady carried his own

303

bag of tricks. During the previous hour he and the ghost-hunter had worked out the sort of cage that would be required to snare the guardian. At the back of Brady's mind was an image of Ellen Bancroft, months before, being flung screaming to the ceiling and strangled by a so-called 'trapped' elemental. He hoped that Cochrane had judged the power of the guardian correctly.

Susan Blanford was sitting with the silent Kathy Goddard in the warm lounge next door. The television flickered, but she had turned the sound down, watching the Channel Four news by vision alone. Brady walked very quickly about the lounge placing open dishes of dilute nitric acid in which he had dissolved a little common salt at the four corners. He made the invisible seals of the archangels, ensuring that Susan saw him do so and understood what he was doing. With her staunch faith she was well protected against weak psychic attack anyway: her faith was a means of concentrating the mind, always a potent defensive mechanism against the tenuous tendrils of some questing psychic form.

On the settee, Kathy Goddard sat staring out of the window into the darkening night. Her hair was dishevelled. Her lips were wet. Her eyes were dark-rimmed and narrowed, her hands clasped as if locked in her lap. When Brady passed in front of her she never blinked nor took her gaze from the direction of the window. But she suddenly started to whisper . . .

Susan Blanford rose from her own seat and stood by Brady, nervously listening to the gabble of hissed sound emerging from the woman's lips. It was gibberish, a sound almost frightening because of its alienness. The forms of words were there, but without sense, without meaning. Still she stared out into the night.

'What do I do about this?' Susan asked.

'I don't know. At least its communication again.'

'She sounds mad to me.'

'Just shocked. Shall we leave Mary with you? Or Ed?'

Susan shook her head. 'You need them all if you're going to lift those people out of the mines. I'll be all right. I just don't want her to get violent.'

Kathy Goddard murmured on, her lips moving, her eyes fixed straight ahead.

Then, just as Brady was stepping past her to lead the others up to Pitthurst Hill, the distressed woman shouted out 'YES!'

It startled Brady. He turned to look at her, and Kathy Goddard looked back over her shoulder; her pale eyes, her vacant stare engaged with Brady's gaze in a frighteningly compelling way.

The woman smiled, her lips quivering. 'He's alive,' she rasped. 'My Jack's alive. He's alive. I can hear him. Bring him back to me. My Jack. My Jack. He's calling for me . . .'

Then tears rolled from her eyes, and Susan Blanford sat down with her, hugging her. Brady turned from the room and followed the others out into the night.

They drove in the Land Rover as close to the wood-topped hill as they could. The clouds were bright, the trees a stark and unwelcoming castle above them. Without using torches they walked up the steep track, and only when they were in the shelter of the beechwood, and Cochrane had erected a tarpaulin screen, did they illuminate the stone slab and prepare to descend.

Mary Kitting was shaking with nerves. 'Why couldn't we do this during the day?' she said, holding on to her husband's arms as she watched Brady and Cochrane sprinkle chemicals around the shaft.

'It's as dark down there by day as by night,' Cochrane murmured. 'And every minute is precious.' He straightened slightly and glanced towards the brightness in the distance that was Anerley. Brady tugged his sleeve.

'Concentrate.'

'Sorry,' said Cochrane. 'I just keep getting this prickly feeling on my neck. I'm sure they're here.'

'They'll be close,' Brady murmured, 'but if they were in Anerley they'd be on the hill by now. We have a little time.'

'Hurry!' hissed John Kitting. 'If we've got to go down there, let's go down!'

'I'm not going down,' muttered Ed Blanford. 'Nothing would make me go back down.'

He was a bulky, shivering figure in the dim light, his breath frosting, his eyes gleaming. He still carried the shotgun.

What Brady was doing was making a trap around the entrance to the vertical access shaft. He explained briefly: 'If anything . . . *unnatural* comes out while we're down there, or when we open the entrance, this wall will hold it for a few minutes.'

'What wall?' asked Mary Kitting.

Brady held up a small clay gargoyle, a hideous shape, with the point of an iron nail showing above its head. It nestled in the palm of his hand. Moments later he excavated a shallow trench a few feet from the shaft and buried the object. He had buried eight of them, forming a thin psychic wall similar to that which protected his house in Berkshire.

'Right,' he said. 'I'm ready.'

Cochrane checked two of his meters, then glanced at the small wristlet he wore. 'No psychic energy that I can detect.'

'Good. Come on . . .'

He and Cochrane began to lever the stone slab upright. John Kitting lent a hand. As the dark shaft was exposed, so an eerie humming sound reached their ears from below. They stood and listened to the noise for a moment.

'Goddard? Could that be Goddard?' Ed Blanford shuffled closer. 'No. It's wind. Just wind.'

They fixed the first rope to a tree, tied a sliding loop in one end and dropped it down the shaft. Cochrane descended first, cautiously exploring the first gallery by torchlight before coming to rest on the rock floor. Ben Kitting's body was twisted and grinning, the arms reaching up to the land above. But no spirit inhabited the cold flesh. Cochrane quickly looped the rope around the dead man's shoulders, and his son and Dan Brady hauled the farmer back to spiritual safety. John Kitting closed his eyes as he saw the grimacing death-mask on his father, but he shed no tears and made no sound.

Brady followed Cochrane down to the first gallery. His skin crawled. The dank air, the musty smell of rock, closed in about him. Each time he shone his bright torch down one of the tunnels that led away from this first gallery, he expected to see the rapid motion of the guardian approaching them, defending its shrine.

John Kitting was the third down into the mines. He knocked his head on the low rock roof and swore loudly. By the time he was down, Brady had reconstructed the protective circle, big enough to contain the three men. Ed Blanford dropped Brady's pack down last of all, with the heavy coils of the second rope.

'This is where it gets tough,' Cochrane said. 'This way.'

He led the other two along the maze of tunnels, stooping below the damp roof, keeping the torchbeam directed ahead, but glancing about nervously each time the party came to a junction of tunnels. A cool breeze was fresh on their faces. The distant sound of humming came neither closer nor receded. It seemed to sing at them from all around, a monotonous wailing, not human, but not totally natural.

At the second pit they stopped and stared into the shadowy depths. 'It's about thirty feet down,' Cochrane said. 'That's quite a haul, John.'

'Ed is determined: he won't come down with us. And I don't want Mary here . . . So we'll have to manage.'

'If we get the bodies to the gallery below, I can come up and help haul,' Brady said.

'This is going to take hours,' Kitting murmured, and shivered violently in the cold, claustrophobic chamber.

Holding on hard to the rope, Kitting watched as Brady and Cochrane slid out of sight. He dropped to a crouch, then, his back against hard rock, the torch held before him moving in slow sweeps from left to right and back again, regularly checking each tunnel. Brady had made him a small protective circle, but Kitting could not believe that such a simple pattern could protect him against ghosts.

At the bottom of the shaft Brady unpacked four black-surfaced mirrors and set them up at the corners of a square; he linked them with gold wire and smeared a circle of pungent-smelling unguent around them, leaving two small gaps in the line.

Cochrane watched him carefully, not questioning. Brady passed him a small bottle of the same material. 'To close the circle is to close the cage.'

'I understand. But you're not thinking of trapping the guardian *here*?'

'This is a fail-safe only,' Brady agreed.

'Maybe we should have set traps further up . . .'

Brady laughed, despite his feeling of discomfort. 'How many mirrors do you think I carry with me?'

Now at last, Brady came close to the shrine itself. The wind was stronger. It smelled slightly, and he analysed the various aromas: faeces, sweat, urine, decay – all these things just hinted at. More powerfully, more noticeably, a smell like scorching. Also, the smell of autumn, a natural odour that he associated with woodland on a damp, cold night.

They approached the broken seal and crouched by the plaster wall while Brady ran his finger across the un-mistakable sign of Arachne. There was no movement behind them, nor any sound from the shadowy place beyond the seal. For a moment the walls seemed to close in

308

on Brady, and a hot sweat broke out on his skin. He pushed hard against the cold rock walls, and the discomfort passed.

'I smelled the fear,' Cochrane said. 'I expect the guardian got a good sniff too.'

'Then let's be careful,' Brady said quickly, sharply. The moment of claustrophobia had passed, but reluctantly he had to agree with the ghost-hunter: that surge of panic would have manifested itself in a non-physiological way as well.

Cochrane ducked and slipped into the shrine. Brady drew a breath and followed through, straightening up and looking around as Cochrane's torch flickered around the walls of the place.

At last the light settled on the bizarre grouping of human figures in the centre of the chamber, 'Christ al-bloody-mighty,' Brady whispered, shocked, and slowly settled to a crouch, unwilling to approach the silent forms, frightened, yet fascinated, by his first confrontation with an end-product of Arachne's programme of abduction.

Eight bodies; eight families shattered; eight lives stolen for a purpose as obscure, now, as it had been for months.

Cochrane was walking around the edge of the chamber, staring at each sleeping face in turn. Brady followed his movement. His heart was thundering. Even though he knew that none of his family were here, he had a terrifying image of a similar shrine, perhaps a thousand miles away, where Alison lay as peacefully, or Dominick, perhaps Marianna too; on their backs, hands folded on their chests, eyes half closed, breathing as slow and as shallow as that of a dying man.

The torch illuminated the grotesque, shrunken features of an obvious corpse, a woman, the hair spread about the face. 'I think she was young when she came here. It looks as if she's been drained. Blonde, though. Not your wife . . .'

Again the torch moved. A man, this time, the cheek-bones proud from the skull, the sockets glazed and empty-looking. 'Middle-aged man,' Cochrane said. 'And this chap's on his way.'

The light of the torch was resting on another man. The features were shrunken, but the chest rose imperceptibly every few seconds. Cochrane moved round. 'This girl I recognize.'

Brady rose, in the darkness, and stepped towards the figures. Cochrane had the beam of the torch on the face of an attractive girl of about fifteen. Her features were familiar to Brady too.

'A hitch-hiker,' Cochrane said. 'She was shown on TV a while ago. Vanished on the A1, remember? And here she is.' He was thoughtfully silent for a moment. 'How many others, I wonder?'

'Look at your wrist . . .' Brady whispered, and Cochrane raised his arm. The small watch-like gauge was faintly glowing. Cochrane took a step backwards and the glow went away. In the still place the two men stared at each other. 'The guardian,' Cochrane said. 'It's sensed us.'

He played the torch on to the totem. For a second Brady didn't see the object that was the central focus of the shrine. He had pulled a lamp from his pack and turned it on. A brighter, more friendly light filled the shrine. Shadows were banished, and the thump of his heart died away.

He saw two things, then, that made him start with shock.

The first was the jewelled object, the totem. It lay on a raised platform of rock, gleaming brightly, seeming to mock him. 'Oh my God!' he whispered, and stepped closer, staring at its hideously decorated head, the grimacing, obscene face with its horns curling down to its cheeks. The slit eyes watched him. The stretched, grinning mouth laughed silently at him.

Remember me, remember me? it seemed to whisper.

And Brady *did* remember, and the image of how it had been used on his wife, Alison, made his heart ache and his

310

head spin. Such a vile object, used in such a vile way. Had the rape been all part of the ritual? Or had it just been for the cruel fun of the collectors? Seeing the totem, revered here in this way, protected by a guardian, nourished by the bodies of stolen families, he came a step closer to understanding the design, the deliberate purpose, of that cold, Christmas night when so much of his world had been destroyed by Arachne.

Cochrane could see that Brady recognized the totem. He watched his colleague, frowning slightly, then said, 'You okay?'

Brady nodded solemnly. He pointed to the shaft. 'It was used . . . It was carried . . .' He looked up at the ghost-hunter, the words jamming up in his mouth. 'That night. When my family were taken. One of the beasts was carrying *that*.'

'Or a totem like it,' Cochrane corrected.

'There are other shrines?'

'I'm sure of it. It's part of the purpose.'

For a moment or two Brady could do nothing but watch the other man. Suspicions and uncertainties filled his mind. Cochrane knew more than he had told Brady. The question was: would he, over the next day or so, correct that omission?

Who *was* Cochrane? Just a simple ghost-hunter, drawn into a bigger game? Or was he a part of that bigger game, and not letting on?

Cochrane had dropped to a crouch, holding his wrist towards the totem. 'I think the guardian is back within it. Kitting released the thing when he touched the totem. Maybe Jack Goddard *is* safe.' He looked up. 'Have you got your trap ready?'

Brady reached for his pack again, to take out the bits and pieces of the snare that would restrain the guardian when they finally released it. As he did so, Cochrane said, 'That's the boy whose ghost has been seen around . . .'

And when Brady followed Cochrane's pointed finger to

one of the legs of the spider shrine, he got a second shock . . .

For a moment all blood drained from his face. He frowned, stepped round the shrine and looked down at the peaceful features of the youth. He was a boy of about twelve years of age. His hair was dishevelled. His feet were muddy. His skin was scratched. He was wearing a grey school jumper and long flannel trousers. Though his skin was a ghastly shade of yellow-grey, his chest rose and fell with a more regular rhythm that the others. Somehow he seemed more alive.

Brady was looking at Ellen Bancroft's son, Justin.

'Oh Ellen, Ellen,' Brady said under his breath, and shook his head. He felt like crying. He wondered if Ellen had any sense, any feeling at all about the continuing existence of her child in this shadowland, this half-death.

'I know this boy,' Brady said aloud. 'He's the son of the woman who first helped me.'

'The American?'

'Ellen Bancroft, yes.'

'The one who's now a ghost in your house?'

'The same. She begged me to find her husband and son, to avenge her. She can't get release from me, from the house, until she's sure that they're either dead, or safe.'

Cochrane looked down thoughtfully. 'He looks very alive to me. Half a battle won for your friendly ghost. Is her husband here?'

Brady shook his head. He reached out to touch the dirt on the boy's school shoes. 'It was no ghost those farmers saw prowling around . . .'

'That's what I thought,' Cochrane agreed. 'The boy himself. I don't think he was fully conscious, but he was called, or sent . . . or just self-motivated to leave the shrine.' Cochrane glanced round. 'How did he get out? There's always a cool breeze in here.'

They walked around the walls of the chamber. Where the rock wall was more folded and cracked than elsewhere

312

and the rubble spill was piled quite high, they found the narrow passage out of the shrine; it was like a split in the floor, hardly big enough, Brady would have thought, for even the boy to have wormed through. But Justin Bancroft was a very skinny lad, and somehow he had managed to wriggle through that gap and into the wider space below. The passage led to the surface, and on several occasions over the previous weeks, the boy had entered the real world, wandering about the farmland at night, before being compelled back to his place by the totem.

Cochrane had voiced the question: had Justin been called, or sent? Who was controlling his movement in the autumn world above the mines?

From a long way off came the sound of a voice. Brady nearly jumped out of his skin, but soon recognized John Kitting's call of 'hurry'. The young man was edgy and nervous waiting alone in the dark. It was time to begin dismantling the shrine.

Brady half expected the guardian to rise in protection the moment they touched the first body, but though Cochrane's wristlet indicated his awareness of some restless psychic energy in the chamber, the spirit remained quiescent; the totem lay sparkling and evil in the middle of the floor. Brady's snare was a discreet system of mirrors, gold and iron built around it, silently waiting to trap the elemental.

They took Justin Bancroft first, lifting the sleeping boy by legs and arms and shuffling backwards along the corridor, until they came to the vertical shaft. They waited together as Brady tied the loop of rope below the boy's shoulders. John Kitting tugged at the rope, and the slumped body was winched into the darkness.

The dismantling took hours. They brought all five of the remaining living into the chamber where the rope lay. Then Cochrane went up to help Kitting haul the victims to the

313

upper gallery. The totem now lay alone and unnourished. The eerie howling grew in volume, and a rustling sound came from the shrine chamber itself, like the sound of leathery wings being stretched and tried.

Only when all six bodies had been hauled to where Ed Blanford was waiting to drag them to the surface did Brady and Cochrane return to the totem.

'It knows we're here,' Cochrane whispered. 'I can feel it. It's waiting. Unsure.'

'Perhaps it senses the trap.'

'It senses us. Kitting released it by touching it. What worries me is that if one of us reaches to do the same thing, it'll grab the hand.'

They stared down at the phallic totem. The grinning demon-face almost winked at them, daring them to touch it, willing them to call the guardian out . . .

Brady touched his neck. A few months before the skin had been black, the muscles and tendons below the skin aching and bruised. No human hand had inflicted the terrible wound upon him. An elemental of great power, created by a human mind, had wrapped invisible fingers around his throat and tried to end his life.

Instead, Brady had survived, and the elemental and its creator had been the organisms to succumb to mortality.

'I'll touch the totem,' Brady said. 'You get by the entrance. If it goes wrong, if it possesses me, for God's sake get out of the mines and try again.'

'If it goes wrong,' Cochrane said wryly, 'the dung will close over our heads. There are no heroes here, Dan. And no false optimists. We've got one shot. It'd better be on target.'

Brady smiled. What Cochrane said was true. If it went wrong now, there was no hope for anyone at all involved with the Pitthurst Hill shrine. Arachne would swallow them into its maw, and spit out their bones. And would repair the shrine. And go away . . .

And everything that Dan Brady had achieved would be

lost. Arachne would return to a firmer footing as they moved inexorably towards the conclusion of their purpose.

No. It was inconceivable that anything should go wrong now. He had fought psychic attack, and won. This guardian was an echo, an energy source of diminishing power. It had been called out once, and that would have dissipated its power. Second time lucky . . .

Brady reached down, picked up the totem by its base and banged it hard on the rock, before dropping the cold object and staggering back, body and mind tensed, ready for action.

The moment that Brady touched the totem the whole shrine shuddered, as if it were undermined by an earthquake. In the air before him a tall grey shape formed, a creature out of a nightmare. He glimpsed bat-like wings and a broad grinning mouth; eyes like the blank, faceted domes of an insect's eyes. Limbs cracked and jerked as the hideous apparition reached for him, the glistening mouth opening to engulf him. A moment later it became a grey blur, an amorphous shape writhing and thrashing about as the psychic snare took it. It screeched, long and loud, a deafening sound. The shrine was filled with a stink worse than the smell of a rotting animal's body.

Then the greyness vanished. The shrine became suddenly, strangely silent and still. Dust settled slowly.

Brady glanced round and saw Cochrane cowering in the shrine's entrance.

'Got it,' Brady said. And smiled.

'You can keep it,' Cochrane said back.

Brady stepped forward and gingerly reached for the totem. This time, as his fingers closed around the golden shaft, there was no shaking, no sound. He picked up the ritual object and cradled it in the palm of his left hand, his right index finger tracing out the features of the ghoulish face designed upon it.

As he had picked it up, so something inside had moved, rattling. He had not failed to notice the fact.

315

Indeed, as he passed the totem to Cochrane he hesitated, holding onto the object even as Cochrane tried to take it. 'There's something inside,' he said.

Cochrane nodded. 'I know.'

'What, I wonder?'

Cochrane smiled. 'A piece of bone, Dan.'

'More than a piece of bone, I think.'

'A hell of a lot more.'

The moment of pause between them passed. Cochrane took the totem and turned from the shrine. Brady carefully closed the snare, keeping the mirrors facing each other. He wound the gold wire around them, then covered the whole trap with black cotton before placing it in his pack and following Cochrane to the surface.

Arachne's shrine had been dismantled.

And somewhere, in the maze of tunnels that formed these ancient mines, a farmer called Jack Goddard might still be alive . . .

PART THREE
The Siege

7

If Nancy Cochrane's thoughts could kill, then at eight-fifteen, on the morning after the dismantling of the shrine, her father would have been in very severe trouble.

Nancy sat on the hard single bed in the room she shared with Geoff Cochrane. The sleeping-bag was neatly folded at the bottom of the bed. She herself was dressed, and she sat with her school-bag on her lap, angry and staring hard at the bedroom door.

She had hardly slept a wink, and this bodily denial registered clearly in the shadows round her eyes, and the dishevelled appearance of her hair. Her mouth felt like the proverbial parrot's armpit, but she had not felt like breakfast. A half-hour of Mrs Buxton's prattle was more than she could have tolerated.

Her father had infuriated her. He had left her alone for more than a day He wasn't even planning to pick her up from school until late afternoon. The *least* he could have done was ring her this morning. She had sat in her room, listening for the phone, but all she had heard was Mrs Buxton's breakfast preparations, and the mindless patter of the Radio One DJ.

Now, Mrs Buxton was coming slowly up the stairs. Nancy could hear the woman's breathing, and the gentle creak of the wooden staircase. She watched the bedroom door. A floorboard on the landing shifted with a distant groan. Then there was silence. Nancy watched the gap below the door, wondering what was happening. Slowly her anxiety rose. She clutched her school-bag tighter, frowning as she waited for something to happen. What on earth was Mrs Buxton doing?

Then the door was opened. There was no knock. The handle turned and the bedroom door opened, and Mrs Buxton stood there, staring at the girl. She was fully dressed for the street, and looked in a very bad mood.

'I've finished with breakfast. It's school-time, now.'

'I didn't want breakfast,' Nancy said, watching the old woman's solemn face. Mrs Buxton stared at her, then shook her head.

'Growing girl like you ought to eat breakfast. Sets you up for the day.' She tut-tutted. 'I've made you some sandwiches. But I've got to go out, so I don't have time to cook you anything more substantial.'

She held up a small greaseproof-papered pack. 'Come on, my dear. The school whistle waits for no one.'

'I'm not going to school,' Nancy said. 'I'll work at home.'

Mrs Buxton laughed. 'Will you, indeed? I can understand the way you feel, Nancy. I hated school myself.' She became conspiratorial, stepping into the room and gently urging Nancy from the bed. 'I can't say that I see the point of half the lessons. Learn more from reading a cornflakes packet. But these things, dear . . . Oh well, they're sent to try us. Now off you go . . .'

'I really don't *want* to go to school,' Nancy insisted, turning round and confronting the startled landlady.

Mrs Buxton frowned. 'But you've got to. Your father said . . .'

'My father's an idiot! It's not safe for me to go to school. I'll just wait here, if you don't mind. I shan't touch anything.'

Mrs Buxton chuckled. 'Well, now. What a spirit. I don't think I'd better tell your poor father what you just said . . . Come on, love. It's not going to be that bad.'

'*Please!*' Nancy shrieked. 'Listen to me!' Mrs Buxton looked shocked, then frowned as Nancy went on, 'It really *isn't* safe for me to go to school. Let me just stay here . . .'

'Stay here indeed!' The landlady was getting impatient.

320

'Nobody ever liked school, young lady, and nobody I know ever regretted going. Now no more of your nonsense. The thought of it, indeed, staying here while I go out! I've got to lock up, Nancy, and I don't have a spare key. I can't take the chance of you going out and leaving the place open to any vandal to come in.'

Infuriated with the woman's patronizing tone, Nancy said, 'I'm not stupid, Mrs Buxton. If I say I won't go out, I won't go out!'

'I didn't say you were stupid, child,' the landlady said, as she propelled the girl down the stairs. 'But you're just a youngster. All children are forgetful. I can just see what would happen. An ice-cream van, out you go into the road, slam goes the door, and out you're locked.'

And despite her protests and pleading, Nancy Cochrane found herself outside the house, on a crisp autumn morning, being led by an insistent middle-aged woman to the gates of the school.

Geoff Cochrane let the Buxton number ring fifteen times, then gently placed the receiver back in its cradle. He rubbed his eyes and pushed a hand through his hair, sweeping it back from his haggard, weary face.

'Christ, I'm tired.'

'We should sleep for a bit,' Brady said from across the room. 'But not yet.'

They had finished with the shrine just an hour or so before. Brady could hardly believe that it had taken them so long, but as the night progressed so they had slowed down, taking more and more time to do simple things. The six people from the shrine were now safely bedded down in the largest of the upstairs rooms. Susan Blanford was attending to them. The farmers slept noisily in the dining-room, wrapped up in blankets, anoraks and sleeping-bags.

The lounge, being a deep room with only a single

window to the outside, had been taken over for other purposes . . . Cochrane had made a prison for the totem, a way of keeping it that was probably safer than a safe itself.

Geoff Cochrane picked up a smelly wool blanket and draped it around his shoulders, then wandered over towards where Brady was crouched, staring at the object of their night's work.

'Who were you calling?' Brady asked.

'My daughter, Nancy. She's obviously safely off to school. Best place for her, probably. I'll leave her there until midday.'

'Good. Come and look at this.'

The totem lay face down. Brady had orientated the shaft along the line of magnetic east and west, to reduce its potency should any lingering energy from its previous guardian remain. The object was covered with two strips of black silk in the form of a cross. The two ghost-hunters had constructed an elaborate containing-circle around the totem, consisting of dry earth, nitric acid and slivers of iron. At the main compass-points were four small mirrors, reflecting into the circle.

Geoff Cochrane had added his own extra touch to this prison for the totem and its main occupant: a fine white powder, sprinkled evenly around the golden shaft. He had not told Brady what the powder was, but Brady had already noticed that it had the faintest of garlic smells, and he guessed it to be a combination of dried woodland roots and some inorganic marker.

What he noticed now was that the powder was marked with thin rippling lines, like tide lines, reaching out from the middle of the totem toward the middle of the room. As he watched, so the white powder shifted slightly, and another wave appeared.

'Is this what you were looking for with your powder?' Brady asked, and the ghost-hunter came over to him, crouching beside the circle, but careful not to lean inside.

Cochrane nodded. His breath was very unpleasant as he

322

spoke. 'Something inside had prowled outside in the last couple of hours.'

Brady said 'It didn't prowl very far.'

'Probably just reached a few inches, testing the air. Looking around, perhaps.'

'Looking around at what?'

Cochrane shrugged. 'It doesn't know what's going on, but it knows things have changed.'

Brady stared at the ghost-hunter, curious about, and made anxious by, the unstated knowledge which the other man possessed. Who the hell *was* Geoff Cochrane? Or *what*? Could a simple ghost-hunter have encountered Arachne in such a way that he understood far more of their purpose than Brady had managed to learn?

Brady kept thinking of an old man called William Farmer whom he had encountered a few months before.

William Farmer. And his niece Kelly, a tiny, ten year old girl who had spoken and behaved like an adult. Farmer and the girl had teamed up. Together they had formed what Brady knew was called an *accumulator*, and as such they had been used by Arachne. The combined minds of the old man and the young girl had formed a storehouse for ancient and malevolent spirits, spirits brought to them in various ways. But the power of the 'gods and demons' that Farmer and his niece had stored in their collective grey matter had allowed the two of them to break away from Arachne, and to begin to wage war against the enemy that had tried to use them.

What had that old man said to him?

All across England, across the world, there are those of us, once recruited, who have broken away, who have turned their powers against *Arachne.*

Was Cochrane, in reality, such a recruit, one who had fled the fold and now either ran from his would-be masters, or circled them warily, waiting for a chance to wound the beast?

Brady said, 'This "it" you refer to . . . this main occupant . . . what is its nature, Geoff? How the hell do you know so much about the totem?'

'Two and two made four,' Cochrane said, and rose to his feet.

'What's in the totem?'

Brady stood up as well and tried to engage the other man's eyes, but Cochrane just stared down at the circle, his face white and haunted.

'I'll show you,' he said at last, and reached out to push Brady gently back from the area of the prison. 'If something strange happens, just keep calm . . . don't panic. It was the guardian that was the real danger. I don't *think* there's any danger now.'

'I'll trust you,' Brady said.

Geoff Cochrane picked up the totem. As he did so he sucked in his breath, a sign of his tension. He held the fingers of both hands in an approximation of a horned head, and used the extended fingers to lift the strange object.

When it was clear of the circle he relaxed, but now he himself stepped inside the ring, turning to face Brady.

'Better safe than sorry,' he said.

Brady said nothing. Cochrane turned the phallic totem over in his hand, touching the markings and the evil face. He held the totem up. 'Look. There's dried blood on the horns –'

'I don't want to know,' Brady said, feeling momentarily weak.

Cochrane, remembering what Brady had told him of the way the object had been used, looked slightly embarrassed. 'Sorry.'

Now he began to twist the totem's head. After a moment it gave, sliding away from the main body. It's neck was silvery-smooth. From the container, Cochrane slipped the sharp piece of bone he had already hinted lay inside.

The bone lay in his right palm. He placed the empty

324

container on the floor, moving with exaggerated slowness. Then he used two fingers to turn the fragment over cautiously.

'Not much to look at . . .' he said.

Brady agreed. The bone was six inches long and about the thickness of a finger. It had been broken from a larger fragment and several of its edges were raw and jagged. It was brilliantly white. Over its surface, shapes and marks had been pecked out by pointed tools. A sequence of twenty-eight dots, in a snaking row that doubled back on itself; two 'runes', one of which Brady recognized as 'thorn'; shapes and figures of a primitive design. And at one end, an eye, opened and watching.

'Carved boned,' Brady said. 'The original totem.'

But Geoff Cochrane shook his head. 'Not a totem. Not really. In one sense the bone is dead, ancient. A piece of fossil. But it's *alive*, Dan. It's as alive as you or I. Or perhaps I should say it's as alive as an unborn child.' He watched Brady peculiarly. 'And that's what I believe this to be, Dan. An unborn. A foetus. The whole shrine was not a place of reverence. It was an incubation chamber. The totem is the incubatorium. The eight people around it were quite simply its spiritual nourishment. It had already consumed the life of two of them. In a few months, years perhaps, it would have ingested the life-essence of them all. Growing in strength. Growing in power. Coming alive again, alive after millennia in the darkness. The bone is an embryo, Dan. It won't change its shape or form, but the entity trapped in its calcite and phosphorus, the *thing* that lives in the crystal lattice of this bone – that creature, and others like it, will form again in the real world, metaphysical, insubstantial, desperately powerful. Call it a god or a demon. Call it what you want. Once, such things ruled man. Soon, if Arachne have their way, they will rule man again. Only this time, there will be men who rule the spirits of the gods themselves!'

For a long minute Brady just stared at the insignificant

piece of bone and thought of the immense power it contained – if Cochrane was right. Had he now taken another step closer to understanding Arachne?

The pattern had emerged before and was now becoming clearer. Arachne were raising the past, using old magic and new magic. They were summoning the forces of mind and belief from all the ages, powerful forces, each the expression of a culture's secret knowledge and hidden talent.

First there had been the Nordic spirit, still inhabiting the talisman that he wore. Then the gods of the North American Indians, dispatched to England in a strange Indian girl to be added to the accumulator, the old man and his niece.

Each age, each civilization, had tried to form a magic of its own, to understand the secret life of nature, and of time. Each magic, drawing on an incomplete inheritance from other times, had been shaped for the magician – spells for one, herbs for another, sacrifices for a third, mathematics for a fourth, computers for a fifth . . .

It occurred to Brady now that Arachne were using *all* of magic. In that way they might well fill in the gaps in knowledge that had plagued the dabblers in the secret arts for so many centuries. Combine Roman, Greek, Celtic and mediaeval sorcery, and though much would overlap, each would plug the mystery-gaps of the others. A worldwide cookbook of magic: Celtic gods summoned by computer; the transmutation of lead into gold using neolithic symbol magic . . .

All for a goal that Arachne called the Time of Change.

And if Brady was right, and all of history's hells were loosed upon the world, the expression Time of Change seemed far too soft. As far as humankind were concerned, if Arachne won the day then only one expression seemed appropriate:

Total eclipse.

From within the circle, Geoff Cochrane was watching

326

him coldly. 'You've gone white. Like death,' he said, and Brady shrugged.

'I feel a little shaken,' he murmured, then asked, 'How do you know all this about the totem? How can you possibly know?'

'It was told to me in dreams, Dan. This is why I can't be sure I'm right. In dreams I saw the spider. In dreams I saw this totem – or one like it. In dreams . . .' He frowned as he trailed off, shaking slightly. It was as if he was cold. He placed the bone fragment back into the container, then looked up sharply. Brady thought he had been about to say something and had changed his mind. 'In dreams I've seen a lot of things, and most of them make no sense to me. There is a name like 'magondog', and other things like that . . .'

Magondathog! thought Brady. *Yes. I've heard that name too. Where it will all finish. The place where the final act will occur. The time of change. The roundelay. The incomprehensible ritual, always hinted at, never explained.*

'All of this,' Cochrane went on, waving the totem, 'all that I *think* about this is speculation.'

'Why would they have used it as a rape weapon?' Brady said quietly, trying to detach himself from the pain he felt for Alison. 'Why that?'

Cochrane nodded slowly, staring at the demon. 'If this *is* an unborn god – or something that was once thought of as a god – then perhaps . . .'

'The life had to be started by a simulated act of procreation.'

'Something like that,' Cochrane agreed gently. 'A ritual using, with the pain of the woman generating the first growth.'

Could this very totem have been the one that had been used at Christmas? Was Alison – a part of her, a fragment of her heart and of her agony – still within the bone?

The thought was too much to bear. Brady was too tired,

327

and too on edge, to accommodate the extra anguish that such considerations evoked within him.

Cochrane replaced the totem and stepped from the circle.

The two men slept, a brief snatch of rest, lasting no more than an hour. When Brady woke up and went to the kitchen he could see that the day was overcast and dreary, with a strong threat of rain in the air. The farmers were gathered around the table, talking softly over the remains of cooked breakfasts. Brady sat down among them and drank a cup of strong coffee.

Kathy Goddard, he was told, was restless, very disturbed. But she wasn't violent. Everybody was sure that she would snap out of her strange state of mind soon, and be able to contribute more constructively to the search for her husband.

As for the people from the shrine . . . Susan Blanford's words were dull, she herself heavy-eyed with fatigue and anxiety: 'It's hard to tell if they're this side of death or that side of living.'

Brady went to see for himself.

They had made the Blanfords' main bedroom into the ward, with beds round the walls, and the six silent people lay on their backs, eyes closed, gently breathing. Brady walked around them, staring at each in turn. Their skins were all cold. When he peeled back their eyelids he could see that their eyes had rolled up, as if they were dead. When he listened to their hearts it was sometimes hard to hear the beat. And as he and Cochrane had discovered the night before, their limbs were stiff and ungiving, as if a form of rigor was setting in.

Susan Blanford was right; it was hard to know which side of life or death these unfortunate creatures occupied.

The night before, Brady had spent nearly an hour sitting by Justin. He sat on the bed again now, and stared at the

328

grey features of the unconscious lad. He was a good-looking child. Unlike the others behind the lids his eyes were wild and alert. They seemed to stare at Brady, as if begging him to understand some unspoken message.

Ellen's husband, Michael, was not among the occupants of this shrine. Perhaps he too was lying beneath rock and earth, but a thousand miles away. Perhaps Arachne had taken him for another purpose.

Perhaps he was already dead.

But last night, Brady had called a trusted – and trustworthy – friend, and asked him to go to his house, Brooks Corner. There to tell the ghost of Ellen Bancroft that her son had been found.

Half the anguish of the spirit would fade away. Her release from the mortal realm, when it came, would be that much easier.

Cochrane called to him. Brady tugged on his heavy waterproof and went outside into the yard between the farm buildings where John and Mary Kitting were already at work making the small farm complex into a fortress.

The farm buildings, consisting of the house, two machinery sheds and two barns, formed an imperfect square; but the buildings were of brick, and with few windows on the outside. The farmers had used sacks of manure, heavy machinery, blocks of wood and bales of barbed wire to block the gaps between the main structures. It was Brady's job now to erect as much in the way of psychic defences as he could, both outside the 'castle' and inside. Working with Cochrane, he approached the task readily, recruiting Susan Blanford to help make the *zona magnetica*, with its clay and iron gargoyles. The Blanfords' daughter, Sophie had arrived and taken over the supervision of the seven patients. Her horror, her confusion and her requests for medical supplies were all ignored in favour of a concentrated effort to make the Blanford farm secure against attack by Arachne.

329

When she repeated her urgent request for certain supplies from a chemist, Cochrane told her that he would be picking Nancy up from school at one o'clock. He would fetch the things she needed then. And he added to Brady, 'I'll include some iodine and sticking plaster. Knowing Nancy, I'm going to be needing them.'

He laughed, then went back to work.

Unknown to her father, Nancy's irritation with him had all but vanished during the first half of the morning. She had arrived at school, taken her place in the classroom and shared in the growing disturbance resulting from Miss Bowman's absence. At ten past nine the door to the classroom was flung open and the headmaster entered, struggling beneath a tall pile of the children's edition of *Treasure Island*.

There was a strained, excited hush. Even Sarah Biggs fell silent, watching as the balding, red-faced man walked, without a word, between the desks distributing the reading matter.

When all the pupils had their tatty paperbacks, the headmaster instructed them to start reading. He would test them on chapter one after the morning break.

'Where's Miss Bowman?' Sarah asked, brazenly. 'Is she ill, sir?'

'Has she run away with Mr Trenchard?' Faith Brooker murmured, causing a ripple of laughter among those who had heard her.

'Silence!' the headmaster said. 'Miss Bowman is ill. I shall be supervising you for the day.'

Miss Bowman was ill. The words were like music to Nancy Cochrane's ear. She smiled, relaxed and opened her book. The world suddenly seemed a less threatening place . . .

Until at ten-thirty Miss Bowman arrived.

She came into the classroom, wearing the same clothes

330

she had been wearing the day before. She looked dishevelled and tired, her hair uncombed, her face pale and without any obvious traces of make-up. The effect was to make her eyes look small and her mouth very pinched. The headmaster, who had been sitting at the front desk marking essays, rose and talked quickly and quietly with the woman. Then he left, looking angry and unhappy.

Miss Bowman unpacked her attaché case, then addressed the whole class. 'Continue reading. The test will take place as planned.'

She stood at the front, staring into the middle distance. There was a murmur of whispered conversation. Nancy watched the woman, her heart beating fast. She dreaded Miss Bowman looking at her, but as she stared at the teacher, she almost willed there to be a meeting of eyes.

Miss Bowman obliged.

The contact of eyes was like an electric shock. One moment the woman had been staring into space, the next her whole awareness seemed to be burrowing into Nancy's consciousness, stripping away the flesh and bone, squeezing the grey stuff below her skull. The effect on Nancy was like a sudden, shattering fright. The teacher's gaze was hypnotic, draining. All the energy drained from Nancy. Her limbs felt listless, numb. She slumped in her chair, and felt her jaw go slack. Miss Bowman seemed to come closer, to loom larger . . .

Those eyes, that evil stare . . .

Then the classroom door opened and the headmaster returned. The moment of contact was broken. Miss Bowman seemed almost irritated as she conferred again with the headmaster, and the class continued to murmur and giggle, taking every advantage of this break in routine.

Nancy decided, then and there, that at the mid-morning break she was going to run from the school. She watched the clock above the door, praying for the eleven-fifteen break in classes to arrive.

At eleven-fifteen there was a general movement to put

books into desks and go to the playground for milk and buns.

Miss Bowman stood at the front and said loudly, 'Keep your books on your desks.'

'But Miss Bowman,' Sarah protested. The teacher looked at her and the girl's voice trailed away.

'Yes, Sarah?'

'It's time for our break miss,' the terrified girl managed to splutter.

'There will be no break this morning. Milk will come to the class for those who order it. The headmaster tells me you have not behaved well. Therefore we will have the test on *Treasure Island*.'

Nancy sat, numbed with shock, outraged. Her hands shook as she held her book. Her head felt dizzy. Miss Bowman smiled sweetly, a gesture riddled with sarcasm. Her gaze roamed around the room, then settled again on Nancy. 'Well, my dears,' she said, 'we have a little catching up to do. Nancy, you don't seem to be reading.'

'I've read it before, miss,' Nancy said.

'Have you, indeed. Then you can come out to the front and tell us all about it. Come on.'

Slowly, Nancy rose from her seat and stepped up to the raised platform at the front of the room. As she walked, so Miss Bowman watched her, and there was a sparkle of triumph in the woman's eyes, the touch of a smile on her lips. Nancy felt cold, her legs shaking, her stomach knotted tightly with tension. She was ready to run. That was all she could do, now: run from the room, from the school, out of Anerley. There was something wrong with Miss Bowman, something *terribly* wrong. There was a contact of minds, and all Nancy could feel was a brooding, blood-stained darkness.

As she stepped up beside the teacher she began to smell something, an odour of sharp decay, the foul stench she had come to associate with both death and the super-natural.

332

She didn't take her gaze from the teacher. The sound of the class receded, like the sea beyond a rise of sand dunes.

Miss Bowman turned from the class, reaching towards the blackboard with a piece of white chalk. She said something to Nancy, but Nancy did not hear the words through the rushing of blood in her ears, the inward wailing of warning to her. As the teacher turned away, so the smile increased. For a second, as Nancy watched, Miss Bowman's face changed, distorted. Her eyes narrowed and glowed, her mouth seemed to gape, exposing a toothless darkness within, her cheeks shrank, the skin turning yellowy and waxy.

The grotesque features faded as quickly as they had come. Probably no one in the class would have seen them, but Nancy Cochrane was an exceptional girl with exceptional talents.

It was a corpse which walked here and talked here, a corpse which had focussed upon her and recognized her as a girl of talent. The human side of Miss Bowman had been taken from her. She was possessed. She was not what she seemed. She was part death, and the part of her which was death knew that Nancy knew . . .

The teacher's gaze rested on her. The pale face frowned. The lips moved. Nancy felt, rather than heard, the classroom ripple with mirth, the underhand giggling that releases the tension of embarrassment. Nancy had been standing at the front of the class for several minutes, silent, terrified.

Miss Bowman watched her. There was no doubt that each now knew the nature of the other.

'The class may take its break,' Miss Bowman said, and the words sounded faint and far-away. But the rest of the class erupted noisily from its seats, the mob of boys and girls surging towards the door. Nancy realized that she was to be left alone with Miss Bowman. The woman's hypnotic stare kept her rooted to the spot.

Then Faith Brooker came up to the teacher and said

something. Nancy saw the flicker of annoyance on the woman's face. And the hypnotic hold broke.

Nancy turned and fled. Miss Bowman almost screeched at her to come back, but she thrust herself among the throng of bodies, shoved and fought her way to the door, despite angry protests and childish threats.

She burst out into the corridor and ran frantically towards the main hall. Behind her she heard her name angrily called. Glancing back she saw Miss Bowman, a towering, white-faced apparition of hate moving easily through the children in the corridor, approaching her.

Somewhere, a whistle blew. The break was ended. Nancy's idea of getting to the school gates became abruptly impractical. (In any case, the gates would be locked. She had known that even as she had run). From every door to the outside, children streamed back into the school, a tidal wave of chattering, running bodies. Nancy felt despair, but the adrenalin pumped into her blood, and she struggled to escape the teacher, who was still shouting to her.

She turned down a corridor, darted through the games-room and doubled back on her route. Miss Bowman was nowhere to be seen. Nancy crouched slightly and walked with the moving crowd, and when she came to the girls' toilets she darted inside and made her way to one of the closets, closing the door, and sitting, shaking, on the covered seat.

She listened to the chatter and laughter of the girls outside, the running of taps, the flushing of toilets, the patter of feet. Slowly the sounds died away. A single girl ran water, humming to herself. Then that tap, too, was staunched and whoever it was left the washroom, slamming the door behind her.

Nancy remained breathlessly quiet, listening to the silence. If anyone came into the washroom she would hear the door. Her heart raced in anticipation of that gentle sound, but it never came. After five minutes she began to calm down and started to plan her escape from the school.

334

First, a careful walk though the main hall to the far doors. Then a dash across the playground, in view of the kitchens only, to the grass bank where the exercise bars were. The metal railings were lower than normal, and she was certain she could scale them and get to the roadway beyond.

Time to go, she thought, and began to ease herself off the undignified seat. The silence in the washroom was unnerving and her heart fluttered again. She reached for the lock on the door . . .

The door was struck a blow so powerful that she screamed and flung herself back against the cistern.

A second blow ripped the lock from its casing. The door flung open and banged shut again, and in that instant Nancy saw the grinning, toothless mouth of the creature that inhabited Miss Bowman. It was standing there, one hand extended, nails long and sharp.

Slowly it pushed the door open. Now it was the teacher who stood there, mouth stretched in a smile, eyes narrowed and triumphant.

Nancy flung herself at the woman, head down, arms flailing. She heard the teacher grunt with surprise and pain as the child's head winded her. Claws slashed across Nancy's neck and back, tearing her dress. The woman uttered an unearthly wail and pursued the child to the door, reaching for her.

Nancy flung the door of the washroom wide. Miss Bowman's hands closed on her shoulders, tugging her back. Nancy twisted and pulled the door behind her, banging it against the teacher's right arm.

The grip relaxed. Nancy fled into the corridor beyond, screamed once, a shrill, piercing cry, and ran blindly and without awareness of pain towards the main school doors.

She reached the playground, conscious of the thundering footfall behind her. She crossed the playground. A voice shouted at her. The tarmac rang with the sound of pursuit. The green railings loomed closer.

Nancy leapt for them like a cat, hauling herself up, grabbing at the bladed points of the rails. She tore her dress again as she tumbled across the fencing onto the pavement. Her ankle ached, but she picked herself up and ran on, still aware that someone behind was almost on her.

There was the screeching sound of a wild animal at bay. Nancy stumbled and picked herself up, then turned to look back at the school.

Miss Bowman was balanced on the railings, skirts blowing in the wind, eyes wide, mouth tense with anger. She stared at Nancy, teetering on the fencing. Then, with a single wild leap, she came down on to the road, toppled and fell. Slowly she picked herself up, moving purposefully, like a cat about to leap. Her gaze never left the girl, and she was making a throaty noise, a low growl, the sound of desperate hate . . .

Nancy turned away again, took a deep breath and ran for her life.

8

Geoff Cochrane pulled the Land Rover into the side of the road and watched the thronging mass of children in the playground of St Mary's. It was well into the lunchtime break, almost time, in fact, for the classes to be called back for the afternoon.

'Which one's your daughter?' Sophie Blanford asked from the passenger seat.

For a second Cochrane didn't realize she was being funny. Then he smiled. There were hundreds of little girls racing about the wide playing area. It was like a battleground in there. If Nancy was in the thick of it he'd never spot her.

But Cochrane hadn't expected Nancy to be anywhere but by the main school gate, anxiously looking for him. He drove the Land Rover slowly along the boundary of the school, looking for his daughter. But he couldn't see her.

Possibly she *was* playing, despite what she said about the other girls in the class. Perhaps she was still inside, sulking, or reading in some quiet corner.

'Listen,' he said, 'let's get you to the hospital and the chemist, and I'll come back for Nancy later.'

Sophie shrugged. 'Fine by me.' She was a tall, rather ungainly woman, wearing her dark blue nurse's uniform and a warm black cape. After her initial shock at the nature of the nursing her father had asked her to do, she had accepted the situation calmly. But she needed blood, drip-feeds and other equipment that could only be borrowed from a hospital. There was a small hospital four miles from Anerley. She knew two of the doctors there; she had been

337

out with one of them, and maintained friendly contact with him. She felt she could obtain the equipment she needed without arousing too much suspicion.

'Come on then,' Cochrane said, making the sudden decision. He glanced for a last time at the school. If he could see Nancy, he'd bring her away with him now. But he couldn't, so she would have to sit through the afternoon. She'd be safe enough.

The young farmer, John Kitting, shovelled the last dirt into the last shallow pit that Brady had excavated, covering the last clay and iron gargoyle. He patted the earth down, then stood on it. Brady watched him. Kitting looked up and said, 'What next?'

'That's it,' Brady said, and looked around. It was mid-afternoon. They had done well to defend the farm complex so quickly, although he had to admit that the defences were not as strong, nor as rigorously designed, as he would have liked.

Mary Kitting brought out two mugs of strong, rather bitter tea. Brady was grateful for the drink. He felt cold, and very strange. Although John Kitting had accepted him, there was a coolness towards him from all the local folk. They were nervous of Brady, not understanding him, not liking the strange way he had come to Anerley.

'Those few bits of clay can keep ghosts away? Can that really be true?' John Kitting asked the question between sips of tea.

'It's called a *zona magnetica*,' Brady said. 'For the best psychic defence you need several zones. We'll have to make do with the two.'

He looked at the small, ground-level braziers that burned in two circles, one outside the farm buildings, one inside. He had brought the herbs – mandragora, henbane, hecate and the rest – with him. The braziers had been cobbled together out of copper pots, aluminium saucepans

338

and other household items, and were not perfect by any means.

Brady toured the buildings outside, John Kitting trudging along behind him. High brick walls marked the outer sides of the barns and the machinery sheds. The house had outer windows which were now covered with thick planking and barbed wire, except for small gaps where a shotgun could be poked through with devastating effect. The two wide entrances into the quadrangle had been plugged by a threshing machine, two tractors, a baler, sacks of fertilizer and more evilly barbed iron wire. Only a two-foot-wide alleyway remained from outside to inside, and Brady checked the ground outside this to ensure that his carefully laid trap could not be detected. The turf had been laid down again over the mirror and mercury snare. The triggering wires running below the ground were quite invisible.

All of the physical defences had been made as resistant to psychic battering as it was possible to get, with a brazier of discouraging organic fumes, and a linen-wrapped talisman in each location. Brady carried a few of the Roman mosaic tiles wherever he went. The bulk of the ancient flooring, which he had excavated from his own land and which had still been ringing with the echo of a violent deed committed upon it some two thousand years before, had been built into the main wall around his own house.

The psychic echo in each tile was a potent discourager to any elemental that might be sent in to disperse the physical barriers at the alleyways.

Before he stepped back into the compound, Brady scanned the land around. The clouds were heavy, but bright, and the rolling hills around the farm were stark ridges, where solitary trees stood in wind-blown sil-houette. No human movement could be seen on that bare horizon. The road to Anerley wound out of sight, and in the distance Brady could see the traffic on the main road west. The Blanford farm was bleak, isolated and uncannily

339

silent, save for the whispering of the cold autumn wind in the hollow places of the farm buildings.

Into that silence, as he stood and 'felt' for Arachne, came an ominous, distant clicking. The hairs on his body pricked with excitement. He stepped away from the farm, out of the protecting circle of mandrake.

The sound was not an auditory manifestation. It was registering *inside* his skull, tickling his sixth or seventh senses.

A regular clicking, like ratchets on an old machine. Then one or two aerial *thumps*. On the wind there was the faintest of sharp smells, the stench of rot, but so fleeting that he hardly had time to notice it.

The land around remained deserted of movement and of life, and the eerie clicking died away.

Brady would have smiled, but his face was rigid with a combination of fright and excitement.

He had seen nothing, but the farm had just been probed. Something, an elemental perhaps, or a curious mind, had drifted close enough to scent the mandragora.

Arachne were here.

At last.

He went back through the alley and into the quadrangle. The Kittings were inside the main building, cleaning up after the dirty work of the hours before. Susan Blanford was chopping meat for the evening meal. The sound of hammering told of Ed Blanford finishing the boarding up of windows from the inside. Brady had expected Geoff Cochrane and Sophie to have returned by now. They were probably having difficulty getting the medical equipment, he thought. He hoped they would hurry back. There was, otherwise, the strongest of possibilities of their being caught *outside* the defended farm.

Brady wanted Cochrane's expertise around him. And not just that. Cochrane, though he had revealed much about Arachne, still knew more. Brady was convinced of that.

As he stepped into the kitchen, Susan said, 'Ah, there

you are. The boy . . . the one you know . . . he's saying something. Just a gabble, but it sounds like words.'

The woman wiped her hands on a cloth and led Brady through to the ward. The room was in semi-darkness, and very cool. Fresh air was blowing in the half-opened windows, and an electric fan kept the air circulating. Even so, there was an unpleasant smell in the place, partly the chemicals that Sophie had used to wash the bodies as she had examined them, partly the slight seepage of bodily waste from the healthier of the victims.

The room, normally silent, was now filled with a strange whisper. Justin, his eyes closed, was murmuring feebly, occasionally hissing, licking his lips and speaking his gabble of words in punctuated bursts. His hands were clenched and his head moved from side to side. Brady noticed that he, alone of the six people in the room, had a better colour, a less deathly pallor.

He smoothed the boy's hair back from his wet face, and felt the tinge of warmth in the skin. He put his ear close to Justin's mouth and tried to discern the words.

After a while he realized that Justin was saying 'mummy'. He was calling for Ellen Bancroft, begging her to come, calling her from his fever dream. He also murmured, 'yes', and 'coming' and occasionally, within the burble of incoherent sound, Brady thought he heard the boy say 'frightened'.

He touched a cool sponge to Justin's face, mopped up the oozing sweat. 'He's beginning to come round. I'm sure of it.'

Susan said, 'God be praised. If just one of them lives to love another day, then we'll have done something of worth.'

Brady examined each of the others in turn. The girl, lost while hitchhiking on the A1, was slightly warmer than the rest, but dry to the touch, silent, still very ill. The remaining four were still cold.

The noise of Ed Blanford's hammering stopped.

Distantly, Brady heard him stretching and easing his aching arms. A moment later came the sound of the back door slamming.

'That must be Geoff,' Brady said, and went downstairs. He was puzzled to find no one in the kitchen. He called for Cochrane, but there was no answer. Ed Blanford followed him through to the kitchen.

'Did you see Geoff Cochrane? And Sophie?' Brady asked.

Blanford shook his head. 'Heard the back door go, though.'

From the other room came Susan's call. 'Kathy Goddard's gone!' The woman appeared in the kitchen doorway, white-faced, frightened for her friend. 'What are we going to do? She's not safe out there, not alone.'

'Damn!' said Brady. Picking up his coat he raced outside, calling for the woman. When he reached the narrow exit from the quadrangle he saw her. She was running up the hill, towards Pitthurst Wood. Brady shouted her name, but she didn't respond.

He went in pursuit of her.

At the outskirts of Anerley, where new estates clustered in yellow brick monotony, a woman walked her dog. She was middle-aged, and dressed in anorak and tight slacks. She walked briskly, the terrier padding along beside her, its tongue lolling.

Suddenly the dog began to strain at the leash. The woman stopped and tugged at her pet.

'Not here. Wait till we find some nice grass.'

The dog whined and barked. It was sniffing at the wooden palings of a garden fence, beyond which was a dense growth of chrysanthemum. 'Come on. Sammy. Don't fuss there . . .'

The dog scratched at the fencing. There was a rustle of movement in the flower patch beyond. It was probably

342

another dog, and the woman didn't want Sammy fraternizing, not now, not when she was in such a hurry.

She went up to the fence and peered over.

And gasped with shock.

A small, white-faced girl huddled there, eyes wide, hair dishevelled. She stared up at the woman, looking distraught and quite appallingly terrified.

'Why, who are you?' The woman said, managing only the first two words before the cowering creature screamed shrilly, leapt up and slapped her hard in the face. The girl scrambled on to the fence, scratching the woman and ignoring the terrier's frantic barking. Then she jumped to the pavement and run away, legs pounding, dress flapping.

In seconds the girl had disappeared among the estate houses.

The woman tenderly touched her face, then reached down to calm her pet. 'Well, I don't know. Some children are so *rude*. There, there, Sammy. She's gone now. Nasty girl gone away.'

The dog quietened down.

Half a mile outside the town, on the main road to the west, a man driving a battered Vauxhall Chevette saw the girl walking along the roadside. She moved in a funny, jerky way – walking, then running, then stopping and peering into the farmland to her left, as if searching for something.

As he approached her he slowed down. She glanced at the car and started to run. He drove past her, twisting round to get a better look.

She was very pretty. She was untidy and dirty, and she had a big tear in her frock. But her hair was long and silky, and her wide eyes and prim little mouth were almost grown-up in their attractiveness to the man.

He stopped the car, wiped his palms on his jeans and stepped out. The girl paused, staring at him. She glanced nervously about, but held her ground. The man, who was thin and middle-aged, and looked rather pallid and nervous, clearly frightened her slightly.

He would have to put her at ease. 'Are you lost, lovey?'

She said nothing.

He said, 'Perhaps I can give you a lift somewhere. Where d'you live?'

Still nothing. He took a step forward. Two cars drove by, faces peering at him, but neither stopped. The girl had tensed slightly and he reached out a hand to her. 'Don't be frightened. I live in Anerley. Let me help you.'

'I'm all right, thank you,' the girl said. Her voice was shaky. The man watched her, his knees trembling, his stomach clenched. She was the prettiest child he had ever seen.

'Come for a ride with me,' he said. 'I feel like an ice-cream, and I know a good place. Then I can take you home. I know all the people round here, all farms.'

'Do you know a farmer who carries a shotgun?' she asked.

'Of course I do. He lives over there . . .' He pointed over the low hill, where the girl had been looking. 'Would you like me to take you there?'

The girl stood indecisively for a moment, then stepped forward, looking nervously up at him. He smiled pleasantly.

'Yes, please,' she said. He reached out a hand and she took it, although she kept her grip loose.

'What's your name?'

'Nancy.'

'I'm Simon. Not much of a car, is it?'

He held the door open for her. As she climbed into the passenger seat he reached down and gently, almost as if helping her in, touched her through her dress.

She screeched with indignation, turned and punched him; a small, bunched fist, accurately driven into his genitals. It knocked him back with shock and pain, and the girl twisted out of his grasp and fled. He pursued her,

344

limping, for a few yards, then stopped. She had leapt across the ditch in the grass verge, and over the low wire fencing that bounded the fields.

The last he saw of her she was running full pace towards a clump of woodland that stretched up the rise and into the distance.

By the time Dan Brady had caught up with Kathy Goddard, he was almost unconscious with the effort of running. The woman, despite being in her mid-thirties, was tremendously fit. Obsession gave her extra energy. She had seen something, or heard something, or simply cracked. Whatever, she led Brady a merry chase, and they were a mile from the farm by the time he caught her. She stopped, stared towards the distant woodland which spread above the dismantled shrine. If she hadn't chosen that moment to pause, Brady might never have caught her. When he staggered up to her she jumped, as if – despite his continually calling her – she had been unaware of his pursuit.

'Kathy, come back to the farm. It's not safe out here.'

'Leave me alone. Jack's here. Let me go!'

'Kathy, it's dangerous. Jack isn't here. You're imagining things!'

Brady glanced quickly around, to confirm that no other human form was visible. He saw only deserted land, wind-whipped trees.

'I *saw* him,' Kathy Goddard cried out. She turned to stare towards Pitthurst Hill. Brady reached out and stopped her from running away again. She turned angry, tired eyes upon him. 'Who the hell *are* you?'

'A friend,' Brady said, realizing that this was – in one sense – the first time that the woman had actually seen him.

She came closer, almost growling. 'I saw him. He called to me. He's my husband, you must let me *go*!'

As she said the word 'go' she struggled in Brady's grip,

345

kicking out at him. He took the blows, turning the woman so that she was less dangerous.

'Listen to me!'

She calmed down slightly. Then she started to cry, a bitter sound that reminded Brady of the ghost of Ellen Bancroft weeping.

Brady drew her closer, hugging her. 'I saw him,' Kathy said. 'I saw him outside the window. He called to me. I've got to find him. Oh God, I've *got* to find him. He's so lost. He's so lost . . .'

'We'll find him together,' Brady said. 'We'll all go and look for Jack. But if we go together it's less dangerous. Kathy, you must stay in the safety of the farmhouse. Come on . . .'

She struggled with Brady once more. Then, with a whining sound and a flood of tears, she abandoned herself to his stronger pull, letting him lead her back to the relative safety of the Blanford farm.

'Where the hell *is* she?'

Geoff Cochrane opened the door of the Land Rover and climbed down to the road. The playground of St Mary's school was filled with children, all enjoying their brief afternoon break. Cochrane had fully expected Nancy to be here waiting for him by now. But try though he did, he could not make out her shape or clothing in the milling throng that played and ran across the grey yard.

Sophie Blanford said, 'Look, do hurry, will you? I've got to get this lot back to the farm.'

Cochrane turned to her, stared at her, then saw the sense of her words. He tossed her the keys. 'I assume you can drive?'

'Of course I can bloody drive,' the girl snapped. 'What are you going to do?'

'I'll fetch Nancy and follow you out by taxi, or something.'

346

Sophie shifted across into the driver's seat and closed the door. 'I'll send Brady for you, if you tell me where you'll be.'

'Good idea,' Cochrane said. 'I'll phone the farm.'

The Land Rover sped off. Cochrane crossed the road and drew the attention of the janitor, who was walking along the outer limit of the playground. The gates of St Mary's were always locked, a fussy habit that Cochrane had never encountered before. The janitor let him in and he walked through the bustle of children, occasionally asking one of them, 'Do you know Nancy Cochrane?'

A whistle sounded. The playground was evacuated, streams of kids pouring back into the main building. Cochrane followed them in, speaking to the teacher on the steps who had blown the whistle.

'I'm looking for Nancy Cochrane's class.'

'Which teacher?'

'Miss . . . Bowman, I think.'

'Room 12.'

'Much obliged.'

He walked along the corridor, peering in through the stippled glass windows at the desks, the children, the trappings of the junior school. He had long since forgotten his own school days, but the hundreds of crayoned and painted sheets that decorated the walls of each classroom invoked fond memories. He was amused to see, in one class, a computer display screen. He watched for a second as two small boys worked on it. No more than eight years old, he thought to himself, and they can handle a tool like a computer that has always confused me and always will.

At room 12 he paused. It was not Miss Bowman who sat behind the desk, talking to the class. It was a middle-aged man; in fact, he recognized the man now as the head-master.

He knocked on the door. The headmaster beckoned him in. He entered the class, which stood up with much

347

scraping and shuffling. Without any signal from the teacher the whole group sat down again, minimum courtesy demonstrated.

'Sorry to interrupt the class, but I wondered if I could take Nancy away with me a little early.'

As he spoke he glanced around, frowning slightly. Where was she? At the back? Why the hell hadn't she said anything? It was quite unlike her to remain so quiet.

'She seems to have taken her leave already,' the headmaster said.

Cochrane felt his blood chill. He smiled. 'I don't understand.'

'She left school . . . when was it? Does anybody know?'

One of the girls in the front row put up her hand. 'After the morning break, sir.'

The headmaster glanced at Cochrane. 'She's probably at home now. I hope there's nothing wrong with the girl.'

'I'm sure there's not.'

Where was she?

'We do try to encourage the bringing of notes, or the use of the phone by parents who wish their children to take half days. It *is* a school, after all, and we do have responsibility for the pupils.'

'Yes,' said Cochrane fully. 'I'm sorry. She left this morning, you say . . .'

'So it would seem. The teacher who takes this class was ill. The two of them seem to have left together.'

'She's awful. I don't like her. She's cold. We never laugh. I'm frightened, daddy . . .

Nonsense. Frightened of what?

Miss Bowman. There's something funny about her. Something not right. Daddy, I'm scared . . .

'Oh my God,' Cochrane breathed.

The headmaster frowned. 'Is something wrong?'

'I'd like a word. Outside.'

They stepped out of the class into the corridor.

348

'Where does she live?'

'Who?'

'Miss Bowman.'

The headmaster looked rather perturbed. 'I don't think it would be proper for me to tell you that. What on earth is the matter, Mr Cochrane?'

What do I do? Slap him round the head? Reason with him? Cry?

'I think my daughter is in danger . . .'

'From Miss Bowman? I hardly think so.'

'If she's gone home with her, I want to know. I need my daughter to come with me now. If you won't tell me where she lives, will you at least ring the woman? Will you make contact for me?'

The headmaster stared at him. Here is a man, Cochrane thought, who has been shaped by the taking of responsibility only for infants. He is a school fixture, a mind moulded by simplicity. He doesn't understand what I'm saying, and wouldn't know what to do to help me for the best.

The man said, 'Why do you think your daughter is in danger?'

'She has to . . . she has to take medication. She forgot to take it this morning. She isn't very responsible. I wouldn't want Miss Bowman to have a crisis on her hands.'

Oh how *well* the headmaster understood, now.

'My dear man, why didn't you tell me? Of course you can have the woman's address. Go to my office. My secretary has it on record. Tell her I sent you.'

'Thanks,' said Cochrane, and raced off.

Behind him, a moment later, his name was called. Turning, he saw the girl from the front row. She approached him cautiously. She watched him with an expression midway between curiosity and mischievousness.

'Hello,' Cochrane said.

'I'm Sarah Biggs.'

'Hello, Sarah.'

'It's about Cock – I mean, Nancy.'

Cochrane dropped to a crouch before the child. She looked angelic, very sweet. 'What about Nancy?'

'You see, I'm her best friend.'

Cochrane was surprised. 'I didn't think she had any friends here.'

'Oh *yes*. There's me. We're really *very* good friends. Cocky – I mean, Nancy – Nancy and me are best friends, we play together all the time.'

Cochrane extended his hand and Sarah took it, smiling at him. Cochrane said, 'Very nice to meet you. But I really must go, Sarah. I'm worried about Nancy . . .'

'That's why I excused myself from the class,' the girl said. 'I heard what you said to the headmaster. The thing is . . .' She looked around, as if uncomfortable. 'Miss Bowman is a very strange person. She seemed to have a hold over Nancy. And this morning at break Nancy ran away from her, screaming. And Miss Bowman chased after her. I don't know why she would do that, do you, Mr Cochrane?'

'What do you mean . . . *chased* her?'

'Like she was angry with her. She was shouting at Nancy. Nancy just ran and ran. She climbed over the school railings. I saw her. This was after the break. And the thing is . . . Miss Bowman climbed over after her. What do you think is the matter with Miss Bowman?'

Cochrane ignored the girl's question. He suddenly felt flushed with panic. Nancy had fled the school, pursued by the teacher she had been afraid of. She had tried to warn her father and he had ignored her. What the hell was Miss Bowman? Part of Arachne? That hardly seemed possible. The teacher had been here before the shrine had been breached.

Unless . . .

'Oh my dear God,' Cochrane said aloud. 'The guardian . . . the bloody guardian . . .'

'I'm sorry, Mr Cochrane?' Sarah Biggs prompted.

He looked down at her. 'Thanks,' he said. 'Go back to class now.'

He turned from the girl and raced to the headmaster's office, to get Miss Bowman's address.

They wouldn't have set up a shrine without a watcher in the town. Damn and blast it! The watcher was my daughter's teacher. And each recognized the other.

Run, Nancy. Run for your life!

It was after dusk when Brady heard a car pull up outside the main farmhouse. Doors slammed and the car pulled away. A moment later he saw Geoff Cochrane walking slowly round to the narrow entrance-way through the machinery barrier.

Brady went towards him, puzzled as to why he was alone. Sophie Blanford had arrived back hours ago, with all the equipment she needed. They had all expected Cochrane to ring for a lift as soon as he had fetched his daughter from the school.

'Geoff?'

As Brady came close his heart sank. Cochrane's face was wretched. Tears poured from his eyes and his lips wet and sagging.

'What's happened?' Brady asked quietly. He half knew the answer.

'Nancy . . .' Cochrane whispered.

Brady took him by the arm and steadied him. Cochrane leaned heavily against him. Brady could feel the other man shaking.

'Tell me about it, Geoff.'

The ghost-hunter sobbed. His face creased in agony, and he shook his head, saying repeatedly, 'Oh God, oh God, oh God . . .'

'Geoff! Tell me about it! Is she . . .?' Did he dare say it? He dared to say it. 'Is she dead?'

351

'I don't *know*!' cried the other man. 'Oh Christ, Dan. Where is she? Where *is* she?'

'What happened?'

'I went to pick her up from school. She wasn't there. She ran off this morning, pursued by her teacher. Her bloody *teacher*. I went to the place we've been staying, but no sign of her. I went to the teacher's house, but it doesn't exist. Miss Bowman.' He turned haunted eyes on Brady. 'Just my luck, eh? I put my daughter into a class where the teacher is one of them . . .'

'Arachne? Are you sure?'

He shook his head. 'No. No, I'm not sure. Oh *God*!' He started to shake, biting his finger to try and stifle his scream of despair and anguish. 'I'm dead without her, Dan. Dead . . . I've *got* to find her '

'Come inside and get yourself a stiff drink. We'll look for her as soon as is practicable. She's an enterprising girl, from everything you tell me. I'm sure she'll be all right.'

'She's lost, Dan,' he said. 'She's out there, somewhere. Hiding, I'm sure of it. But she doesn't know where the farms are. She never came here. She'll be looking for me. She'll be getting frantic. I've got to find her, Dan. I've got to find her before *they* get here.'

He must have felt Brady's sudden hesitation, sudden shock. He stopped, wiped his eyes on his sleeve and fixed Brady with a quizzical, almost fatalistic stare.

'Don't tell me,' he said softly. 'They're here already.'

Brady nodded.

'They're here already.'

9

They were here! They were here! She could *feel* them. She could almost smell them! After so long they had returned to Anerley. Now there would be liberation; now she could join them in the proper pursuit of the greater purpose, the great awakening.

She walked briskly through the main street, all thoughts of the Cochrane girl gone from her mind now.

Miss Bowman felt joy; yet it was a joy tinged with fear. When they had been in Anerley before they had spoken to her, touched her, embraced her; she had been prepared for her task in an intimate and demanding way, but she had never seen them. They had been dark shapes in a dark room. Only their hands, their lips, their whispered voices, the cold hard feel of their bodies against hers. Her mind had opened. Her awareness had widened. She had formed the link with the guardian in the shrine, and had settled down to life in Anerley, as a teacher, as a spinster . . . as a watcher.

Joy and fear. Miss Bowman felt excitement, too. But it was excitement tinged with apprehension . . .

The shrine had been broken. The unborn had been disturbed. She had called for help as soon as it had happened, but it was *her* shrine, *her* watch. Would they be angry? Yes, of course they would be angry. But not with her. She was just the outside guardian. They would punish those who had interfered with the sanctity of the chamber. And they would set up a new watcher, and take *her* with them. She had served her apprenticeship. Now she would go on to greater things, help serve the greater purpose.

As she walked and ran through the jostling high street, she looked among the blank country faces for the darker faces of Arachne. She watched for those who watched her. She sought the dark features, the brooding countenances of the collectors whom she had summoned.

She could *feel* them. Every hair on her body, every muscle in her limbs, everything twitched and tingled with the psychic contact.

Miss Bowman began to smile, then to laugh. She abandoned all thought of Nancy Cochrane and the fact that the girl had made a mind-contact with her, spotting her own guardian spirit.

She made her way through the side-streets to the house that Arachne owned. It was not the address she had given the school. She wanted no one, no teacher, no pupil innocently knocking at her door. The house had been bought for her by unseen, unknown people. It was small, rather drab, but it stood alone, away from other houses, and was screened by trees, bushes and a wooden fence. The curtains in all the rooms were closed.

She entered her house and took a deep breath. They were not here. But they would be.

The place was in darkness. She walked slowly from empty room to empty room. Empty food tins lay scattered everywhere. Rotting clothing was piled in one corner. The bare floorboards creaked as she walked. The cold-water tap in the decaying bathroom dripped noisily and irritatingly. Her bed was a pile of blankets, with a sleeping-bag. In the kitchen was the only furniture, a table and four chairs, with a small double gas ring for cooking. She owned four plates, and they were filthy. On the table was a small fortune in paper money. She had no bank account and was paid in cash. She spent very little money, enough to keep two sets of smartish clothes, and to buy sufficient foodstuffs to keep the body around her soul reasonably healthy.

Each night she sat in the darkness and stared into space, listening to mice foraging among the empty tins, smelling the sweet decay of the place, dreaming of Arachne, of the time they would come for her.

They were here now.

She sat down at the table, staring at a chink of fading light that showed through the kitchen curtains. Her heart began to beat fast. In the darkness, in the silence, there was just the gleam of her bright, wide eyes and the sound of her steady, excited breathing.

Soon she heard movement. She smiled.

They were here!

Cool air touched her neck, ruffled her hair. She folded her hands on the table in front of her, heart beating loudly, mind reaching for contact with her masters.

A door opened and closed. A lock rattled. The curtains moved, then were still, and the chink of light vanished. Outside the kitchen the floorboards groaned gently and a tin was moved as someone came across the bare-floored lounge towards her.

Suddenly they were in the room with her, four of them, tall dark shapes, their breathing a hoarse, rasping sound. Two were behind her, two in front. She tried to see details of their faces, but the blackness was absolute.

Then light flickered briefly and fire was struck to the wick of a black candle. The flame was small and dim, but it was held towards her and now, by its feeble light, she saw the faces of her masters.

She almost cried out in alarm, but she remained silent. *This was not right.*

They were not men. They were beasts. The blank-eyed face of a horse looked down upon her. Next to it the grinning features of a pig, the snout split through, the eyes tiny and dead. She twisted in her chair and looked up at the two who stood behind, gasping with horror as she faced the glistening jaws of a goat, the skull split and spread to form a living mask over the human face below. In the shadows

355

behind the goat was a human figure with the face of a hyena, grinning, malevolent.

'Have you come for me?' she asked, alarmed.

Hands touched her shoulders, pushing her forward towards the table. Yet behind her, the goat-faced man had stepped away. There was a fifth presence in the room. The hands were huge, the fingers digging painfully into her flesh.

'You were the watcher of our unborn lord.'

'Yes. I summoned you when the chamber was broken.'

She couldn't tell which of them was speaking. The candle-flame guttered, then was still. She stared at it, feeling the hands on her shoulders crushing harder into her bones.

'You should have known that the unborn lord was in danger. Your purpose was to be the eyes in the town.'

'I was diligent,' she gasped, the pain becoming excruciating. She tried to look up at the horse. She could just see the drip of saliva from its slack lips, the bright facets of its broad teeth.

'You failed,' the horse said. 'The shrine should not have been opened. We were not summoned soon enough.'

'I heard the cry from the guardian. I called at once. What more could I have done?'

'You were the eyes in the town. No man should have gone to the hill without your knowing. No stranger should have come to the hill without your knowing. You were the eyes and ears of the town. You have betrayed us. You have betrayed the unborn.'

'No! Oh please, no! I did everything I could. I've been faithful to the purpose. Take me with you, now. *Please. I want to travel with you. I want to serve. I called you when I knew of the breech!*'

'Too late,' whispered the horse, bending close. The unseen hands on her shoulders moved slightly, twisting her head so that it strained on the neck-bones to stare up at

356

the gathered beasts. She sobbed and shook, immobile, her arms limp by her sides, her body pressed down on the table, breasts crushed against the table's edge. Her head was moved, her nose pinched, her eyes poked so that they watered. A stinking finger entered her mouth, tugged at her tongue, pulled her tongue from between her lips and twisted it so that she started to choke.

The hands were on her face. The four beasts watched her, the candle-light making their death-masks writhe and twist, grinning faces, dead-eyed, yet sinisterly aware.

The horse leaned forward. The cold, wet lips sucked at her face, a demon's death-kiss. The goat leaned down, the lips flopping about her own, the cold teeth nipping at her. Then the pig, its dripping snout pushed against her mouth, a snort of laughter accompanying the moment of condemnation. Finally, the dog-like beast, the hyena, its breathing a sort of braying as it stooped to impart its farewell.

Her head turned further round, and she felt the bones give. The noise was like the cracking of a branch. Still her head was twisted, until again it faced downwards to the table.

Then there was a blow like a pile-driver, that split the table in two below the sad, dead face of Miss Ruth Bowman.

'Drink this,' Brady said, pushing a large glass of Blanford's precious brandy into Geoff Cochrane's hands. Cochrane shook his head and tried to pass it back.

'I don't want it. Anyway, I remember what you told me. Alcohol makes a body more susceptible to psychic attack.'

But Brady was insistent. 'I said *drink* it. Drink it slowly. Relax as you drink it. You're more susceptible to psychic attack in your panicking state of mind. The lesser of two evils, Geoff, and brandy is sweet to the palate . . .'

357

Cochrane stared down at the glass, then raised it to his lips. He sipped, then drained the spirit. Immediately he choked, but he smiled, then took a deep breath and sighed.

'What the hell am I going to do, Dan?'

'Look for her, of course. But look for her in a calculated, careful way.'

Tears rolled from Cochrane's eyes. His lips quivered. Brady watched him, feeling a terrible sympathy. He couldn't condemn the man for this display of emotion. He remembered all too well how painful it was to adjust to loss . . .

Cochrane said, 'I'm lost without her, Dan . . .'

'I know,' said Brady, soothingly. 'I understand completely.'

Geoff Cochrane looked up at him. Then he seemed to realize something and nodded. 'Your own daughter . . . Marina?'

'Marianna.'

'Marianna,' Cochrane repeated. 'Do you miss her most of all?'

'I miss them all,' Brady said softly. Then he decided to be truthful, to fight his own surge of sadness and pain. 'But yes. Yes, I suppose I miss Marianna in particular. We were very close. Fathers and daughters. We had . . . we had something special, a special understanding.'

'A special love,' Cochrane whispered.

'That too,' Brady replied. 'Yes. A special love. She, above all, haunts my waking hours. But I intend to find them *all*, Geoff. I shan't be content with just one, not even if that one is Marianna. I want Dominick and I want Alison too. I want them all.' He leaned towards the ghost-hunter. 'I'm greedy, you see. I shall keep hunting these bastards until I have my family back, safe with me . . .'

'And then?'

Brady smiled. 'And then I shall keep hunting them. You know well enough, Geoff . . . people like you and me, people with a special knowledge of this force . . . these

358

bastards . . . We have a special privilege. We have a special role. Whether I like it or not, last Christmas my life changed. I'll get my family back, but we shall never be a normal family again.'

'You must be sad at the thought of that,' murmured Cochrane.

'I suppose a part of me is sad. But I'm beyond that sort of feeling, now. I have hate. I have determination. I want the blood of certain creatures who attacked me and raped Alison. When I have that blood something in me will be satisfied, but then . . . Then, I suppose, I must make amends for my violent revenge. I shall have to continue to hunt Arachne, hunt them down, destroy them . . .'

He trailed off, watching Cochrane as the ghost-hunter frowned, became less distraught, listening to Brady's words.

'Are you afraid of them?'

'Yes. And that doesn't mean a damn thing. I'm afraid of a runaway train. I'm afraid of heights. So what? Fear is merely one aspect, one part of the programme of the machine that is Dan Brady. A killing machine. A hunting machine. And that's what I am, isn't it? Height six feet two. Weight one hundred and sixty pounds. Codename: *Nemesis*. Wind him up, let him loose. Arachne know I'm here. I know they know. That shared knowledge makes me more dangerous to them than anything else in the world that they might encounter.' He smiled as he saw Cochrane look sceptical. 'And that arrogance keeps me running blind, Geoff. I'm on target, and running blind. But goddamn – as an old friend of mine used to say – I'm one hell of a dangerous blind man!'

Cochrane stood up, thoughtful and still very distraught. He walked over to the window that looked on to the quadrangle of the farm.

'I'm out of my depth,' he said quietly. 'And without Nancy . . . to lose Nancy . . .'

Brady sat down on the arm of the sofa. 'We're all out of

our depths, Geoff. You'll just have to learn to hold your breath. But to be more practical . . . how do you know Nancy isn't hiding somewhere safe?'

'But *where*?' Cochrane turned from the window. 'Where would she go? Where does she know?'

'She might come here.'

But Cochrane shook his head. 'She came with me on the first night. But she was half-asleep with exhaustion, and we came here by taxi, and after dark. She knows of Ed Blanford only as the farmer with the shotgun.'

'She might make her way back to your digs.'

'Mrs Buxton is in. I saw her. If Nancy turns up there she'll ring. But it was the obvious place for her to go, and she hadn't been there at any time after she ran from the school . . .'

Brady thought hard, trying to work out a way in which he might help the ghost-hunter. But there was nothing he could offer except the appearance of support. He said, 'Put yourself in her place, Geoff. You're terrified by a teacher. The teacher chases you. You run from the school. Now: would it occur to Nancy *not* to go to her digs, an obvious place. Would she avoid that obvious location?'

Cochrane nodded slowly. He leaned against the window, his hands in his pockets. 'Yes. I think that's the way her mind would work. She's a bright kid, given to occasional moments of panic and bad judgement . . . but bright.'

'All right. She's running. She won't go to your lodging-house. Will she go to the police? Or to a church?'

'No. I'd say not. I'd say she would try and find me. She'd follow her nose and try and get out of Anerley, looking for the farm.'

'Would she know the way to go? Would she know which road to take out of Anerley?'

'Probably not, except that . . . well, each day when I've seen her off I've gone back the way we came. I suppose, as a matter of instinct, she'd run from the school in that

360

direction, which would bring her out west of the town . . . on the right track.'

Brady stood and went to peer out into the darkness.

'It's a strong probability, then, that your daughter is somewhere between here and Anerley, hiding in woods, or a ditch, or in the garden of a house.'

Geoff Cochrane shivered violently. He said, in a voice edged heavily with despair, 'One small girl, alone, half-naked in a freezing night. One tiny girl with a mind that will be radiating like a beacon to Arachne. They'll spot her from half a mile away . . .'

Brady hadn't really understood the girl's talents, but he could do nothing other than believe her father. 'I hadn't thought of that,' he said. 'You're right, Geoff. We've got to go out again and look for her.'

As they slipped away from the farmhouse, crouched low, carrying a small haversack of Cochrane's 'tricks' and a shotgun, Kathy Goddard watched them anxiously from the darkened bathroom.

What are they doing? They've got a gun . . . Oh God, they're going to . . .

She tried to force the thought away. It came back, like a bad dream.

They're going to kill Jack. The spirit has him. They're going to shoot my Jack . . .

She watched the darting figures of Brady and Cochrane slip out of the farmyard, ducking down behind machinery and surveying the land beyond before they proceeded further. As soon as they were gone from sight she turned from the window, ready to hunt for her husband on her own.

As she reached the landing she gasped with shock and stood quite still. The ragged boy, the one from the shrine, stood there at the top of the stairs. He blinked as he stared at Kathy. His skin was pale, but normal-looking as if he

361

were ill and not in some half-dead state. His hair was dishevelled, his breathing hoarse, noisy.

'Where am I?' he said.

'You're safe,' Kathy replied, and approached him slowly.

'Where's . . . where's mum?' He looked around, frowning.

'She's safe,' Kathy said. As she drew level with him she smelled him, a strange, chemical odour, some balm or skin-cream, perhaps, that Sophie Blanford had applied to the unconscious patients. Where *was* Sophie? Wasn't she looking after her patients? Was she neglecting them?

Kathy had no time to stop and worry. She darted past the boy and down the stairs. He stood, staring at her, his face a pallid mask of puzzlement. He kept asking where his mother was. Kathy felt a tingle of something like concern, or sadness, but a greater concern was occupying her now. They were hunting Jack. They were hunting him with guns. They thought he would have gone mad, being trapped down those mines. Mad or possessed, in either case they were going to kill him. But her Jack wasn't mad. He had called to her. She had seen him. She had seen him, up on the hill, beckoning to her. He wasn't mad. He was just scared.

Kathy knew where to go to find him. Brady and Cochrane would go up to the wood, searching near the old pits. But Jack would have gone home, of course he would. It was so obvious to her now. He would have gone back to the farm, and be hiding there, wondering what was happening!

She walked quietly to the back door and stepped out into the night. She could hear Susan Blanford down in the cellar. There was no sign of Ed. The Kittings were in the lounge, talking.

Kathy Goddard made her escape from the Blanford farm as easily as a cat leaves a garden. Without a glance behind her she passed through the gap between the barricades, then began to run along the road, towards her farm, a mile away.

Soon she could see the light in the kitchen and the warm glow of the standard lamp behind the net curtains of the lounge. The yellow beacons called to her, and she hastened her step. Then she slowed, frowning . . .

Who had put the lights on?

The children were away; the farm-hands would have gone home. There was no one at the farm. Except Jack, of course.

Of course! Jack. Jack was in the kitchen, probably using up all the cheese as usual. Kathy ran even faster, though her lungs ached and her skin was clammy with sweat.

She slowed again as she approached the farm's gates. Somewhere in the confusion and dizziness that was her mind a voice of warning whispered to her. She so desperately wanted to take it for granted that Jack had come home and was sitting, waiting for her, chewing his way through a cheese sandwich while he watched the farming programmes on the TV. So much of her mind was committed to the return to normality that the voice of reason, the sigh of warning, was easier to block out, and to ignore.

She called his name as she entered the gate and ran to the back door. She went into the kitchen.

'Jack! Oh God, it *is* you! Oh thank God, thank God. You're safe!'

'Kath. Where have you been?'

She ran across the kitchen and hugged him. Only when she had hugged him and sobbed on his shoulders for a minute, or perhaps longer, did she pull back, still holding on to his arms, unwilling to let the contact end.

She was partly aware of the wood that littered the kitchen. He had chopped the kitchen table into a hundred pieces. Half the kitchen units had been destroyed, a scatter of formica-coated blue fragments on the floor and work surfaces. He had also dragged in several logs and reduced them to strips of firewood no thicker than paperback books. The whole kitchen was *filled* with wood, and the walls, and the work surfaces, and the floor, were gouged and ripped where the axe had struck them.

'What have you been doing?' she asked, looking about her. He still held the axe in his right hand. It was long, heavy-bladed. The dark grey whetstone lay on the floor amongst the wood litter.

'I was cold,' he said softly, staring at her. 'I was chopping wood for the fire.'

She looked up at him, alarm beginning to chase away the shadows of madness. He was wild-eyed, white-faced. His hair stuck out at odd angles, and there was blood on his scalp and on his cheeks, and Kathy could see how he had torn whole locks of hair from his head. He was smiling at her, watching her through eyes whose pupils were hugely dilated.

'But you've cut so much,' she whispered.

'I was *very* cold,' he replied, his voice a cruel mockery of her own whispered tones.

'And you've chopped up the table . . .' She looked around, the blood beginning to pound rhythmically in her ears. She frowned as the true destruction about her began to impinge upon her senses. 'And the cupboards, and the floor . . .'

She looked up. 'You've even chopped the ceiling.'

He had stepped towards her. She stared at him. Her words, then, would have sounded comical in any other circumstance; but for Kathy Goddard they were the first desperate words of understanding, a softly spoken cry of sanity from her disturbed mind.

'Is everything all right, Jack?'

'Fine,' he said. 'Except that I cut myself. Sharpening the axe.'

He held up his left hand. It was red and raw with blood. Two fingers were missing.

'Oh my God . . .' Kathy moaned, and her legs went to jelly. She collapsed to the floor, scattering the shards of wood. She could hear Jack saying, 'You left me in the darkness. I was trapped in the darkness. I was terrified. It was so cold, Kathy. So cold down there, and that thing following me, and Kitting. Following me. I just kept running and running, but it was so cold down there, and there was no light.' He loomed over her. 'Why did you leave me, Kathy? Why didn't you come and get me. It took me ages to find the hole. I could smell the air. It was so fresh. But when I woke up everyone was gone. And there was just that *thing*. Oh Kathy, Kathy, where were you, where did you go? I was so cold. I was so cold. I'm still cold. Must make a fire. Must get warm . . .'

As he talked to her, so he continued to chop firewood into smaller and smaller pieces, the axe rising and falling, a rhythmic movement, punctuating his talk.

'Oh Kathy, Kathy. I was so cold. But you're here now. And we'll be warm together. Warm together. Warm together.'

10

They came to the main road. Brady was breathless, but fear and grief kept Cochrane running without pain.

'Wait,' Brady called, and in the darkness the ghost-hunter stopped and turned to look around him.

'No time to lose!' he hissed. 'For pity's sake, Dan. Not a minute to waste.'

A car screeched along the road, headlights blinding until the driver saw the two pedestrians and dipped the beam. The clouds were light and scudding, bringing an unnatural brightness to the farmland around them. The ridges were clear against the pale night sky. In the distance, Anerley was a vague glow above dark trees.

When Brady had his breath again they began to trot towards the town. Every hundred yards Cochrane stopped and called Nancy's name. His voice, at first quite hushed, afraid of attracting Arachne should they be around, had soon risen to a full-blooded cry. The name of the girl echoed across the bleak black landscape, but only wind answered the call.

'We should split up,' Brady said. 'I'll go over the road and explore the farmland to the north.'

'Good idea,' Cochrane said, but at that moment stopped and hissed, 'No! Wait!'

Brady came up to him. The ghost-hunter was turning slowly about, eyes closed. 'What is it?' Brady asked.

'She was here,' Cochrane whispered. Tears squeezed from his closed eyes. When his eyes opened, they were huge and moist. 'Christ!' he said bitterly, and his lips quivered.

'What can you feel?'

'Distress. Danger. She ran, I'm sure she ran. But she was here. I can almost hear her . . .'

'You never cease to surprise me,' Brady said.

Cochrane shrugged, shivering slightly as he looked around. 'We shared more when she was younger. When June went . . . it came back a lot. She was *here*, Dan. And something frightened her . . . she ran . . .'

'Maybe she got away then. Maybe it wasn't them.'

A ridge of trees led up the hill to the nearest rise. It divided two farms, a thick, dense strip of tangled deciduous wood. Cochrane stared at it, then made a decision. 'We should follow the hill. If I were her I'd have run for that shelter. She knows how to use wood and leaf litter to hide. *Come on!*'

Brady crossed to the other side of the winding band of trees and together they half ran, half walked back towards the haunted farmland, struggling up the steep rise and calling for Nancy. They disturbed birds, foxes and smaller mammalian life, but no girl ran screaming and overjoyed from a hiding place in the dense brush.

Soon they stood together, exhausted and disappointed, staring into the distance, to the dark place that was the Blanford farm, and north of the farm to the steep hill with its patch of haunted wood. Cochrane sucked in his breath with surprise, and even Brady felt his heart murmur with alarm.

There were lights on Pitthurst Hill, flickering lights, like torches being moved about among the trees.

Crouched low, the two of them ran a further half-mile or so towards Pitthurst Hill. Although Cochrane still called for Nancy he did so now in a hushed voice, hoping that the wind would carry his whisper of concern to wherever she lay, hiding and frozen.

Soon, even this last token effort to find his daughter ceased. He became a silent, grim-faced man. He didn't respond to Brady's voice, he was hardly even aware of his

367

companion. His situation was so desperate that he had closed himself off from the world, lost in his thoughts, lost in his despair.

To Dan Brady, the movement on the hill was a typical piece of arrogance, the sort of indifferent caution that he had come to associate with Arachne. They must have spent months up on the hill preparing their shrine, and no one had known they were there, nor had anyone ever noticed that they had been there. If they had wanted to return in absolute secrecy they could have done so.

Perhaps the group that had come to inspect the damaged shrine were not aware of the need for secrecy. The way they weaved their lights about was an easy advertisement for their presence . . .

Perhaps that, too, was part of their plan. To attract – moths to a beacon – those who had disturbed their sanctuary.

It was that thought that made Dan Brady suddenly tug at Cochrane's sleeve, stopping the man in mid-step and dragging him down on to the bare field. The wind whipped about them. Brady felt exposed, naked in the midst of the empty space. But the field was dark, and they were two dark shapes against the ground.

'I don't think we should go closer,' he said.

Cochrane stared at him without speaking. After a moment he whispered his daughter's name.

Brady said, 'We're not going to find her, Geoff. Face facts. If she's in the area, then I hope she's got her head down. If not, then the police will have her soon enough. Geoff, we've got to get back to the farm. They'll be at the farm within hours. We owe it to the Blanfords . . . We promised we would look after them . . . Without us they're at Arachne's mercy.'

'You go,' Cochrane murmured. He looked up at the hill. 'I'll keep searching.'

'You'll do no good!' Brady insisted. 'Come on Geoff. Give it up.'

368

Cochrane allowed himself to be hauled to his feet and dragged around the hill towards the Blanford farm. They scrambled over a wire fence and stumbled across a ploughed field, where the furrows were deep and the clods like boulders. A brook babbled its way merrily down the hill and they leapt it, all the time keeping low, watching the lights in the wood.

In fact, they came closer to Pitthurst Wood than Brady had intended. At one point, crouched behind the brambly bushes that grew over an old field border, they could see the shape of figures among the trees, human figures, three or four in number. Their heads seemed abnormally large for their bodies. Torchlight illuminated beast-like features. Brady heard voices. There was no laughter, only anger. Some of the voices called, strange animal sounds echoing across the nightscape. Others were human, hailing others of their kind. 'Here!' Brady heard a man call, and another responded, 'And here.'

There was the sound of stone being chiselled. There was a crack, as if a tree's branch was being broken by force. The eerie cries persisted, as did the human calling. The activity in the wood was frantic, puzzled, becoming more angry.

Around Brady the air clicked, like ratchets . . . a slow, metallic sound that set his hair standing on end.

He grabbed Cochrane, and they raced towards the farm. Suddenly thunder echoed about them, bowling them over. An icy blast of wind blew against them, coming from the hill. Brady struggled to his feet, blinking and squinting into the blast of air. Something like a billowing cloud, glowing, tenuous, was rolling towards them. As it came closer it resolved into a complex of threshing shapes, faceless bodies, disembodied heads, immense animal faces like cloud shapes, glimpsed then lost as the whole manifestation blew towards them.

'Move!' Bready screamed, and the two men fled. Ahead of them a wall of brilliant fire burst from the ground. Brady felt Geoff Cochrane hesitate, but he dragged him through the inferno with a cry of, 'It'll only burn as much as you believe it can. It's illusion!'

The flames receded before them, raging higher, then curling towards them, fingers of orange fire that licked at their legs. Brady ran, denying the fire its existence, though Cochrane screeched with pain, not strong enough to fully deny the manifestation its physical presence.

The fire went. Thunder cracked and the shock wave threw the two men forward again. The amorphous shape behind them loomed above them, tendrils of ghostly white reaching towards them.

Brady faced it and made the elaborate shape of the pentagram in the air. A combination of his own belief and the inheritance of occult meaning made of that simple gesture a powerful blow back to the pursuing elemental. The cloud-like mass faded, shrinking to a single glowing point of mind energy that vanished into the earth . . .

A wall of earth surged upwards! It came at Brady with a sound like a scream of rock being torn from its bed. Brady staggered backwards, and again made an air sign, chanting an invocation to the protecting angels Michael, Gabriel, Uriel and Raphael. The dirt wall rose higher. Grains of earth, moist lumps of clay, flew at the two men; stinging blows sent them running backwards, away from the ghostly twisting of the ground.

As they ran, the earth wave followed them, reaching towards them. Dirt and rock were flung upwards and forwards, turfs and roots wrenched from the ground and mangled, by the energy of the mind that controlled the bizarre attack.

The wave spread about them, reaching from fifty to a hundred feet in either direction. The icy wind still stung and sang around their ears. Brady ran until his heart threatened to burst, and as Geoff Cochrane raced for safety he began to whine, a steadily rising note of panic that he sustained as if with a single breath.

There was someone walking from the farm buildings!

'Go back!' Brady screamed, waving as he ran.

Then he saw who it was.

'Justin! Go back!'

The boy was already out on the unprotected land, walking towards Brady as if he couldn't see him. His hair blew in the wind. His pale features seemed quite blank.

As Brady reached him he swept him up into his arms, flinging him heavily over his shoulder. Cochrane darted ahead into the safe alley through the piled machinery. A moment later Brady crossed the *zona magnetica*, flung himself into the security of the farm buildings and collapsed beneath Justin's struggling weight.

The wave of earth beached against the cold farm walls smashing noisily against the bare brick like an ocean-wave breaking against a promenade. Earth shot up into the night heavens and came down, a dark, grainy spray, inside the compound. Outside the walls the bank of earth was ten feet high. The machinery and the alleyway through the blockade were covered with dirt, which trickled noisily into a stable pattern as the power behind its movement withdrew, and the displaced land grew cold and silent again.

The farmers had seen what had happened, and an atmosphere of shocked silence pervaded the warm farmhouse kitchen. Ed Blanford was outside, shotgun at the ready, poking at the dirt-fall as if some clue as to what had happened might be found among its cold grains.

Susan Blanford was rubbing her hands together nervously, ashen-faced and concerned, looking from Brady to Justin and shaking her head. The Kittings stood together in numb silence, overwhelmed by events, ready to do what they were told.

Dan Brady asked, 'When did Justin slip away? I found him walking out on the fields.'

371

Susan said, 'Must've been when I was down the cellar. We heard sounds down there and I got worried, so I went down with a torch and a spade in case . . .'

'In case what?' Cochrane asked coldly. He was shivering, his arms wrapped around his body as he stared out into the quadrangle. Brady knew what he was thinking about. He wondered now if he could continue to count on the ghost-hunter's full co-operation and assistance.

Susan Blanford hadn't known what she was looking for and said so, and then added dully, 'Kathy Goddard's gone too.'

'Again?' Brady sighed. She had probably become lost in the darkness, looking for a husband she would probably never find. 'Damn,' he whispered.

'Is she in danger?' John Kitting asked, and Brady felt like shouting at him.

Instead he wearily said, 'Yes, John. As much danger as we are. Only we're defended. We have a chance. I told you to keep a tight watch on her . . .'

'That . . . whatever it was . . .' Mary Kitting said, pointing out to the barn where the earth-wave had broken. 'Was that them? These people you're worried about?'

'They're here,' Brady agreed. 'They're on the hill, looking at the old mines. Cochrane and I gave ourselves away and they saw us. What you saw was a simple demonstration of their power, but they know where to look now.'

'Will they kill Kathy?' Mary asked quietly.

'If she stumbled upon them, then probably yes. It depends on where she goes. She could be safe. But if we're to have a chance of surviving and trapping Arachne . . .' He tapped the table and looked at each in turn. 'We *must* stay here. And watch out for Justin . . . and the others,' he added.

Justin stood, staring up at him. The boy's face was grimy and wet, his eyes huge, sad pools. Brady dropped to a crouch before him, brushing at the lad's hair.

372

How like Ellen he looked. The same solemn mouth, the same intense gaze and a touch of the same warmth. He didn't know Dan Brady from Adam, but he knew, already, that Brady was a friend.

'I want to go home,' he said quietly, and Brady smiled.

'You will go home with me, Justin. As soon as we've made this place safe for these good people, I'll take you home.'

'Where's mummy and daddy?'

'A long way from here,' Brady said. What did he tell the lad? How could he break the news of his mother's death at this difficult moment?

Justin said, 'She keeps calling me. I can hear her. Where is she?'

Frowning, Brady said, 'When does she call?'

'When I'm sleeping. She calls my name. Where is she? Is she lost?'

'Not lost, Justin. But a long way away . . .'

'I want to go home. I'm frightened.' The boy had begun to tremble. Brady took him by the shoulders and shook him slightly. 'To go home you're going to have to become a big man, very quickly. Things have changed at home. There will be a lot of things to get used to.'

Justin stared at him blankly, then nodded. 'Mummy said that to me.'

'When you were sleeping?'

Justin nodded. 'I wasn't really sleeping,' he said, brightening slightly. 'I was in a dark room. There were other people there as well. The whole room was full of whispering. I was quite frightened at first, but I soon got used to it. Mummy kept calling to me and I couldn't get out of the room. But there was a tunnel. I used to make tunnels at Aunt Betty's. I'm good at it. I went out of the tunnel, but it was night-time. I didn't know where I was. I *was* sort of sleeping, I suppose. Mummy was calling me home, but I didn't know where that was. She said she had gone a long way away, but she could see me and hear me, and that a man called Dan would look after me. She kept calling. It was really funny. I suppose I *must* have been sleeping, mustn't I? Sometimes I'd wake up and be back in the dark room.'

Brady smiled at the youngster. 'You were sleeping then, but you're awake now.' Justin grinned at him. 'And by the way,' Brady said, extending his hand. 'I'm Dan.'

Justin shook hands. Brady stood up. The boy was coated not just with dirt, but with the aura and the influence of the shrine. He would make a natural target for psychic attack. Brady said, 'And now that you're awake I want you to do something for me. Go upstairs, and as quickly and as efficiently as possible, have a bath.'

Justin's face dropped. 'Now?'

'Now.' Brady glanced at Susan Blanford. 'He needs a change of clothes too. Can you oblige?'

Without speaking, the woman indicated that she could.

'One that was lost is returned,' Cochrane whispered as Susan Blanford led the boy from the room. He spoke in a sort of hallowed, religious tone, then turned damp, dark eyes on Brady. 'Can you work the miracle twice, Dan?'

'Pull yourself together, Geoff,' Brady said quietly but curtly. He walked into the lounge and crossed to the corner where the silent totem lay, in its weak psychic cage. The pattern of ripples in the white powder that surrounded it had spread, to form two strange-looking wings, as if the gold shaft were the body of some primeval butterfly. At any moment the whole eerie creature might take wing.

Inside the cylinder, locked into the matrix of the bone, an ancient intelligence waited and listened, sensing the strange air outside its golden home, sniffing for the cause of its sleep being disturbed. It was young. It was hardly formed. It could do no more damage to them than could a foetal human kicking blindly at the soft wall of its mother's womb.

Not yet, at least.

It lay in sleep and dreamed. Perhaps it dreamed of the

374

time on the earth when the minds of men had created it, had brought it into existence from their own dreams and beliefs in nature. They had shaped a god to rule them; the god had become demon when other men, with other beliefs, had come to the same land. The demon had passed into memory, back into nature, soon to become nothing but folklore. And yet it had remained a potent source of power, locked in that same memory, alive still in the natural world of brooks, trees, fields and living earth.

Arachne had found the way to call it forth. They had found the way to give rebirth to the ancient wisdom. In a bone, in a fragment of crystal, in a piece of shaped stone, in all these things, across all the world, the past was growing again. The unborn lords of those times when magic and the supernatural had been real presences in the world were now babes in their cold, silent wombs . . . drawing on the life-power of human beings, gestating slowly in their shrines, ready to be called upon again to participate in . . .

In what?

All Brady knew was that soon – months away, perhaps years – there would be a time of change. It was called the 'roundelay', a name which meant nothing to him beyond its mediaeval concept. Somewhere in the north, at a place called *Magondathog* (a name he had heard whilst he had been dying) there would be a time of change, a time when the course of the world would alter.

Marianna, his daughter, was important to that change, because she possessed a special talent. Alison and Dominick too had been taken because they could be used to advance Arachne's purpose. Perhaps they now lay in a shrine, as Justin had lain. Perhaps they were dead. Perhaps the probing mind of the growing life-form had not yet tapped the essence of their lives.

How to find the other shrines? How to locate the places in the earth where his family might, even now, be silently sleeping?

He shivered violently. For a moment it had felt as if he

375

was being watched, probed . . . almost certainly he was. His head spun slightly and the room turned cold. Blinking hard, he tried to shake off the sudden brightness, a greyness around him, like ice-coated stone. The flickering presence of the stoneworld did not last, although the illusion favoured him with a moment's sensation of howling wind, and the whip and crack of a tree's branches against a towering pinnacle of rock.

Above him, in the real world of the Blanford's farmhouse, there was a sudden movement and the breaking of a glass bottle . . .

The man she had tagged 'Ronnie', because of his resemblance to the Great Train Robber, Ronnie Biggs sat bolt upright on his makeshift bed. Sophie Blanford was holding the wrist of the young woman tagged A One, feeling how the pulse surged fast, then slowed almost to nothing. From the corner of her eyes she saw the man suddenly begin to twist and turn, but she ignored him, glancing at him occasionally, intending to check him over next.

The sudden movement startled her. The drip-feed bottle connected to his arm toppled and smashed. She saw it happening and ran across the bedroom to try to save it.

Ronnie's eyes were open and staring, but they were not human eyes. His mouth gaped and a great thick stream of translucent liquid poured over his lower lip, soaking into the sheet.

He made a bizarre gurgling sound, then turned his head to face the nurse. Sophie Blanford began to shake, but she steeled herself and went over to him, pushing on his shoulders so that he lay back again.

Across the room the man tagged Chaplin began to murmur, his body twisting slightly, first to the left, then the right.

376

Dan Brady stepped into the bedroom looking anxiously at the nurse.

'What happened?'

'They're beginning to get lively.'

'Waking up, you mean. Are they snapping out of the coma?'

Sophie stared down at the bulging eyes of Ronnie. 'I'm not sure,' she said quietly. 'You'd better come and see this.'

When Brady stepped up beside her he gasped.

She had first noticed it about an hour before. All of the shrine victims' eyes had rolled up, exposing only the white cornea. Then, over the minutes, the cornea had engorged with blood. Below the closed lids of those who still appeared to be sleeping, the eyes were brilliant red orbs, bulging in the sockets.

Sophie Blanford had never seen anything like it.

'I'm not sure if they're becoming conscious or . . .' She looked nervously at Brady. 'Or becoming active whilst still *unconscious.*'

'The farm is protected against any outside influence,' Brady said in a murmur. He shook his head. 'It *oughtn't* to be possible for anyone outside to affect these people . . .'

'Something's happening, though,' Sophie said. 'They're becoming increasingly agitated, increasingly disturbed.'

'Body functions?'

'They're all beginning to pass urine. You can probably smell that . . .'

Brady had noticed, but it hadn't bothered him.

'Their heart activity is really weird. It races, then slows and sometimes stops for as long as a minute. Their skin temperature changes, but their basal temperature has remained two degrees below normal since I got here. I've tested the motor reflexes, too. They all *function*, but at about half the speed I'd expect . . .'

'But they're all unconscious.'

'That wouldn't make a difference. Their bodies are slowed down. The agitation, perhaps the blood engorgement of the mucosa and the cornea, may be the effect of their bodies *returning* to normal and perhaps . . . I don't know . . .' She looked at Brady and shrugged. 'Perhaps fighting off some hypnotic programme or drug-induced catharsis?'

Brady said, 'I'll send John Kitting up to keep an eye on them with you. I don't want them blundering about in the farmyard like Justin. If he came out of it, so can they . . .'

Except, he thought to himself, that Justin probably had never been as deeply *in* the trance as these others. As he had been placed into the shrine he had begun to bridge the space between two worlds, the world of reality and the shadowland where the spirits of the dead went first, before moving onwards to the higher planes of existence. Half in, half out of that shadowland, his mother, Ellen Bancroft, had seen him and called to him. Her awareness of him had made her cry. It accounted for the ghost's peculiar behaviour over the last few weeks. But as Justin had begun to pass into that shadowland, allowing Ellen to glimpse him, so her interaction with his unconscious mind had kept him more alive than the others.

Ellen had saved her son from sinking as deeply into the trance state as these others. It was the only explanation that made any sense. She had been aware of him, but not of where he was. Confused and distressed, peering beyond the defence zones of Brady's house whenever he made a break in those barriers, she had called to her son, desperately trying to get him to come home.

Brady ran down the stairs to call for John Kitting.

From outside came the deafening double blast of a shotgun being discharged.

When Brady reached the kitchen, Ed Blanford came thrusting in through the back door, white-faced and furious. The gun was broken at the breach and acrid smoke still drifted up from the long barrels.

378

'Where's that box of cartridges? Damn them!'

He went to a cupboard and took down a large box packed full of orange twelve-bore cartridges. He emptied them on to the work-surface, slotted two into the gun, then loaded his pockets with the rest.

Brady was already at the back door, peering at the bizarre activity. Earth was being flung high into the air. The machinery which physically blocked the gaps between the buildings was rattling and vibrating, as if shaken by giant hands. An uncanny light hung over that end of the farm complex, a shifting green and grey aura which darted from left to right, then seemed to surge forward trying to overcome the walls of invisible defences.

'They can't get through!' Brady yelled. A wind began to blow, and the roofs of the barns began to bang and twist, splinters of wood and brick flew about the yard.

One way in, Brady thought. *Come on, my beauties. One way in, and we'll have you. Capture the mind and the body won't be able to run . . .*

One way in . . .

He stepped out into the yard, watching the psychic attack as it shifted round to the east. Doors banged and glass shattered. The huge baling machine that stood there was shaken violently, but it stood its ground. An unearthly shrieking accompanied the attack now, a howling on the wind, a sound that spoke of frustration and anger to Brady.

Blanford pushed past him roughly, glanced round, saw where the grey-green aura was and ran that way.

'Ed! Don't waste shells!'

'I'll show these bastards. Attack *my* farm, will they!' He raised the gun and blew a great hole in the sky. The discharge knocked him back. The lead bore appeared as two grey streaks in the night, widening and striking the aura, which absorbed the impact without worry. Blanford reloaded, screaming blue murder at the invisible hands that were trying to wrench the barricades down. He shot again and again. Tiles and windows shattered. He gouged a

379

huge hole in one of his barns. The baling machine rang and juddered, two long strakes bending beneath the impact of a badly placed shot.

'You can't hurt them,' Brady shouted at the man. 'Save your energy. They can't get in!'

'There's men out there somewhere!' Blanford replied, as he frantically reloaded. 'Twelve-bore will stop them right enough.'

Brady glanced in the direction of Pitthurst Hill.

How close had they come, he wondered? Were they close by, black shapes in a dark land, peering through their animal faces as a chubby farmer shot blindly into the night, watched by the angular, uncertain form of the man they were beginning to find a very great nuisance?

Arachne knew that a ghost-hunter was in the area. The signs and circular traps from the mines would have told them that. But they couldn't yet know – could they – that Daniel Brady was here, waiting for them?

He turned away from the farmyard, ears ringing, mind dulled by the repeated discharge of the shotgun. Blanford had almost worked it out of his system. He was breathless, frightened, watching as the attack changed position again, moving round to the front of the house and sending dirt, leaves and branches flying at the barricaded windows that overlooked the road to Anerley.

Inside the house the phone began to ring, and Brady heard Cochrane's delighted cry of '*Nancy!*'

11

Geoff Cochrane snatched the receiver from its cradle. 'Nancy!' he said loudly, his back to Susan Blanford and Dan Brady.

For a moment or two there was just silence. Slowly then, Cochrane let his arm lower, taking the receiver away from his ear.

'Who is it?' Brady asked.

'I don't know . . .' Cochrane breathed, his voice hardly audible. 'They're just laughing . . .'

Brady took the receiver from the shaken man and listened. There was a sound like static, a crackling, hissing sound. Emerging through the static there was, indeed, the sound of laughter. The connection sounded like no phone connection Brady had ever encountered. Somehow, the beasts beyond the farmhouse had tapped into the phone lines.

'Who is this?' Brady asked, and the laughter stopped. A voice hissed and rasped down the line.

'Give us back what you have stolen.'

'What have we stolen?' Brady said.

'Give us back what you took from the sanctuary,' rasped the voice. 'No harm will come to you.'

'The only thing we took from the mines is a gold phallus. It has a piece of bone inside it. We're thinking of giving the bone to the dog; there're some jewels in the object. Should be worth something when we've prised them out.'

As he spoke he turned and watched the others. Five blank, frightened faces stared at him, all of them intuiting who was on the other end of the line.

The voice of Arachne was silent for a long, long moment. Brady could hear the breathing of the man. He could almost see the puzzled expression on the beast's face, the frantic glances to his companions.

Then: 'Who is this? Are you the ghost-hunter?'

'No,' said Brady quietly. 'I hunt more powerful game.'

'Who are you?'

'That's a good question,' Brady said. 'Ask George Campbell. Oh no, you can't, can you. He died in the fire. I saw him die. Perhaps you'd better ask Alan Keeton. I liked Alan. Until I found out he was one of you. Oh that's right. How silly of me. He's dead too. Out in the Norfolk marshes. Well now, let me see. You could have asked Simon Moss, but . . .' Brady laughed. 'Well, I'm afraid I saw him off too. He made a very pretty sight, up in the tree. I didn't realize I had the strength. Quite surprised myself. Three down, though. Three down and, by my reckoning, four to go.'

This time the silence was longer. For a second it seemed as if the line had been disconnected. Then the voice hissed back along the wire, a tired, angry voice now:

'Brady . . .' it said, and in the speaking of the name was all the weary irritation that Brady's continual presence as an enemy of Arachne could evoke. *Not you again. Not Dan Brady . . .*

'I know what your totem is,' Brady said. 'I know about the unborn life it contains. I know what your purpose is . . .' He raised his eyebrows to Cochrane, as if to say, *a little lie never hurt anyone*, but Cochrane just watched him grimly. 'I know, too, how to destroy your precious piece of the primal past. I grilled Simon Moss at about gas mark five. Gas mark nine for your bone sliver should destroy the unborn nicely . . .'

'You will not destroy the life in the shard,' Arachne said menacingly. Brady couldn't tell whether this was an order, or a statement of his certain failure.

'I'll let you know,' Brady said calmly. 'Heat. Fire.

382

Burning in a brazier of mandrake. Immersion in nitric acid. There are many things to try. And your unborn can throw whatever it likes against me. I can see beyond illusion, and the thing is too young to have real power.'

'The unborn must not be destroyed,' Arachne said, the rasping voice filled with urgency.

'Come and get it, then,' Brady said.

'Return the totem. No one will be harmed.'

'It's too late for that.'

'*Return the totem*! What is it you want from us?'

'Three people who are precious to me. Four people's lives. The return of my family. The death of those who abused us.'

He waited for the voice of Arachne to answer him, but for a long while there was just the sibilant sound. He was about to place the receiver down when the voice spoke one last time to him.

'Give us back the totem.'

'I shall destroy it first. I shall die rather than give it back to you.' *Come and get it. Come into the farm and get it!*

'You're a fool, Brady.'

There was a loud shriek, then a click, and the line went dead. Brady pressed the cradle lever and jiggled it, but the phone was disconnected.

Cochrane said, 'Did they say anything about Nancy?'

'Not a thing,' Brady replied. 'But they knew about you.'

'Thank God,' murmured Geoff Cochrane. 'If they'd got her they would have mentioned it. She's still safe. She's lost, but she's still safe . . .'

So cold. So cold. Must keep alert, though. Must keep moving. But so cold. Can't go on much longer. Need to sleep. Find a warm place, wait out the night.

No! Remember the films. They always say keep moving. Don't give in to sleep. Don't give in to cold . . .

Nancy Cochrane took a deep breath and emerged from

383

the ditch where she had been huddling for the last – how long? Half an hour? More? She brushed aside the twigs and leaves she had used to cover herself. She was still in the patchy woodland that ran up and across the hill. Memories of that man's hand upon her were painful and terrifying. He had not been one of the evil ones she knew were here. He had just been a maniac, a child-attacker. She had come close to being as clumsy as her wretched father. Like father like daughter, she thought bitterly. Always making mistakes at the most critical of times.

Still she had got away from the attacker. He had not pursued her. Thank God. And she had been hiding for ages.

It was pitch-dark. It was freezing. The evil ones knew about her now. They had passed by her, just a few feet away. One of them had called her name. They had sounded like friends, calling for her, urging her to come out to them, but she wouldn't be tricked twice. The voice had changed. It had even sounded like her father, but as tricks went that was the oldest one in the book.

She had closed off her mind, lain absolutely still and waited for the hunters to pass by.

Now, as she emerged into the night, her frock saturated with cold ditch-water, she wondered which way to go. The best bet, she decided, was to creep back into Anerley. If she went to the police they would warm her up and give her a cup of tea, and eventually her father would come for her. It was the only way, she realized. She didn't dare send the police looking around the farms. She had a pretty good idea that someone – or some persons – had been killed during this ghost-hunt. Her father would not thank her for landing him in trouble with the police.

But she *had* to get warm, and she *had* to get to safety.

So: an innocent touch of amnesia. And wait it out.

Mrs Buxton's was not safe. If these people knew of her, they would know where she had been staying. No, the police station was the only answer.

But as she turned down the hill, towards the road again,

from a long way away came the sound of a gunshot.

Immediately her heart raced. Her mind filled with the sleepy image of the old farmer, his shotgun nursed so lovingly below his shoulder. A second shot came. It allowed her to plot the direction a little better.

Over the hill and far away, but perhaps no more than a mile. Should she take the chance? She glanced at the night glow of the hidden town, and at the scudding clouds above the far ridges.

A third shot came and she made the decision. She would take the chance that it was the farmer who was making that noise. And that her father would be somewhere in the vicinity.

She raced up the hill, running fast and low until she collapsed breathless on to the ground, half laughing, sucking breath into her body in great gasps. The sweat glowed on her skin and a flush of warmth coursed through her limbs. *Better.* She ran on, reaching the top of the first hill and staring out across the cloudlit land. A shot came and orientated her, slightly to the right. She scampered down the hill, arms wheeling. She tripped and stumbled. A few paces later she ricked her ankle in an unseen ditch. She sat down on a thistle and nearly screamed out loud.

After that she decided that a more cautious movement was called for. She walked briskly, trying to see the ground ahead of her. She had to negotiate a barbed-wire fence in the darkness, and in doing so she tore her frock yet again. The garment flapped loosely about her body, half ripped off.

The sequence of shots had ended, but she was heading in the right direction now, she was sure.

And when she came over the next rise of ground she could see light ahead of her.

A sixth sense cautioned her to drop to the ground and peer intently at the distant activity. It was among woodland. Perhaps that was the woodland which her father had been interested in. He had said the name to her, but Nancy was notoriously forgetful when it came to names. Nevertheless, the flashing of lights among the trees gave an idea of movement, and it was like a beckoning flame to a cold, lonely moth.

At a crouch she negotiated the intervening farmland. From the bottom of the hill she couldn't see the movement, but the trees were tall, stark shapes against the light clouds. Behaving with commendable care she ran two hundred yards to the left, so that she could climb the hill well away from where she had seen the darting beams of torches.

Soon she heard voices.

At the top of the hill she dodged into cover behind a gnarled, wind-twisted tree, clutching hold of the cracked bark as she searched the gloom for movement. The voices seemed more distant. Wind rustled foliage, blew cold and sharp from the open land. She made her way from tree to tree, puzzled as to why there were no longer any torches.

Then, ahead of her, a light flickered. A tall, dark man-shape passed between her and the light source. He seemed to be wearing a dark robe, and a helmet . . . His head seemed huge.

She decided, then, that despite her caution, she had behaved very imprudently, coming this close to the night activity. The shots had come from away to the right. She should make her way there without delay.

She dropped to a crouch again and turned away from the hovering, masked figure . . .

And found herself staring at the decaying head of a horse!

Its dead eyes gleamed; its fleshy lips hung limp over tall, yellowing teeth. A strained breathing issued from its throat. It hovered there, inches from her own face; then the mouth opened and it snapped at her!

With a scream she tumbled backwards. She heard laughter. She ran blindly, tripped, and glanced up to where a dead pig peered down at her. A hand clutched her shoulder but she shook it off and ran again. She struck a

386

tree, bruising her face. Beyond the tree the split and smelly face of a huge hound loomed down towards her, growling as its muzzle brushed against her nose.

'Get off me!' she shrieked, and fled through the trees again. All around her the wood was alive with light. The trees were black tendrils against the flashing yellow, and among them, swaying and closing in on her, were the shapes of tall, beast-faced men.

The woodland filled with the sound of their eerie, unearthly laughter.

Stumbling over a jutting tree-root, she slipped slightly on the earth, and felt herself dropping into a badger's set, or some other tunnel in the ground. Almost frantic with panic she scrabbled and crawled deeper into the earth, feeling the tree close over her head, enclose her body. The tunnel was wide but low, and stank of dead things. She crawled for several feet, eyes closed to stop the fine dirt and dust getting into them.

The passage narrowed and clutched at her. She wiggled and squirmed, but she could get no further. Ahead of her there was just darkness, though a cool wind blew from that direction.

She lay there, in absolute silence, listening to the absolute stillness. The voices could not be heard. The earth did not vibrate with footfalls.

Total silence.

And then, in the Stygian gloom before her, something moved. It crept closer, scratching softly on the earth. Her eyes widened as a terrible fear possessed her.

A man's finger touched her on the nose, then a hand grabbed her face!

Another hand closed firmly around her leg and began to tug her back to the surface of the hill.

For a second Brady hesitated, reaching towards the shining totem, but not letting his hand waver inside the

387

small circle. Then he smiled and snatched up the object, rising to his feet and rapidly detaching the head from the body. He let the piece of bone slide out from the container and held the cold fragment against his face.

Around him the room shimmered and brightened. Ice touched his limbs. Wind ruffled his hair. A grey, bleak landscape stretched away from him. A creature moaned deeply, stalking him . . .

And faded. The room came back, the chairs, the glass cabinet, the dusty books, the worn, deep-pile carpet.

'Try all you like, little unborn one,' Brady said quietly. 'I can see through your illusions.'

He popped the marked bone back into its patterned container and screwed the head back on, tossing the cylinder into the air, spinning, and catching it as it fell.

John Kitting watched him from the doorway, shaking his head.

'Taking a bit of a chance, aren't you?'

Brady said, 'Not in the least. This is one devil I've got to know well enough to understand its limitations.'

Outside in the yard, the safe place between the house and the barn, Geoff Cochrane was a solitary, stationary figure, standing by the open land, staring towards the invisible hill. Weird, blue lightning flickered in that direction, shimmering strikes of fire that played about both cloud and earth. No thunder followed the discharges, though.

'Seen anything?' Brady asked as he came up behind the man.

Without looking round, Cochrane shook his head. 'They're out there, though. They're watching us.'

'They've been doing that for some time.'

Cochrane glanced at him. His eyes brimmed with tears. 'They have Nancy. I'm sure of it.'

'Sixth sense?'

The ghost-hunter nodded. 'I went very cold, very chilled. There was nothing to hear, but I could hear a scream. There was nothing to feel, but . . . a hand was holding my face. They've got her, Brady. I know they have.'

'Time will tell,' Brady said, feeling uncomfortable with Cochrane's sudden use of his surname. He cradled the totem for a moment, then lifted it above his head, holding it in both hands. Cochrane detected the movement, glanced round and saw what Brady was doing. He gasped with surprise, frowning. 'What the hell . . .?'

Not letting go with either hand, Brady waved the totem from right to left, slowly, mocking the watching men. This close to the edge of the psychic defences around the farm, he wasn't going to trust that a stray tendril of mind energy wouldn't reach out and snatch the incubatorium from his fingers.

'What the hell are you doing?' Cochrane finished.

'I believe the word is "taunting".'

'Taunting Arachne?'

'Not the Wizard of Oz.'

Ignoring the sarcasm, Cochrane said, 'But why?'

Brady lowered his arms, holding the cold cylinder tight. Unseen fingers seemed to pluck at the flesh of his arms, a most uncomfortable feeling. 'I think we ought to face the fact that we've been too clever,' he said. 'Or more accurately, not clever enough.'

'The trap, you mean?'

'They're not going to take the bait,' Brady said. 'I suppose it was hoping for miracles that Arachne would just walk in here, arrogant to the last, to claim back their property.'

'There's still time,' Cochrane whispered, frowning, but Brady shook his head.

'The way in is clear. The way in is free. If they were going to try, they would have tried already.' He stared into the darkness, his teeth on edge, his mind dizzy with frustration and nervous contemplation of what might happen next.

'You mean, we've endangered the farmers for nothing?'

Brady looked sharply at the ghost-hunter. 'I don't recommend that we say that to them. Blanford is jumpy enough as it is. That bloody shotgun will do one of us damage if we're not careful.'

For a second they contemplated the unsafe land beyond the yard in silence. Cochrane said, 'And you think by taunting them with their embryo they'll overcome their shyness and come streaming in to the farmyard? Taking the bait by irritation?'

'All I want,' Brady murmured, 'is one of them, a stalker, a watcher, anything to snare the body by snaring the mind . . . Ideally I'd like to get one of *them*. I want to ask so much . . . I need to know so much . . .'

'From what you've told me,' Cochrane said, 'you've let several of them slip through your fingers. The man you burned, the boy in Norfolk . . .'

'Arachne have a habit of dying when I get hold of them, I admit that,' Brady said. 'I've never had one of them close enough to question without my natural vengeful instincts destroying them . . .' He looked curiously at Cochrane. 'Or is that true, I wonder?'

Geoff Cochrane stared at him blankly for a moment, then grasped what Brady meant. He looked both worried and amused. 'Me? Not me . . .'

'I'm not so sure. Not everyone remains faithful to the mother spider.'

Cochrane shook his head. 'I'm sure that's true. But not me. I'm not one of them. Never have been –'

'Nevertheless!' Brady said suddenly, reaching out to stop Cochrane walking back to the house. The two men's eyes met and the air about them became electric with tension.

Coldly, Geoff Cochrane said, 'Nevertheless what, Mr Brady?'

'You know too much,' Brady said. 'For someone who isn't involved, you know far too much . . .'

390

He knew that Cochrane would strike him. The man's face flushed almost purple, his eyes narrowed, his jaw clenched. He flung his fist at Brady, and Brady countered the blow. The two men staggered, locked in a strange, violent embrace. Brady was hampered by holding on to the totem. After a few seconds Cochrane's anger subsided, even though he continued to cling to Dan Brady like a wrestler circling his opponent.

'I didn't say I wasn't involved . . . Dan,' he said, hesitating before he used Brady's first name. 'I'm not one of them, but I didn't say I wasn't involved . . .'

His fingers dug into Brady's shoulders, a bruising grip that bespoke both tension and – strangely – need.

'Tell me about it,' Dan Brady said softly.

'Yes,' said the ghost-hunter. 'Yes. I think I need to tell someone . . .'

His name was being called. He turned towards the open land, stared at the darkness, listened to the wind and the haunting cry . . .

'BRAAAIIIIDEEEEE . . .

'BRAAAIIIIDEEEEE . . .'

The voice was a man's. The name was called from a great distance, each syllable emphasized, lingering . . .

The voice of a demon. Summoning him.

Dan Brady glanced quickly at Cochrane, then passed the ghost-hunter the totem. 'You'd better hold this.'

'After what I've told you? You still trust me?'

Brady grinned. 'I don't trust the man in you one inch. Just hold the totem safe. For the moment.'

Cochrane accepted the object, cradling it gingerly in his hands. With a last glance at him, Brady turned away.

Towards the voice.

They took her. They won her. They possessed her. Don't ask me how. One day she was . . . she was just June Cochrane.

391

Lovely June. I loved her so much. The next. The next, she was one of them . . .

'BRAAAIIIIDEEEE. . .'

Like a hound howling. Like a dog wailing. An animal's voice, a supernatural voice, the voice of death. Brady stood in the passage between the blockading machinery. He searched the darkness . . .

Saw the movement.

What could I do? I knew she was lost. Possessed. She tried to kill me. Twice. Once with a carving knife. Then with a garden fork. She screamed at me. She laughed at me, spat, scratched. Something had gone wrong . . . she was neither one of them, nor June. Something . . . wrong . . . Tried to kill Nancy, with a stocking, strangling her in her sleep . . .

Brady stood at the limit of the protective field. The blue lightning flashed distantly, an eerie light in the blackness. They walked towards him. Still the haunting cry came from afar, the sound of his name, calling him.

I had to kill her. What else could I do? We went to Cornwall. She had times of quietness, times when she was less possessed. Almost normal. We walked on the cliffs. I hardly remember doing it. I pushed her over. I killed her. What else could I do?

They stood before him, black shapes in a bleak night, the wind catching their dark clothing, the lights of the farm highlighting the hideous animal masks they wore.

But they had failed with her. I know that now. As she fell, as she went over the edge, she screamed out to me. It wasn't fear. It was relief. She screamed: Thank God for this; I love you, Geoff. *Think of that, Brady. Thank God for this. I love you. As she went to her death. She knew. She knew she was possessed. The last moment was ours. I love her for that.*

Cold wind in the time of stillness. Brady facing Arachne, one against four, the man against the beasts, studying what he could see of them, wondering why they had called him.

Thereafter . . . what? She was there, always there. In my dreams. Talking to me, warning me. She showed me the signs:

the spider, the labyrinth, the totem. She told me of the
purpose. Wherever she was, she was like your Ellen, close to the
earth. She knew about them, and what she knew she told me.
Oh God, I loved her for that. Such strength, Brady. The same
strength as little Nancy. I can't lose them both. Not both. Not
June and Nancy . . . understand me, Brady. Not in control
. . . Can't lose them both . . . Not both . . .

Sophie Blanford reached over to peel back the eyelids of
the woman she had named A One. The eyes were white
again, and Sophie gave a little smile of relief. But the
eyeballs were still rolled up as if the woman was dead.
That continued to puzzle her.

Behind her there was movement. Sophie closed the
woman's eyes again and straightened up from the bedside.

The woman blinked alert, lying there staring up
through eyes that were normal, deep-coloured and wide
with apprehension. The sudden return to awareness
startled Sophie . . .

A hand touched her shoulder and she started with shock,
turning quickly then gasping aloud.

Three of the shrine victims stood there, close to her,
staring at her through wide eyes. Ronnie was reaching out
to her, his blood-red orbs frightening in his ashen face.
The man Chaplin too retained the bizarre syndrome. But
the woman Medusa, an older woman with wild, spiky hair,
was normal. On the bed the girl Dorothy was sitting bolt
upright, looking around her. She too seemed normal again.

'Ronnie . . .' Sophie breathed, and reached up to take
the extended hand.

The man's mouth opened and a low-pitched sound
emerged, something like a scream, but a scream that he
seemed to be shaping into words. He darted at her, and the
hand closed round her throat. Chaplin moved to her too
and the two men toppled her to the ground.

Her voice was a single, shrill cry for help. Ronnie was

393

strong and he turned her over, face down to the ground. She heard a glass glucose bottle being smashed, and from the corner of her eye, as she struggled beneath the powerful grip of the two men, she saw Ronnie raising the jagged edge above her head.

'Oh God, no!' she screamed. 'Somebody . . . HELP!'

The broken glass slashed down, cutting through the back of her neck in a powerful sawing motion.

Acting quickly, Brady stooped and smeared the circle of mandrake and hellbore around his feet. The four beasts before him swayed and made sounds like laughter. Brady straightened up and painted the five-pointed star that defined the limits of the pentagram in the air towards them. His hand tired as he marked space in this way, and his skin tingled, but the resistance was only token. On his chest the skull talisman seemed to grow hot, but he placed a hand upon it, willing the spirit within to keep quiet.

A man with the face of a horse stepped forward a little, emerging further into the spill of light from the farm. He was still a long way away and he shouted across the intervening distance. 'All we want is the totem. Give us the totem, Brady and your friends will be left alone.'

'The totem is in the house. It's there for you to take. If you can.'

The horse laughed. 'The trap was too simple-minded. Besides, your talisman warned us first . . .' Brady touched the necklet, running his fingers over the cold stone skull. Warned them first? He guessed that the presence of the talisman's radiating psyche in the farm grounds had been one protective presence too many, and Arachne had decided to act with caution.

Damn, he thought. But he couldn't take the talisman off.

'The unborn will be destroyed,' Brady said. 'If I can't destroy you, then I'll destroy one of your summoned powers. Anything to slow you in the purpose . . .'

394

'You are a small thorn pricking the skin of a very large beast,' the horse said. 'What you are about to destroy will draw a spot of blood. That is all. Bring the totem to us, Brady and come over to us. With the talents you have developed the future holds a rich treasure for you.'

'You hold the only treasure I want.'

'Your family are safe. You can be reunited with them.'

The words were like thrills of shock in Brady's body. His family were safe . . . He could be reunited . . .

But he had heard of their safety before. He had thought himself reunited with Alison once before, only to have the moment of joy snatched from him . . .

'Bring them to the farm,' he said. 'Bring them by dawn and the totem will be returned.'

'You ask too much,' the horse said.

'If they are safe, they can travel. Have them here by dawn and I shall hand the totem to you.'

'Not possible!' the horse shouted, his voice sounding edged with anger. 'They are too far . . .'

'Where are they?' Brady demanded. 'If you know, then tell me.'

'The girl is far in the north. The woman is in a . . . safe place . . . near London. The boy is on the island in the west . . .'

'Which island?' Brady shouted.

'*Give us back the totem!*' Impatience made the voice of the horse sound almost shrill.

'Bring *one* of them by dawn and the totem is yours. One of my family . . . And one of you, tied, stripped and prepared to die. You play with life and death so easily there must be one among you prepared to sacrifice his life for the unborn . . . One member of my family, any of them . . .'

Fire leapt from the earth before Brady, a great wall of cold, silent flame, yards wide, the height of a house. He turned away and stepped back through the alley . . .

Cochrane stood there, staring at him blankly.

And John Kitting, whose white face and blazing eyes set warning bells going in Brady's head.

'Bastard!' hissed the farmer, and the man's fist struck out and hit Brady on the side of the face, sending him sprawling. Cochrane stood above him, cradling the totem. Kitting stepped over him, reached down and made to grab for Brady's lapels, to haul him back to his feet. As he moved he said, 'Bargain with our lives, will you? It's six feet under for you, you b –'

His words were staunched by the sound of the shotgun in the house . . .

The first shot blew away the top of Ronnie's head, knocking the corpse eight feet across the room, still clutching the broken glucose bottle. Tears in his eyes, Ed Blanford stepped into the bedroom, staring down at the twitching, bleeding body of his daughter.

Susan Blanford pushed past him and screamed, 'Oh no! Oh God no!' She ran to the girl, dropped to her knees and touched the deep gash on her neck. The girl moaned, but her hand reached out and gripped her mother's arm. 'Oh thank God . . .'

Blanford turned the shotgun on Chaplin and blew a hole through the man's stomach. The other victims of the shrine began to scream. The girl, A One held her hands over her ears, shaking her head in total confusion.

Blanford blew away her confusion as he blew away her face.

Calmly, not moving from the doorway, ignoring Susan Blanford's pleas for him to stop, Blanford turned the gun on Medusa, and then on the girl child. He killed every man, woman and child who had been saved from the shrine.

When he had finished, the far wall of the bedroom was bright and running with blood.

Kitting straightened up and Brady scrabbled to his feet, angrily pushing the young farmer aside. For a second the three men stared blankly at the house, then Brady and John Kitting started to run. They burst in through the back door and flung themselves to the stairs. Justin Bancroft huddled in a corner of the lounge, terrified by the shots. Brady glanced at him quickly, then pounded up the stairs to the door of the bedroom where the ward was established.

In the middle of the room Ed Blanford stood sobbing above the body of his daughter Sophie. Susan was screaming, 'Put the gun down, Ed. Put the gun down!'

Brady felt sick as he saw the mayhem. Blanford said, 'Those bastards brought this on us. Our Sophie . . . They said we were safe . . . I'll get 'em . . .'

What had happened here? In a way, Brady already knew. Arachne had probed into the house with their minds, using the narrow gap in the psychic defences. They had summoned the dead, brought life back to the coma victims and turned them against the farmers . . .

'Put the bloody gun down, Ed!' Brady shouted from the doorway, and Blanford saw him.

In a single, smooth motion he had brought up the weapon and fired both barrels. Only Brady's alertness saved him. He darted back on to the landing as the great cone of death blasted and gouged its way through door-jamb, plaster and ceiling.

He didn't linger. He almost jumped downstairs. Blanford raced after him, shooting again and destroying the grandfather clock in the hall . . .

'Blanford's gone mad!' he yelled as he slammed and locked the lounge door where Justin was huddled. If Blanford was after him and Cochrane, then perhaps the boy would escape the wrath.

He slammed the kitchen door behind him, locked it

397

from the kitchen side, then went out into the yard and frantically looked about for something with which to defend himself. John and Mary Kitting were huddled together in the cold night.

'You've brought this on yourself, Brady,' Kitting shouted angrily. 'You bargained with our lives . . .'

'No such thing!' Brady snapped back. 'I had to know how powerful they were, what they knew, where their weakness lay . . . I was bargaining with nothing. Where's Geoff?'

They all looked around.

'Christ Almighty, what's he doing?'

Geoff Cochrane was running through the alley, out into the unprotected night. He was holding the totem, waving it above his head. Deafened for a moment by Blanford's shotgun, as it was used to break through the kitchen door, Brady heard Cochrane's frantic cry of 'Don't harm her!'

He went in pursuit of the ghost-hunter.

He had known that Nancy was among them. He had felt it, long minutes before. He had felt her cry, sensed her fear. It had tickled and tugged at a part of his mind which marked him as more powerful, and yet less strong than other men.

He had stood in the farmyard, listening to the wind, knowing just *knowing* that Nancy had been captured. He had watched as Brady confronted the four beast shapes, the limbs of the body of Arachne, and he had felt the same anger, the same sense of betrayal as John Kitting.

But as Brady had run into the house, drawn by Blanford's frantic firing. Cochrane had felt himself drawn to the edge of the circle again. He had stood there, clutching the totem, and peered out into the night.

And he had seen her.

'Nancy! Oh Christ, NANCY!'

In a ragged, flapping frock, held off the ground by two of the animal men, she had called to him. She had been struggling in their grasp, and had screamed for him.

I can't let her die. I can't lose her. They'll let her live if I bring them the totem.

'Don't harm her!'

He began to run. Behind him, Dan Brady's voice was hysterical with anger, with panic. 'Cochrane, don't do it! Geoff, come *back*!'

He ran frantically. The beasts extended their arms to him. Nancy struggled and screamed. She seemed to recede from him. He reached for her. He drew back his arm to throw the totem.

Someone struck him from behind, and he went sprawling. He knew it was Brady even as the earth hit him in the face.

And then the world changed . . .

It was like a blast of anger. The child, disturbed in its metal womb and disorientated by the sudden lack of vital life force around it, kicked out violently. Its scream of irritation was an icy, blasting wind.

Around them, dazzling white and grey. Dark rocks rose from the maelstrom. Trees whipped and whined in the deafening, terrifying storm-wind. Dust whirled about the ghost-grey land, stinging, blinding. Leaves, twigs and fragments of thorn sang past like projectiles, breaking skin, adding danger to confusion.

Somewhere in the chaos, Geoff Cochrane screamed his daughter's name. Bowled over, and then flung against a crag of glittering white stone, Brady squinted through the dust-laden wind, through the white glare, and saw the grey shape of the ghost-hunter stumbling and reaching into nowhere.

He called for Nancy again, and then again . . .

A shotgun fired. The sound was a dull thud against the screaming storm. Brady hauled himself to his feet, leaning

399

against the rock. He stared into the white landscape. He saw Blanford clinging on to a hawthorn tree which was bending almost double. The man held the gun in one hand. He discharged the second barrel. The ground in front of Brady churned and showered dirt into the storm, fragments of earth that were whipped away by the furious elements.

Ed Blanford lurched from the security of the tree. Head low, and reloading the gun as he staggered, he came towards Brady.

Brady looked around frantically. Where was the totem? The damned totem! What had Cochrane done with it?

He went after the ghost-hunter, shouting at him frantically. The wind made his ears ache, froze his skin. He held a hand in front of his eyes, trying to filter out the driving dust and stone.

'Cochrane!' he screamed.

Ahead of him he heard a voice, equally urgent, calling, 'Nancy!'

Suddenly it was there . . . on the ground before him, unmoved, as if the wind could not touch it. It gleamed in the stark white light. The grinning demon face was red with blood and the eyes that peered through the sticky fluid seemed to glower at him. The mouth, once a mocking grin, now was turned down, a furious scowl. Suddenly it jumped and jerked, twisting on the ground as if the life inside it turned and thrashed, angry and alone, and perhaps afraid.

Brady hesitated for a second, then reached down and snatched the ice-cold totem.

From the ground before him a tall thing grew, rising from the earth so fast that he could hardly comprehend the way it expanded and changed its shape, towering over him. He gasped with shock and took a step back . . .

Dark, gleaming eyes leaning to peer down at him . . .

He saw the waving branches of sharp-thorned trees growing, horn-like, from its head, the great shield of leaf

400

and bark that was the mask upon its face, the quivering tendrils of fern and heather that were the hairs upon its body. The tree-thing rustled and creaked as it bent towards him. Its breath was sour and strong against the wind. Weeds and creepers wound about its legs, animated and alive.

A cone of death blasted past him, shattering through the torso of the beast, but causing no damage, no wound. Brady knew that the shot had been meant for him. He staggered away from the dark form, clutching the totem. Behind him a heavy footfall shook the earth. A twenty-foot-high crag of rock crumbled and shattered. A tree, its branches waving and shaking, seemed to rise behind the ruined stone.

Blanford pursued him. The wind took away his voice, but kept the farmer's shots from firing true. Brady stumbled from tree to rock, desperately seeking shelter . . .

And suddenly a pig leapt at him. Strong hands grappled with him. A foul liquid dropped from the grinning, gaping mouth upon his own lips. He stumbled and the pig leaned down towards him, wrestling with the totem. Beside the pig the slack-jawed head of a mastiff appeared, huge and black, its tiny eyes glittering with awareness. It sniffed at him, and a human laugh sounded from within the mouth. More hands struck at him . . .

Between one blink and the next, the head of the pig had vanished. A raw, red neck spouted blood into the wind, and the body collapsed. The mastiff howled and straightened up, and as it did so it too was suddenly headless, and the dark-robed body was running in circles before collapsing in a heap of gore-drenched clothing.

Around Brady the air was darkening, a bizarre gloom in the startling white and grey light. Blanford approached, the shotgun held towards him. Brady struggled to his feet.

'I've got you now, you bastard!' yelled the farmer. Behind him two dark human figures came quickly towards him. Their heads were strange, and through the dust-storm and the glare of light, Brady could see the face of a horse. The other was indistinct.

The darkness closed in. The earth thumped and vibrated and large, jagged shards of rock began to fly about the air, some coming very close indeed to Brady's huddled, shivering body.

'Say your prayers!' screamed the farmer, and raised the gun.

'Destroy this totem!' Brady shouted back frantically. 'Not me. The totem!'

'You caused it all. You and that ghost-hunter!'

'*This* caused it. Get me later. For your daughter's sake, destroy *this* now!'

As he shouted at Blanford, so Brady flung the totem into the air. It flashed bright yellow in the glaring sky. The wind whipped it away from Brady, towards the farmer. The gun remained on Brady for a second. The two beast-faced men behind Blanford were almost on him, their robes flapping about their legs, their bodies hunched against the storm-wind.

Blanford's gaze on Brady was cold, half-blind, persistent. Brady felt his spirits sink. He had lost. The farmer would shoot him.

The totem began to fall back to the earth.

And then Ed Blanford whipped round the shotgun, raised it and emptied both barrels into the air. The second shot sent the totem spinning into the distance and into oblivion, a shattered, twisted metal box, peppered with lead shot.

There was a terrifying scream. The whole earth tilted. Brady sprawled on the ground. A sound like the crack of thunder nearly deafened him, and where the two beasts had been now there were just two horribly crushed shapes. A single hand stretched up from one of them, the fingers slowly curling into the palm . . .

The whiteness faded. The wind dropped.

402

A cold, dark night returned, silent save for two sounds:

The distant whimpering of a girl.

And Geoff Cochrane's cry of, 'Nancy! Thank God. Thank God.'

12

They huddled in the bright, warm kitchen of Ed and Susan Blanford's farm. Cochrane hugged Nancy to him. Nancy slept on his shoulder, a fragile, filthy shape, her arms draped around his neck. John and Mary Kitting sat stern-faced, yet no longer hostile, watching father and daughter united, still thinking over the bizarre events they had witnessed from a distance.

From the lounge came the sound of sobbing. Ed Blanford's sobbing. Anger, fear, frustration, all of them had finally emerged as tears.

His daughter Sophie was in no danger. She sat in the lounge too, her neck swathed in bandages, her eyes hollow and bloodshot, but her spirits high. The bottle had cut the muscle of her neck, but not the bone or nerve.

Nevertheless, Brady couldn't help feeling thankful for one small mercy: Blanford had thrust two handfuls of cartridges into his jacket pocket. Steadily, with monotonous determination, he had used them up. He had destroyed the totem, and had come for Brady . . .

But the cartridge with which he had ended the embryonic life of the tree-thing had been his last.

If not for that, he would have blown Dan Brady to hell and back. It had taken an hour to calm the man down to the point of tears, an hour and a struggle with the shotgun . . .

'What the hell am I going to do now?' he had wailed. 'I've got five dead bodies in my bedroom, and two headless corpses out on the field. All down to me. All *my* doing. What the hell am I going to *do*?'

Brady had already discussed with John Kitting the

disposal of the bodies into the Pitthurst Hill mines. And not just the seven that Blanford had destroyed with his shotgun, but the four others which the embryo had crushed. The master had destroyed the servants. As punishment.

There was one policeman and one policeman only who should see the results of the terror, a man who knew about Brady's quest, and understood – and *believed* – that what they were up against was part-supernatural and considerably murderous.

The problem, of course, was the two dead farmers, Jack Goddard and Ben Kitting. Ben's body could not be hidden. And Jack's body was still lost.

The sooner that the understanding policeman got here the better, Brady thought.

'You knew that the shotgun could destroy the totem, then?' Cochrane breathed, as Nancy murmured and slumbered on against his neck.

Brady took a deep breath and stretched, then rubbed the sore place on his shoulder where he had been bruised during the pursuit.

'I was sure that fire would do it. They say that silver shot is effective. But no, I didn't know. I just thought: high-energy lead shot, hot and hard . . . That's enough of a kick to ensure an abortion . . .'

'What happens now?'

'I suggest that you, for your part, take Nancy and get the hell away. I'll explain what happened here. No one wants revenge any more . . . do they?' He looked at John Kitting, who shook his head.

'Your children are safe,' Brady said to Mary. 'It would be nice if Nancy Cochrane could be safe too . . . Safe from being taken away from her father, as might happen . . .'

'I agree with you,' John Kitting said tiredly. 'Let him go. As long as no harm, by law or otherwise, comes to us, that's fine.'

Mary Kitting nodded. 'Let them go.'

She rose from the table and looked at her husband. 'I think Kathy Goddard will have gone back to her farm. If she's very distressed she's going to need a friend. Do you want to come?'

Kitting thought about it for a moment, then shook his head. 'I don't suppose there's any danger now.' He looked at Brady, who nodded.

'All danger has fled,' Brady said. 'The sleeping creature killed its own, an act of anger.'

'Then I'll go and see if she's at the farm.'

She leaned down and kissed her husband. He smiled at her. She got her coat and went to the back door, turning as she did so. 'What *did* happen to Jack Goddard, I wonder?'

'If he's trapped in the mines we'll find him,' her husband said.

Mary Kitting left the house to walk the half mile or so to the Goddard farm.

'Get going, Geoff,' Brady said. 'Unless . . .'

'Unless what?'

'There's something else you can tell me about them, about you . . . about anything?'

Cochrane smiled, his eyes hard, penetrating. 'Nothing at all, Dan. I'm just sorry that you didn't get closer to your family. I feel for you, believe me. I feel for you very strongly.'

'I came closer in a way,' Brady said. 'I'm sure, now, that Alison is in a shrine like this. And I found a boy who was lost, and whom I can now return to normal life. He's not the son I would have chosen to find, but he's the son of someone I care for very much, and there is a sense of achievement in that. I feel good about it, Geoff. And for the first time in months I feel hope, do you know that? Hope!'

'You've found one child. You can find your own children.'

Brady grinned. 'Exactly! God alone knows, Geoff, hope

406

is something wonderful. Life is hope. Hope is strength!'

'Good luck, Dan. If I come across anything at all, I know where to get in touch with you.'

He rose from the table, carrying Nancy in his arms. As he made the movement she stirred and woke up.

She looked around at the kitchen, then smiled. 'Where's this?'

'A farm. But we're going home. Well, to Mrs Buxton's, anyway.'

The girl made a sound of disapproval. She closed her eyes and snuggled into his arms again, saying as she settled down for transport home, 'I intend to have a few firm words with you tomorrow, *daddy*. A few well-chosen words about *integrity*. And *promises*. Home, James.'

With a glance at Brady, and the smile of an (almost) worried man, Geoff Cochrane went out into the night, to where the Land Rover was parked.

Soon the engine revved, the headlights flashed on and the vehicle vanished into the distance, taking the ghost-hunter out of Brady's life.

Mary Kitting sensed that something was wrong, even from the gate to the farm complex. A single light was on in the house, in the kitchen. She walked slowly towards the back door. There was a strange sound coming from inside the house. At first she couldn't identify it. Then . . .

Someone was chopping wood. The sound of the axe striking wood went on and on, a regular, powerful blow which hesitated only briefly before continuing.

She peered in through the kitchen window and gasped with shock.

Jack Goddard was squatting on the floor, legs spread, face blank, hands covered in blood. In one hand he held the big axe. In the other a thin piece of wood which he was chopping steadily into smaller and smaller fragments. As he chopped, so he talked. She could see his lips moving.

407

Jack was alive. Thank God. But . . . but what was he doing?

She opened the back door and stepped tenatively into the kitchen. Again she gasped. She looked around at the destruction – the ceiling plaster cut away exposing the wooden strakes beneath, the floorboards gouged, the units smashed, the table, the chairs, all reduced to firewood.

'What are you doing, Jack?' she asked, and Jack Goddard looked up at her, then slowly climbed to his feet.

'Cold,' he said. 'So cold. Chopping wood for a fire. So cold. Have you brought me something to chop?'

'Where's Kathy?' Mary Kitting asked. 'Where's your wife?'

Jack Goddard grinned.

'I'm here,' Kathy Goddard said from the door, making Mary jump with shock. She turned. A weary, bedraggled-looking woman stood there, and Mary hardly recognized her.

'Kathy. Are you all right?'

Kathy Goddard smiled thinly. 'Like the new décor?' she said quietly, then laughed. She pushed past Mary into the room and deposited three large logs in front of her husband.

Jack Goddard sat down on the floor, grinning happily. He started to chop.

'Soon be warm,' he said. 'Soon be warm.'

CODA

Two days later Daniel Brady came back to his house in Berkshire. It was early evening. The ordeal was over.

'Here we are,' he said to Justin Bancroft, and held the door of the car open. The pale-faced boy stepped out and looked through the wrought-iron gates at the tall, silent building beyond.

'Is mummy here?'

Brady squeezed the boy's hand reassuringly. 'Mummy died. I talked to you about it . . .'

'I know,' Justin said quietly. 'I mean . . . is she . . .?' He looked up at Brady.

'She's there,' Brady said softly. 'I'm sure you'll hear her.'

'I want to see her,' the boy said.

'Maybe she'll let you. But whatever happens, you're safe now, and I care for your mother too much to send you away.'

Justin smiled up at Brady. 'We'll look for daddy together.'

'In the *holidays*,' Brady said with mock seriousness. 'Only in the school holidays . . .'

He led Justin to the door and unlocked it. The two of them stepped inside . . .

She knows we're here.

The whole house seemed to tremble. If Justin felt nothing, Brady felt it acutely. The air was still, yet there was movement everywhere: curtains, floorboards, light fittings. The house vibrated with tension, with expectation . . .

With excitement.

Brady walked with Justin into the lounge. The room was cold. He walked to the kitchen, to the study, the dining-room . . . nothing.

Nothing specific. Just the sensation of someone breathlessly waiting for them.

'Where's mummy?' the boy asked.

'She's here.'

He led Justin upstairs and at last he found her. She had withdrawn to the main bedroom. Locked in the stonework, she watched as Brady brought her son to her.

Justin was aware of her immediately. His hand tugged out of Brady's and he walked quickly into the room, turning round, looking up towards the ceiling. He was smiling. 'I can hear her! It's like when I was asleep and she was calling. I can hear mummy!'

Brady was delighted. He glanced around the room, then stepped back into the hall, closing the door of the bedroom, leaving mother and son alone for a while.

He went downstairs and out into the garden, shivering in the cool dusk as he walked slowly about the grounds, inspecting the defences that kept his house secure.

It had been his best shot yet – a whole group of collectors sent to handle a situation that they had been ill-equipped to tackle. He could have learned so much! And he had learned so little. Arachne had slipped through his fingers, fatally punished by the product of their own manipulation with the secret forces of time and nature.

And he had not even come close to his family. He remembered the words of the 'horse':

The girl is far in the north. The woman is in a safe place near London. The boy is on the island in the west.

Alison near London! But she was in a shrine, he *knew* she was in a shrine. It made sense, the 'mother' of the unborn buried with the embryo. Alison was sleeping somewhere below the earth. A shrine near London. Perhaps a shrine close to his own house! The thought made his stomach knot with frustration.

410

Marianna was far in the north. And Dominick was on an island – no, *the* island in the west. An island off the west coat, a secret place.

It was information that Brady could not dignify with the word 'tangible', but it added to his hope that his family were alive.

Arachne – the horse – had given away so little, and yet so much. Their need of the totem had overridden caution, and, unbelievably, they had answered him. But the totem had held the key; without it they had known they were lost. They had begun to bargain for their precious god.

And Brady had let the opportunity slip away!

A safe place. The far north. An island in the west . . .

'Hang on, kids,' he whispered to the gathering gloom. 'I'll find you soon. I swear it. I'll find you, and bring you home . . .'

'Dan!'

He turned and looked up at the bedroom window. Justin was leaning out, smiling at him.

'Had a good chat?' Brady called.

'Mummy wants to talk to you,' the boy called back.

Brady stepped into the house and went to the lounge. It felt warm there. The spectral presence of Ellen Bancroft was all around him, making his hair prickle, blowing cool air in his face. The sadness that had infested the house a few weeks before had gone. The place felt bright and cheery again.

He sat at the table and drew the message pad across to him, holding a pencil loosely in his right hand. Justin stood beside him, watching. There were tears in the boy's eyes and drying streaks across his face. But he was happy.

After a moment Brady's hand moved. The pencil made random scratches on the paper: circles, doodles, angular designs. And then it wrote words, simple words. Joyous words.

Thankyouthankyou.Danohdan. THANKYOU. Happy. HappyDan.Justmichael. Oh DAN. Thankyou.

411